DESTINED TO RISE

EMMIE HAMILTON

DESTINED TO RISE

Copyright © 2023 Emmie Hamilton

This book is a work of fiction. Names, characters, places, and incidents are either a product of the author's imagination or are used fictitiously. Any resemblance to a real person, either living or dead, locations, or events are purely coincidental and is not intended by the author.

All rights reserved. No part of this book may be reproduced or used in any manner without the prior written permission of the copyright owner, except for the use of brief quotations in a book review.

Innulum Press is an imprint created and owned by Emmie Hamilton.
For more information, please visit emmiehamilton.com

Paperback: 979-8-9879638-1-4
First paperback edition October 2023.

Edited by Quinn Nichols
Cover design by Franziska Stern: coverdungeon.com
Layout by Evenstar Books: evenstarbooks.com

Printed in United States of America.

DESTINED
TO
RISE

For Oliver –
My heart, my innulum, my forever journey.
This, as all the others, is for you.

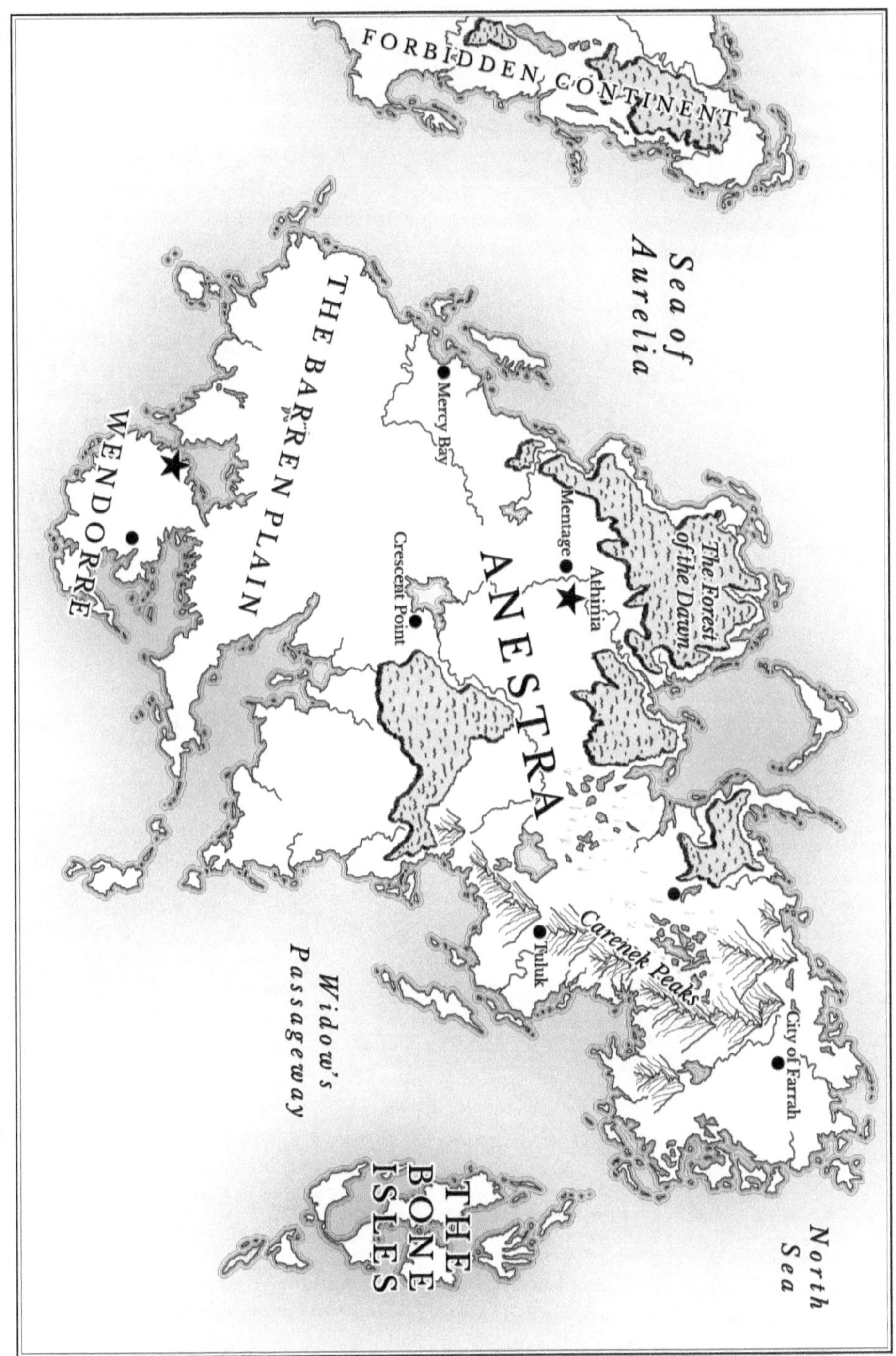

FORBIDDEN CONTINENT
Sea of Aurelia
Mercy Bay
WENDORRE
THE BARREN PLAIN
Crescent Point
Mentage
Athinia
The Forest of the Dawn
ANESTRA
Widow's Passageway
Tuluk
Carenek Peaks
City of Farrah
THE BONE ISLES
North Sea

A NOTE TO THE READER

Dear Reader,

We have come to the end of the journey, and what a messy one it is. Faria, Nellie, Hunter, and Ander all have their share of trauma to work through, and while this book is filled with light and hope, there is also an ocean of darkness to navigate.

As always, I strive to be as transparent as possible, and while this book is quite tame, there are still elements that can be distressing for some, including: torture, gore, violence, , manipulation, mentions of child neglect, and death.

Thank you, as always, to anyone who decides this book is worth a piece of their time. I've grieved with these characters, mourned their losses, celebrated their victories, and now I leave them in your hands to do the same.

Much love,

Emmie

PROLOGUE

DARROC

Pain. Burning, wretched agony. And silence.

Darroc L'Azare had never known such suffering in his life. Not physically, like he did each time he shredded a piece of his soul and sanity to create new monsters in the hope of perfecting the warlock race. Not emotionally, like when he watched his mother suffer in her final days or when he murdered his father out of revenge for giving their magic away for a hopeless cause. Not mentally, like when his willpower was tested after he failed for centuries to get what he wanted.

This—this agony he felt, this empty, burning, everlasting, fire consuming him from the inside out—was something he hadn't experienced before.

And it was because of her. Moira.

His mother.

He had known, or at least he had hoped, back when he did such frivolous things, that his mother was still alive. She *was* a phoenix after all, and even though she was the first and only of her kind he knew of, the fact he'd seen her regenerate from her ashes once before led him to believe she could do it again. He scoffed in indignation at the hope that he'd had, the hope his father had harbored when he'd accidentally turned his wife into the creature she was in a last attempt to keep her evermore, because he loved her so much he couldn't let her go.

Darroc had learned from that moment that love was nothing but a dangerous distraction from what was important. A strong and healthy race, powerful magic, and domination. He had vowed to never let love make him as fragile as it had his father.

And yet, even after dedicating long centuries to those very goals he'd strived for since he had murdered his father and was shunned by his people, he found himself in the exact position he never wanted to be in.

Alone. Desperate. Weak.

And it was because of his mother—the only female he had ever felt something for. The only one who had ever loved him back, once upon a time.

But time had a way of blurring reality, of making memories seem prettier than they were. Rage filled him, competing with the flaming agony of burning from the inside out.

Darroc had looked for her after she had disappeared and stolen the warlocks' power. It wasn't his mother's fault, exactly. The warlock queen strengthened the king's magic. A king was never at the height of his power without a queen there to bolster it. But his father had poured the last of his magic into his mother as she lay dying, and when she turned to ash, she was transformed into another thing entirely. She couldn't have known that by leaving the warlocks were left for ruin.

Or, at least, that had been Darroc's rationalization in the first few decades before his heart had fossilized.

But after his people cast him out for killing the king, after the last kernel of power failed to transfer to him, he set out on a mission to find the phoenix and return the power to his people. He would have done anything to keep her there, even clipped her wings and kept her in a cage if that was what it took to prove that he rightfully deserved to rule and restore his people's faith in him. But the more he searched for her, the angrier he got. How dare she abandon them? How dare she let her people rot and die out so she could have her freedom? Instead, he focused on what he could change to give his people what they needed. More magic.

The depths of the many realms he'd had to travel to find the answers to what he sought, the depraved things he'd had to witness and subject himself to, the sacrifices he'd had to make, all helped him to become stronger, something more, something *other*.

Except now, none of that mattered. He was convinced he was dying, or coming as close to dying as he could. He wasn't entirely certain there was any way for him to truly die without a Spell of Unmaking, and luckily, he was the only one with knowledge on how to properly utilize it.

Taking a deep breath, he slowly opened his eyes and waited for them to adjust to the darkness—a special modification he'd given to himself during one of his many experiments. Shapes started to form: A rough rock wall surrounding him on three sides, forms protruding from the ceiling like stalactites. He was in a cave, or underground somewhere. An entrance was not discernable in his periphery, so it must have been behind him.

Awareness started to come back to his limbs and it was then that he realized there was nothing tangible holding him in place. He did not feel the rough edges of cold metal, nor the frayed tethers of thick rope. Something magical bound him, something more powerful than him.

It was his mother's magic.

He still couldn't wrap his head around seeing her a year prior. At killing those she called family. At giving her a chance to survive, though he presumed she'd died in the fire he'd set on the dilapidated shack they had lived in.

And to see his mother for the first time, standing with his estranged wife—the elf he made queen of the warlocks, who fought on the side of his wretched traitor creations—marked her as his enemy as well.

Any shard of compassion, any remnant of care he might have had for her burned the second she wrapped him in her fiery embrace. Darroc grunted against a painful lance through his stomach. The agony. If only it would end so he could think clearly, so he could plan his next move.

He turned inwardly to assess the damage being inflicted on his body. He knew it was a magical attack on him as the whips of fire he felt lick along his skin and through the sinew of his muscles were not really there. He had enough claim over his awareness to know this was an induced hallucination.

That didn't stop the searing torment though. He bit back a scream, bile rising up his throat as another slash tore through his insides.

Was it the power of the phoenix that was torturing him now? The burning sensation, the feeling that his insides were turning to ash. He'd never felt anything like it before.

Fury consumed him. She was a traitor to her people, and thought it fit to torture her only son? He couldn't wait to get his hands on her. Capturing her wouldn't be enough. Nor would the torture. No, he would run as many experiments as he could until she died. And when she returned, he would do it again. And again. He would figure out the secret of the phoenix, learn what song needed to be sung to have her under his complete control, and then he would make more of them to command at his whim.

For a brief moment, relief flooded his veins as the pain slackened, allowing Darroc to feel the blood oath connection he had made with Ander as the boy approached the Change. He didn't know what powers would settle within him. The past few years had been tumultuous enough having to deal with the unpredictable and rapidly changing nature of his abilities and the pathetic way the boy seemed to grow a conscience.

He tugged on the cord of power he felt from the blood oath and forced his will through the connection. *The Eternal Flame*, he thought. *Now.*

Undoubtedly, Ander was with Faria. He thought he had put the boy through enough to get rid of his bleeding heart, but apparently not. The number of times Ander had called out for his mother, for his father. The dreams that tortured him. It had taken years of grooming, of teaching him what true power looked like, of learning to fear and be feared, and just when he finally had him under his grasp, the first of his powers had emerged.

Val powers.

Darroc couldn't fathom how Ander had developed such abilities when the Val had been extinct for a thousand years. Their power had been almost unmatched. That they were created from the Fae, direct descendants of the gods, meant that some of their power had been an inkling of what ran through the gods' veins as well.

They had been feared, created merely as weapons, and bred for the sole purpose of ensuring a never-ending line of protection to the Agostonna family.

They had almost defeated the warlocks. They had almost defeated *him*. But he'd still been young then and his creatures were not as easily controlled. Darroc hadn't yet figured out how to make the perfect warlock. He hadn't learned what dark spells were needed to control them, to draw his essence into them. And when the Val gave up their power, when they all killed themselves for the sake of the Agostonna's ruling Anestra, they thought it meant the end of him as well.

But they didn't know he'd already lost his mortality by then. They didn't realize it would take more to kill him.

Darroc wasn't sure how much his influence would work on a Val. They'd traveled through the realms together, as he'd rallied other races to work against the Agostonna's, as he'd promised riches and wealth and freedom to roam the land whenever they wanted. He'd trained the young boy as best as he could. The deals he'd made with the Lord of Storms and Seas alone were almost enough to make him regret taking the boy and allowing the god of another realm to see the rare possession he had in Ander. If Darroc hadn't needed to learn the essence of a particular creature in that god's realm, one not found in any other, then he would have called the whole thing off.

Of course, he had no intention of following through with the deals he'd made once he became king, but they didn't need to know that. They just had to agree to fight for him when the time came.

But he needed a backup plan and having a Val at his disposal meant he was finally able to get the one thing that guaranteed his success: The Eternal Flame.

"You won't get it, you know."

Thoughts ceased as he craned his neck, trying to find the source of that musical voice he'd spent decades once longing to hear again.

Light footsteps slowly approached him. With them came the familiar scent of fresh wildflowers, citrus, and the ocean—all reminiscent of Wendorre. Or at least Wendorre of the past. It filled him with an ache he didn't want to acknowledge. He was vulnerable enough being at her mercy.

A ring of fire grew around them with each step Moira took. She stood in front of him, her tanned skin, sharp cheekbones, and wild red curls. Similar to how he remembered her, yet different as well. She didn't look at him with love as she once would have, nor with familiarity. She looked at him as though he were a scour she wished to vanquish from the earth.

"Mother."

She smirked at him and raised a brow. "Am I? I don't believe I am anymore."

He knew he shouldn't have responded or given any indication he was affected by her words, but his reply came out with a sneer. "No, you abandoned our people to live freely. Why would you still hold your title as Mother? You stopped being that when you stopped being the queen."

"You think I live in freedom? That the agony of dying and coming back to life again isn't a cage?" She laughed, its derision echoing back at him. "You have fallen so far down this path of evil, your awareness of the world is severely lacking."

She stepped closer to Darroc and took a moment to observe him as he struggled against the invisible binds that held him down.

"And you falsely accuse me of choosing to not be the queen. I believe I begged my husband to let me go into the Beyond, and he refused. And when I gave up my magic, it was in the hopes that the warlocks would survive without me. Clearly, the Fates intervened and did what they wanted with it."

"I've seen the source of our magic. I meant to take it off Queen Amira's dying body except it wasn't there."

"Of course not," she said, staring at him with disgust. "Why would it be there when it didn't belong to her?"

"We finally agree on something. I got rid of her so I could take it back."

"Back? It is already with the rightful owner."

He paused and tried to think through the pain, now a dull ache throughout his body. "*I* am the only rightful owner."

She snorted, something he remembered as uncharacteristic of her. "You're the only rightful owner of a warlock *queen's* magic? Please. Use your sense."

The haze cleared from his head as he thought about the words she used. One word, specifically. "You can't mean …"

"Yes, it's already integrated into her," the delight in her voice echoed in the chamber.

It amplified his anger, clearing his head quicker.

"Good on you for making her queen. She needs only to step on Wendorre soil and the power will be restored."

"I will siphon it from her dead body."

She rolled her eyes. "You are no longer a warlock. Wasn't that what you prided yourself on? That you were able to become something *other*? Do you really believe my people's magic would work for you now?"

Darroc had never fathomed that thought. Had he changed so much that the magic promised to him would no longer recognize him as its owner? "Once I have the Eternal Flame, it won't matter."

"Ah, yes, which brings us back to the beginning." Her cheekbones became sharper in the harsh light. Fire from the well inside her reflected in her pupils and a smile that was not entirely sane crossed her face.

For a moment he wondered if her act of repeatedly dying and coming back to life unhinged her.

"Let's see how much this *other* body of yours can handle."

Good … Make it hurt.

Screams, agony, and fire unlike any he had known vibrated through his bones. He was charring from the inside out; would be nothing but ash. He would destroy her, he promised himself. He would destroy every bit of what she was and do it again when the phoenix flew once again.

Her smile grew wider.

The pain burned on.

PART I

ONE

FARIA

"**H**unter?"

Acrid air seared her lungs as Faria gasped for breath, unwilling to believe that the male she spent months mourning over was now standing in front of her. Hot magma seeped from giant black rocks surrounding them and a river of lava glowed menacingly in the red light of day.

Steam misted hazily in front of her eyes though she did nothing to move it away, relishing the burn instead, wishing this wasn't a dream. The Fates wouldn't be so cruel, would they?

"Faria," his melodic voice vibrated through her, shocking her from her awed state. Deep green eyes slit against the burning fog as another gush of heat blasted through them on a wind that smelled of misery and fire. "Come back with me."

Really? The first thing he thought to do was command his queen? Indignation burned her as much as the flames from the realm they stood in. Soft choking sounds rasped next to her as Faria finally remembered she wasn't the only one who stood in front of a wrathful Val Prince.

"I must stop Ander before he's forced to give Darroc the weapon he needs to destroy Anestra. I am not going anywhere without him." She scanned the perimeter, noting almost nothing except for a lone volcano in the distance.

"It is said that only Val can survive in this realm. Allow me to get him, so you can return this *creature,*" he spat the word at Jamison, "to safety before he dies here."

Faria glanced down at a kneeling Jamison, the heat from the rocks burning holes through his pants. He had started to look worse for wear upon entering this realm; his blond hair was matted with blood and a large gash ran down his left cheek. A darker, more menacing crimson stain soaked through his shirt.

A flare of alarm ran through her. There had been no time to assess if he was well enough to go with her to this realm. He had grabbed her hand as she disappeared in Ander's power and she couldn't tell him the dangers he would face.

"I will not leave without my son. Bring him to safety," Faria implored Hunter.

Hunter crossed his arms, his feet planted firmly to the rocky terrain. To Faria, it looked as though he was ready to have an argument about it in the middle of a realm set in a relentless blaze. She looked closer at him, taking in the curled lip, the hardened planes of his face, the danger that seemed to pour off him. This was not the same Hunter she once knew. The darkness leaching from him felt almost familiar in a way as if mirrored within herself. Faria wondered what had happened to him in the time that he abandoned her to Darroc and then again after he died.

"Do not force my hand, Hunter. I am your queen now—or have you changed your allegiance in your absence?"

He waited a beat, then two; his jaw clenching. The show of emotion was surprising. If anything, he used to be stoic, so dispassionate that she used to beg him for some type of … anything. Now, she wasn't sure she liked what she saw.

She forced his name out. "Hunter."

"Fine, but I am coming back for you."

"There is no need." She softened her defensive stance, allowing a shadow of relief to surface. "Ander will return me after I help him. Go back to Anestra. You have a war to prepare for."

Hunter gave her a curt nod and grabbed Jamison by the cuff of his arm before disappearing from the realm.

Faria sighed to herself. One problem at a time. She didn't have space to worry about Jamison, Hunter, Ander, and her people. At least she could hold onto the hope that the scars and burns on Jamison's skin would heal in time. If not, she'd try to heal him herself as soon as she returned with Ander.

Now that she was truly alone, Faria turned toward the lone volcano in the distance and prayed that was where she needed to go. If she remembered what Moira said correctly, the Eternal Flame was meant to be in the middle of an inactive volcano. That was the only lead she had to go on.

Sweat poured down Faria's back as she picked up the pace as best as she could with the smoke filling her lungs. She still had plenty of energy left since she'd barely fought in the battle on Earth against Darroc, and now that she could feel the magic of the warlocks swirling inside her, she was more powerful than ever. Despite that, Faria hesitated to use any magic she had access to so as not to deplete her energy reserves; she didn't know what she'd need to use against Ander if he decided to fight her, or if there were dangerous creatures hidden among the lava and flames.

She felt it suddenly: A tug on the cord deep inside her. The *innulum* pulsed strong, even more so than it had on Earth. It was sharp enough for her breath to falter. A sense of unease ripped through her. Something was wrong with Ander.

A roaring screech echoed throughout the land, followed by another. Faria could see through the hazy clouds an outline of large black wings and curved talons pointed toward the ground. A team of … dragons? *No,* those were *Drogosterra.* They flew in formation around the volcano she headed toward before falling into its rocky mouth.

Pieces of her flesh seared violently as Faria continued in the blazing heat of that godsforsaken realm. A column of steam issued from the ground and Faria thought she heard laughter, as if the land mocked her for being weak in that hellscape. Delirium had set in, she thought, because she couldn't have heard voices in a land no one sane enough to inhabit. Had it always been that way? Or had it once been viable, teeming with green and life and rain? Water … She desperately needed water.

Faria couldn't fathom what could have happened to make the land this way if it hadn't always been like that from the beginning.

Now soaked through, her clothes were heavy and her eyes stung with sweat. She felt pieces of her hair singe and wondered, as each step brought her closer toward the volcano, if she was a Val at all. Perhaps she allowed hope—or ignorance—to take precedence rather than her common sense.

Her powers could have come from anywhere. Maybe she was an elf with extra abilities and would now burn as surely as Jamison had started to.

Soon the rocky terrain gave way to a smoother path. Rough stone transformed into hardened obsidian sand and her feet sunk into its glassy depths as she approached the lone volcano. A single *Drogosterra* roared high above her. At any moment she was prepared for it to swoop down and release a breath of fire on her.

She stopped, bent over at the knees, struggling to get air in her lungs. She couldn't go on; it just couldn't be done. She wasn't right, she wasn't built for this world. Wasn't built for this life.

Toxic fumes surrounded her and Faria sank to the ground, the searing rock tearing holes through her pants. She tried to scream but her voice was too raw.

Faria wanted to waste away there, but the force of the *innulum* brought her to her feet. She stumbled, barely catching herself before falling back to the ground. Ander was in trouble. The panic eroded her sense of helplessness and was replaced by desperation to both save her son and hurry back to her people. She couldn't allow herself to break down, not yet.

She dragged herself forward along a rough-hewn path littered with puddles of molten magma. Monuments of huge stone beasts stood sentry outside of an arched opening, like watchdogs of a barren cemetery. The detail on the statues was impeccable as she approached—their violet-veined wings, the obsidian scales that glittered from the radiant spray of lava. Faria paused, marveling at their beauty, and wondered what manner of people would have created such art in a desolate place. Their eyes glowed a brilliant cerise at her approach.

Pulsing, hot magma slid out of the statues' gaping eye sockets until a steady stream of red tears flowed down their stony faces. After a moment, another crimson river gushed from their mouths and fell to the ground in a straight line.

It made no sound; there was no hissing of fire against rock, no popping as stone and slate melted and burned. All around Faria, a moat of liquid lava surrounded the volcano, as if activating what had long slumbered. She smiled grimly. It seemed her presence activated something within the land, or at least within this landmark.

A roaring screech from a *Drogosterra* caused Faria to jump, shaking the direction her thoughts had started to take. She walked through an old stone archway that appeared to be made from the same rocky material as the monuments, though there was something odd about it.

Straining her eyes, she caught the flash of winking gemstone as she approached. A faint green shimmering light pulsated as Faria walked through the doorway.

She made it only a few steps inside before another force pulled from deep inside her. The feeling of sharp claws latched onto her heart, ripping it from her chest. Faria gasped in pain, clutching her body to keep it safely locked in place. She let the force lead the way as she tore down a winding, rocky path that led deep into the mountain.

Ander.

She knew the *innulum* was telling her something had happened to him. She approached another arched entryway that extended hundreds of feet into the air, beyond which a body lay slumped to the ground. The gleam of chestnut hair and dark clothing told her the prone figure belonged to her son, but still, she gave pause.

The shadowed outline of another presence, taller than any she had seen before, leaned over Ander. In his hands, he held the Eternal Flame, its blue light bright as the Flame gently flickered and seemingly soaked into the stranger's dark hands. He turned his head and looked at Faria, eyes of pure gold staring back at her.

She took a sharp intake of breath as a primal fear and disbelief filled her. There was a sense of familiarity like she should have known who this being was.

He unfolded himself to his full height, and though most of his face was still shrouded in shadow, he gave a slight bow in Faria's direction, as if acknowledging the queen she was. Then he faded out of existence.

Tiny pebbles shook the ground as a low rumbling echoed in the large chamber. Ander lay next to a large dais, whose stand cracked down the middle from the increasingly violent shaking. The acrid scent of sulfur and the heat of the magma pooled within the belly of the volcano, which exhaled an anguished breath as if the mountain realized what it'd held onto for so long, was no longer there.

Stumbling to Ander's side, Faria's hands hovered over his body, her heart hammering as a blue light flashed out from her fingertips. He stirred, then brushed her away.

"I'm fine," he mumbled, grunting as he turned onto his side.

"You don't sound fine," she hissed, frantically searching his body for injuries. "What happened?"

"I had it," he said, breathless and defeated. He lay still, staring at the ceiling with vacant eyes. "I had it in my hands. The legends are true. We really can handle it."

"So that was another Val?"

"I wouldn't know. It's not like foster daddy took me to see my blood relatives, did he?" his voice was bitter, the anger making the sharp planes of his face starker.

Faria ignored the pain of regret and sadness that ebbed into her. "He seemed familiar, in a way. What else could he be, to overcome a new Val growing into his powers? What other manner of being can wield the Flame?"

"Yeah, I don't know!" Ander yelled over the clamoring of cracking stone, shakily getting to his feet. He rubbed at a spot in his chest. "But we better hope he isn't an evil bastard like Darroc."

"Speaking of, we must go back to Anestra. I have to defend my land and my people and it's the best place for me to protect you."

Ander looked down at her, his expression unreadable. "Darroc will find me no matter where I am, and it's better I don't lead him straight to your door."

"I won't hear of it," Faria said, anger strengthening her voice. "You're my son and I will protect you."

"Yeah, you've done a great job of that so far."

They stared at each other, each with the stubborn fire inherited from their respective parents, each of whom they felt let down by. The ground shook harder and a single *Drogosterra*, who had been flying in circles near the ceiling, suddenly dove down at them.

"We need to leave, now." Ander grabbed Faria's hand as she looked up, watching the mythical dragon beast, whose eyes seemed filled with a curious hope and sadness. It was then that Faria remembered how the Val used to ride *Drogosterra* into battle, and she wondered if they somehow got separated. If the dragons had been here for centuries, waiting to be rescued.

Faria extended her other hand to the beast, her fingertips just barely grazing its snout as Ander's power melted over them, squeezing the air from her lungs as darkness descended.

TWO

FARIA

Chaos.

Screams of terror.

A screeching roar, the torrent of wind with the flap of wings, voices shouting:

"*What is it?*"

"*It's one of Darroc's!*"

"*It's the queen! Protect the queen!*"

A stampede of footsteps rumbled the ground as armor clashed and the sound of arrows being pulled back from stretched bowstrings reverberated around her. Faria tried to open her eyes, but the blazing sunshine and crisp, cool air were a shock to her system. Hard snow blanketed the ground and Faria's boots, still sweltering from the fire realm, hissed against the frozen land.

Her realm. She was in Anestra, finally back where she belonged. She let out a ragged cough, spluttering the last of the sulphuric ash from her throat as hands suddenly tore at her, pushing her in several directions, eager to save her from whatever it was they thought she needed protection from.

"Ander!" she gasped, feeling his hand tear away from hers. Faria searched the crowd frantically, the faces all a blur until she finally landed on one.

Dark green eyes with a blazing golden halo around the center stared back at her, but they didn't belong to Ander. Hunter raised his eyes to the sky, his expression unreadable as he took a defensive stance, squaring his shoulders and planting his feet firmly against the ground. Faria followed his gaze until her sight adjusted enough to see the source of the widespread panic.

A *Drogosterra* circled high above them, out of range of the arrows now loosening from their bows. It released a warning bellow.

"Stop it!" a voice shouted. "Don't hurt it!"

Nellie shoved her way toward Faria, knocking people to the ground to reach her queen. Faria breathed a sigh of relief, thankful that Nellie appeared unharmed, apart from being caked in mud and blood, and her curly hair wildly out of place.

"Thank the goddesses," Faria breathed into her friend's neck as she pulled her in a quick embrace.

"Faria, you have to tell them to stop shooting! They think you're in danger."

It didn't get past Faria that Nellie still used her full name rather than the name of endearment she longed to hear from her friend. Faria knew she needed to make time to properly apologize to her.

Faria turned to face her people, a mixture of civilians and those trained in the Anestrian army, along with the Royal Guard. Their weapons were well made, but much of their armor seemed to fit poorly as if grabbed at random and hastily put on. She made a mental note to prioritize proper attire for battle if they had the time.

"Stand down!" Faria shouted.

A few elves hesitated, though their arrows remained docked.

This was her first official order as the queen of Anestra, yet she held no sway over a few archers. What use was it to rule a queendom? Familiar feelings of inadequacy crept up her spine and bitterness coated her throat as she ordered them to stand down again.

"Listen to your queen," Hunter's deep voice rumbled behind her.

She sensed him step close, felt his space impress upon hers. Whatever darkness had come over him, she knew, was on display to her people. They shrank back immediately. She tempered her annoyance at their easy compliance with him by staying focused on the beast in front of them.

The *Drogosterra* took advantage of the pause and dove. Its wings spread over the light of the sun, allowing the rays to highlight the crimson veins running through its wingspan. The Anestrians' fear was palpable, though she knew, for some reason, this dragon wouldn't hurt them. It would have already if it wished.

It landed in front of Ander. The force of its impact on the ground sprayed all surrounding them with flecks of dirt and snow. The Elven

Royal Guard scattered out of its way, dragging with them those who were rooted in shock.

Ander tensed as he looked up the length of the dragon's snout and beyond to its scaly body. *Don't provoke it,* Faria begged inwardly. *Don't cause it offense.*

The *Drogosterra* was large, a dark gray mass like rumbling storm clouds on the horizon. Its wings spread wide, webs of deep red veins weaving through them more evident up close. It was huge, much larger than what Nellie had turned into, but Faria could tell this one was just a youngling. Did it recognize itself in Ander? An outsider, or perhaps feeling alone?

Faria stole a glance at Hunter, who scrutinized their son and the *Drogosterra* closely, though he made no move to intervene. Of course, Faria thought, he would have had plenty of experience with *Drogosterra*, given their history of riding into battle together. They used to be more than mere partners, but companions.

Ander straightened. His full height was still far below the snout of the *Drogosterra*. Faria watched as it dipped its head until it was eye level with Ander. A growl rumbled from deep within its belly and trailed up its throat. Whisps of gray smoke exhaled from its nostrils, a brimstone scent catching in the brisk wind.

Hunter slowly reached for a dagger at his side, his fist gripping the handle as he gently eased it from its sheath. What did he think he would do with such a tiny weapon to that massive beast?

A wave of pressure brushed against Faria's side as Nellie started to vibrate in preparation to shift.

"Do. Nothing." Faria's voice was quiet, but firm.

The pressure immediately eased, though a distinct static remained in the air.

Faria watched her son maintain eye contact with the *Drogosterra* and reach his hand toward its snout. Her concern multiplied tenfold as his hand lingered over its protruding fangs, but the *innulum* didn't give off a warning. That alone put her at ease. That Hunter had done nothing more than change his stance to one of protection comforted her further, for she did the same.

A shimmering silver glow emanated from Ander's exposed tattoos and for a moment Faria was distracted by their beauty. They were similar to Hunter's and her own, though the symbols were organized in a different way. Hers flowed delicately and weaved on her arm and across her torso in soft waves, the symbols dancing with each other. Hunters were thicker, bolder, and more striking. They were placed on his body in a way that told a story if one knew how to decipher it. Ander's, however, almost looked like violent slashes intermingling with a script Faria couldn't understand. It was frightening and mesmerizing. She wondered if he was cold in the frigid air.

A murmur of shock and wonder rippled among the Anestrians. Bows relaxed and taut strings loosened as arrows hung at their sides. Soft whispers traveled throughout the crowd as if they were afraid to startle the creature before them. The Guard watched transfixed as Ander's hand came to rest upon the *Drogosterra*.

Nellie gasped beside her and Faria had the urge to echo the sentiment as the *Drogosterra* snorted. A violet flash trailed down Ander's arm, sparking the iridescent designs into a frenzy of life. The *innulum* inside Faria turned warm and images flashed through her mind: those of violence, war, brimstone, sadness, loneliness. It nearly brought Faria to her knees as she tried to decipher them as quickly as they came.

As if sensing her distress, Hunter was by her side, moving quicker than she was able to track. He brushed his shoulder against hers, murmuring something low that even her exceptional elven hearing couldn't pick up. Immediately the tension within her eased and she released a slow breath, careful not to let her people see her distress.

Hunter's essence brushed across her mind and for a moment Faria let the barrier she built between them fall. *"The pain you feel belongs to the Drogosterra. She is letting Ander glimpse inside of her to know her true nature and because you are connected to him through the* innulum, *you are feeling pieces of it as well."*

Ander's hand remained fixed on the *Drogosterra*, and the longer he held on, the brighter the violet light shone. Faria took hesitant steps toward her son and watched as he turned his palm over, revealing a network of symbols as if they were burned onto his skin—another tattoo, another marking, another bond she couldn't prevent from taking place. Perhaps this one wouldn't be as dangerous, though. Perhaps it wouldn't be permanent.

"He is Marked," Hunter said, his tone a mixture of awe and something Faria thought might have been longing. "The *Drogosterra* marked him as hers to protect. In return, he must do the same. All in the name of the Agostonna line."

"That doesn't make sense," Nellie said. "Ander is the next in the

Agostonna line. He's next to be king somewhere in the far, far, so very far, future." She nodded at Faria earnestly. "Not at all any time soon because you are going to live forever."

"He is also inherently a Val soldier and we cannot ignore or forfeit the bond of our *Drogosterra*. We weren't made to ignore the call."

"So, he's just automatically a soldier just because he's a Val? Does he not get to choose what he wants?" Faria asked fiercely. She didn't care what ancient magic might have created them she would not let Ander live his life without the ability to choose what he wanted for himself.

Ander looked up from the intricate designs emblazoned on his fingers, his eyes roaming across the Anestrians and landing lastly on Faria. "I don't …" He glanced at King Dennison, a man he hadn't met yet, who helped to rule the country Ander would one day inherit if he wished, and then at his father. "I can't. I don't know you." He started backing away from the *Drogosterra*, a low growl crawling up its throat. "It's too much."

The shape of his body shimmered as Ander prepared to shimmer out of existence. The *Drogosterra* whined, thrashing its tail in protest. It took off into the sky and veered north toward the Forest of the Dawn and further out to sea. Its wings whooshed once, twice, before disappearing over the golden forest.

"Ander, don't," Faria pleaded, her hand reaching out to touch his arm. "There's still Darroc to consider. We don't know where he is. You're safest here."

"It doesn't matter," Ander said as his body vibrated with the first of him disappearing. "When he's ready for me, I'll be forced to go to him, anyway."

The gut-wrenching pain of loss and something deeper filled Faria. She had never had a chance to be a proper mother, to watch her son grow up, to protect him from harm or teach him the dangers of the world. Never had a chance to show him strength through love and compassion. She had no idea what he could have gone through, of the horrors he had likely faced. And even now, even when he was in her grasp, she still could do nothing to help him.

She swallowed down the well of helplessness as she watched her son disappear. Ander was a man now, whether she was able to reconcile that fact or not. She had to trust he knew what he was doing, or at least respect his boundaries and let him sort through his feelings. Her people needed her now. *I am their queen*, she reminded herself. *I must protect them.*

Faria stood among the mix of shapeshifters, elves, humans, and warlocks. Her eyes shifted over to Hunter. And Val. She was queen to all and knew almost nothing about the life she had to lead and the land she now had to rule.

A flurry of items on her to-do list flooded her mind. She needed all the newcomers to sign the Blood Contract. She had to learn what their numbers were, what their battle strategy was, what she missed out on during her time on Earth. She needed to check on Jamison and speak to Nellie, needed to figure out what to do about the *Drogosterra* now roaming her realm. To learn more about what it meant to be a warlock queen and in what other ways, besides healing from the brink of death, her abilities might change. Perhaps Endo could help with that. She needed to know more about every power that shimmered and grew beneath her veins.

More than anything, she needed to speak to Hunter.

Eyes burned in the back of Faria's head and she felt a pressure against her mind. She had resealed the wall she briefly let down and wasn't ready for the intimacy of regular contact again. Not yet. The darkness within him scared her, and if she cared to admit it, she felt her own kernel of shadow taking root deep within her soul.

There were many times in the past year when she'd felt that shadow grow within her. She truly believed Darroc had implanted something evil inside her when she thought she was pregnant with his baby. It stirred in her blood and haunted her dreams. The whispers, the feeling of constantly being watched.

But now after seeing Hunter, after feeling the darkness emanating from him, she wondered if it was something other than that.

Faria walked to King Dennison, briefly acknowledging those who fell to their knees as she passed and making a mental note of those who chose not to show her deference. She had never cared about it before, but now that it was clear her people weren't ready to follow her lead, she'd have to figure out what to do about it.

"What do you need of me, Father?"

King Dennison wrapped his daughter in his arms and she immediately melted into his embrace. His familiar scent of sweat, leather, and cinnamon and the scratchy feel of his beard against her cheek comforted her in a way she hadn't realized she needed. Faria swallowed the sudden impulse to cry. She knew there was a fair share of trauma to face, but in this moment, she wanted nothing more than to crumple in her father's arms and feel protected for once. She wished he could take care of everything for her. She wished her mother were still alive. Wished she didn't feel like she was so incapable of doing what she needed to do.

"Nothing, my darling," her father murmured in her ear. "First you eat, you sleep, then when you wake we will begin a new day together."

"But there is still too much to take care of. The shapeshifters, the treaty—"

"I will prepare for the treaty. Nellie will take care of the shifters." He put his arm around her shoulders and led her back toward *Mentage*, her home. The sprawling white mansion looked different to her now. Larger, and despite the hundreds of people stationed throughout the fields, emptier.

"Take time for yourself first, love. You cannot lead if you are not whole."

Then I cannot lead at all, Faria thought bitterly. Broken pieces of who she once was were reduced to nothing but ashes. Yet, she had no choice. She nodded her agreement and let her father take her away to find a moment of serenity.

THREE

ANDER

Leaves crunched beneath his boots as Ander landed on the hard ground, the scent of wet pine and woodsmoke filling the air around him. He raised his eyes, noting an overcast sky and impending darkness. It was probably late afternoon if he had to guess. He knew he must have looked like hell and probably smelled even worse, especially after spending any amount of time in the fire realm. He sniffed at his clothes. Sulfur and sweat.

He didn't want to show up at her house like this—a mess of a male, whose powers were barely under control, bound to a psychotic murderer, and now dealing with the new trauma of being the same age as his mother, who was alive and not dead, as Darroc had convinced him of so long ago. That would have been easier than the truth: That she abandoned him.

That wasn't fair, not really. He knew she was telling the truth; could see the devastation on her face. He didn't understand how time was so different between realms, or that it was only a few weeks for her that he had been gone, yet it was eighteen years for him. His life had been lost to time, something he'd never understood until that moment. He never cared to think about something as grand as Time whenever he and Darroc had gone through the Gate. He still didn't fully understand why Darroc wanted him.

Ander edged through the trees lining an oversized yard, lost in his thoughts. He had loved him, in his own way. Darroc. Ander was treated well as a boy until he reached around his tenth year of life. He had birthday presents and was taken to see the most magical places. He didn't want for anything growing up, though instead of toys, Darroc would buy him things he didn't care so much about. Parcels of land, crystals from other realms. He thought he'd had a strange father, but was grateful at least he had one.

It was weird now to think of Darroc as a father, but if he married his mother then he supposed that was who he would have been anyway. Except fathers weren't supposed to subject their children to the types of terrors Ander had gone through. They didn't allow their sons, adoptive or not, to lie, steal, or learn the art of manipulation. To murder.

The nightmares Ander had for years after the first time he'd killed still haunted him. He was barely twelve years old, visiting the human realm, learning the different terrain and those who lived within it. A gross under-exaggeration, considering Darroc's idea of "learning" meant he performed twisted autopsies at least once a month.

Ander had only just started to learn the extent to which Darroc would go to get what he wanted. He knew he'd been power hungry, knew he sought to take back control of Wendorre. Knew, even, that Darroc wished to create more warlocks. It was why Darroc had forced so many magical implements on him as a child, to see if perhaps anything useful in him stirred.

Darroc couldn't have known, as Ander did not realize himself until he started to go through the Change, that he was Val.

A darkness had started in him, in the center of his mind and his chest. Every time his heart beat it spread a little more through his body. He didn't know what it was, at first, not until he had given in to impulses that festered as time went on. Every annoyance, every bit of anything that made him angry, had turned him violent and bloodthirsty.

By then, Ander was more afraid and dependent on Darroc, who seemed to always encourage the darkness to spread. He didn't know if it was something Darroc had done to him, some sort of spell or magic placed on Ander to turn him into an amoral killing machine, but when Darroc gave him a target, it helped ease the pressure he felt inside.

It wasn't until Ander felt compelled to go to Anestra that he started to realize the truth or at least some of what lies were told to him. He meant to travel to Wendorre, to see the land of his father. Then maybe he would feel more connected to something rather than so alone.

Except it wasn't Wendorre he was attracted to, but *Mentage*. When he found a male who looked exactly like him, whose tattoos shone the way his did, whose eyes had the same golden halo, he knew he'd been lied to. And when they made brief eye contact before Ander panicked and disappeared, he knew he had seen his real father.

And now his feelings were twisted. He was supposed to hate his mother, resent her for having him go through the horror of living with Darroc, yet there was something inside him, something the darkness couldn't touch. The *innulum*, she called it. He felt it even now, trying to pull him back to her. He knew, without knowing how, that she was telling the truth. That she never meant to cause him harm. That this wasn't her fault.

But it didn't take away the sins he had committed, the unparalleled pain he had caused. And now with the virus on Earth killing the shapeshifters, Ander was ready to take any punishment the Fates deemed worthy to bestow on him.

Ander hadn't meant to do it. He was supposed to kill the clan leader outright, but he was hoping a disease would appease Darroc instead. Longer suffering maybe? He didn't know what the goal was other than to not murder any creature again. Ander hadn't expected the disease to evolve and spread like it had; he didn't know he would destroy an entire race.

Ander's shoulders slumped under the weight of all he had endured as he peered up at a house in the distance. A light flickered on in the upstairs bedroom and the outline of a girl shadowed the window. He slid back under the cover of trees lining her property. He didn't know why he showed up there of all places he could have gone to, covered in muck, smelling of sweat and ash, with more psychological trauma than he knew what to deal with.

The window slid open and Jane's soft voice carried over to him in the still night air. "Ander?"

Maybe if he didn't respond, she would forget he was there.

"I know you're there. Come inside before someone sees you."

He couldn't resist Jane's honeyed voice, and not for the first time, he was grateful he didn't kill her as he was once tasked to do. He'd shot an arrow straight through her heart on Darroc's orders only a few months ago and thank the gods she had survived. Now he hoped she had strength enough to endure what he could not stop from revealing to her.

Who knew, maybe she could help stop the sickness he'd caused. Or better yet, maybe she'd turn out to be a Celestial—a mythical soldier of the apocalypse, like the Earth's version of a Val. It was possible, actually. She was, after all, a Guardian of Earth.

FOUR

NELLIE

*H*oly *heck on wheels.*

Nellie wouldn't say her life had been bereft of trauma, being that her mother was murdered, she was banished from her clan and had felt, to the marrow, the deep terror of ceasing to exist. Then there was having to hide who she really was lest she be discovered and crucified.

She had lived her life in a perpetual state of anxiety that bordered on paranoia. But there was something about a deranged psychopathic murderer killing her friends and destroying an entire species that hit differently, and she wasn't sure she would come out of it whole.

"Nellie," his voice carried through the crowd and she felt both relief and a prickling of annoyance come over her.

She'd wanted to see Endo for so long. Had believed in him. Now they were in the same place, but she wasn't the same as she was when she'd left. Witnessing the destruction Darroc wrought over the two realms she'd visited—and likely more than that—had her second-guessing Endo's loyalties. Who blindly followed someone they had never met? She could understand wanting to restore his race's power, as the warlocks had been close extinction for centuries. She understood wanting to bring back health and happiness to his people. But she could not understand doing so at the risk of innocent lives, and that was exactly what Endo did.

Nellie might not have had a male's attention in entirely too many years, and Endo may have always had the best of intentions, but returning home to him mattered less to Nellie now that she saw the reality of the situation. She used to love herself a morally gray man, but if they were all like Endo, then they were just morally lame.

She walked on, weaving her way through the crowd, though she felt him pursue her. Nellie was about to turn around and tell him to back the heck off when she heard another voice call her name.

Her ears perked up in attention and she veered over to the shapeshifters. Standing awkwardly in a group together on the edges of the Forest of the Dawn, they looked worse for wear. Ripped, bloodstained clothing, injuries still weeping with ferocity, some even had chunks of flesh missing that the healers were desperately trying to attend to. Everything was such a whirlwind. They endured their battles. Their losses.

Luck.

Ripples of grief sent shockwaves through Nellie. She hadn't taken the proper time to process or mourn all that had happened in the past few days—heck, even the past few weeks—and she wasn't sure she was ready to confront it now. But memories rushed through her whether she wanted them to or not.

Nellie had adored Luck, though she knew him for such a short time. His laughter was infectious and his smile felt like a galaxy of suns radiating after an eternity of darkness. It felt good to be in his presence, and his loss was a shadow hanging over her. She could tell the other shifters felt the same.

Nellie waved to Tommy, her former mate, then walked to Marisa, who stood at the head of her clan. She couldn't have been much older than Nellie's own twenty-two, and for her to lead a group at such an age, during times like these, must have been a great burden for her.

"Hey," Nellie said, her hand clasping Marisa's shoulder in comfort. "What can I do for you guys?"

"Are we near an ocean?" Marisa asked. She buzzed with a strange sort of energy. "We can feel it, the water calling to us."

Her face took on a desperate look, and Nellie observed the others who all had a similar expression of need and hope on their faces. They looked over their shoulders occasionally past the Forest of the Dawn, where Nellie knew the Sea of Aurelia lay just beyond the dense forest.

Nellie pondered. "Anestra is surrounded by water on all sides," she explained. "If you travel a few hundred leagues in this direction"—Nellie pointed south—"you'll end up at the Sea of Aurelia. I've never seen anything like it before. Not on Earth, at least.

"The waters are clear and appear to have changing colors underneath as if gemstones lay beneath. The way the sun hits at sunset makes it feel like it's infused with magic.

"We have a large port town there," Nellie continued. "Mercy Bay. It's probably the second-largest city, after Athinia. Where Athinia has lots of shops, restaurants, an art district, and is the center for education and the arts, Mercy Bay is where the shipping, trade, and similar business happens. Lots of seaside restaurants and nightlife, but also the ability to sail to other countries.

"We still have trade set up with Wendorre, in the south, and though no one has said it, I think we send supplies over to the Forbidden Continent as well."

Marisa's clan grew excited and stole longing glances in the direction Nellie pointed. Marisa explained, "For so long, we'd been confined to lakes and rivers, but my people belong in the ocean. According to our clan's legend, it was my ancestor who was the first siren to walk the Earth. She had birthed a siren, and on it went. No matter who the father was, the children always were sirens. Males and females alike."

Nellie wouldn't say she had a particularly strong tactical instinct, but she had a feeling there was a way they could both get what they wanted if King Dennison agreed. Former king? She needed to double-check proper titles now that Faria had been deemed a queen. Or was she? Without a ceremony? Did it matter?

"There are things you will have to do here at *Mentage*: sign the Contract, learn the rules. As far as I know, I'm the only shapeshifter who has lived here in centuries and I did so in hiding. While I know Faria will accept our kind, we all still have our place to make it work. Assuming you don't want to return to Earth, let's see what King Dennison will want and need from us. Take a bit of time getting to know *Mentage* and Athinia, train with our soldiers, and rest. Goodness, we all need rest. After that, I have an idea for how we might be able to give you what you want."

Marisa looked into each of her clan's eyes. The disappointment was apparent. They had been starved from the ocean for weeks or longer, and now they were in a place filled with magic and endless sea, a new home they could build upon, and were still denied the chance to experience it. Still, hope remained.

"Yes," she said finally. "I don't believe there is anything left for us on Earth, especially not with the disease running as it is. We are so grateful to Faria, and will do what we need to earn our place here."

"You guys are gonna love it. And when we have a moment, you're trying our world-famous honey cheesecake."

A few elves tentatively approached with what appeared to be tonics and water.

"For now, let our people take care of you guys. You can trust them."

Nellie hadn't recognized the healers who approached, but they didn't seem shocked to see shapeshifters, at least. There was no prejudice or distrust in their eyes. Still, she couldn't help but say, "Take care of them, or I'll turn into a *Drogosterra* and eat you."

Nellie turned away from Marisa and found Jamison on a makeshift pallet surrounded by another group of healers. She felt compelled to take care of them all, the shifters. Faria needed them here, but it was Nellie who had convinced them to come. More than that, they were her people. She might have grown to feel part of Anestra, but she had never lived there openly as herself. Now, there were a few dozen of her kind here, all ready and willing to defend a land and people they'd never met for the sake of ridding all the realms of the evil that stained their lives.

They were all there for one mission, and while Marisa promised to stay, the others hadn't. Nellie selfishly wanted them to.

She knelt in the grass next to a groaning Jamison, who grimaced before turning it into a lazy smile. "You idiot," she said gently. "Why did you grab onto her? Didn't you know what would happen to you?"

"No," he said gruffly. "I didn't. But I said I would protect Faria for as long as she let me."

"And how did you expect to protect her, being a useless charred lump in a realm that murders any not built to survive there?"

"Okay, okay, enough with the lecturing." His skin was coated in a sheen of sweat despite the frigid winter air. Jamison's eyes shifted past her shoulder. "Tommy mentioned something about staying in the Forest for a while. Have you spoken to him?"

Nellie shook her head. "There has been way too much happening, and besides, that chapter is closed. I'm sure Faria won't mind him staying where he feels safest after he signs the Contract. What else is on your mind?"

"That him?" Jamison's voice took on a hard edge. "The one she grieved for?"

Nellie followed his line of sight until her eyes landed on Hunter. His back was to them, but she could tell he was listening to every word they said from across the way.

She nodded. "Yes. They are who the Fates decided should be together."

"Faria can make her own decisions."

Nellie's chuckle turned to a cough at Jamison's dark look. "Yes, she can. And you will find that she will still choose Hunter, every time. And if you don't want a Val soldier turning you inside out, I'd suggest you not say anything more. He can probably hear us."

Jamison's mouth tightened. He gasped as a tonic was poured over his weeping blisters.

"Also, you look terrible," Nellie said.

"Thanks for stating the obvious," he groaned. His gray eyes burned into hers suddenly. "Tell me what happened. To Luck."

A painful lump formed in her throat and she tried to swallow it down as the memories flashed through her. "I tried to save him," she whispered thickly, the knot in her throat attempting to keep the words in. She forced them out anyway, "Darroc's creatures just wouldn't stop coming. Darroc was gone but the compulsion he had over them, over the more feral ones, was relentless. Wave after wave. We fought so much and when we thought it was over, there was a final push."

She shook her head, unable to continue, unable to tear the images from her mind. The body parts scattered on the ground, the screams, the unnatural screeches as organs were spilled on the land. Yeah, she'd been through trauma, all right. She wondered if any of the mind healers would have time for her. A lot of time.

Tears trickled out of Jamison's slanted eyes and trailed through his temples. "He was my best friend. It's my fault, what happened to him. If I were there—"

"Don't do that," Nellie interrupted forcefully. "Don't think of the what ifs or put the blame on yourself. He was an excellent fighter. An excellent leader. You being there wouldn't have changed anything, other than you bearing witness to it."

"What happened to his body?"

"We had a funeral pyre before coming here and made sure he and the other fallen were honored properly." Something else she'd never forget. The smell of burning flesh and the hours it took to finish.

"You know … I need a new second …" Jamison trailed off.

"If you're implying it should be me, I should remind you that we aren't even from the same clan."

"We're all one clan now, aren't we?"

Nellie considered that. It was how she thought of it when she was training them and again when they were all battling together on Earth, so there shouldn't have been a reason to think differently now. Didn't she just inwardly claim them as hers, anyway?

Still, Nellie snorted. "As if I'd be second best to anyone." She smirked at him and placed her hand on the least raw part of his flesh. "I'll check on you later. Please eat and get some rest. They will take good care of you."

Nellie turned around and slammed head-first into a hard body.

"Nellie."

She took a deep breath, trying not to pay attention to his the scent of sea mist and aftershave. She knew when she first arrived and jumped into his arms that maybe she was being too hasty, but it felt good to see Endo, and even better to be back in Anestra. Her emotions took over, and she didn't want that to happen again this time. Now that she had a bit of time to process, something felt off.

"Hey, I've been trying to talk to you," Endo said as he closed in on her.

Nellie took a step back in return and the gesture didn't pass him by.

His eyebrows furrowed and he jutted his chin in defiance.

"I've had to make my rounds, Endo. Not to mention, I'm starving from all the shifting, stink worse than my grandmother's underpants, and desperately need to sleep for no less than seventeen years."

"Of course," Endo said quickly, his face clearing. "I only meant that King Dennison wishes to speak with you along with the rest of the Royal Guard."

Nellie perked up at that. It had been a while since she'd been with the Guard, and she forgot that she was a member as well. They might be a great distraction for her, but *gods*, her bed was desperately shrieking her name.

"Right," Nellie said, turning toward the barracks. "I assume they're in the meeting house?"

"No, they're in the Council Room," he said, placing his hand on the small of her back and leading her to the mansion. "I'll walk with you there."

"I've got her," Hunter's voice cut through the beginning of Nellie's protestations.

A sense of cautious relief coursed through her. The darkness seeping from Hunter was palpable and she didn't know if she'd rather take her chances having an awkward conversation with Endo. It didn't feel evil, just … angry? Agitated? Dangerous.

Now that the Val was out in the open and he didn't have to hide himself anymore, it seemed as though Hunter was letting it all out.

"Oh, okay …" Endo's voice trailed off as he glanced between the two of them. "See you later, Nellie."

Nellie stared after Endo for a moment before falling in step next to Hunter. "I don't know if I should thank you or not, but can I just say, wow, this whole vibe you have going is delicious."

A ghost of a smile haunted Hunter's face. "Still have that same humor, do you?"

"It's really all I have going for me," Nellie sighed.

"There are things I want to discuss with you," Hunter started.

"If it's anything to do with Faria, the answer is there is no way in heck I'm getting involved in your mess."

"After you've rested, I need you to turn into a *Drogosterra*."

Unexpected request. "Ahh, yes. Heard of my beautiful beastly prowess, I'm sure?"

"You need to find the youngling that flew off when Ander disappeared. I need you to talk to her."

Nellie suppressed a bubble of laughter and looked up at Hunter. His face was devoid of emotion, not that there was much anyway, but she wanted to believe he was joking. "Umm ... you need me ... to talk to a dragon?"

"*Drogosterra.* They're more than dragons. They're incredibly intelligent creatures and bond quickly with their soldiers. It was why they were created; the entire reason for their existence is to have a bond with us. That one felt compelled toward Ander for some reason, and Ander seemingly abandoning her has put us in a precarious situation."

Nellie pretended to understand what precarious situation he was referring to. "Well, you're coming with me, right? I know nothing about *Drogosterra,* even though I battle as one like the Boss B I am. How am I supposed to soothe a giant creature I know nothing about?"

"It would be more than soothing. I want you to train her."

"Train her." Maybe she was delirious with lack of sleep, but he couldn't possibly have suggested that she—a human, a shapeshifter, a twenty-two-year-old hormone-crazy girl whose middle name was mischief—train a dragon.

"Yes. To fight with us."

"And you, a Val soldier, who you just said they were created for, cannot do this?"

Hunter shook his head and gripped his hand against the bow he held. The tattoos under his skin shifted with the movement. "There are still so many things locked inside me. Memories, abilities. I can't remember so much and it has nothing to do with me living a thousand years. Someone or something is preventing me from seeing properly who I am and what I can do."

Nellie wanted to know more but the angrier he got, the more the darkness threatened to rip the air from her lungs. "Can I ask you something?"

He sighed almost imperceptibly. "You can always ask, but I might not answer."

"Typical," she said, but without the joking gusto she normally carried. "Listen … don't take this the wrong way, but … you're grim now, my dude."

"Care to elaborate?" his tone was saturated with boredom, but the way he shifted his shoulders suggested he knew exactly what she was talking about.

"Whatever it is, Faria has it, too," she continued in a quiet voice. "She mentioned she felt the same from Ander. She kept wondering if Darroc did something to them if there was a seed of darkness planted within her when she thought he impregnated her."

Hunter flexed his jaw hard enough that Nellie heard a crack. "It isn't something Darroc did to any of us. It's called the *malosin obsinae*. It's an added ... hmm ... reflex, is the closest comparison you would understand. The legend is that the Fae placed it in us when we were created so we would have no compunctions over doing whatever was necessary to protect the Agostonna's."

Nellie was shocked that he offered any type of explanation and was about to ask if he was feeling all right when he continued.

"It's something we have to fight to control once it starts to form, but then it acts as another limb, doing what we desire of it with barely a second thought. Has she done something? Said something?"

"No, not really." Nellie wanted to tread carefully as she had only just started to get back into Faria's good graces and didn't want her friend mad at her for saying anything behind her back. "It's just that she seems to be motivated by emotion more than anything."

"That's nothing new," he said.

"No, but when we were battling Darroc, she had this plan ... to take things into her own hands. She said she didn't want anyone else dying because of her and it's ... It's almost an obsession. And her powers have increased tenfold. She healed a girl who was almost dead, who then turned out to be Darroc's mother, which was wild, and—"

"Wait, what?" Hunter stopped in his tracks and grabbed Nellie's arm, halting her footsteps as well. "Darroc's mother?"

"Yeah, okay. Well, long story short, Darroc's mom is a phoenix, and she—"

"The same seen here a year ago?"

"I mean, probably, how many phoenixes are supposed to exist? Anyways, turns out she's just been living and dying for centuries. So this time she was dying and Faria healed her. I mean, basically raised her from the dead."

"And those powers worked on Earth?" Hunter stared off into the distance.

Nellie wished she could get inside his head to see what he was thinking about. "Yes, that was the strange thing," she said, starting again toward *Mentage*. "This blue light emanated from her, and the girl kept calling her 'my queen, my queen.' Well, anyways, turns out that Moira, the girl, used to live in Anestra until Darroc almost killed her."

"Really," Hunter said.

"Yes, okay, I'll spill all that tea later. The point is, Moira is the Wendorrian queen. *Was* the Wendorrian queen. There was this bracelet of power—once Faria put it on, it sort of seeped into her and then she had—I don't know—not new abilities, but … something extra."

"Mhmm …"

"Are you listening to me?"

"Yes, Nellie, of course. I'm assuming that once Faria steps on Wendorre land and claims it as hers, then that's when the warlocks will feel the change within them as well."

Nellie's heart ached for the warlocks who had to watch their people suffer for centuries. At the heart of it, they just wanted their lives to be what they were. Originally, that was once Darroc's mission as well.

If Faria could somehow make it happen for them, unite both countries, or at least … restore what was lost? Who knows how that could change the tide against Darroc. They needed every warlock possible and to have them at full strength would potentially be a game changer.

Nellie and Hunter walked up the stone steps that led to a patio outside of the dining hall at *Mentage*. Blue veins interspersed throughout the white stone, like glinting ice in the dull wintery sun. Hunter led Nellie through glass double doors and entered the vast room.

Wooden beams crossed along the ceiling in elaborate arches and the Agostonna banner hung from the rafters. *Mentage* felt different from the last time Nellie was there, the night Queen Amira died. It wasn't run down, necessarily, but everything seemed to be shrouded in shadow.

"*Mentage* is only as strong as its queen," Hunter said as if reading her thoughts.

For all she knew, he probably did.

"And though Faria technically is its queen; she has yet to complete the binding ceremony to make it so."

"Can she catch a break for once?" Nellie wondered aloud. "If she's binding her essence to everyone else, what will she have left to give herself?"

As they stopped outside the Council Chamber, Hunter had nothing to say.

FIVE

FARIA

The nightmares, the visions. Would they ever stop?

A cave, a set of scales—she had seen this all before. A fire. Hooded beings, their faces too dark for her to tell who they belong to. A fleet of *Drogosterra*. Armor made of scales. Screams. Endless agony. Ash. A phoenix.

Faria awoke in bed, a cold sweat slicking the sheets she lay upon. Tiny dust motes floated in the rays of the setting sun, her breath disturbing their path to nowhere. She longed to be as carefree to float where her body wished to go. What a wonderful feeling it must be, to let go.

A knock sounded at the door and she let out a huff of laughter. Typical. For a moment she wondered which helper her mother sent to her, which outfit she was meant to wear that day.

Then she remembered.

Faria glanced around her room, her eyes settling on the wardrobe full of dresses and skirts, silks and lace her mother insisted she wear and a deep sadness welled inside. There was so much left unsaid. So many things she would never know the answers to. The one letter … It wasn't enough.

"Enter."

Faria heard the door to the outer chamber open, then another soft knock on her bedroom door. She sighed, unsure if it was relief she felt over it not being Nellie, as she would have barged in without the courtesy of manners. It was still too early to be bombarded by her endless energy.

A head full of silver hair peeked through the door and then a wisp of a woman appeared. She moved the way a shadow grew long throughout the day, graceful and patient, whose presence made itself known with each passing hour. She was a godmother to Faria, an adoptive mother to Nellie, and the only member of the Secret Keepers whose identity wasn't so secret.

"Faline!" Faria gasped before throwing herself in the woman's arms.

Unabashedly, tears flowed down her cheeks and pooled against Faline's cotton shirt. She smelled of lavender and myrrh, of old tomes and tradition. Of the Autumn Garden, the scent of leaves just before they changed.

"Hush now," Faline said, rubbing circles into Faria's back. "It's all right, child. Everything is fine."

Faria sniveled, uncaring about the snot dripping down her face. "Nothing is fine, Faline. You know that."

"What I know is that not one moment has broken you, yet. Every challenge you faced, every hardship you endured, it strengthened you. Fifi, you are not the same young elf that left here. You have evolved, as we all must, in the currents of grief." Faline grasped Faria's shoulders and pushed away from her. "There is so much we have to discuss and plan. But first I must know, are your abilities under control?"

Faline looked between Faria's eyes, and not for the first time, the young queen felt as though Faline were reading her like one of her many precious tomes. And this time, Faria knew she didn't have the luxury or time to lie to her.

"There is … something. A lot of somethings, actually." Faria fingered a loose thread on her quilt, tracing the golden whorls and symbols adorning it. "News here spreads fast, so I'm not sure what you've heard …" She took a deep breath and squared her shoulders, looking at Faline head-on. If she was the queen of Anestra then she had to at least give off an air of confidence. "I have the warlocks' power. I feel it churning inside me. It burns and cools and feels as though there is a constant ache under my skin and all it wants to do is … blossom."

Faline searched her face, her arms, her skin, but hesitated to say anything.

"What is it?" Faria asked. "Just say it."

"Are you sure this feeling isn't because you're Val?"

Why was she turned into a Val? Did it make her a Val soldier, like Hunter? A protector? A Val queen? The more questions she had, the less the answers seemed to come.

She tried to swallow past the lump in her throat. It took her a long time to admit to herself that she might be Val and it was still hard to accept she wasn't an elf, though that had never felt right to her either. No, now she knew where she belonged, but she didn't have a firm grasp on that, either. There were only three of them in existence, as far as she was aware, and with the Fae still missing, she had no one to ask for an explanation.

"I know it's warlock because of the way it feels in my body. My blood can taste its essence; it knows every strand of this power's being. The part that makes me Val is all-encompassing, but this feels like pieces of a whole. It wants to get out, though I don't know how to do it."

"I might have an idea on that," Faline said. "Technically, you are the warlock queen, however, you aren't officially queen until you step foot into Wendorre. I think once you are there, the magic will do what it needs to."

"Go to Wendorre?" That journey would take weeks, at best, without a threat on their heels. "How am I to manage that? Not only that, but surely Darroc would have some sort of fail-safe put into place? Something to trap me once I was there?"

"Hmm … perhaps," Faline said, considering. "Given that he never told you to claim your right as queen you'd need to step on the land, we can assume he had alternative motives. More than that, he believed he would rule Anestra, and the only way for him to do that would be to make sure you weren't around. He thought he needed your power, so yes, I'd conclude you would have been trapped somewhere."

"And yet, it's something you want me to risk, now?"

"No, child. That's something you must speak to others about. Your father, and especially your Royal Guard."

My Royal Guard. It was so official, the thing she left unsaid hanging between them in the tense silence that followed.

"Speaking of ..." Faline trailed off, looking at the chamber around her.

Faria followed her eyes from the wardrobe to the balcony doors leading out to the Spring Garden. Faria had a feeling she knew what Faline would say. Her throat constricted in anticipation.

"The royal chambers are yours now," Faline finished gently. "Your father moved out the day after ... you were gone. He said it wasn't right anymore to sleep in a place that didn't belong to him."

A place without her mother is what he meant. Goddess above, she was so selfish, still. So many things were happening to her, yes, but they were happening to those she cared about as well.

The entire walk back to her rooms, which she insisted on going to when her father tried to drag her to the other side of *Mentage*, he had only asked about her or stayed quiet. Was he waiting for reciprocity? For a shared moment of grief?

"We have people available who can pack up this side and move your belongings over. Or you can stay here if you wish. Of course, you can do whatever you desire now."

Faria sighed as she rose from the bed and headed to the wardrobe. "Where to sleep should be last on anyone's list of worries, should it not?"

Faline gave a small smile. "Of course. Though, you would also have access to the queen's personal library, which I hear is filled with more than just historical ditties from when the goddesses roamed the earth."

A huff of laughter escaped Faria's lips. "Sounds like Nellie will get more use out of that than I would."

"Have you two mended things?"

Faria turned away from Faline and opened the wardrobe, if only for something to do. The grief at seeing the silks and colorful fabrics made her ache for her mother. She tossed aside dress after dress. The sweet floral and cinnamon scent that clung to her mother's skin was seeped into the clothing and Faria buried her face in the chiffon sleeve of an evening gown. *That was a mistake.*

What was it Faline said? Right, Nellie. Focus on her instead. Faria didn't know exactly what it was that hurt her more when it came to Nellie. The fact that she had lied to Faria for as long as she'd known her was hard to get over, though it was understandable. Nellie had to keep herself safe and couldn't tell anyone about her being a shapeshifter. Though, for all the talk about them being like sisters, it seemed maybe there would have been a hint of … something different. Even if there was, Faria could admit she wouldn't have seen it. She loved her people, but she was so preoccupied with herself, she might not have noticed.

Like when Nellie spent so long trying to get Faria alone last year. Nellie had tried to explain that Darroc was evil, that Faria was feeding into exactly what he wanted from her. At the time, Faria only took it as an attack against her character. And if she was being honest with herself, she felt shame about it as well because Nellie was right. She had fed into it. She had desperately wanted to explore the darkness that seeped the land, and she'd been caught up in its temptation. She couldn't handle that Nellie called her out on it.

It came down to the feeling of abandonment. That Nellie stayed away during the entire time Faria was grieving, when she was pregnant and sick, she thought of all the ways she wished she could have ended herself if the life she'd grown did not prevent such a thing from happening. Nellie never checked on her at all, and she knew everyone would have known by then what happened to her.

"We have an understanding," Faria said, her voice harder than she meant it to be. "We went through a lot in the three weeks we were on Earth, but we haven't cleared the air entirely."

"It will come in time. Repairing relationships is a lot harder than it is to break them. Difficult feelings aren't easy to erase. Memory never seems to truly forget."

Faria snorted. That was the truth. Given she already had an extended life, goddesses willing, she knew it would be a long time before she ever truly forgave anyone for abandoning her.

What a hypocrite I am, she thought. *I've abandoned everyone.*

"There's one other thing," Faria said, pulling on a black tunic to go with the dark pants she found at the bottom of her wardrobe.

"Hmm, it isn't like you to be so forthcoming with information."

Faria knew Faline meant it as a joke but she couldn't help but feel uncomfortable with the truth of it. "I am queen now, aren't I? I have to share all the necessary information."

Faline, who had been readying a cup of tea, stopped to focus on the young queen. "Go on, child."

"There is a darkness in me," Faria started. "Originally, I thought Darroc had succeeded in planting his seed of evil when he impregnated me. When I realized who Ander's father was, I was relieved, knowing that my worst fears weren't true. And yet, it grows still. It didn't leave when I gave birth nor at any time after. I suppose for me it has only been … a month? Since I had Ander, but I would have thought …"

The ticking of a clock and distant voices in the fields beyond the garden trickled their way between their thoughts.

"It grows, Faline. It isn't warlock, it isn't any of my abilities. It feels like something that was always there, but more so now. And I'm worried I won't be able to control it. It makes me impulsive, emotional, irrational."

"Stress can do that to anyone, especially someone who has been through as much as you."

"It isn't stress, and even if it were, that doesn't instill much confidence in having me as queen."

"There is still time to worry about your confidence as queen." Faline picked up a brush and swept it through Faria's unkempt hair.

The action soothed Faria, though she did wish she had taken the time to fix her hair while bathing the previous night. At least then, Faline wouldn't have felt the need to take care of her in this way.

"We need to do the formal ceremony and the blood rites to the land before you are officially Anestra's queen."

"Surely we won't be dallying with a traditional ceremony and party after in a time like this?"

"No, no. But the ceremony will have to be done soon. Today, if possible."

Anxiety welled in Faria. Was she ready for this? She'd been claiming herself queen for weeks now, but could she truly manage it? "Why the rush?"

Faline worked her fingers along Faria's scalp, gathering pieces of hair to make traditional elven braids. "With the shifters on the land, you need to have them sign the Contract to prevent any violence, just in case. And that can't happen until the land accepts you as hers."

Right. The shifters. The Contract. She had learned about the importance of it, of course, but she never thought of the possibility of the land rejecting her.

Another knock at the door produced a steward with a tray of food for her. Cinnamon rolls and fresh strawberries. Why would the kitchens take the time to produce a luxury like cinnamon rolls on the cusp of battle? Was this also something she'd need to address as queen?

"The good food is to keep spirits up," Faline said as if reading her mind. "We aren't in the middle of a battle now, are we? Let's enjoy the little luxuries until we can't anymore. If we all find one ritual that makes us happy, then we will always find happiness within each day, no?"

Faline's unending wisdom brought tears to Faria's eyes. Happiness. When had she last felt it? Truly? "I shall speak to my father about the ceremony."

"One last thing," Faline said as she made her way to the door. "You might want to speak to Hunter about that darkness of yours."

"I don't think so," Faria said quickly. "I'm not willing to share any vulnerabilities with him."

"I'm not forcing a relationship of trust onto you, child. That darkness you feel—Hunter has the same. It rolls off him, and while it's not evil, it is significant and has been driving his own emotional decisions lately. I believe he knows what it's called and why you have it."

Faria flashed back to her memories—were they her memories?—of the body she saw, bloodied and broken. Crispin. Hunter had done that to him.

She shook her head, unable to believe he was capable of it, and yet, wouldn't she do anything to protect what she deemed as hers? Was she capable of the same?

Mercy ruled her heart, but was it vengeance that grasped her soul?

Another knock at the door shook her from her macabre thoughts. It was just a result of the trauma, the loss. Nothing more. She was probably overthinking things.

Faria quickly tossed on a pair of black boots and regarded herself in the mirror. Faline had done her hair in the way her mother had always worn it: elven braids from the crown down to the root, then pulled back in a way that accented her strong cheekbones. She had bags under her eyes and her frown was filled with more than just disdain for her position. There was a sadness in the downward turn, one that she hadn't had even at her lowest. She might have been queen, but she didn't feel strong enough for the job.

Faria took a bite of cinnamon roll. The warm gooey sweetness slid down her throat and she moaned in appreciation. She had truly missed *Mentage's* cooking.

She swung the door open, her food sticking in her throat as she let her unexpected guest in. He took up the space of a man twice his size. The bright yellow halos surrounding his impossibly green eyes. The infuriating half-smirk he still had the audacity to give her, even after everything.

"Hello, *Princess.*"

That nickname. She hated it once because she didn't want to be a princess, and now she hated it because the name belonged to him. She swallowed and affected a look of boredom, or so she hoped, even though her insides were a tempestuous storm ready to raze the land.

"There is no princess in Anestra. What you meant to say was, Hello, Queen."

SIX

ANDER

He knew he shouldn't have gone to her. He knew Darroc could be anywhere, or one of his spies, at least. He had minions everywhere, keeping tabs on all his *possessions*. Yet, when Ander appeared back on Earth, did he know he would end up at her house? That she would see him?

"Ander," his name drifted to him on the wind, the angelic whisper bringing him instant comfort. "What the hell are you doing here?"

Ahh, there she was. He smirked to himself. Try to kill a girl one time and they never seemed to let that go. He walked to where Jane stood in her window, the crunch of leaves under his heavy boots mixing with the acrid scent of sulfur still clinging to his skin. *What am I doing here?*

"Why are you still out there? Hurry up!"

He climbed in through the window and stood in her bedroom,

staring down at her short frame. The space in her room felt distorted as if it were trying to move to accommodate him.

"Cripes, you stink."

He rubbed his neck, self-conscious to be near her, but he failed to find the words to explain his appearance or why he came to be at her house at all.

"Hello! Are you going to say anything? What are you doing here?" The muted light in the bedroom accentuated the golden streaks of her chestnut hair.

He stared into her dark eyes and noticed that while her words were hostile, her eyebrows were drawn in a frown. She was concerned for him.

"I, umm ..." Why couldn't he speak around her? "I don't know. I don't know where to go." He glanced down at his clothes, the charred holes allowing patches of his skin to peek through. It was stupid to show up there. Ander made to run a hand through his hair before his eye caught on the swirled pattern etched into his palm where the *Drogosterra* had breathed into him. He regretted leaving as he had.

He rubbed the design and felt heat swirling from it. Sadness filled him and for a moment he thought he heard the preening moan from the *Drogosterra* he left behind.

"So you go to your enemy's house? Is that wise?"

Ander shook his head and redirected his focus to the spirited girl standing in front of him. Jane had her hand on a jutted-out hip and waited impatiently for a response.

"Still can't forget a bit of attempted murder? Is that what makes an enemy?"

She scoffed. "No, asshole, because of the havoc you're wreaking on the Earth. Are you ever going to attempt to heal this sickness spreading to everyone? This is a global issue. The human population is quickly reducing."

A stone of despair took root in his stomach. It was easy to forget, for a moment, of the absolute destruction he caused. Ander was so tired of endless murder without reason or explanation and thought he would be able to save the clan leader afterward. It turned out that maybe all his abilities weren't under his control.

"I should probably start by apologizing …"

"Don't bother. You wouldn't know what to apologize for, anyway."

"Everything."

"Well, you can start with the stench pouring off you. Why do you smell like you slept in a freaking hole in the ground?"

"I practically did," he mumbled. "Look, I'm putting you in danger just by being here. This was a bad idea."

She stepped closer to him, her tiny frame completely dwarfed by his. He couldn't take the pity in her eyes.

"This was a mistake," he said again before she would say something comforting and break his resolve.

"Look … take a shower at least. I can find some clothes for you. But if any of my guardians ask if I've been with you, I will deny it until my last breath."

He went to the ensuite, then turned back toward her. "Why are you being nice to me? I've never apologized for anything, I've never … We aren't even friends. Why offer me kindness?"

She gave him a small smile. "If I allow you a memory, will you be able to see it?"

"I think so."

She placed her hand on his arm and a liquid heat seared through his skin and traveled into his blood until—

Burning pain steals the breath from my body before I realize my heart has stopped beating.

It had been there moments ago. I'd felt it as Liz updated me with the daily hot gossip. We had just been taking our usual walk around the parking lot during our free period, talking about how Jesse cheated on Marlene at Conor's party last Friday, but I was instead thinking about how wasted I'd gotten even though I'd only had one beer. I am like, 99 percent sure that I made out with some kid I never even saw before which is so not like me, and then Bam! Pain tears through me so quickly and viciously, it felt like an arrow went straight through my heart. I glance down and see the black metal shaft sticking out before my head slams against the pavement.

"Oh my God! Jane!" Liz pulls at the fiery hair plastered to my forehead in the sticky heat.

The pavement burns through my flesh. I am almost positive I am actively getting third-degree burns from it. I can imagine the headlines now, Florida Girl Gets Shot; Dies From Pavement Burns.

"Jane! Someone shot you! Like, with an arrow."

Besides the fact that what has just happened to me is completely obvious, I can barely process anything past her shrieking at me.

It doesn't strike me as weird to be assaulted by an arrow in the middle of the day in my high school parking lot, or that once the arrow hit me, my muscles were completely paralyzed. It's most absurd to me that despite what has just happened to me, Liz keeps talking as if I can hear or understand her through the shock of being shot.

Sirens shriek through the parking lot—I can still hear and understand my surroundings, thank god. EMTs rush over and attempt to talk to me. Though I can process what they want, I froze.

They place me on the gurney and I start to panic. Frantic whispers shoot through the gathering crowd. I try making out what's being said to prepare myself for the utter embarrassment I'll have to endure tomorrow.

"Gently. Don't move the arrow," one of the EMT's hiss.

"Where's the blood?"

"There's no blood? Why isn't she bleeding?"

Oh man, is that Conor? How humiliating. It sounds like half the school surrounds me and this is the opposite of the kind of gossip I want going around about me.

Actually, why am I even thinking anything at all? My body is paralyzed from the arrow and my heart stopped freaking beating. Shouldn't I be dead?

This must be some sort of alternate reality. Or maybe an I'm-in-a coma-and-floating-over-my-body type of dream situation. That's possible, right? Yeah, that has to be it.

Latex fingers search for a pulse and the stench of coffee breath wafts over me. This seems entirely too realistic for a coma dream. If I wasn't completely petrified by the weapon sticking out of me, I would have given him a piece of my mind about how rude it is to breathe on someone. Especially when everyone is sick with some sort of serious flu right now.

As I'm lifted into the ambulance, my eyes fall in line with something shining in the trees surrounding the parking lot. It looks like the sun is reflecting off something and it isn't until the doors slam shut that I realize I'm looking at a huge metallic bow, held by a boy I think I know. His eyes shine, though I feel like I can see them flash in my mind as if they are a memory attempting to resurface. Green with a yellow halo shining around the pupils. I remember thinking they were so beautiful when I first saw them … which was … when?

We peel out of the parking lot. After a minute I realize we're riding in silence. Isn't this a serious medical emergency? Where the heck are the sirens? I'm freaking paralyzed. By an arrow.

"Jane Emory Novak, my name is Santana," Coffee Breath says to me. "I'm so glad we were the ones to arrive first." He moves into my line of vision and gives me a smile as if we're long-lost friends. "It is such an honor to finally meet you."

"Tan, can we save the pleasantries for later and help me out here?" that voice doesn't sound as friendly, but it can be because she is gasping for air.

Santana's hands hover over my eyes, brown skin covering my face in shadow. Cold air whips around me as purple electric volts trickle out of his hands and carry themselves over my face, racing toward the arrow.

My body feels (feels! It feels something!) warm and tingly, and after what seems like a freaking eternity, I'm finally able to move my face.

"What the actual heck is happening right now?" my voice sounds like razors cutting through cheesecloth—scratchy and static.

"Don't try to talk until we get this thing out of you," Miss Warm and Sweet says to me. "The spell could be irreversible if it shifts."

"Pardon? Spell?" I'm not one for following directions.

"We're almost done, Jane." Sweat travels down Santana's forehead.

After another minute, the bed jolts as if the ambulance drove over a speed bump before I realize it was the force of the arrow being ejected from me that lifted my body off the gurney. Sharp prickles of pin-needled pain spread down my limbs and into my fingers and toes. My tongue is swollen from where I must have bitten it when my head hit the pavement from the force of the arrow. My mouth is like sandpaper against a tin roof, and hunger tears through me. Apparently nearly dying makes a person hungry. Everything seems in working order except for one minor thing.

"Um, where is my freaking heartbeat?" I'm also not one for beating around the bush.

"It will return shortly when the poison leaves your veins." Bedside manners aren't in Miss Warm and Sweet's repertoire. She lifts my arm and lets it flop down again. Bubblegum-pink-colored hair enters my vision followed by shrewd hazel eyes frowning down at me.

"I don't need bedside manners. It doesn't get the job done."

"I didn't say anything!" Stunned that she read my thoughts, I lie there, embarrassment flushing me for a moment, but wouldn't you know, I'm not one for subtlety. "Okay, peaches, who are you? Where in the world am I and what the heck are you guys?" Smooth.

"Jane, I am Santana, this is Lindy, and we are your Guides." Ocean Eyes stared down at me, wrapping me in their cozy tide.

His smile is dazzling but annoyance prickles behind my eyes as I feel my headache spread with impatience.

"Guides?"

"Guides. You know, leaders. Teachers. Of Everlife."

Peaches is on the verge of making me go as crazy as the nut who shot me.

"What are you saying?"

"Jane, you are a Celestial, and you were lanced with the Spear of the Fallen."

Ander's head swam as the visions left and the last echoes of voices receded from his ears. The Spear of the Fallen. He hadn't heard anyone call his arrows that before. Darroc had gifted him a quiver of black arrows he'd said were spelled to never miss their mark. Why was the Spear of the Fallen significant?

"I showed you that memory because you couldn't have killed me. You thought shooting me in the heart would have ended me, but it wouldn't have. Your arrow would have leeched whatever made me a Celestial, but I can't die until every ounce is gone." She shifted closer to Ander, her hand sliding down his arm until she grasped his fingers. "I know you've been misguided. I've learned a lot since my Guides made themselves known to me."

It didn't make him feel better, but he supposed he could come to terms with his murder attempt having failed anyway. Darroc must have known about her; it was the only explanation for why Darroc wanted Ander to eliminate her.

"Does Darroc know?" Ander had to make sure. He needed to make sense of it all, of what his role was supposed to be in all this.

"He knows there are those on Earth who are meant to fight in the apocalypse. Soldiers. If he could eliminate them, he'd have more of a chance of dominating all the realms."

"Why does he think himself a god?"

"The better question is, how can we work together to stop him? Look, my guardians would have a fit if they knew Darroc's prodigy was in my house, but for the sake of both of us, take a shower. I'll order us some food and then maybe we can figure out how to work together."

Ander had shown up at Jane's house for a reason. Maybe this was it.

SEVEN

NELLIE

"We need you to train the *Drogosterra*."

Nellie had entered the Council Room five minutes prior, and besides the Royal Guard showering her with a chorus of "Welcome home!" and asking for stories of her adventures, King Dennison got straight to the point. Hunter had warned her already about going after the flying Nessie, but she had hoped he wasn't serious about *training* it. She was a *Drogosterra* for basically a day. That thing had been one its whole life. How was she supposed to train it for anything?

"Sorry, train? Like a puppy? Shall I teach it to fetch?"

"I'm going to overlook that tone as exhaustion or perhaps stress," King Dennison said, his voice lacking the usual humor he was known to have, "but the request remains the same. You are to look for the *Drogosterra*.

You are to communicate with it, let it know that we are friends, or at the very least that it isn't allowed to eat anyone and keep destruction to an absolute minimum."

"Um …" Nellie didn't know exactly how to tell King Dennison he must be trippin' but … he must be. "Look, I can absolutely go on the hunt for it. But for you to assume I can communicate with it feels like a bit much. I'm just a human."

"No, you're not," the room said in unison.

"Nellie," Johanna, leader of the Royal Guard, said, "remember what I said last year? There is only ever one true shapeshifter at a time. That's you. You can't be human. And even if you were, you already know you can communicate with others. How else were you able to train the shifters you brought over when they were in their animal form?"

"How do you know I trained them?" Nellie asked. "Could you guys see in the other realm?"

"No," Reed said. His lanky body leaned against the wall as if he were in pain. "But why else would they have collectively decided to come to our aid?"

Nellie wondered what had happened to him while she was on Earth.

"But we also fought Darroc's creatures," Reed continued, "and there is no way anyone untrained would have survived. That those shifters are still here says as much as we'd thought with your involvement with them."

Nellie was embarrassed by the turn of the conversation. For so long, she stayed quiet, as much in the shadows as she could. From living a nomadic life with her mother to keeping her head down and out of trouble with her clan, and then once she was banished, she had to be another person, hiding who she was. She was never given the opportunity for a leadership role, until recently when Queen Amira demanded it of her. But to say that it was because of her that any shapeshifters survived …

"It was Faria's idea to train them. I wanted nothing to do with it. If I'm being honest, I was happy to let them rot for what they put me through. I don't deserve any praise at all."

"What matters most is that you were willing to change," King Dennison said. "You saw past your need for vengeance and followed your queen." He placed his hand on Nellie's shoulder. "You have never failed to follow your queen, no matter how difficult the task she asked of you was. A proper leader knows when to follow. And I guarantee those dozens of shifters, not just from your own clan, but multiple, will still look to you for guidance from now on."

"And," Enis added, "the one named Marisa was telling Jamison all about what you'd done for them when he followed Queen Faria into the fire realm. Our healers were hanging on to every word she said. You will be spoken about for a long time to come." She paused a moment. "What is she, by the way? Marisa? She gives off the most interesting aura."

"A siren, I think. Or some variation of one. I haven't heard the full history yet."

"That might actually be useful," Wilhelm said.

Nellie scrutinized Wil the way she had Reed. His stocky body was hunched over the wooden table; a sling wrapped around his arm. Nellie had never seen him so tired, but she was glad to see that both he and Reed survived Darroc's creatures. At least one love story needed to work out.

"There's news that Mercy Bay has been reporting disturbances in the ocean. Fish gone missing, the colors muted without their usual vibrancy. A few who charter boats to do a spice trade along the coast even reported an island missing."

Endo piped in then. Nellie hadn't noticed him lurking in the corner and her discomfort rose again. What was it that left her feeling so uneasy? She'd gone to bat for him over and over. Believed in him, knew he would come back to the right side. But … why hadn't he tried to rally together the other warlocks? Perhaps the ones who also felt cheated by Darroc and were ashamed of their alliances? Others who wanted to prove their loyalty to Anestra and the Agostonna crown that had never let them down?

Why did he spend so much time, so close to all the inner workings of the Royal Guard? Had he become a member while she was gone? She knew it was only three weeks for her, but nearly a year had passed for them. He could have said or done anything to make up for leaving, as she'd hoped he would have. Plus, Endo was just as skilled as Hunter in most forms of combat since he'd lived at *Mentage* for the past fifteen years, at least.

And yet … did it not strike anyone else as suspicious? How could they be sure he wasn't under a spell of Darroc's? No one knew Callum was except for Nellie, who was promptly ignored, until it was too late.

Endo's ocean eyes shifted from the map laid out on the table in front of them and suddenly pierced through her. She'd always loved them, thought the deep cerulean was like waves she wanted to swim in for hours. But now, were they colder? Stormier? His eyebrows drew down in concern the longer he stared at her.

Cripes, she forgot he could read emotions. He was going to know she found him suspicious or at the very least, that the fun feelings she once had for him were gone.

"We've also had reports from Wendorre," Endo said, reverting his attention to the map. "A few warlocks stationed down there waiting for signs of Darroc made friends with some sailors who just came back from near Widow's Passageway."

"Widow's Passageway?" Enis said. Her left eye was swollen to a deep purple.

Nellie wondered why she hadn't seen a healer about it. Their tonics could have healed it in an hour, tops.

Enis shifted her short black hair behind a pointed ear. "Why would anyone travel over there? It's impassable."

"Warlocks are excellent navigators," Endo said, his voice lowered in annoyance. "We've been traveling through there for centuries."

"So, those are all your ships wrecked along the mountain cliff then?"

"There used to be three islands that made up the oasis," he went on, ignoring the jab. "Now there are more. And, besides that, there have been reports of something lurking in the waters."

"The ocean has always been filled with lots of sea creatures we don't understand," Nellie said. "I'm sure it's like that here as it is on Earth. What does that matter?"

"They say it's eerie, having land pop up out of nowhere and more creatures to go along with it."

"What did the creature look like?"

"Don't know, just that it has tentacles."

"So your excellent navigating seamen saw an octopus and thought to report it?" Nellie didn't understand where he was going with this.

"It isn't an octopus. Now that we have a siren—who I assume needs water to shift—she can explore for us and see what's happening."

King Dennison interrupted before Nellie could give him a scathing reply. There was no way she would let anyone use the shifters as some sort of tool for convenience or hobby. "Endo. You're not here to decide what the shifters will or won't do, especially not to satisfy your curiosities. Am I clear?"

"Yes," Endo said, taking a step back against the wall.

Nellie noticed a movement to her right and realized Hunter stood behind her. She hadn't heard him come back to the Council Room after he'd dropped her off there. His face remained impassive, so she couldn't tell what he'd thought of what Endo said.

"Don't you think Faria should be a part of this meeting?" Hunter said. "We would never have a meeting without Queen Amira, and to plan what to do, no matter how small, without Faria won't instill confidence in her as a leader."

"Thank you for telling me what I should or should not do with my daughter," the king replied tersely.

Nellie raised her eyebrows. It was unlike King Dennison to not be filled with compassion and empathy. He was normally laid back, and though he was the commander of their army, he was always willing to share a laugh. The past year had taken a toll on him.

Nellie eyed each of the Royal Guard, their faces haggard, their bent armor riddled with bite marks and bloodstains. The past year had damaged everyone.

"Faria needs to first perform the ceremony so we can have the shifters sign the Contract. Then we will continue with war and strategy."

"Um—" Reed tried to interrupt.

"I think Faria will want to visit with her people," Nellie piped in. "She was most concerned about them in her absence and extremely frustrated about having to choose between them or Ander."

"Ahem, but—" Reed tried again, lifting his arm in an attempt to get their attention.

"We need to meet with Faria," Johanna said. "We must start getting a clear idea of how we will work together and start sharing expectations."

Voices rose in a crescendo, each one attempting to be the loudest in the room.

No one heard the door open.

"If you are all quite done deciding my future," a quiet voice backed with strength and clarity rang out.

Immediately the disparaging voices ceased. A pulse rippled through the room and the fire in the hearth flared in response. Nellie had the sudden urge to bare her neck as if she were a beta in a shifter clan.

Faria stood in front of the door, her hands clasped in front of her, shoulders thrown back and chin held high. She wore black pants and a dark tunic, something she normally would have worn when the world was a different place. Her wavy dark hair was untamed, though the front was woven back in three braids, extending from her temple. It was a look Queen Amira often wore.

"Thank you for taking the liberty to discuss what I shall be doing with my life. It is reassuring to know not much has changed in my absence."

She looked at each person pointedly. "Due to the emergent situation we find ourselves in, it is imperative I first do the blood ceremony with the land. There is no point in me giving orders and demanding the respect of a queen if I am, in fact, not a queen." She took a breath and stepped further into the room.

Gooseflesh rippled across Nellie's arms and the hair on her neck stood on end. The power emanating from Faria far exceeded what she felt from her on Earth. It was as if being back home, back where her ancestors were from, where she was Fae-blessed, with her feet touching the same ground the gods had roamed a millennia before, all heightened her magic.

"If I am blessed enough to have the land accept me, then I will see my people. They need to know I am all right and I will help the healers or those in the kitchen or on the fields as I normally would. Normalcy matters right now. It will also give me the opportunity to check on the shifters and have it known they are not to be harmed. They can sign the Contract then.

"After that, I will meet with the Royal Guard, and you, Father, to catch up on what you have done so far with training and accepting help from allies. After that …" she trailed off, looking from Hunter to Endo. Then her eyes landed on Nellie before shifting back to Hunter again.

The silence was heavy.

Energy rumbled from Hunter. Nellie recognized it as the darkness she had felt on her walk over with him. The fire in the hearth shifted colors, briefly, from orange to crimson to navy with a black center. It was different from the violet and green that used to show when their powers combined. What did it mean?

"After that, Hunter and I must discuss our son."

King Dennison eyed the fire and then stared at his daughter for a moment before he broke the tense silence, "Let us start with the ceremony then. The sooner we do that, the sooner the work to heal and protect can begin."

Faria waited until everyone filed out of the Council Room until all that was left was her, Nellie, and Hunter. He ran his hand through his hair as if he was suddenly uncomfortable, and Nellie watched as Faria looked anywhere but at him. To her surprise, Faria grabbed Nellie's arm and looped her own through it. The queen rushed Nellie out of the door before Hunter could say anything. Nellie heard a frustrated sigh behind them.

"So, I hear you're going after the *Drogosterra*."

Nellie almost asked how, but remembered that elves had exceptional hearing and Faria was basically an elf on steroids. She wouldn't have been surprised if Faria had heard from her chambers on the other side of *Mentage*.

"Yeah, gotta wrestle up Nessie and somehow train her to listen to me, a faux *Drogosterra*."

"Nessie?"

"Like, the Loch Ness monster?" Nellie said. "We need to catch you up on Earth legends."

Faria seemed distracted as she eyed the paintings on the walls, her head cocked to the side as if she heard something no one else could.

Nellie glanced around the hall they walked down, noting the stone walls, the torches, the floor-to-ceiling windows. *Mentage* was a quirky mix of ancient and modern, and while the feeling was different, everything else looked much the same as she remembered.

Faria cleared her throat. "Well, anyway, why would you call yourself a faux *Drogosterra*?"

"Because in the words of the great Christina Perri, 'I'm only human.'"

"You're no more human than I am. The proof is evident in the fact that our weapons changed once they were glazed in your blood. I may not know enough about humans, but I do know their blood doesn't have magical properties like that."

"So you think it's true then? I fully become whatever I shift into? I still retain my human mind, my knowledge, my instincts."

"Yes. And I think my father is right. There should be a way for you to communicate to the fawn and at least help to keep it under control until we can get Ander back here."

Nellie looked out the windows to a busy lawn before the Forest of the Dawn. She longed to just be in the Phoenix Fire eating a slice of honey cheesecake, not contemplating whether or not she could train a dragon.

"I'm sorry, did you just call it a *fawn*?" A fawn to Nellie was a sweet baby deer, not a dragon the size of a city apartment complex.

"I'll admit I don't know much about *Drogosterra* being that I didn't think they truly existed, but yes. That one was certainly a baby."

"It was larger than a school bus. How can you be sure?"

"Because," Hunter interrupted from behind them, probably annoyed at having been left out of the conversation for so long, "an adult *Drogosterra* is four times that size and wouldn't have been scared of a few dozen arrows being shot at it. An adult *Drogosterra* would have protected its target and taken out everyone else. That fawn only cared for Ander and the way she left was her way of having a tantrum."

Nellie felt the strength of attention on her and turned to Faria. Her queen pointedly stared at her, then her eyes shifted back toward Hunter. It took a few moments and an elbow to the gut for her to realize that Faria wanted Nellie to ask him more.

"What do you mean by Ander rejecting her? It just seemed to me like Ander was gonna pet it and then she left." Nellie glanced back at Hunter, who smirked at Faria's back, willing to play the game.

"Sometimes Val soldiers were lucky enough to have a *Drogosterra* pick them. It's a type of bond that if accepted, they swear to protect each other, always put each other first, etcetera."

"Sounds romantic," Nellie said. "If this story is about to take a weird turn, I have to tell you I draw the line at bestiality."

"For someone who regularly turns into beasts, that seems hard to believe."

Nellie opened and shut her mouth several times, unsure how to respond to an accurate, yet extremely wrong statement. "Anyway, this dragon pup chose Ander, and now what? Does he have to accept her back? And if this is something meant for Val soldiers, then why did she choose Ander? He isn't a soldier. There isn't even an army."

"I don't know why that *Drogosterra* decided to follow him, nor why she chose him. Things don't seem to be playing out the same way as centuries before. Perhaps there are more *Drogosterra* out there, ready to commit themselves to any race, not just Val."

"Perhaps there are more Val out there," Faria mumbled to herself.

"I would know," Hunter replied tersely. "We are it."

"Hmm," Faria said, seemingly lost in thought.

"You don't think so?" Nellie asked as they rounded the corner to Faria's wing. She wondered why she hadn't moved herself to the Royal wing yet. Nellie had heard there were some spicy novels hidden away in the private royal library. She'd kill to get her hands on those.

"I don't know what to think, other than everything we think we know is either a lie or has been a misdirection. The Fae are not gone, as one turned me into a Val. The *Drogosterra* did not disappear, as we saw several flying in the fire realm. It's logical to think there could be more across many realms. We did not know shifters still existed, nor did we realize the expanse of different species within the shifter race. I mean, sirens? They are mythical to everyone, are they not? And yet I have a group of them on my lands.

"It stands to reason that given the Gate of all Realms seems to be stabilizing, which according to Moira was only because the Val were coming to power again, that certainly there are more of them." Faria glanced back at Hunter. "Perhaps whoever you've been reporting to has been keeping something from you."

Hunter clenched his jaw but remained silent.

EIGHT

FARIA

The ground was covered in a frozen layer of ice and snow, and though the sun shone, the wind bit through their clothing and armor as they headed out onto a terrace leading to the Spring Garden. Faria led the way, thinking of the only place where the Fae's old magic allowed for the garden to bloom in perpetuity. It was one of her favorite places in all of Anestra—not that she'd been to many places—and she thought it would be fitting to be surrounded by the blooming trees as a symbol for her own new life. The life of a queen.

Though she'd hoped to keep it a quiet ceremony, a crowd started to form once their processional was noticed. It was silly to want to keep it from her people. Goddess knew they needed something to look forward to, and elves were a traditional type. Too traditional. *This land was built on archaic rituals*, Faria thought, not for the first time. Tradition, she knew, kept people together. It gave them expectations, rules to follow, and a purposeful pathway into a hopeful future. A party for this, a ceremony for that, a parade at this time. Religious freedom was allowed, so all the races could live in harmony, but that just meant the previous Agostonna rulers went harder on their self-proclaimed traditions. Faria hated it. It was part of the reason she wanted to change the rules, to break the mold, to transform their land as their people transformed.

It could not, however, begin that day. She knew there was little to nothing she could do about the land accepting her as its new owner unless the Fae wanted to honor them with another visit.

Faria walked along the stone pathway leading into the garden and breathed a sigh as a wall of warm air seasoned with the scents of jasmine and honey greeted her. She was grateful for the Fae magic that still lingered and filled Anestra with extraordinary beauty, allowing it to become ingrained in the souls of her people.

She scoffed at the irony of how the Fae left and yet their presence was still evident in everything they were as a people.

Faria passed by the jade fountain with the mythical beasts displayed: the lion, the bear, the stag, and the phoenix. The conversation she'd had with Darroc, when he told the story of his people and their lost magic, filled her with a surprising sense of sadness. She remembered thinking how she wished she knew more about her own legends and was envious of Darroc for knowing so much about his people.

Of course, she hadn't known at the time that the story he told was autobiographical rather than a legend, but the sentiment remained the same. Maybe she would take a peek at the royal library and see what she could find about the creation of Anestra, on the story of the gods that used to roam the lands before the goddesses banished them.

A stone wall surrounded the garden, but Faria watched as the crowd of humans, elves, warlocks, and even shapeshifters grew. *What a spectacle.* She sighed, wishing again for privacy, if only to save her from the embarrassment if something went wrong. What if the land rejected her?

Whispers felt like screams as her sensitive ears picked up the murmuring.

"Our queen."

"She's doing it now."

"Why didn't they tell us?"

"Should we inform the kitchens?"

"Will we have a celebration after?"

She closed her eyes and focused on blocking out the noise and instead tried to feel what the land wanted her to feel. She removed her boots and stripped her hands of the gloves she wore and knelt on the ground, wanting to touch the ancient power that ran deep through her land. She was getting better at distinguishing the type of magic she felt, especially now that she had the warlocks' magic running through her.

She could feel the essence of the warlocks in the plants that grew, the soil that remained fertile. She could feel the elves in the minerals and water soaked into the earth. Everything worked in tandem, in a beautiful harmony. And just underneath that, there was something else. Something she had never noticed before.

Faria dug her fingers through the dirt and rested her forehead against the ground. Her skin grew hot as gasps from the onlookers threatened to break her concentration. A tugging sensation pulled within her, knocking against her mind's door. She swatted against it as if it was a fly, annoyed at his distraction. She wasn't ready to let Hunter in and allow her confused emotions to interfere with what she felt in that moment. Faria believed the land would accept her, but she still didn't want any misplaced negative feelings feeding into the ground that she was about to pour her blood onto.

"Well, that's something you don't see every day," Nellie whispered.

Curious, Faria paused to let the voices of her people back in.

She's glowing.

Look at her skin, look at those markings.

I don't remember this happening with Queen Amira.

Queen Amira. Her mother's name echoed as the sentiment was repeated. The ceremony was meant to be an entire affair, topped with days of celebrating, foreign embassies staying in Anestra, and beautiful displays of magic. Athinia would be bursting with guests, street vendors selling their wares, and specialty food items created for such an event. The kitchens would need weeks to prepare, and they would have started receiving guests months in advance.

At least, that was what Faria was told. Of course, she wasn't alive for her mother's official coronation but she'd learned what to expect when it was her turn. She'd learned, specifically, how she was supposed to conduct herself. Proper dancing, proper curtseying, names of important people and their families, what they contributed to Anestra's economy.

This—what she was doing—felt more fitting to her. An informal gathering, letting all those who came to her father's call to arms to bear witness to what was happening. Not just the diplomats or the people she was meant to put on airs for, but those who were willing to shed blood, to give their lives to protect their land.

Hunter's warm caress eased down Faria's back in a sign of comfort. She inhaled, allowing the warmth coming from her to melt into the ground. She felt recognition in return. Her father's presence drew close to her. She turned her head and peered up at him, unsure of what was meant to come next.

King Dennison, wearing a simple black tunic and pants, stood tall next to her. Wil was beside him, holding a silk pillow with something placed atop it that Faria couldn't see from her kneeled position. A moment later, her father lifted a black dagger. It glinted with a blood-red sheen in the sunlight. A Val weapon. It was a wonder she'd gone from never seeing one to only seeing Hunter with one, and now they seemed to be everywhere. Was that always the ceremonial knife?

"Today is a day unlike any other we will see in Anestra during our lifetime. The honor of having Faria Agostonna as heir to the throne, and inheritor to this land is one I cannot properly convey." Dennison cleared his throat and placed a hand on Faria's shoulder.

She kept her eyes averted, half listening to her father's speech. The other half of her attention was focused on keeping her magic reigned, and the darkness that threatened to release itself with all the energy streaming through her at bay.

King Dennison continued, his voice carrying the strength of a male who lived several lifetimes, who had known loss and fear and persevered anyway. Faria hoped she could be more like him when she grew up. "This particular heir is unlike any other we have had. She is our Elven queen, Warlock queen, Val princess, and Fae-blessed. Let those of us gathered who are old enough to know the ancient blessing say it now, in a plea to allow the land to accept who we have chosen to lead us."

Her father spoke words in a language Faria didn't understand, but others seemed to. Raised voices echoed the words back to the king. Faline stepped up and joined the others as their voices droned on in a low buzz.

A weird prickling sensation ran over Faria's skin, and her already glowing light shone a little brighter. She felt a pull from her *innulum* and knew it was Ander, probably curious about what was happening to her. She was curious herself.

The chanting stopped and Hunter placed his hand on top of the dagger, adding in his own part in the Val language.

"Is this added specially for Faria?" Nellie asked aloud.

Faria was glad Nellie asked as she was wondering the same. There couldn't have been another Val that had a part in her mother's ceremony, so it must have been newly added. Faria wondered why she couldn't understand the language he spoke when she seemed to understand other parts of herself better. She'd have to figure out a way to learn the language. Maybe that was in the royal libraries as well, because goddess knew she didn't want to ask Hunter to teach her anything else.

Without warning, a tremor passed through the ground. The vibration shot up through her knees and into her body. Her eyes darted to her father, Nellie, and even Hunter to see if any of them reacted. None of them acted as if anything was different, and Faria had no choice but to assume it was a normal part of the ceremony.

Faria released a breath. She needed to say something to the land now if she recalled correctly, and then they could finally move on with what they needed to do. Relief wasn't something she was accustomed to feeling lately, not when every piece of her had been on edge since the moment she gave birth and had to flee for her life. Flashes of that night filled her mind, of Ander screaming, of seeing Hunter's mangled dead body on the ground. She clenched her jaw. She refused to give in to the images. Later, she could fall apart. Later, she could feel the pain, the loss, the endless winding river of grief carving a canyon straight through her.

Faria coaxed her power into the ground, intending to reacquaint herself with a sense of its life force, but where once it was vibrant, now it felt as if it hesitated. A pulse radiated from deep within the earth, just a shadow of vibration. The source of it was far away, whatever it was, and Faria felt it moments before struck it *Mentage*.

She jumped to her feet, dirt trailing down from her knees only seconds before Hunter was on the alert. They shared a glance, confusion and wariness exchanged. A few of the stronger elves with more magic in the crowd gasped as if they, too, could feel something but weren't quite sure what it was.

Birds shot out of the trees of the Forest of the Dawn, squawking their way into the sky and away from where Faria could feel the pulse originating. A cry bore from the earth and a rush of unnatural wind suffused them. A crack of thunder *boomed* as though the earth had been cleaved in two.

Hunter whipped his head toward the east. "It can't be," he whispered.

"Is it Athinia?" King Dennison demanded. "More?"

"No," Faria breathed. Her city was fine, though she could hear shouts of surprise and confusion. The thunderous crack sounded past the city by leagues. But nothing was on that side of the country save for endless farmland before they stopped at Carenek Peaks.

Faline paled. "The mountains?"

Faria searched the crowd for Nellie but her friend's eyes were narrowed on Endo. Then she heard Nellie say, "Didn't you spend weeks trying to get through the mountains?"

Endo eyed her, seemingly unwilling to respond, before he said, "It's impossible. I reported it as such. Those mountains are completely sealed shut against what lay beyond."

Something nagged at the back of Faria's mind, a piece of history that Faline had taught her years ago, during one of the many lessons she had ignored.

"The Crystal of Light," Nellie said. She turned to Endo and demanded, "Is this Darroc? Did you know about this?"

"Whoa, Nellie, relax. I don't know anything."

Faria's heart raced as she tried to think. "Faline, please remind me, besides Farrah's tomb and the Crystal of Light, what else is—"

An unholy roar shrieked its way toward them and Faria heard screams from endless miles away. She looked at Hunter, fear in her eyes.

He asked, "Do you hear that?"

"Is it the Forsaken?" Faria felt the blood drain from her face. The Forsaken were mythical creatures created by Farrah's concubine sworn to protect the goddess' resting place. No one had seen them before, so it was truly a legend, but if it was true …

"How many, Faline?" the king asked. "How many were protecting Farrah's tomb?"

Faria knew he asked Faline because she was a member of the secret keepers.

Faline shook her head. "There was no real … all guesstimation. It could be one or it could be a few hundred."

"We don't need any more creatures roaming free across this land," Hunter said, double-checking the knives strapped against his body. "Nellie, find the *Drogosterra*."

"But I'm needed now. I can't take a joy ride all over the country hoping to find it when I could be doing something. I could, I don't know, breathe fire on these new beasts."

"No," Faria said, her voice resolute. "We must protect the people, but these are creatures held captive for centuries or longer. Since Farrah went to rest. And if they are out, if the magic on the mountain range is broken, we must divide our resources. Hunter and I will investigate the creatures. They deserve to stay alive at all costs. Faline will gather more information. Nellie will go after the *Drogosterra*. The Royal Guard will decide who amongst you can spare and send a team of people to inspect the mountains."

"What can I do?" Endo asked.

Nellie interrupted, "Stay here with the king." She crossed her arms.

Faria cocked her head. Endo used to teach her how to use weapons when she was younger. He used to speak of Wendorre, of what he was learning before he left. "No," Faria said. "You will take a team of shifters.

Marisa and Jamison, if he is well enough, and whoever wants to follow and you will sail around the country to the other side. Toward Widow's Passageway."

Endo looked excited by the news.

"You want him to explore the area he wanted to?" Nellie asked, incredulous.

"Yes. It was once impossible to get through there. And if the mountains are now passable, it stands to reason other areas will be as well. Do reconnaissance. See how far you can safely go. Do not stop to explore; we don't know what is a trap set by Darroc. Report to our sentries in the mountains once you get to that side and they will relay the information back to us. If it's Darroc, we will prepare immediately."

"And if it's something worse?" Hunter asked.

"Unless the gods themselves have awoken, there is nothing more dangerous than Darroc."

Perhaps it was her naivete, but the look on Faline's and Hunter's faces made her think that wasn't quite right.

"You heard her," Dennison said. "Protect the land, protect the people. Gather as much intelligence as possible. Meet back in a fortnight."

PART II

NINE

HUNTER

The *malosin obsinae* grew stronger every day.

He thought it would settle once Faria came back, once his obsession with keeping her safe was abated. He didn't, however, expect her to block the bond so thoroughly. There were times, such as during the ceremony, he was able to give her a calming stroke down her back when he thought he felt a glimmer of anxiety shimmer through her.

It was a punch to the gut every time she rejected him. More than that, Hunter felt generally more unwell and more uneasy as it went on. It was as though his equilibrium was off, and only she could set the balance right again. He was sure she must have felt the same, or at least a similar sense of agitation.

"Don't stand so close to me," Faria said as they walked on.

He smirked. She definitely felt something. He'd take anger over indifference any day. Gods knew he gave into his anger as much as he could if only to distract himself from the incessant ache.

"Whatever you say, Princess," he responded, knowing it would rankle her. It shouldn't give him as much satisfaction as it did to watch her shoulders tense, though he gave her credit for not responding this time.

Hunter eased up, allowing a fraction more space between them. They walked toward a footbridge that separated *Mentage* from the road to Athinia. Hunter hoped they'd have a bit more privacy to discuss what they had to do. Each of them was strapped with a quiver and bow, along with various knives and daggers hidden throughout their bodies. Hunter wasn't sure what to expect from the Forsaken making an appearance if they actually existed, but he hoped there would be just one of them.

"Let's go over here," he said, lightly brushing her to get her attention. She shifted away from his touch.

"You probably don't want prying eyes as we practice sieving—how to make you appear where you want in the Val way."

Hunter saw the nearly imperceptible tightening of her fists and was ready for her to show some sign of something—anything—but her face was emotionless.

"We do not have time to waste on you teaching me a trick of the Val. Our people could be hurt, and that animal or multiple of them could be lying dead somewhere from an attack against them. Bring me there and teach me your tricks after things have calmed down."

"We don't have the luxury of waiting until things calm down. You must learn as much as you can to be the best queen for your people."

Faria turned to him and bared her teeth. "Don't you dare presume to tell me I haven't been doing what is best for my people." Her chest heaved.

He slowly looked her up and down, taking in her combative stance, the flush of her skin as it pressed against her tunic, her knuckles pale as her fists clenched. He reached his consciousness out to her, but as ever, her mind was an impenetrable wall.

Hunter tried to hold his anger back but doing so agitated the darkness within him. She couldn't keep rejecting him like this. It would only serve to hurt them both, not to mention, the more she rejected her true nature, the more unpredictable it would become as it found ways to lash out.

Why couldn't she see that?

At the rising of his *malosin obsinae*, he felt an answering call within her. It was silent, like the curiosity of a cat wanting to figure out what might be lurking in the shadows. Hunter pressed a tendril against her and her *malosin* pressed back.

They stood inches apart but Faria's eyes flew open at the metaphysical contact. The heat from her skin pressed into him, and for a moment, he thought he saw black flames in her eyes.

"There is still much I need to teach you, Princess." His darkness played with hers and he savored the touch, though it barely satiated the connection the bond demanded of them. "This thing inside of us, the *malosin obsinae*, it can be difficult to contain. Let me in."

Faria closed her eyes and tilted her head as if his words had a nullifying effect on her anger.

He wondered for a moment if this was another Val secret that had been tucked away in the recesses of his mind. The ability to make a person agreeable. That would have come in handy countless times with her in the past.

"What are you doing to me?" she murmured breathlessly. "I feel like I'm on fire."

"The longer you deny our bond, the more painful it will become."

"No," she replied, her voice almost dream-like. A series of emotions flittered across her face. "This feels good. And if this is from me denying the bond then I see no reason to not continue."

A flash of frustration tore through him, followed by confusion. Did the bond not affect her the same as it did him? Or maybe she was feeling the effects of something else?

He took a furtive glance around. Birds chirped within the golden leaves of the Forest, a wind blew in with the crisp scent of another winter storm approaching. He didn't understand what was going on with her, but they didn't have time to figure it out. The longer they stood there debating the intricacies of their relationship, the more danger their people were in.

"We do not have time for this. Act like a queen or I'm going to continue to treat you like the spoiled *princess* you are behaving like."

Her face contorted into an affronted look and she seemed moments away from incinerating him with that dark fire inside her before she swallowed down the flames and said in a controlled voice, "We will deal with this later. Take us to the mountains. Training, or talks thereof, shall be when time is not pressing against us."

Hunter was surprised she bit back her retort, but they finally agreed they didn't have time to mess around. Faria held out her arm to him, and he gave her the barest graze with the tips of his fingertips, not wanting to acknowledge the burning ache of longing he knew touching her would emphasize.

A squeezing sensation like being sucked into a vacuum engulfed them, taking his breath away with a gasp before they landed, crunching down in the silence of the mountains. Hunter's ears perked and he closed his eyes, focusing on his other senses. The sting of the wind as it traveled down the icy mountains bit his cheeks, the powder of the snow was soft beneath his footsteps, the wet cold of it threatening to seep through his boots. He felt the heat from Faria to his right, could sense the mountains looming ahead of him, but he could not hear or feel the presence of another.

"I've never been out there," Faria said, looking around with interest. "It's hard for me to judge if anything is different …" her voice trailed off.

Hunter followed her gaze to what caught her attention. The white-capped mountain range ran straight through Anestra, and their size was daunting. A snow-covered forest lined the base, golden leaves glinting in the sunlight as if gemstones clung to their branches. The mountains were giants standing watch over the land.

In all his memory, the mountains remained impassable, and it was only through the ancient tomes of Anestra's history that they knew the goddess Farrah's tomb existed on the other side, along with a city that boasted the largest library seen. It was said that scholars traveled from far and wide to study in the hidden city, its seclusion allowing for proper absorption and practice of knowledge and magic. Many experiments were meant to be run out there, far away from where any mishaps could potentially harm others. Much of what was known about the city was based on rumor only, as most who had traveled to the city to learn created a new life for themselves away from mainland Anestra.

The mountains had sealed themselves when Farrah was laid to rest, ensuring that no others would disturb her slumber, or steal the core of her power with the Crystal of Light. And, as a failsafe, the Forsaken were said to protect Farrah from invaders.

Carenek Peaks were more than a beacon or a landmark. Dwarves dwelled beneath them, governed by themselves in their own territory. The colossal peaks protected the dwarves' home while providing Anestra with protection. The mountains were shrouded in superstition, with those living in the villages closest to them always reporting strange, mournful howls, or the tinkering of music on a wind.

Now, as Hunter followed Faria's gaze, he realized the cause of the screams they'd heard from a distance. It wasn't because the Forsaken got loose.

The mountains were cleaved in two.

Massive trees collapsed on the ground; their once golden leaves shriveled in a crimson death. Thick roots stretched toward the sky, reaching for help that hadn't come. A once shimmering lake that sat before the forest overflowed, creating swirling waters that froze on impact.

But *gods* those mountains.

The peaks had been unpassable for centuries, ever since he was first tasked to defend the Agostonna bloodline, and now they were split open. He had to ask the Elders about it, or at least the one most like a father to him, Jacobi. He must have some idea what could have caused this.

"Do you think it was Darroc?" Faria asked, turning to face Hunter with true fear in her eyes.

He would do anything to take that look away, to protect her as he was meant to. It was hard to reassure her when he was uncertain of anything. "Darroc doesn't have the power to cleave the world in two. Besides, nothing is so important to him that he'd ruin the very land he seeks to rule."

Faria's face turned stormy. Before Hunter could decipher it, his mate turned on her heel and headed toward the mountains.

"Where are you going now, Princess?"

"The mountains are open. They are on my land. I'm seeing what's on the other side."

"You gonna walk?" He chuckled at her back as he slowly meandered behind her, keeping his senses open to potential unknown dangers.

There were no footsteps in the snow, nothing to suggest any wild creature or being had been in the vicinity. She had the right idea in investigating closer.

"It will take you nearly a day to walk around that lake, especially now that it seems to have tripled in size. And then another day and a half with no rest in between to get to the mountain. And then who knows how long it'll take to make it through the pass."

She huffed a breath, the vapor rising in a cloud above her. Hunter watched as the snow melted beneath her boots, and he wondered again about the fire inside her, the power she harbored from the phoenix.

"Fine, take me there."

He wanted to argue, to push her to learn the magic of the Val hidden within herself. But there didn't appear to be immediate danger and the sooner they figured out what was happening, the better.

Hunter tilted his head toward his queen and gave a mock bow. "Your wish is my command."

TEN

NELLIE

Un-*freaking*-believable.

It figured that when something really cool finally happened in Anestra, she was sent on a babysitting mission. What if there were insane creatures tearing people apart?

Not that Nellie wanted there to be insane creatures tearing people apart, but for the first time in goddess knew how long, Anestra was finally showing a bit of personality. And Nellie wanted to be in the action.

Instead, she headed north over the Forest of the Dawn, searching the skies for the *Drogosterra* having a temper tantrum. Okay, that was a bit hypocritical as she was the one currently having the temper tantrum, but still.

Nellie also had to admit that she would have loved to see what was happening between Hunter and Faria. There was no way Faria would have let him train her to do that cool jump thing Val did, but how would it have been to see their darkness play with each other?

Instead, Nellie soared the freezing skies through tiny needles of ice that incessantly battered against her wings. It wasn't painful but it irritated her. She huffed out a breath through her snout and tried to focus on what she was able to experience rather than what she was missing out on. Not just anyone could turn into a mythical dragon and soar above the continent the way she could.

An ocean of trees was a white-capped golden wave beneath her as the leaves reflected the mid-afternoon sun. The Forest of the Dawn stretched for miles, though Nellie could beyond the northernmost point of Anestra ending in a sheer cliff face before plunging to the choppy seas below. Though she was familiar with some parts of the Forest, Nellie hadn't quite grasped its enormity. She wondered if all parts of it had been thoroughly explored and if the Fae magic that kept it alive had other secrets that had yet to be revealed.

Nellie flapped her powerful wings and urged her body to move quicker. She had no idea how she would speak to a dragon, but she wanted to get this task over with and revert to some semblance of reality. It was funny how her whole life her mother would have done whatever possible to shield Nellie from the magic of the world. Now, she was surrounded by more than she could have dreamed of.

The ocean grew closer, its gray depths surprisingly dull compared to the other seas around the continent. Seeing it reminded her of the first time she went into the Pacific Ocean and her mother had to save her from drowning. Her mother. If there was one thing Nellie could relate to Faria on, it was the feeling she had when she realized how many secrets her mother had kept from her.

Nellie and her queen had more in common than she realized. Both of their mothers were murdered at the hands of Darroc. Her own mother, quite literally, had her heart torn out by him. She had nothing left of her mother's, except for that locket Tommy had saved for her. A necklace her mother had worn for as long as she could remember. Nellie made a mental note to find where it went in the chaos and keep it close to her. She didn't want to lose the last piece of her mother she had.

There was something Darroc had said to her that bothered her, something about her smelling familiar. It didn't sit right with Nellie. Of course, he could have been referring to his time in Anestra as they both lived at *Mentage* for a while, but it seemed like there was something more to it. Darroc was unhinged, so maybe she didn't need to put too much thought into it.

Or maybe she should.

Nellie finally reached the coast of Anestra and glided along the craggy cliff that made up the walls of the continent. Tiny islands wound their way around the cliff and Nellie wondered if those islands had always been there or if it was the kind that mysteriously popped up as Endo claimed.

She swooped in a wide arc, easing her way closer to the mountains to look for anything amiss. Or those sweet creatures she was missing out on. Not seeing anything, she gained altitude to get her bearings. Even as high as she was, she still couldn't see past the peaks, though there was a disturbance off in the distance. Nellie lowered one of her inner lids to keep out the water stinging her eyes and focused.

Trees from the forest were toppled over and what looked to be a huge, glistening crater reflected glaring sunlight back at her. Not a crater, but water. The only lake she knew of was tiny, little more than a pond, so what exactly was she looking at?

What the fluff? The mountains were … She headed back inland to get a better view. Yeah, they were split in half. Nellie couldn't begin to imagine what could have caused it, but she knew it couldn't have been Darroc. He was a snake, performing his tricks like the wasting spell he put on *Mentage.* If he knew how to break the earth, or even something on a much smaller scale, he would have revealed that card already. For mountains that have been impenetrable for as long as Nellie had been taught, she knew there was nothing short of an act of god that could have done such a thing.

Nellie shifted her body, catching an updraft, and veered back toward the archipelago she had seen. She wanted to explore the mountain range and see what was past it, but she'd have to leave it up to Hunter and Faria to figure out.

Though it was freezing at her altitude, Nellie tried to enjoy the heat of the sun against her scales. If there was one thing she loved, it was feeling the vitamin D—

Hail pounded against her skin, pelting shards of ice into the thin membrane of her wings. Pain lanced through her and steam rose in the air, clouding her immediate pathway. *What the f—*

Bright skies shone again and the rocky archipelago appeared below her, a barren series of eight islands nestled in a blanket of jewel-toned waters.

Ummm, Nellie thought, *what just happened?*

She flew in a wide circle, doubling back the way she came. The sun glared against the—

Thunderous clouds cracked and lightning flashed as she—

A crisp winter wind kissed her wings as she flew through clear skies again.

Nellie hovered, trying to discern if she was starting to lose her mind or if there was a cause to the sudden shift. There was nothing but the archipelago directly below her and empty skies all around her. There was nothing to indicate a change in weather, or, gods above, a change in realm.

Where did the lightning go? Where were the storm clouds and the hail pelting against her scales?

Maybe she had imagined it. She had been overwhelmed by the thought of what happened to the mountains and the implications of the forces great enough to move the earth as it did. Or she was sleep-deprived. That was probably it. Shifting into a *Drogosterra* took a lot of energy and flying the leagues had exhausted her. Plus, she didn't think to bring snacks for when she turned back into a human. She honestly didn't know what a *Drogosterra* ate and didn't seem likely to find out.

Below her, a low growl carried on the wind and Nellie felt pressure in her head, almost like a sense of danger was telling her to turn around except it didn't feel like intuition. It was more as if someone or something were trying to push her in a different direction.

She scanned the largest island and spotted the deep crimson veins of a wing nearly camouflaged with the rock it sat upon.

Nellie hovered above the *Drogosterra* and felt an influx of emotions. Sadness, anger, defensiveness. It was hard to decipher if they were all coming from her or not. The growl turned into a one of warning before breaking off into a pained lament.

She wasn't sure what to do. Say something like, "I come in peace?" And how would she say anything anyway?

What are you? the question drifted across her mind. Not words, but the impression of them, backed by a curious and defensive air.

Nellie hovered in the sky and debated how to respond. Should she open her mouth as if to speak? Should she think at the *Drogosterra* and hope the thoughts traveled down to where she lay?

Enemy?

It was wary, and Nellie hurried to reassure her that she was not an enemy. *Friend!* Nellie thought, yelling the word in the dragon's direction, *I am friend!*

Friend is loud.

Nellie laughed to herself. *Sorry, I don't know how this works. Can I sit with you?*

You will hurt me.

No! Nellie replied. The poor thing was probably traumatized from everyone shooting arrows at her. Or did she mean emotionally, like Ander's abandonment? *I wish to speak.*

Share minds?

Was that the *Drogosterra* meaning of speaking to each other? *Yes, share minds.*

A general feeling of assent was directed her way, so Nellie swooped down toward the island and cautiously landed next to the *Drogosterra*, minding the sharp rocks jutting from the ground. The air was warmer down here, tropical almost, and Nellie thought she could smell a faint tinge of freshly cracked coconut in the air. It reminded her of the smell of American beaches in the summer. Suntan lotion and sweat with the brine of the ocean mixed in. Being as far north as they were, she was surprised to feel any warmth at all, let alone heat.

The water surrounding the island was even more mesmerizing up close. The jewel tones she saw from the sky deepened in color, and at this short distance, she could see beautiful schools of rainbow fish, brightly colored coral, and what might be actual gemstones drifting in the current. Curious, she extended a claw toward the water, her talon just inches from the surface before she felt a sharp snap across the back of her head.

Do not touch that!

Nellie glanced at the *Drogosterra*, who gave her a look as if she was a complete idiot—an impressive feat for a dragon.

Why not? She could admit it was strange, but this was unexplored territory. She had no idea the oceans here were the same as in Mercy Bay. For all she knew, all the water surrounding Anestra was meant to look like this. Mercy Bay's ocean wasn't dangerous, so she had no reason to believe this would be.

It is not from here. Dangerous. Will get lost in the Nothing for a long time, like the rest of us did.

The rest of you? Nellie glanced back at the ocean, then slowly retracted her claw. She'd had enough of that sort of trauma to last her several lifetimes. *Are there others like you?*

Lost.

Nellie wanted to ask more but the *Drogosterra* sniffed at her, then leaned in and sniffed at her chest.

Um, it's a bit rude to go there without asking first, Nellie said, trying and failing in her large body to properly scoot away.

What are you? the *Drogosterra* asked again. *Your scent is different. Ahhh …* The *Drogosterra* nuzzled her snout down Nellie's chest toward her belly.

Nellie was starting to get alarmed that this would accidentally end up in territory she wanted absolutely nothing to do with.

You have one fire but not two. You are us and not us. How?

Nellie took a wing and gently nudged the *Drogosterra* away from traveling toward any other parts of her. *It is hard to explain what I am. What do you mean 'one fire but not two?'*

The dragon shifted onto her side, exposing her belly to Nellie. *Scent me,* she thought toward her. *We know to whom we belong from what is inside. One fire for rage, for protection, the other fire is deeper. We never show but it is a different scent. It helps us find family and the one we bond with.*

Nellie hesitated but leaned her snout in close and tried to breathe whatever it was the dragon wanted her to. She couldn't believe she was sniffing what basically equated to a dinosaur's belly when she could be exploring the ruins beyond the mountains. She couldn't believe a lot about her life, but here she was.

She inhaled, and the brimstone that lay inside the *Drogosterra* filled her nostrils. *Okay, so it can set me on fire, good to know.* She moved her snout a polite distance lower, taking care not to get too close to any parts she didn't want to analyze up close.

Closer, friend.

Nellie closed her eyes and made a mental note to never tell Hunter about this moment if only to avoid any future bestiality joke he might make with her. She rested her snout against the dragon's upper belly and inhaled. Images flashed through Nellie's mind at once, too quickly to make sense of. Verdant rolling hills, a gleaming forest of gold and crimson, wildflowers bursting everywhere, *Drogosterra* flying, children laughing, feasts, and music. Drums? A beating echoed in her mind, her body, her heart. The sound dissipated when she opened her eyes.

The dragon looked at her sadly. *Home.*

Those trees, the gold and crimson. This is your home, right? You are from here? Was that Anestra I saw?

This is home to my Weyr. My family. But it is not what it was. Where is the light? Everything is dark. Broken. Missing. Lost.

Slow down, Nellie thought at the rush of emotions that threatened to choke her. *This land is different, but it is under attack. We are trying to protect it. And I have to ask you to help us.*

I will help my chosen but he left me. He is dark but I recognize him. He is made from me. We are forged from the same creator. He will learn if he comes back. Will he come back?

Yes, Nellie said. *What do you mean by 'forged from the same creator?'*

They made us. All of us. Not you, though. I do not know what created you.

Okay, rude. Was it the Fae who made you?

What is 'Fae?'

Nellie tried to conjure an image to her mind, but her only idea of what a Fae looked like were the hunky males in the romances she liked to read. She was fairly positive they wouldn't look like that, just as the elves didn't look anything like what Tolkien described. Still, Nellie pictured someone who looked like an elf, with elongated ears and elegant limbs. She tried to picture the elemental magic they possessed and images of Faria and her mother. It was the closest she could come to explaining. Then she brought Hunter's image to her mind, his iridescent tattoos. She tried to convey that the Val were said to be created by Fae, so perhaps it would be in their image.

Ahh, the children of the creators, the *Drogosterra* thought the words excitedly. Huffs of smoke issued from her nose. *They are in the image of the creators, yes. With similar powers, yes!*

So the Fae created you then? Nellie confirmed.

I still do not understand this word. The mother creator is kind. She raised us, made sure her children bonded with us. She loves all of us and my Weyr was happy to protect her and all of the children she bore and made. But something happened. It was the start of the darkness. We felt it, the shift. She said it was her fault, and her lover's. She said it was too much power and the only way to balance it was for her to put her power to rest. Her lover did the same. They created the many worlds to try to disperse the power but it was still too great. Then they made the decision to leave us.

But it was okay because they would still be here and their children would protect us and we were tasked to protect the land. They thought the darkness would be gone. They found beings, ones that encouraged darkness, and banished them before they left. Things were okay for a few years but it started again. They said it was inevitable, her and her lover. They had to do the long sleep. So he put his power into the flames and she put hers into the jewels and they both slumber.

Wait, Nellie said. *I'm sorry, are you referring to the goddess Farrah? And her consort, the god Alexei?*

Farrrrrahhhhh. Yes, mother creator, mother creator.

You're telling me Farrah created the Val? Not the Fae?

She had many, many, many children everywhere. Maybe they are Fae you speak of. She is mother. I do not know what you are.

Nellie tried to put the new pieces of information together. The mountains had split open. She just said she couldn't imagine what act of god could have done it. But ... was it the act of a god? A goddess? No. Impossible.

Just as Nellie was about to ask the *Drogosterra* more questions, a sonic boom echoed, and a blinding white flash of light spread from the very mountains she'd just—

Thought ceased as she lost consciousness.

ELEVEN

ANDER

Freshly showered, Ander stepped in front of the foggy mirror and wiped the condensation away. He hated to look at himself. When he was a kid, he resented not looking like Darroc. That was his father, after all, and yet there was nothing similar about them. Darroc had pale brown skin and eyes so dark his pupils often blended into the irises. Darroc was tall and thin, his bones jutted out against his skin.

Ander, on the other hand, looked perpetually sun-kissed. His light brown hair had red and blond highlights and his green eyes had a golden halo around his pupils that glowed at times. He was tall and naturally muscular, though he worked out his aggression through exercise and gained muscle from being in a constant state of angst.

Sometimes he would look at himself and wonder how much of his mother was apparent in his features. Was it his angular jaw? The unusual way his ears tapered at the top? His strong cheekbones or almond-shaped eyes?

Ander studied the tattoos writhing underneath his skin. They'd been more active since he met his mother, whatever that meant. His powers grew stronger as well. He was eighteen in just a few days. Or had it happened already? He stopped paying attention. He lived his whole life according to someone else's rules of time, so what did it matter to him what age he represented now? He felt like he lived and suffered through several lifetimes.

Now that he was clean, he took a closer look at the imprint left on his hand. The marking was faint and thin scars raised from his skin extending down his forearm. He knew little of *Drogosterra*. Darroc had educated him in all manner of creatures, but the *Drogosterra* were his least favorite. Darroc had called them little more than beasts, unable to be tamed. It wasn't until Ander came across a book, in the human realm of all places that he learned a bit more about *Drogosterra* and the fabled way they connected to elves and Fae. The lore was wrong, as it often was when humans shared information, but the thought of it was the same.

And now the proof was marked on his skin and, he was surprised to realize, in his mind. He didn't think he could communicate with her, but he felt a new presence. Something separate from what he shared with his mother, something different than the pressure of the blood command Darroc had placed on him. This felt like something gentle, and secure. It gave him peace of mind, even if it scared the hell out of him.

Ander felt badly about leaving the way he had, but being around his family, if he could call them that, in his ancestral home was too much. And then to have a freaking dragon connect with him. He was a walking disaster and nothing but a danger magnet, especially with Darroc keeping tabs on him.

Even now he felt eyes on him. *Wait.* Ander stilled, reaching his senses out for any unusual sound. Muted steps up the stairs sounded like light feet against carpet. There was no one else in the house, so he knew that to be Jane. *What is …* Was that a quiet sigh or the breeze rustling through the treetops in the distance?

Ander whipped his head to the bathroom window, seeing only his reflection. Slowly, he raised the window and peered into the darkness, nothing but the faint outline of trees lining the yard. Even with his lowlight vision, he was unable to make out more than the nearly empty branches against the shadows.

"Ander?" A soft knock against the bathroom door broke his concentration. "I have some pizza here, and we still have a few more things to discuss."

Ander let out a soft sigh and opened the door, wiping his dripping hair with a towel. He'd put on the sweatpants Jane had given him, though his shirt remained on her bed. He tried to hide his disgust as he looked down at Jane holding a paper plate of greasy pizza. Spicy pepperoni and cheese smell drifted under his nose and his stomach growled, despite never acquiring the taste for the human delicacy. When was the last time he'd eaten?

"Umm … here," Jane said, shoving the plate against his chest. He caught it haphazardly, careful not to let the cheese slide off the plate.

He saw her rosy cheeks before she turned away and busied herself with papers on her desk.

"You all right?" he asked, smirking at her turned back.

Jane snorted. "As if there'd be a reason I wouldn't be, other than being stuck with you." She turned back to him with a half smile of her own. "Why are you here, Ander?"

He was about to answer her before noticing her face cloud over. "What's wrong?"

"I don't know, I feel funny," Jane said. Her already pale skin turned pallid in the glare of her bedroom light. "It's almost a fuzzy, a buzzing—"

"Is it the pizza? Because humans have a weird—"

Ander flashed to Jane's side and caught her before she fainted, gently lowering her onto the floor. He wanted to use his power, his ability, whatever it was that allowed him to seek out a weakness in a person's body, but he was scared he would accidentally make her sick or worse. He hadn't scanned someone since the day Darroc had ordered him to murder the shifter clan leader and inadvertently started the plague that ravaged the land.

Separate flashes of pink and blue light illuminated the darkened bedroom. Two figures appeared before Ander. He recognized the bubble gum curls of the one Jane called Miss Warm and Sweet—Lindy, and the other named Santana. They were the EMTs who worked to remove the arrow from Jane's chest. Her guides.

"Move," Bubble Gum said, pushing him aside with surprising force.

He got up from his knees and stood next to the window, far enough away for them not to worry about him getting in their way, but close enough to see what they were doing.

The guides crouched on their knees and hovered their hands over Jane's body similar to how he'd seen his mother do when he'd spied her healing the young girl—Darroc's mother. It was similar to what he could do as well, except where they healed, he caused destruction. Gold light trickled from their fingers and entered her body. He watched the light travel under her skin. It took him a moment to realize it was traveling through her veins. *Well, that's new.* He wanted to join them, to see what it was they were doing. Maybe his power would teach him how to heal properly.

"Don't even think about it, young killer," Bubble Gum said. "You step near her and I don't care how much our power won't affect you, I will make sure whatever I do will maim you for eternity."

"Shh, Lindy, I think I see it," Santana said. "Look. It's the virus."

The guides looked at each other, then back up at Ander. "See what you have done," Bubble Gum hissed. "She is meant to be one of many to protect the humans from the end of days. What do you think will happen if you finally succeed in your mission? One attempt on her life wasn't enough for you?"

"Look," Santana said. "Her body is fighting it. Watch what happens."

Bubble Gum refocused her attention on Jane.

Ander took the opportunity to put on his shirt and jacket, then stepped closer to her.

"It's just popping it out of existence," Santana said.

"Possibilities: she's chosen so she has extra protection."

"That's most likely but we never had a charge who was immune to illness before. They might be hard to kill, but she would still be sick for a while."

"This looks different than the shifters who have natural immunity," Santana said. "Look at the way her white blood cells are almost lining up, already on the defensive."

"Show me," Ander said, trying to keep the desperation out of his voice. "Let me see what's happening. If I can replicate it, I can save the others."

"We know exactly what your idea of saving others looks like," Lindy sneered.

It took Ander a moment before he realized what she was referring to. The wolf shifter from just a few days ago.

Ander caught wind of a shifter who had deflected from her pack and lived on her own. He'd heard the female was sick, incredibly sick, and could be heard begging from her bedroom window for someone to help her. Ander had been searching for someone to test his ability on to see if he could heal the rot he'd caused, and a lone shifter with no pack to call her family was the perfect test subject.

Ander had sifted outside her house, which doubled as a storefront selling crystals, stones, and from the smell of it, a lot of incense. He inhaled again. The stench of infection underlined the patchouli and rose.

The sign on the door read Closed even though it was normal business hours. He tried the door handle anyway and turned it a degree too far to the right until he heard a subtle click and the door swung open. Ander's eyes watered and he tried to breathe through his mouth instead, tasting the sickness on the back of his tongue. The door creaked closed behind him, leaving a sliver of sunlight in an otherwise darkened and dusty shop.

Ander walked by shelves displayed with tarot cards, jewelry, and stones he knew for a fact were not authentic. He could thank Darroc for that knowledge. He'd visited a realm when he was younger filled with mystics, and there he learned how to discern real stone from fake, to feel the proper vibrations and energy each one gave off. He glanced quickly around, noting the only real stone in the shop was rainbow moonstone. Fitting, for a shifter.

In the back of the shop lay a glass counter with a display case underneath, presenting daggers of various designs laid out on small velvet pillows. The most unassuming one caught his eye. There was just enough reflection of light from behind the closed window shade for the blackened blade to give off a blood-red sheen. Of all the assortment of daggers this shifter tried to sell, she probably never realized she had something as priceless as a Val weapon under her nose.

Ander slid the glass case open and slipped the dagger off its pillow and into its protective sheath. He placed it in one of many inside pockets of his leather jacket, then proceeded up the set of stairs behind the cash register. He didn't feel bad about stealing from a dying woman; she was about to lose everything anyway.

Ragged breathing grew louder as he approached and a wet cough echoed through the upstairs. He knew she could hear him. Unless the virus inhibited her senses. The door to the bedroom was ajar, soft moans trickling out on stale air. Ander's boots echoed down the hallway, a reaper on his way to his latest victim. He pushed open the door, though he was unprepared for the sight before him.

A small woman lay on the bed, her body crumpled in on itself, wrapped in torn crocheted blankets. The lump shivered, the layers of fabric doing nothing to soothe her fever. Blood dripped from eyes that were nearly lifeless, filmed over with a white sheen. Her skin was yellowed, which Ander knew to be a sign of jaundice. Her liver wasn't working properly, which wasn't a surprise as it appeared nearly everything had broken down.

"An angel," she croaked, staring at the spot where he stood sentry at the door. "An angel has finally come to take me into the Beyond." Tears of relief streamed down her face and she seemed to relax deeper into her mattress.

Ander swallowed against the bile inching up his throat. "An agent of death," he said. "Though I would like to try to help if I can."

"Please." She latched her hand onto him faster than he thought possible in her state. Her fingers turned white with the grip she had on his arm. "Put me out of my misery."

Ander swallowed hard. How could he have been capable of something like this? He was only seventeen. It shouldn't have been possible. He was created wrong. No one should have the ability to harm another in this way. "What is your name?"

"Stacey," she said, the last of her energy leaving her. She closed her eyes, her breathing rapid and shallow.

Ander recognized it as the final moments before the permanent sleep. He gently removed her hand and placed it against her chest. He used his power to look inside, to search for the disease and a way to eradicate it, but it was everywhere. It was too much. He followed the faltering beat of her heart and pressed his will against it. Moments later, she was dead.

He set her home on fire and left, hating himself just a bit more than before he'd arrived.

"Please," Ander pleaded, coming back to the present. There was no sense in explaining to two strangers the truth of the matter. At the heart of it, he had killed her, in more ways than one. "I won't do anything but watch what happens. I have to try to fix this."

Santana looked at the one called Lindy, shrugging his shoulder.

Lindy huffed a breath of annoyance. "If one thing goes wrong, I mean, if her breathing falters for even a second, I will burn you to a crisp and laugh while I do it."

Ander shook his head. How did he always end up with the bloodthirsty weirdos?

He laid his hands over Jane in the way he'd seen his mother do. Sky blue light emanated from his hands and rested along Jane's body. He closed his eyes, visualizing the light permeating her skin, ghosting through barriers until he could see what was happening at a cellular level. Yellow oblong shapes in her blood—a virus.

Suddenly, something in Jane's blood rose like a tidal wave and drowned the virus. As it settled, the virus was gone, no trace to be had.

Her blood, Ander noticed, had a silvery sheen to it, as if it were imbued with something alien. "Why does her blood look like that?"

"Like what?" Santana asked after a slight hesitation.

"Like it has been imbued with mercury or something."

More silence, then a throat cleared. "You can see that?" Lindy asked.

"Of course I can," Ander said, his irritation becoming evident. He wanted to dive deeper and figure it out, but he couldn't be sure something wouldn't happen to her in the process. "Whatever it is, it's unlike what I've seen in others. It is destroying the virus."

"She is touched by the Creator," Santana said. "She was one of several humans chosen to guide the human realm in the apocalypse. The Creator kissed her brow when she was a child, activating the spell. It keeps Jane safe, allows her to recover quicker, and delays her death."

"You're speaking too much, Tan," Lindy said through clenched teeth.

Ander opened his eyes, staring at the strange woman. Besides having bright pink hair and eyes like ice, the deep groove of the wrinkles in her skin were more apparent when she frowned at him.

"Whatever it is, that's what will save everyone. Can we replicate it?" Ander asked.

"What do you want us to do, drain her?" Lindy huffed. "The audacity you possess to still attempt murder. In front of her guides, no less—"

"I said replicate it. Not drain her. We need more blood than her body would be able to produce anyway. Can your creator-touched blood be replicated? If we are to save the others, this is the way."

Lindy opened her mouth to respond, but instead of Ander hearing her undoubtedly nasty retort, white-hot pain blazed through him, followed by a sense of fear so complete he thought he was about to face his own death.

He groaned, dropping to his knees. Images flashed in his mind. Ocean. Mountains. White light. Was it Darroc? Was he free and on his way to Anestra? Nauseated by the pain, Ander had no choice but to follow it to its source. He closed his eyes and screamed as he let himself be dragged through space and time, praying he wouldn't be too late.

TWELVE

FARIA

The earth cleaved in two.

Of all the shocking events Faria had experienced in the past year of her life, the one that lay before her far exceeded anything she could have imagined. Faria tried to remember the dreams she'd been having, the so-called *visions* that had plagued her for over a year, and yet none of them had revealed the Carenek Peaks broken in half. Fear clamped down on her as she thought of the possibilities of what could have done such a thing. Darroc was her biggest fear and greatest threat, but she didn't think he had that type of power in him.

It had to be someone or something that could control the earth, or the elements at the very least. She thought back to last year when she'd had little control over her emotions and the way they affected the weather.

She'd been throwing daggers at the trees in the Forest of the Dawn, turning the weapons to ice, setting them ablaze, watching the thunderclouds roll in, wildflowers bursting at her feet before shriveling in decay.

In her overwhelming grief, she'd even poured the weight of her emotions into the ground, wishing it would break open and swallow her whole, wishing she could cleave the earth in two just to bring Hunter back from the dead.

Faria stole a glance in his direction, considering him for a moment. The things she was willing to do, willing to sacrifice, to have him alive and with her again shocked her now, given her hesitation toward him. She knew part of it was ego, part of it was pride, but she also felt so abandoned by him. His loyalty to the Elders, to those who told him what he was or wasn't allowed to say, upset her, especially when she gave her blind loyalty to him and based her happiness on his reaction to her.

A lot had changed in a year and she was nowhere near the naive girl she used to be. And while the feelings she had for Hunter were still strong, she wasn't quite ready to let the pain go. She didn't know how.

They walked along the fallen woods, the golden leaves still gleaming with life, though they had no reason to shine. Hunter had flashed them to the entrance to see if there were any other markings, footprints, or disturbances in the snow that might give an indication of who might have been there, but no evidence of anyone other than themselves was apparent.

"I don't know how much further I can take us," Hunter said, grunting as he moved a corded branch out of the way. "We can only go where we can see or have been before."

"So, basically, I can't go anywhere, seeing as how my parents didn't think to let me explore the queendom." Faria huffed a laugh. The moment she had a cool gift, one that didn't require her to come up with an elaborate plan to sneak out of her rooms or around the workers at *Mentage*, it wouldn't work properly for her.

"We'll sieve to that spot." He pointed to the distance, just before the shadowy passway between the mountains encroached over the last of the light. "And then we'll have to walk."

The silence within the mountain range unnerved Faria. It was unusual for her not to hear birds chirping, a wild animal rustling in the bushes, the soft murmur of people speaking in the distance. Even if she was the only person around for miles, there still should have been the melody of the earth to listen to. Rivers babbling, the wind rustling through fallen leaves. There was nothing but the sound of their boots shuffling against the dirt ground and their hearts beating in the stillness.

Faria's eyes adjusted to the darkness, one of her natural elven abilities, but there was little to be seen other than the outline of the jagged mountain walls. They walked quietly, but cautiously.

After a while, Faria felt a pressure in her mind, another of Hunter's attempts to see her thoughts. She swatted at it as if it were a fly buzzing in her ear, but it persisted.

"Stop trying to get into my thoughts," she whispered at him, careful not to let her voice carry. "If and when I am ready, I will let you know."

He froze mid-step, narrowing his eyes at her. "I'm not ..." his voice trailed off. Hunter lifted his bow and nocked an arrow, the creaking of the bowstring like the crack of thunder in the silence.

Slowly, Faria mimicked his movements, trying and failing to sense anything in the low light other than the feeling of being watched.

The *malosin obsinae* in Faria unfurled and traveled throughout her body as if searching for the cause of her uneasiness. No matter how deeply it looked, there didn't seem to be anything that didn't belong, both inside her and in their surroundings.

"We are alone," she said, allowing a bit of relief to overcome her.

"Assume nothing, Princess," Hunter said, his voice much closer to her ear than she expected it.

Surprised, Faria whipped her arm out unleashing a lash of darkness at him. A swift pain rippled through her as his *malosin* harnessed what she aimed at him.

"Do not," his teeth brushed against the shell of her ear, "use a weapon you do not understand against someone who has mastered it."

"Have you?" Faria turned around and leaned into him. She felt his surprise as he quickly stepped back before she could bump into him. "Care to tell me what happened with Crispin, *mate?*" The flashes of his shredded body—knowing it was Hunter—left a sour taste in her mouth.

"I was made to protect you and these lands. He was a traitor. I will not justify my actions to you."

"How quickly you wish me to change and yet you are still as obstinate as ever." She turned on her heel and continued on the path between the mountains, letting him trail behind.

He had a way of bringing out the childish behavior in her and if she stayed next to him for a minute longer, she would have probably embarrassed herself unbefitting a queen.

"You really should learn to harness your powers," Hunter said after a time.

The path had started to brighten after what felt like hours. Excitement built at finally learning what was on the other side of the mountains, not just what was in the legendary songs but the ancient tomes on Anestrian history as well.

"I can handle my powers just fine," she replied. "The Fates wouldn't have given them to me if I couldn't handle them."

"The Fates made you go through trials and you still are not queen. The Fates took our son away from us. Do you now trust Them so blindly?"

Pieces of cobalt sky were now visible and a lush verdant valley peeked through the widening at the end of the path. His questions irritated her. She didn't want to think of the Fates just then. She didn't want to think of anything. She wanted to be in the moment and bask in the discovery of something new. She quickened her pace.

"I trust no one blindly, least of all Them, but I also have no control over Them, either, so what am I meant to do? If I should not have this power, then I would not have it."

Hunter grunted and passed her, raising his bow again in a cautionary gesture. "We don't know what's here, Princess. Whether there are legendary beasts or not, something unnatural split the land and it wouldn't be wise to run in unprepared."

"What level of preparedness do you think would help in this situation? We have our magic, we have our weapons, we have heightened senses. This is as prepared as we can be for the unknown."

Faria jogged ahead, the scent of the jasmine and wildflowers enticing her. There was a spice in the air, similar to that of the Forest of the Dawn, but more intense. It was intoxicating, whatever it was, and she longed to be closer to it.

Past the mountain, a brilliant stream of sun shone down on her in the perpetual heat of late spring. The grass was soft and springy beneath her boots, wildflowers reached up past her waist, and her thighs burned pleasantly as she ran up the side of the hill, longing to see—

Breath tore from her lungs as she pulled up short. A horrifying scene lay before her.

Elves, humans, and a species that looked suspiciously like Val were frozen in time. Birds stuck in mid-flight, insects glued to flowers and the ground. Children—Faria had never seen so many—frozen mid-dance, mid-laugh, and mid-run. The clothes they wore were older, woven from what looked to be a golden thread. Their hairstyles were outdated; vintage was an understatement. Their features were different as if in the time they'd been frozen, each of the races had evolved in a minute way.

Shapeshifters.

Faria approached one animal and noticed it was mid-shift. Its teeth were elongated, fangs jutting past its jaw. The ears were round and fur sprouted from its face. A tail had just started to grow but the body was human.

Shapeshifters had lived here, in the open, among everyone else.

Why did their histories say they were persecuted? Why had she learned that even as recently as a few centuries ago, shifters were being murdered for what they were? Intolerance used to be at a high. No one trusted them. Why had they been lied to?

Tables laden with golden plates of fruits, sandwiches, bread, and more, sat in the distance. It looked as though they'd been celebrating, but celebrating what? And who could have done this? Was this the work of the Fae? Large poles were erect with beautiful ribbons hanging down, each one held tightly by a child. Faria recognized it from a human book she'd read. Something about a maypole?

"Most human traditions came from us," Hunter said, his voice tight.

She'd forgotten he was there for a moment and was grateful to have someone to share the burden of this discovery with. Did anyone know? Her mother would have never let this stand, but what could she have done about it with the mountains as impassable as they were?

"Hunter," Faria choked out, trying to keep her sobs at bay. So many people, so many children, and races, and history lost to time. "There are Val here." It was unmistakable from this distance. Their tattoos were still iridescent, though they did not writhe underneath their skin. Were they alive?

He clenched his jaw as he scanned the faces of each one, the only show of emotion he was willing to give. He was a prince, she just remembered. Did he know these people? Were they *his* people?

Powerful magic permeated the air. Faria felt a charge as she walked in between the immobile apparitions as if they were refueling her depleted energy. Their faces were frozen in smiles but the more she looked at them, the more she thought their eyes were wide in fear. Was it just a reflection of what she felt tearing her up inside? What had done this?

They walked past the celebration and found their way to another road, this one packed firmly as though it had been traveled upon frequently. They rounded a bend beside a sparkling river, its current also frozen in time, before a huge city sprawled in front of them.

"What am I looking at?" Faria asked in a hushed voice.

Huge buildings reminded her of the cities in the human realm, though not as many or as tall, but still, the metal gleamed. More shocking was the vehicles. She wasn't even sure *vehicle* was the right word. They looked almost like the trains from the human realm, though much more advanced than what she'd experienced. They appeared to hover in the air. They didn't have technology in this realm, and yet that seemed to be what she was looking at. Perhaps not run by electricity, perhaps it was fueled by magic, but it was far more advanced than anything she had seen in Anestra before. It made Athinia look primitive.

"This was where scholars went to perfect their magic. Warlocks came to perfect their alchemy," Hunter spoke as if he were reading from a text rather than from memory or something he might have experienced. "Val came to learn the art of war. Weapons were likely forged here, the likes of which no one alive would have seen. The brightest minds and most talented hands learned here."

"Why would this be kept hidden?"

They wound their way through the city buildings, marveling at the people trapped in mid-conversation, eating, and drinking outside of taverns. Faria could almost hear the music played by a lute player on the street corner, and almost smell the freshly baked bread from a nearby bakery. She couldn't help but feel their eyes trail over her as if they were fully aware someone was walking amongst them for the first time in millennia.

Endless statues of the goddesses sprinkled the streets around the buildings. This was different from any city she knew of in Anestra. While the Agostonna's allowed all religions in whatever form they took, there wasn't one that overtook another. Here, she could only see those of the three goddesses, the creators of their world.

Faria stopped in front of the largest one, her heart racing. The goddess' features were strikingly familiar. Bright, almond-shaped eyes, high cheekbones, thick curly hair cupping her face. This was Farrah, though the images Faria had seen of her were slightly different than what was erected before her.

Faria's breath faltered when she glanced at the statue next to Farrah. The goddess' hand was clasped with a familiar male's. His ears were elongated into sharpened points and he was of a larger build than she'd known him to be in real life. But the shape of his face, the sharp jaw, the defined cheekbones, the eyes, were all the same.

Something like awe and a strange sense of betrayal filled Faria. She didn't think it could be possible but there was no mistaking it.

The statue was of Hunter.

THIRTEEN

HUNTER

The accusatory look in Faria's eyes almost made him want to laugh at the absurdity of her unsaid jealousy. Except he didn't have a logical explanation for why he looked like Farrah's consort.

Hunter wracked his brain, but the harder he tried to remember his past life, the worse his headache became. He felt the an absurd urge to apologize to Faria, though for what, he didn't know. There was no way he was a god. A Val prince, yes, but not a creator of this realm, nor any other.

"Care to share something, mate?" Faria's chin jutted out.

Hunter suppressed a laugh and shook his head. "I've got nothing, though maybe you'd like to?"

"What could I possibly have to share?" she huffed.

It was bizarre, them arguing over a millennia-old statue in the middle of a frozen city, surrounded by untold technology and beauty, the magic seeping into his pores. Hunter made a show of looking around at the waterfalls that fell off the tall mountainside next to the city, then up to some sort of hovering transportation craft, before giving an exaggerated perusal of Farrah.

"Seems to me the consort isn't the only one with a suspicious likeness," he said it first in jest, but the longer he examined that rendition of Farrah, the more he realized the truth in his words.

And so did Faria.

Hunter watched as she took an annoyed glance at the goddess, unwilling to play his game.

Confusion and something like fear shone through her features. She bit her lip. "What are you playing at?" she murmured.

Though the shape of the face was different, the length of the nose and the curve of the mouth were similar, as was the depiction of the wavy hair Faria often had trouble taming. The resemblance was uncanny.

"That's obviously not me," Faria said, still staring at the statue. "This isn't what the goddess is supposed to look like, either. She had long, straight hair. The illustrations I've seen have her as dark-skinned with almost white hair and shining blue eyes. This statue …"

"Is made from marble," Hunter interjected, "so you can't make a fair assessment. But I agree there seems to be some discrepancies between what we know and what we've been told."

A plethora of emotion swirled within Hunter, creating a maelstrom he wasn't quite sure how to handle. The Elders had lied, multiple times, for centuries. Possibly longer. They were the ones who constantly threatened to unmake him. Who manipulated and controlled every decision Hunter made. His head throbbed, a reminder of the memories they still kept locked away.

He knew he was a Val prince because he remembered being one. He didn't remember the kingdom, though he knew it wasn't on a continent other than Anestra. He remembered his parents, though they were fuzzy memories at best. He remembered his mother's laugh. His father's boisterous singing after having one drink too many. He remembered he'd had a brother who passed away at a very young age from an accidental fall. But he didn't remember names or faces. He didn't remember most of his time growing up.

There was little he remembered from before the final battle in the Great War a millennium ago, other than sacrificing his power with the rest of his people to give the elves one final chance at survival. It worked, but he hadn't died like his people had.

But had they?

His entire existence from that point on was being the sole protector of the Agostonna line. Not once had he encountered another like him. Not once had there been rumors, no matter how hard he looked for a clue, of their survival.

And yet there he stood among the frozen figures of his Val brethren. None looked familiar to him but there was no mistaking what they were. The markings beneath their skin were enough evidence.

Had he ruled over them? Were they distant cousins? Had this land on the other side of the mountains been considered Val territory?

The Elders must have known. He just couldn't think of a reason why they would lie to him.

They ventured further past the city, barely stopping to marvel at the views, the storefronts, the clear advancements in medicine and technology, each lost in their own thoughts.

Before long, a fork in the road appeared. One direction led away from the city and toward what looked like a village, judging by the people outside going about their business. The other path led to a set of stairs that descended in a steep decline.

"I can't bear to see those villagers," Faria said, rubbing her hands up and down her arms as frost coiled like a serpent against her skin. It was a testament to how much the entire scene chilled her.

Hunter knew she couldn't be cold in the heat of the sun's rays, but even if she were, she had the ability to warm herself with her magic. He was just as disturbed as she was.

"Let's head down here," Hunter said.

He still clung to his bow and mentally counted his hidden daggers, if only to comfort himself. He didn't know what still lingered if anything, and he didn't want to be caught unaware. Even with the might of his power, he wasn't sure he could properly protect Faria. Whatever was going on was way beyond his ability to comprehend.

The stone steps built into the side of the mountain were steep and crumbling but still held under their weight. Regardless, Hunter kept his hand out, ready to snatch Faria should she look like she would fall. He was certain she knew why he hovered so close, but he was grateful she didn't say anything.

They rounded a sharp corner and were greeted by a magnificent marble statue of the goddess Farrah, her smile wide and her hands outstretched and cupped in front of her as if holding something precious. Behind her stood a beautiful white stone temple. Columns lined the front, the tops of which were adorned in a floral design. Large windows encased the temple, the sides almost entirely glass. It had a flat roof that tapered at the sides. The lawn in front was covered in botanicals that both looked and smelled like the Spring Garden outside of Faria's rooms at *Mentage*. Ivy crawled up the side of the temple and there was an overgrown wall of jasmine in front of it. Stone benches were placed along certain pathways and there was even a fountain in the middle, this one depicting people, or rather, four other gods and goddesses.

Hunter assumed they were the siblings to Farrah and her consort, though the past few hours had shaken his confidence in any knowledge he thought he had.

"This looks alarmingly like the Spring Garden, doesn't it?" Faria asked, her mouth in a tight line.

"I was thinking the same thing myself," Hunter replied. He picked the most direct path toward the temple. "Let's go this way. Her temple was supposed to be sealed and the Crystal of Light should be inside somewhere. If it's gone, we'll have a whole other set of problems to worry about."

Faria followed him, keeping her distance.

His head throbbed with each step he took. Hunter didn't know if the pain was from his locked memories or her slowly rejecting the bond, but his entire body was starting to feel as though it were under attack and he didn't like it. He tried to keep his mood to himself, his face inscrutable as he was known to do, but it frustrated him. She had to be hurting as well.

Faria was stubborn at the best of times, but if this was from rejecting the bond, it was unbearable.

They both stopped at the entrance to the temple, trepidation filling Hunter at the first of what he deemed to be the worst-case scenarios. The entryway was cracked in half, the thick stone sliced away with force. Tiny cracks ebbed away from the point of contact and shards of marble littered the ground. There was a gap wide enough for Faria and Hunter to pass through side by side.

Hunter peered in before entering, noticing how bright the entrance chamber was. A swirled pattern of tile sparkled in the sunlight streaming in through the windows. He could just make out illustrations on the walls, though he was too far away to see the detail on them. He held out his hand in front of the doorway and concentrated on the feel of magic. It was strongest here, almost making him choke on the air, though when he pressed a little of his own power against it, it moved easily.

There was no protective barrier, or if there was, it wasn't there anymore. Hunter searched the perimeter, paying special attention to the threat of magical traps but there were none.

"Is it safe?" Faria asked.

A faint purple light appeared as if an aura surrounded her body and Hunter wondered if that was meant to be protective or if she was exuding power to see for herself if there was anything to be worried about. He'd never seen her magic presented in that way.

"I don't sense anything. I haven't even had that feeling of being watched since we entered this side of the mountain."

Flashes of light throbbing with the pain in his head started to blur his vision. Hunter couldn't remember the last time he had a headache that wasn't directly related to a fight or training.

He rubbed his forehead. "Me either. Let's go in."

FOURTEEN

HUNTER

Their footsteps echoed off the walls and high ceiling, bouncing playfully back to them. It gave the impression of a troop of people entering the antechamber rather than just the two of them. It was cooler in the temple, and still. Dust motes traveled lazily in the sunbeams trickling through the glass windows. The magic hung like thick humidity, pressing against their bodies, causing them to drag their feet with increasing exhaustion.

Hunter suspected this magic would have forced others to fall asleep or deter them from moving forward. It was gentle, but a being with lesser comparable power to Hunter and Faria would have likely been unconscious for days, rather than hours.

A gasp from the corner caught Hunter's attention.

Faria stood in front of the first of a series of paintings, each appearing to be the continuation of a story. Hunter stood behind Faria, barely a breath away, inhaling her jasmine and honey scent. He resisted the urge to run his fingers through her hair, to grip her hand and assure her that everything would be okay. Instead, he looked at the painting she stared at with horrified fascination.

It was the creation story. Written in Vallean, or maybe it was some variation of it. The language of the gods, perhaps, as they were in a temple devoted to one.

"I can't read it," Faria said. "Can you?"

The illustration showed an immense cosmos; swirling hues of rose and violet danced with gold on a blanket of navy. Splashes of white twinkled within the endless colorful void. It somehow seemed infinite, though it only filled a tiny square of space.

"There once were three sisters from a place far from here. They wanted to explore outside of their worlds and found this one." Hunter walked over to the next one, trying to decipher the words. "They found a world filled with every shade of green and blue, with a sun that gave life. It was beautiful, different from the worlds where they came from. And so they stayed."

The next illustration had six figures, three goddesses and what seemed to be three gods. There were no names and not all of the words made sense to Hunter, but he continued on as best he could, filling in the unknowns with what he thought they meant. "The sisters started to miss their home, so they poured pieces of their magic into the ground and nurtured it until trees with golden leaves grew tall and wildflowers blanketed the land. They were pleased, but after a time, they realized that they were not alone.

"Upon exploration of the land, the sisters discovered that three brothers lived in the southern part of the continent. The brothers also came from Elsewhere and craved a different life. They combined their powers of creation and made the many realms to visit."

Hunter was fully invested in the story. Wanting to know more, needing some sort of answers. He didn't know how much of it was truth, but who would carve lies in a goddess' resting place?

He stepped in front of the next painting, this time of the goddesses standing opposite the gods. He took a moment to decipher the inscription. "I don't understand all of this. It sounds like they created others in their likeness. The goddesses created the Fae in their likeness. The gods created warlocks and … I think this means to say shapeshifters. But neither were happy with the way the others did it." The next illustration showed what appeared to be a scene of sacrifice. "The gods found they had more control over their creations when they were made using blood magic. The goddesses believed this to be an abomination and threatened to banish the gods if they did not cease their abuse of power at once."

The next image was of Farrah and her consort standing separate from the others. "Despite this, Farrah fell in love with someone her sisters were starting to look at as the enemy. They forbade her to have relations with Alexei, but she couldn't help what she felt. Farrah and her consort soon became pregnant, the only child conceived naturally rather than magically. Farrah named her heir to the land.

"The gods were jealous of the baby as they believed it was their right to rule the land, and tried to kill their niece. The brothers were banished to the Forbidden Continent, along with a group of their closest followers. Farrah and Alexei created the first Val and gifted the Fae the proper magic to create more to help protect their bloodline."

"Wait," Faria said, her voice echoing in the chamber. "Are you telling me the Agostonna's are direct descendants of the goddesses?"

Hunter wished he knew what she was thinking. It was silent in the temple and dust floated in the shaft of sunlight streaming in through the windows. He wondered what time it was outside of this place.

"Do you think my mother knew?"

"Your mother held many secrets," Hunter replied. "But we don't know what is in the royal library yet or what the Fates might have told her and shown her during her trials."

"This is Them," Faria exclaimed, running to an illustration on the next wall over.

"Who is Them?" Hunter asked, quickly reading through the artwork she skipped to make sure they weren't missing any major information.

There was only the mention of the goddesses banning the close followers of the gods from stepping foot on the land again with their version of blood magic. The heir to the line must keep the magic in place or else risk invasion. *Hmm, that seems important.* Was there more to the Blood Contract than he thought? Faria needing to be accepted by the land for the magic to work properly was a lot more important than they believed.

"These are the Fates," she breathed, looking at the illustration with a mixture of fear and awe.

Hunter peered closely. It looked like a circle of shadows more than anything, unformed, and yet their presence was immense, even through the painting.

"What does it say?"

Hunter scanned the words. "The creators knew there was too much power for the realm and trusted in their offspring to keep the beauty of their creation going. Before they settled for their … Hm, I'm uncertain … Long sleep? They divided a piece of their consciousness so they could still protect the realm and its inhabitants without being physically there."

The next illustration depicted Farrah and her consort pulling what appeared to be shadows from their bodies and placing them against blurred objects around them.

"Once their collective consciousness was Everywhere and in the Dreaming, the two most powerful creators, Farrah and Alexei, pulled a kernel of their power into objects that could be possessed if the time was necessary to defend the realms against the ultimate evil. The consort put his Flames in his beloved realm of fire, where none but his Val could enter. Farrah kept her Crystal in the eyes of the people, where none but the chosen could possess it.

"Farrah's sisters chose to rest in other realms," Hunter continued, "as did the consort's brothers, but Farrah couldn't bear to leave the land with all her children. Alexei laid her to rest and sealed her in magic that could be broken by none but him at the end of days."

"But the temple was opened," Faria said. "If only her consort could open it … Does that mean he is awakened?"

Hunter shook his head, unable to process much of anything past the unbearable pounding behind his eyes. "Let's find where she rests. Maybe we will know more then."

They walked down a hallway off the chamber, more illustrations of breathtaking flowers, waterfalls, and the brilliant night sky lining the walls. It was beautiful and whimsical with an almost sensual energy radiating from it.

At the end of the hall was a single arched doorway. Painted on the door was a vast ocean with phosphorescent green and blue rippling through the currents underneath an infinite twilight.

Hunter paused at the door, sensing a pulsating energy radiating from inside. A feeling come over him—an intuition more than anything—that he wouldn't be allowed entrance.

He glanced over his shoulder at Faria, who was busy studying the constellations etched onto the ceiling. "Come here, Princess," he said.

She shot him a look of annoyance before stepping beside him.

"What do you feel when you stand here?" he asked.

She smiled sweetly at him. "You mean other than the irritation at having to stand so close to you?"

He smirked knowing she was affected by him by the flush of her cheeks and the way her pupils dilated. "Nice try, Princess. You forget how well I know you, how in sync we are, even if you don't care to recognize it at the moment. Plus, your scent is intoxicating to me."

He watched a torrent of emotions rush through her before she faced forward again.

"What is it you want me to feel? In regards to the door," she finished quickly.

"The energy pulsating from inside. Close your eyes, concentrate. What does it feel like to you?"

Faria closed her eyes.

Hunter took advantage to admire the lines and curves of her face. She looked different to him. Fiercer than he remembered. He could see where Ander got his cheekbones and the shape of his eyes. She looked like her mother, the same strength glowing beneath her skin. She would be a formidable queen as soon as the land accepted her.

"I can feel … warmth. Like sunshine, like love. It's comforting. The energy seems like it's embracing me. I can feel it brush against my skin the way a cat does to its owner when it's ready for attention. Or Nellie," she added with a hint of a smile.

Hunter suspected the magic would have only responded properly to her, especially if the Agostonna's were of the goddesses' bloodline. "I think only you can open the door."

"There's no handle," Faria said, opening her eyes and examining it. She placed her hand against the stone.

Sapphire light glowed where her skin touched it and scanned her. There was a faint click and the stone started to push backward.

"Should I go in alone?"

"Not a chance." He folded his arms and waited for her to enter.

FIFTEEN

FARIA

Faria rolled her eyes and stepped forward into the chamber. An ethereal light appeared.

An opaque sarcophagus stood alone in the center of the room. The white stone walls were at odds with the red dirt floor. The ceiling was shrouded in darkness, and even with her exceptional vision, she couldn't make out what it was made from. A barrage of emotions engulfed her and all at once it was as if she could see and feel the love Farrah and her consort had.

Brief images flooded her and the intensity of who they were to each other reminded Faria of the echo of what she and Hunter had. *It could be like this,* she thought. *If she could just forgive him. If he could just see things from her point of view.*

"What is it, Princess?" Hunter asked. "What are you thinking?" He tried again to brush against her mind.

Though she did not allow him access, the longing she felt for him, for the loneliness to subside, almost broke her resolve. He was right earlier; she did feel the ache of missing him but she also needed to heal and be ready. She spent so much of her time wanting the choice of who to love and right now she was choosing herself.

"You need to forgive me sometime. You won't be able to avoid the call of the bond for long. Eventually, you'll let me back in."

"Not yet."

"This has gone on long enough."

The golden halo in his eyes burned with his anger as he stepped closer to her. She breathed in his scent of sea and spice and wondered again if he was from this land. If he was created from this soil and water and air and the fire of the gods.

"This has just started for me," she hissed. Her voice echoed off the temple walls. "The idea of you being alive, of being here with me for however long it has been."

He closed the distance between them, and she leaned closer, unable to resist the pull that was always there, despite the animosity between them.

"I was always here, always fighting for these people. This land. For you."

"You abandoned me," her words broke with the memory her past trauma evoked. She was overwhelmed by the imprint of undying love seeped within the chamber, so at odds with the pain and resentment she harbored for the past eleven months. "You didn't check on me. You didn't stop Darroc from the twisted games he played on me. Worst of all, you never told me that …" She paused, the pregnant silence filling the space between them with words she wasn't ready to say out loud. The darkness in her rose, setting fire to her limbs, seeking a way out of the cage it had been placed in. "It broke me in a way I don't know can ever be repaired."

He yelled in frustration, a tendril of his *malosin* whipping out and lashing the wall beside him. Tiny pebbles tumbled around them.

"Why can't you be grateful I'm here, that the Fates have ensured we would be together?"

Why can't you just apologize, she didn't say. *Why can't you see that what I had to do to survive life without you fundamentally changed me?* "Maybe the Fates have it wrong."

"So now the gods are wrong?"

"No one is infallible," she said.

Maybe she was being obstinate, but being together in that chamber, with the remnants Alexei and Farrah's love pressing in on them was suffocating. She needed to refocus on the task at hand. They had more important things to worry about than when she would let him in on her thoughts again.

Faria stepped toward the sarcophagi, steeling herself to gaze upon the goddess who looked so much like her, who created this realm and named her family line as the rulers. Hunter groaned behind her. Faria peered over her shoulder at him, concern immediately taking the forefront as he clutched his head.

"What's wrong?" she asked. She'd never known him to be sick or hurt outside of training. She'd never properly seen him in battle, but she was fairly certain that with their advances in alchemy and potions, he'd not be in pain unless something was wrong. "Hunter, what is it? What's happening?"

Hunter fell to his knees, his hands on the sides of his head as if to keep it from falling to pieces.

Alarmed, Faria lowered the mental shield between them and reached out to him. She entered his mind without resistance and instantly regretted it as shockwaves of pain overtake her. "What is this, Hunter?"

"Shield … yourself," he struggled to speak.

She quickly retreated from his mind and threw her walls back up again. The pain ceased but she it resonated throughout her body. Faria grasped her chest, desperate for her breathing to resume normally. She wanted to reach for him, but intuition held her back.

Blinding white light burst from Hunter's body. The force of it threw Faria back into the sarcophagus.

Except there was nothing there.

It was a mirage. Trick of the eyes.

Faria slammed to the floor—the that had once been covered by the coffin's image. Laying there, crumpled and hurting, her hand dangled over a deep, dark chasm in the floor.

Another wave of light came from Hunter as he screamed with the pressure of it, and she felt its energy slam into her. Searing flashes of agony ripped through her. It was too much.

Her final thought rang with alarming clarity.

The grave was empty.

PART III

SIXTEEN

NELLIE

Waves crashed against the rough rock cliff of the island in the middle of the North Sea, spraying Nellie with frigid, salty sea mist. She stirred, wiping the water from her eyes as she came back to consciousness. Warm air covered her body with each exhalation from the *Drogosterra*, making her feel feverish between the heat of its breath and the cold of the winter air.

Nellie sat up, brushing off tiny pebbles embedded in her cheek. She glanced down at her fingers which were attached to her human hands which were attached to her arms that connected to her very human body. *That's interesting.*

She stood tall, stretching her tight muscles. She was absolutely certain she was last a *Drogosterra*, but she had no recollection of changing back into her human body. The last thing she remembered was a bright light. A gust of humid, topical wind had whipped across the island, a stark contrast to the frigid air now slapping her skin.

Skin?

Nellie looked down, taking in her very nude body. *That was a new one,* she thought. She'd always switched bodies with her clothes on and they existed when she switched back. Was it because of that light? Did it somehow burn off her clothes?

Oh, well, at least I'm alone—

"What are you doing with my dragon?"

Nellie let out a long-suffering sigh and cursed the Fates. Of course someone would show up when she was in nothing but her birthday suit. Of course it would be Faria's son. He was practically her nephew for cripes' sake. She stole a quick glance at his alarmed face. Her attractive, not-at-all-related-to-her-in-any-way-so-it-was-not-as-weird-as-it-sounded nephew.

"Excuse me, why are you staring at me? It's a little rude, don't you think?" Nellie thought about running and hiding behind a wing but she needed to retain some of her dignity. Plus, she was a hottie. And they weren't weird about bodies in Anestra so she wasn't going to start with her former human ideals now that she was in front of her queen's son.

Oh god, she thought, *my prince.* She was in nothing but the flesh in front of her *prince.*

"It would be nice to know why my dragon was scared enough to call for me, only for me to find her lying unconscious next to you in the nude. Were you trying something weird?"

"I swear to the goddess if one more person makes a bestiality joke ..."

Ander smirked at her and tossed her his coat. "Really though, what happened?"

"I don't know," Nellie said, placing the leather jacket on her. It was warm and smelled of fresh soap with a subtle undertone of ... *pizza?* "I saw Carenek Peaks were completely split in two when I flew here, and once I got to this archipelago, went through multiple realms even though I know I never left these skies. Then I had to comfort your *Drogosterra*, who was upset that you rejected her, by the way. So I hope you plan on not being a butthead and making it up to her. When we were just starting to understand each other, a blinding flash of light came from the direction of the mountains. Next thing I knew, I woke up naked."

Ander looked her up and down as if wondering if she had a few screws loose before saying, "Don't you know how to switch forms without losing your clothes?"

Nellie rolled her eyes. "Obviously I didn't choose to be naked next to a dragon. On a remote island. In the middle of the ocean. In the dead of winter. In the north."

"Right ... Well, are you hurt?"

"As if you even care," Nellie said, flinging her curls out of her eyes as if it didn't bother her one way or the other. "Now that you're here, though, maybe we should go back to *Mentage* to check in. That light was weird, and your parents were there when I left."

"Your queen is fine," Ander said quickly. "I would have felt it otherwise."

"It's good to know that your *mother* is fine," Nellie said pointedly, "but there's still your father, your grandfather, and basically all of Anestra to worry about. Plus, I've been tasked to train your dragon, so it would be nice if you stayed and kept her happy with me."

Ander walked up to his *Drogosterra* and placed his palm against her snout. There was a brief flash of purple light, then the creature gave a low rumble as she stirred awake. Nellie saw one eye open and watched as its slitted pupil focused on her. The *Drogosterra* sniffed in Nellie's direction, huffing out a steaming breath on her body.

"It's me," Nellie said, though she realized how idiotic it was to speak to a dragon in the human common language as if it would understand. "This is my other form. Well, my true form. My preferred form?"

"Are you going to keep talking or can we just get a move on?" Ander was grumpy and impatient.

Nellie rolled her eyes at him before tossing his coat over his face and switching back to a *Drogosterra*. Once in her dragon form, she communicated with Ander's companion that they were going back to the place where everyone shot arrows at her and to try not to freak out.

I know where we are going. I understand all languages. She lowered herself and allowed Ander to climb onto her back.

Nellie wondered if she would also be able to understand all languages in her *Drogosterra* form.

You are a strange creature. You must have many worshipers.

Nellie cackled to herself and sprang off the rock, eager to get back to *Mentage* and hopefully find some answers, particularly on what that light was.

Ander's *Drogosterra* flew cautiously as if unsure of having something astride her back.

Are you okay? Nellie thought toward her. *You aren't going to harm him.*

My Val is fragile in emotion, she replied. *If I fly fast, he could feel overwhelmed and disappear again.*

He left before because there was too much happening at once, Nellie said. *All of our emotions were fritzed. Plus, he might be of this land, but he didn't grow up here. He doesn't know the queen or his father. He does not look to these people as his, and now that he will be a prince, there may be expectations. He has an evil warlock attached to him. Also, he basically started a pandemic in the human realm."*

Nellie felt ripples of horrified amusement from the *Drogosterra.*

Yes, I think going slow will be good for my Val. He needs some time.

Despite going at a slower pace than Nellie would have wanted or expected, they made it back to Anestra and found themselves in the middle of a maelstrom nothing short of calamity. People of all races ran in every direction, falling over each other, yelling at each other.

Nellie sighed inwardly. Just once she'd like something easy.

Both dragons landed in the thick snow and Ander slid off the back of his. A crowd of people encircled them, though none were giving words of welcome.

Nellie scooched closer to Ander and let out a low growl. She didn't need the power to feel emotions like Endo or to scent them the way some elves could to know that Ander felt extremely uncomfortable and was on the verge of jumping ship again. The hushed whispers she knew would be too loud for his hearing were the final straw.

A quick burst of light and an angry, naked Nellie stood in front of the crowd who emitted gasps of shock and laughter.

"Whatever the heck your problem is, you need to get over it. This is your *prince*." She waited for the laughter to die down, for the embarrassment to show on their faces. There were still too many defiant ones in the crowd for her liking. "Show him respect."

There were a few beats of silence before more protesting and demands to have him sign the treaty before he helped Darroc eliminate them all ensued.

Nellie was astounded. Never had she experienced any Anestrian to be so unwelcoming, but fear dictated behavior, and the stench of it coated the words leaving their mouths. It triggered something in Nellie. For years, Shapeshifters were persecuted, and had they known what she really was five years ago, they would have reacted the same way or worse without ever getting to know her. She wouldn't stand for that type of ignorance.

Faline appeared next to Nellie, wrapping a cloak around her shoulders. She gave her adoptive mother a grateful smile and was about to tear into all the hateful people again before a louder, more stern voice rang out.

"Enough!" King Dennison shouted, silencing the crowd.

The Royal Guard broke up the scene, divvying out tasks for everyone to complete, or else telling the angrier ones to walk it off.

Dennison eyed Nellie and Ander. "We have much to discuss. Meet me in the Council Room in twenty minutes. Clothed." He gave Nellie a pointed look before turning to speak to a warlock.

"He's normally much nicer," Nellie whispered to Ander, careful not to let the king overhear as they trudged through the snow. She pulled the cloak tighter around her, but walking through a foot of snow on the ground barefoot with no pants was nothing short of torture. "But his wife was murdered, his daughter went missing, he lost his grandson, and now the entire land is in jeopardy, so, you know."

"Nice … I'm leaving one set of trauma for another," Ander mumbled.

"I'll meet you at the dining hall in fifteen minutes," Nellie said. "It's just through there, down the lawn, and onto the stone patio. You can't miss all the arches. And if for some reason you do, it's the giant room with tables where, you know, people dine. Flags with the Agostonna crest are hanging from approximately eighty different locations, in case you forget who rules this land." Nellie parted ways and ran to a side entrance closer to her rooms.

Immediately the comforting smell of cinnamon and cloves hit her, a scent that permeated throughout the mansion due to the spiced bark that always lit the fireplaces. She turned the corner and admired the decorations put up for the solstice. Evergreen boughs and wreaths made of gold and crimson leaves donned the walls, while candles were placed strategically to give the home a cozy effect. Side tables situated near every intersection or major entryway had crystal bowls filled with chocolates or freshly baked cookies and stations set up with melted chocolate, tea, or mulled wine.

It was clear that King Dennison tried to keep spirits high during such a traumatic time. Or perhaps it was the Anestrians who wanted to keep his spirits high. Either way, Nellie appreciated the gesture. It was nice to have a bit of normalcy again.

She reached the rooms she shared with Faline. They were modest, just a sitting room and a larger bedroom for both of their beds and a bathroom attached. It made sense when she was a child, but she was twenty-two and wanted her own space. Nellie wondered if Faline would care about her moving into a different section of *Mentage*. Maybe she could convince Faria to head to the royal chambers and she could take Faria's old rooms. The sunken tub in her bathroom was to die for.

Nellie rifled through her clothes, pulling out a pair of soft jeans and a white cashmere sweater. She liked dressing as she used to, the way other humans did in Anestra. Nellie was always filled with longing when she saw them walking around wearing their Doc Martens and crop top sweaters. She had been stuck as a young girl and wasn't able to dress the way she wanted when she wanted to.

But now she could, and comfort was her ultimate goal, especially after a day of flying in the frigid temperatures.

She walked over to her jewelry case which was filled with gemstones from around Anestra. She'd never really had use for them, but they were gifted to her nonetheless, mostly by Faria over the years, who'd wanted nothing to do with the jewelry her mother tried to make her wear.

Nellie rifled through until she found a simple pair of silver hoop earrings. She lifted them out and noticed a chain knotted against the end of one of them. It was her mother's locket. Excited, Nellie put it around her neck and admired it in the mirror. It wasn't the most beautiful necklace, but she was at least able to feel like a piece of her mother was with her. She yawned and cracked her neck, mentally preparing herself for whatever other curveball the king was going to throw her way, and went to meet up with Ander.

And then, she decided, she would go to The Phoenix Fire in Athinia for a giant slice of honey cheesecake.

SEVENTEEN

ANDER

Though he was no stranger to uncomfortable situations, there was little that could rival the awkwardness of his current predicament. Had he murdered sick people before? Yes. Kidnapped not one, but two sirens? Yes. Watched Darroc split apart a loyal follower who questioned why they were wasting their time trying to get through the mountains and did nothing to intervene? Yes.

But to be in the same room as his grandfather, his mother's best friend whom he had just seen naked, an entire guard who looked at him as if he were the one who put a wasting spell on their grounds, and a former follower of Darroc's Ander recalled seeing a time or two, all made Ander feel as though he were having some sort of out of body experience.

"We need to discuss what our next steps are while Faria and Hunter are away," King Dennison said without preamble. "The fact of the matter is, until they're back, we don't know what we're dealing with, but it would be unwise to be unprepared."

"With respect, sir," a short elf with dark pixie hair said, "we have been preparing for the better part of a year. Most of our forces are on these grounds, or near enough to be here within half a day's notice. The rest are interspersed along our waters. Until there is something to fight, what more can we do besides forge more weapons and continue making tonics?"

"Actually," Nellie cut in, rubbing a necklace she now wore.

Ander thought she looked nice in human clothes. Her hazel eyes were bright with excitement and the pink in her cheeks highlighted her freckles. Her energy was infectious and he found himself taking a slight step closer to her, wanting to bask in her glow.

"I have a major update that will give little to no information at all."

The king rubbed his forehead and gave her an exasperated look. Ander had the impression this was a common occurrence.

"Time is of the essence, Nellie. Speak it and we will decide if it's valuable information or not," Dennison said.

"Right, okay. So I'm flying up in the clouds, right, and it's cold but so nice at the same time. Plus, I had that little chamber of fire near my belly so I was also a bit toasty. Anyways," Nellie sped up her story at the looks she received in the chamber room, "I'm flying, admiring the forest. It really is so beautiful from above, you know? Unfortunate you don't have airplanes here because, wow."

"On with it, child," an older woman with a severe demeanor said.

Her hair was stark white and Ander knew that for an elf to have white hair it meant they had been around for centuries. He wondered if it was considered rude here to ask someone their age. "Information. Go."

"I'm getting there! I could see the tip of Anestra in the distance and dark waters beyond, but I looked to my right to admire the view of the mountains and wondered what was happening between Faria and Hunter, because, you know, *awkward*, when I veered toward mountains instead."

"Nellie," the one Ander knew to be called Wilhelm said, "please get on with it. We're all in anticipation."

"They were split. In two. The entire mountain range split open. The forest in front was all plowed down and remember that cute lake that used to be there? It's massive now, probably from the earth splitting. I won't go into the science," Nellie said, winking.

The room was heavy with stunned silence.

"Faline," the king said, turning to the older woman, "what do you know of this? The Secret Keepers?"

The older woman opened and closed her mouth again, shaking her head. "I wouldn't know, Dennison. That is unheard of on every level. I don't think there's a soul still alive who would know what could cause the mountains to split."

"Ander," the king said, his voice breaking a bit at the end of his name.

Ander felt his blood pressure rise at being singled out, then felt a slight pressure as Nellie pressed her shoulder against him as a gesture of comfort. At least, that was what he took it as.

"Would Darroc know how to do that?"

Ander swiftly turned his head to the side. "He would not have sent you a wasting spell if he knew how to manipulate the earth in that physical manner. He doesn't have the strength. The Crystal of Light is safe from him."

"Not if he gets word of this," a tall, dark-skinned elf said. Her eyes were bright yellow, two citrine gemstones sitting in a sea of black. "With the mountains open, anyone could get the Crystal."

"I'm more concerned with what's coming out of there," a shorter guard said. He was thin and favored his right leg. "What creatures could be free, or what if it was sealed for our protection, rather than protection for the inside? What if it's gone now?"

"I am most concerned for my daughter," the king interrupted. "But I will have to trust she and Hunter will come back to us soon with an update. In the meantime, Endo,"—the one who was Darroc's follower stood from his leaned position against the wall—"what are the waters like off the east coast of Wendorre?"

"Sir?" Endo questioned. "The waters …"

"For sailing, Endo. Is there a port that was used often? Will it be easy to acquire a ship?"

Ander could have answered that question. There was almost nothing left besides a few withered warlocks who didn't have it in them to leave their land. There was little to no trade, though he knew the Forbidden Continent helped Anestra supply them with food and goods every now and then. Even so, there were barely any warlocks left to receive them.

"I haven't been there in quite a while, but from what I remember, there was only a small town that would have a ship or maybe two. There is nothing to the east besides the Bone Isles. The west was where merchants were needed."

"Have you finished gathering supplies and your crew to fulfill Faria's request? Head to Wendorre, obtain a ship, then sail north. See if the protective spell is still active from that side of the mountain or if it's just on land."

Ander watched Endo raise his eyebrows and heard his heartbeat quicken. Why was he so interested in going? That sounded like a weeks' long voyage and the last thing he'd ever want to do.

"I'd like you to go with him, Ander," the king said. "With your *Drogosterra*."

Ander stared at his grandfather, trying to figure him out. His cunning blue eyes pierced through him, and Ander was sure whatever talents he had included scanning people. "I never agreed to stay," he said.

A sense of unease rippled through the Royal Guard. Looks of distrust thrown his way.

"I will remain with my dragon, but I don't know this land. I don't know any of you. My sense of trust and loyalty is a little skewed these days," he tried to make it lighthearted but it just came out angry.

Faline said, "Ander, the most you need to trust is that we are on the same side. We must rid this world of all that threatens to destroy it. It was always going to come down to this. It will be us against him. And believe me, no one in any realm will fight harder for your freedom than your mother."

The discomfort Ander felt was more than knowing that no one liked or trusted him, but that they thought to use his mother as a bargaining tool. He didn't know her. He would protect her, yes. The *innulum* all but required him to. But to say that she would fight for him when he'd seen only a few days' worth of evidence of that over the past eighteen years was not something he was ready to hear.

"If you want him and the *Drogosterra* to go, why not just fly?" Nellie countered. She looked as confused as Ander felt. The logic in the plan was missing, which for Dennison being a leader of the Anestrian army, seemed unusual. "The three of us could fly over the mountain range or circle around the island and come at it that way in less than a day," Nellie said.

"Because as a Val, he can protect our people. It will be Endo, Johanna, and three others," Dennison said. "I have already asked one of the shifter leaders and she will bring two more."

"No," Nellie interjected forcefully. "We aren't going through this again. Marisa isn't yours to experiment with. Absolutely not."

"If they want to go, they should go," Dennison said. "They will soon be citizens of this land and with that comes the responsibility of protecting it.

"Sir, with all due respect—"

"This is war, Nellie. This is what it takes. Tough decisions. We must be tactical. Be reasonable and see that this is the most effective way to cover all our bases. The *Drogosterra* will be in the sky and will alert Ander of any danger there. He will be on the ground with our soldiers. Endo will navigate the ship and Marisa or whoever of her clan will explore the water. We must know how to effectively divide our resources ..."

Ander's vision blurred in and out. His ears swam as if he'd immersed them in water and his skin flushed. Time slowed and the room was like static, switching from the Council Room to a darkened cave. He saw movement in the abyss, but just barely. It was the outline of something. Then the king was back speaking to others, probably giving out more orders. Ander didn't know.

He glanced over at Faline, his eyes dragging slowly as if he were drunk. She looked at him curiously and stepped as if she would go to him. He moved his head over more and looked at Nellie, only Nellie was no longer there and instead, was inches from Darroc's face. At least, he thought it was Darroc's face.

His skin had a thin sheen of sweat and he smelled foul, like fetid blood, disease, and decomposition. Darroc's eyes found his and Ander's body flooded with alarm. He wasn't in the cave, not really, but he tried like hell to run backward away from the maniac insanity now housed there.

"I figured it out," his voice cracked as if he'd screamed for hours or days. "I know how to destroy her and then I can finally be free of this death magic she holds over me." He laughed.

The sound crawled under Ander's skin and triggered his impulse to kill and protect.

"Ander." Nellie snapped her fingers and he was firmly back in the Council Room.

Everyone stared at him in alarm, waiting for him to say something.

"What?" he asked, trying to play it cool. He forgot, however, that everyone there was advanced in some way and could hear, scent, or see the changes happening within his body. Silence, waiting for him to say something. "I don't know what happened. I was here, obviously, but I was elsewhere. It looked like a cave. Darroc was strung up on a rock."

"A vision?" Faline asked. "Faria has visions often. An inherited gift?"

That was a question more for herself than him so he didn't bother answering the last part. "It didn't feel like a vision. I was there, but also here. It felt like the current time. I could still hear the echoes of conversation here while listening to what he said there."

"And what did he say?"

"He figured out how to kill her and then he would be free of the death magic she held over him."

"Her meaning …"

"His mother. Moira. The phoenix." Tense silence followed his answer. "There might not be much time before he's unparalyzed from whatever Moira did to him. It was as if she burned away a piece of his soul."

"We need to leave now," Johanna said. "Grab the packs you've prepared already and let's go. There is no time for goodbyes. Ander, I will take care of your things. You will need to jump us to the border if you're comfortable with that."

If he was comfortable? Now they cared about his feelings?

"I'm going too, then," Nellie said, looping her arm through Ander's. "Let's do it."

"Nellie, maybe you should stay with the shapeshifters until they at least sign the Contract," Faline suggested. "They trust you."

"Well, you should trust them first, considering they gave up everything they knew to come here and help defend a country they know nothing about. Come on Ander, let's get our dragon friend ready."

Nellie turned around and led him out into the hall and toward the front entrance. Ander was impressed that she stood her ground to the most important people in the country and that they seemed to respect her decision. He liked that the king listened to everyone equally before making any decision. It was so unlike what he'd grown up with. It was strange, not knowing his place. He was technically a prince and yet he'd never felt more displaced in his life.

"You don't have to keep an eye on me," Ander said, taking care to keep his strides the length of hers. "I'm not going to drop them off in the underworld or something."

"I'm not worried about you," Nellie said, distracted. "Well, I guess in a way I am. I don't like the way people look at you. It's Endo I want to keep an eye on."

"I'd seen him with Darroc a few times. What's he doing here?"

Nellie sighed. "He turned to the dark side, young padawan. Sorry," she continued quickly. "Star Wars reference."

"I know what Star Wars is." He'd spent more than enough time on Earth to learn almost everything about their pop culture. It was fun, but mindless compared to other realms he'd visited. "So what happened?"

"He became a spy, or I guess as much as he could be. He'd leak information to us when there was any to be had. He said he wasn't part of any type of inner circle to know much."

Ander tried to remember more about that one. Endo. He was probably telling the truth. Ander was forced to witness the cruel punishments Darroc would bestow on his closest supporters when they disappointed him and he didn't recall Endo ever being one of them. "So he saw reason, I'm assuming, and came back here."

"I hoped he would but …" Nellie concentrated a little too hard on navigating across the snow-packed lands toward the edge of the Forest of the Dawn where his *Drogosterra* hovered far enough away to not be considered a threat to anyone. "It's just different now. I wanted him so badly to return to us, but it just doesn't feel the same. It's like …"

"Grief hardens you over time," Ander finished her thought for her. "I don't know much about you because you were never on Darroc's radar. And I never picked up on what you were either, but from what I know just of the past few weeks, there has been a lot you've had to come to terms with in a short amount of time. You lost your sovereign, went back to a family who rejected you, something about an ex-boyfriend that I don't know the details of but I'm sure that was confusing, seeing everyone aged when you still looked the same, learning more of your mother's murder, uniting clans, witnessing so much death."

"Wow, color me speechless," Nellie said. "You're quite observant for someone who seemed indifferent to us."

"Confused, not indifferent," Ander replied. "What I was taught and what Faria told me are complete opposites. I've experienced my share of trauma." He cut himself off, worried Nellie would say something about it.

Instead, she nudged his side playfully. "We love a good trauma story here," she said. "You'll fit right in with us, promise." Nellie stopped just shy of the entrance to the Forest of the Dawn and removed her necklace. "Do me a favor and hold on to this for me." She shoved it into his hand before he could object.

He was surprised to realize he didn't want to. It was nice she trusted him with her belongings, like a friend would.

"I can't risk going commando again and somehow losing that. It's the last thing of my mother's that I have."

Something warm cracked through his cold heart. He understood the need to have something of her mother's close to her and kept safe. How many years had he longed for the same?

Ander slid it into one of his inner pockets so he knew it wouldn't risk falling out. "It's my pleasure."

"Thanks!" She beamed at him before rubbing her hands together maniacally. "Let's do this."

She transformed into a *Drogosterra* quicker than he'd ever seen a shapeshifter change and zoomed into the sky.

Footsteps sounded from behind Ander and he turned, his good mood replaced with anxious reluctance. The small group of Anestrians were making their way toward Ander.

He took a deep breath, steeling himself to spend time with his mother's people. "Let's do this."

EIGHTEEN

FARIA

Cold and darkness. Fire and light. Death and rebirth. The visions were confusing, bombarding her quicker than she could decipher until it was just a bedlam of emotion and—

Faria.

A whisper of her name in the onslaught of raw feeling tried to bring her back to the present but it was incessant, the pain and horror and love and—

Awaken, young queen.

Who was calling her name? The voice was unfamiliar; the power it held almost forced her to yield to whatever it asked of her. But it didn't matter because a tidal wave of grief crushed her and she choked on the despair as she drowned in—

Faria Agostonna … Wake up!

Her name was a sharp bark in her ear and Faria's eyes flew open. She dripped in a cold sweat and the dirt from the floor of the tomb clung to the moisture on her skin. Bile burned her throat and she willed her heart to calm down. It was a dream, or vision, or … Whatever it was, wasn't real, despite how real it felt. The residue clung to her memory, but *this* was real; lying alone on the cold floor, staring up into the ceiling of darkness in Farrah's tomb was real.

Faria sat up, slowly at first, then quicker when she realized that hers was the only body within the tomb, but the grave was disturbed as if recently tampered with. She was alone so she didn't know who woke her from her nightmare but … *she was alone.*

"Hunter?"

Faria jumped to her feet, checking for any injury from her fall, but if she'd had any, they'd already healed. She patted herself down. Weapons were still intact. Her well of power...*responsive, good,* she thought as tiny flames rested along her fingertips.

She quickly dropped the shield around her mind and tried to reach out to Hunter. Nothing. The void was louder than any silence and she felt a panic start to rise in her.

At least I know that he can't die this time, she thought. She tried to repress memories from the last time she had awoken to find Hunter's lifeless body in front of her.

Faria strode down the hall that led back to the antechamber with the illustrations of the creation story, pausing just long enough to look at the images she had skipped over in her earlier haste to learn about the Fates.

Three images stood out to her: the first a group of hooded individuals standing over a bloodied body. The second was of Farrah bleeding into the ground. The third was of Farrah and her consort surrounded by people who looked to be a mixture of elves, Val, and animals which she had to assume were shapeshifters, considering what she saw on her way in. She wondered what it meant and made a mental note to ask Hunter if she ever found him.

Faria jumped down the steps to the temple and out into the garden and was immediately hit with the familiar scent of jasmine and spice. Warm sunlight beamed down on her and she stood in the middle of this place that was so foreign to her, its beauty frozen in time, asking herself why. Why was this piece of history kept from their historical records? Why had this place been sealed? Why were so many people stuck here? Were they awake? Could they feel?

It was silent and though Faria could appreciate the beauty, there was something to be feared in the stillness. Farrah was no longer in her tomb. That meant one of three things. First, she was never there to begin with. Second, someone stole her body, but why? Or third, she was awoken by her consort.

Faria didn't want to know what the implication of that meant, but she recalled something Hunter had read. The consort would only awaken the goddess at the world's end. Given that she'd been living in a state of apocalypse for the better part of her recent memory, she worried that was the more likely answer. Besides, if it were true that only Alexei could awaken her, then no one else should have been able to get in.

The grass made a soft shuffling noise under her boots as Faria walked back to the stone steps leading up the cliff face. She stopped at the giant statue of Farrah and looked up into the face that resembled so much of her own. Was she really a descendant of a goddess? Of a creator of the realm? She looked between the statue and the temple. She needed more information.

Faria examined the craftsmanship that went into the statue, the details of the robes Farrah wore, the wave of her hair. She even had a slight dimple in her cheek. Her hands were outstretched and cupped open in front of her, as if in offering. Faria was too short to see what would be in her hands, but the rings the goddess wore on her fingers caught her attention. The veined marble was cut in a way that made them sparkle as if her rings were made of gemstones or crystal.

Oh. My. Goddess. The Crystal of Light.

Hunter had just read that it was kept in plain sight only to be taken by who was worthy of it. *The* Crystal. Farrah's power. Farrah, the creator of their known realms. Farrah … destroyer of realms? What could be powerful enough to move mountains, to break the spell protecting Farrah's tomb if not Farrah herself?

There was no other explanation. And if Farrah and her consort were awake, what would they do to their creations intent on destroying the world? Faria had spent enough time in the human realm to know how much destruction they had all caused. Would Farrah and her consort destroy that realm? What about the innocent people?

Would they destroy hers?

There was no point in jumping to conclusions. She didn't know enough of the history—the proper history. She wasn't even sure how much of what she'd learned was fact.

She searched the base of the marble statue, trying to find an area where she might be able to find purchase and climb it to see what was inside Farrah's hands. The marble was smooth, without a nick or dimple in sight. She turned to the mountain cliff and started climbing the stone stairs.

Once she was about halfway up the cliff face, she turned, studying the statue from a higher elevation. Faria could see over the curve of Farrah's hands, and cupped inside them was …

Nothing.

If that truly was the location of the Crystal of Light, then it was no longer there, which meant their situation was more dire than ever. She needed to find Hunter and hurry back to *Mentage* to warn her father.

Faria raced up the last of the stone steps, hoping Hunter was okay. The void in her mind was painful, its ache starting to spread. She wished she hadn't been so stubborn so she could learn to sieve from place to place rather than waste her energy running everywhere. Maybe Ander would help her. Maybe she'd finally accept things with Hunter were what they were. She could forgive him.

Winded, Faria bent over at the top of the stairs, gasping for breath. She turned toward the city with its strange technologies and vehicles that hovered above the ground. There was something alarming about gazing upon a silent, busy scene. She knew the noise she should hear and the lack of it made her feel as though she were standing in a graveyard.

Faria remembered the village and peered in its direction. An eerie feeling crept over her, like a premonition. She hadn't wanted to see more people, to feel more eyes on her but maybe she could at least get solid evidence that the Val were there. Or perhaps it was her morbid curiosity. Either way, she headed down the lane and walked carefully through the village center.

There were only a few homes and what looked to be several places of worship for both the gods and goddesses. This village seemed different from the scene they entered upon. When they first arrived on this side of the mountains, Hunter and Faria walked in on what looked like a celebration. This, however, looked like … a ritual?

Elves stood in a circle, heads thrown back as if in reverence to the sun. Children stood next to their parents in similar form. It was creepy.

She walked through to the other end of the village and saw, just a few yards away, what looked to be an arena. It was in similar shape and build as the arena at *Mentage*, though that one had seating along the sides and this was wide open. Stranger still was the amount of people that stood on the field.

Faria couldn't get over the feeling of walking through bodies she knew were still alive, even if their hearts were no longer beating. She wished Hunter would return or that Ander would pop in to see what she was up to. For company, of course. Not to save her.

Faria's heart stuttered when she finally realized what she saw. Rows upon rows of elves were lined up in the arena, all positioned with their feet shoulder-width apart and their arms at their sides, palms parallel to the ground. Their eyes were wide open, tendons in their necks straining. They looked as though they were in excruciating pain. A faint silver glow pulsated from them and flowed into the ground.

Alarm bells went off in Faria's head but she crept closer, needing to have some type of confirmation of the absolute horror she stumbled upon. Standing at the edge of the arena, Faria studied the glow from the elves. She reached into her well of power to figure out which abilities would help analyze what the light was when she noticed something strange.

All of the faces looking at her were more oval than elves'. Their ears were pointed into sharp tips, curving slightly at the stop, while their eyes were elongated, tilting upward at the corners. Their hair had a brilliant sheen as if the sun radiated from inside. Everything about them was symmetrical, angled, and beautiful. And every single one of them stared at her in wide-eyed fear.

Bile rose in Faria's throat.

They weren't elves.

They were the Fae.

The Fae that never came to help in the Great War a thousand years ago. The Fae whose magic was steeped into the land. How many times had Faria and Nellie wondered why the magic in the land hadn't faded?

This is why.

Faria reached a hand out toward the closest one. She didn't know what her intentions were; maybe to try to touch one? To comfort? To let them know that now she knew they were there, she'd save them? But if she did, what would happen to Anestra? How much of their magic kept the land alive?

Her intentions mattered little when her hand hit an invisible wall just inches from their bodies. She pounded against it, poured her magic into the air—nothing.

"I'm sorry," Faria whispered, her voice anguished. "As queen to this land, I vow to rescue you. Please, hold on." Before she turned away, she watched a single tear fall down a Fae's cheek.

Faria turned and sprinted back through the village, through the city, sobs wracking her body and fueling her forward. She might not have understood the power to sift through space like the Val, but she could damn near fly with her speed. Adrenaline kept her going, despite her barely having any proper rest in weeks.

Faria ran through the facts in her mind, trying to make some semblance of sense. Farrah and her consort were awake. Farrah broke the mountains. Hunter was missing, again. And the Fae, the *Fae's* magic was being leached and had been for possibly millennia.

The historical records had it wrong. The Secret Keepers had it wrong. Anestra was supposed to be a land of freedom and acceptance. Everyone put in equal work, they ran on the barter system for those who did not have coin or wished to use it. They cared about the protection of all species. It was a prosperous, beautiful land filled with wonder and magic.

And it was filled with unforgivable secrets from the past.

Faria let out a sob and continued on.

NINETEEN

HUNTER

Waves crashed and broke along the cliff face Hunter kneeled upon, his head throbbing intensely, his body screaming for unconsciousness, but somehow he kept healing just enough to remain on the cusp of awareness.

Fire licked his face and he saw the flicker of embers behind his closed eyes and knew, without having to open them, the Elders had summoned him. The same Elders who claimed they protected him—the supposed last Val in existence even though he had seen ample evidence to the contrary. The same Elders who bound his powers and shielded his memories to save his mind from the horrors he'd had to endure.

He had believed them. Hunter had no purpose after losing his family, his brethren, his land. He was prepared to die in the Great War and yet survived and had felt he owed his life to the Elders since then. Jacobi had told him the Fates saved him and placed him in their care, that it was up to them to protect the Agostonna bloodline.

"You lied to me," Hunter growled out. He raised his head and looked at each of the cowled Elders in turn with as much hatred as he could muster. As he raised himself to his full height, he grimaced in pain, ignoring the nauseating need to vomit from the agony as much as he could. "Why?"

The Elders stirred, but none made a move to speak until Jacobi, the one who claimed to look after him, the one who took him under a wing as something more akin to father and son, lowered his hood. He had the ability to unlock Hunter's powers and memories but never did. He said it would be debilitating.

"Where have you been?" Jacobi asked.

Hunter stared into the face of the male he'd grown to care about in his own way. His hair was white, his blue eyes sunken into his sallow-skinned face. He seemed frail but perhaps that was all part of his deceitful plan.

"We lost sight of you shortly after you were in the mountains. What happened? What did you see?"

They lost sight of him in the mountains? Did they see the broken mountain range? It was interesting to learn they couldn't see beyond Carenek Peaks, even with it no longer intact. He extended a thought to Faria, wanting to let her know immediately where he was but he found no connection there, nor did he find any evidence of a bond at all.

"Where is my mate?" he asked, his anger rising to molten fury. "You dare to cut me off from her again?" The darkness swirling in him relished the opportunity to release its power but just as it readied to lash out at the Elders, he felt something like invisible cuffs bind the power inside him.

"Calm yourself."

Low chanting arose from the circle of Elders and Hunter felt their grip on his magic tighten. Everything he learned from Farrah's tomb was made apparent. He couldn't believe he had been so lost and devoid of hope he didn't care to see the evidence that had been laid before him for centuries.

"It's true then," Hunter spat. "You are the warlocks who believed in blood sacrifice to gain special magic for the land. You are the heretics who believed yourself as gods."

"Where would you ever hear such a story?" Jacobi advanced toward Hunter, his hands raised slightly in front of him.

The stench of blood hit Hunter's nostrils and his eyes zeroed in on Jacobi's life essence, droplets falling into the sand between them. The invisible chains tightened inside his body and he suppressed the urge to gasp in pain. Bright lights flickered in his eyes as the pain in his head sharpened to a new height.

Rage and betrayal surged through Hunter. The centuries of lies, of being controlled, of missing his people, his family who might still be alive somewhere. The despair that consumed him for decades over the decision he had made, on his command, to sacrifice their magic to save the Agostonna's. He had been so alone, empty, lost with nothing but his self-hatred for company until Faria came along, and then the Elders had the audacity to interfere between them as well. He hadn't felt so helpless, so *murderous*, in his long life.

Something inside Hunter broke, a dam that had contained his most essential self burst with a flash of brilliant white light. And suddenly he was flooded with both relief from the pain and a surge of adrenaline from the all-encompassing power that had freed itself from inside him. Magic that he'd once tasted but hadn't for so long. He let it run its course through his veins, pump through his heart, nestle into the minute pieces of who he used to be. His tattoos illuminated in the night, rushing under his skin in a frenzy.

The Elders took a collective step back, raising their hands in front of them as if to defend themselves from the onslaught of rage they expected to receive from him.

With barely a thought, Hunter released a shred of his *malosin obsinae* to each of the twelve Elders, raising them in the air, hovering them in place. He was a Val prince. Perhaps even a king now. No power rivaled his own. Except, he suspected, Faria's.

They were matched in every way—the Fates had seen to that. He had been a prisoner inside his own body for far too long and he was eager to release his fear, anguish, and fury on those who held him in place.

"What's your plan, Hunter?" Jacobi asked with a strain in his voice. "You kill us, and then what? You never hear our side of the story, never know what happened to your kin. Never get your memories back."

"I don't need them," Hunter said through clenched teeth. The power tried to overwhelm him and he strained slightly to keep it under control, unused to its might.

"But you still need us," someone quickly spoke up. "You cannot kill us."

"Why is that?"

"We know how to defeat Darroc."

"I believe I can tear that information from your minds, or have you forgotten the frightful power of the Val?"

"You may be able to, but we are the only ones who can execute it."

The hazy fury cleared as realization dawned on Hunter. "The Spell of Unmaking."

"Darroc is no longer a warlock, no longer anything the realms have seen before. Despite Moira's best efforts, she did little more than burn a piece of his soul, leaving him more unhinged than ever. Soon, very soon, he will be in Anestra and then you will need us."

"If you can end him then why keep me prisoner? Just end him."

"Though we are the only ones who can defeat him, you are the only one who can allow us entry back to Anestra," Jacobi explained. He gasped as the *malosin* squeezed his neck, attempting to cut off his windpipe. "We are spelled here until Faria is accepted by the land." The words choked out. "Then she can allow us back in."

"If you think Faria will allow you on her lands, you are as unhinged as Darroc. Not only would she never let anyone who has kept me from her in her good graces, but she absolutely would not grant entry to those who could cause her people harm."

"There will come a point when she needs to choose what is best for her land and what is worth the bigger sacrifice, because believe us, we are the only ones who know the Spell of Unmaking. The only ones who can perform it. Collectively."

Hunter didn't quite believe them but access to his memories did not return with the resurgence of his powers, so he had no way of knowing fact from fiction. He was furious they still thought to manipulate and control him.

Hunter allowed the *malosin* to take over, to give each of the Elders a taste of rage. He grasped each of the Elders as one, binding them as they thought to bind him, and sent a flick down each tendril of darkness. Pleasure rippled through him as bones started to break from the strength of his *malosin obsinae*. The crack of an ankle followed by screams of pain sent shivers through him. *More*, his *malosin* seemed to tell him. *We need more.*

Effortlessly, Hunter gave more to the shadow beast residing within him and he wondered if he would start to lose some of the humanity he clung to. He realized he didn't care.

They should be frightened of him. Of what he would do to them when the time came.

As the *malosin* continued binding and bruising the Elders, Hunter unsheathed a dagger from his waist and held it against Jacobi's throat. He pressed the tip against the pulsing artery in Jacobi's neck, wondering how much blood he could spill before feeling a sense of satisfaction. Hunter still felt like the Elders were lying about something, that they wanted more than to return to Anestra, but until he had the proper time to figure it out, he would at least let them suffer in the meantime.

"I want to bleed every one of you dry," Hunter said, dragging the dagger down Jacobi's neck, a thin trickle of blood following. He inhaled, relishing the scent, but he controlled further impulses to exsanguinate them. "Fortunately for you, I have more important business to attend to. Like returning to my mate." He bared his teeth while the *malosin* pried open their jaws to prevent them from speaking back to him. "I will return when we take care of Darroc. Until then—"

With a final thought, Hunter scraped the *malosin* against their skin and watched with a sick sense of delight as flesh and sinew peeled away from their broken bones. He winked at them and sieved back to Anestra, comforted by knowing that they could not follow.

The ease with which he traveled brought with it a sense of relief and familiarity. He controlled the movement, the place, the time. He knew because he was told, that Val were manipulators of time and space since the different realms operated on their own passage of time, and now he tried to remember the proper way to sieve. Perhaps with more Val in existence, time between realms will balance out as Moira once predicted.

He reached for the bond with Faria and was relieved to feel it come through the in-between space he hovered in, and even more grateful that her end of the bond was open to him. He sent a gentle caress searched for her imprint, knowing her essence would leave an impression on whatever land she stood upon. As if she were a beacon of light, she guided him back to her.

He found her standing on a field on the outskirts of the city past the mountains, walking in between dozens of frozen elves ... *Wait.* With the return of the full might of his power came an intense clarity that had been missing for centuries.

The elongated faces, the slight tonal sound of music that seemed to trickle out of them and pour itself into the ground. The pointed ears and delicate angles of their faces. Those weren't elves like they'd seen when they first entered this side of the mountain range. They were Fae.

The strange energy seeped off them, raising gooseflesh along his skin. With shock and horror, Hunter finally realized what he was looking at. The Fae were somehow pouring their magic into the land.

Faria stood feet away but she gave no indication she could see him. He called out to her in vain. Hunter looked down at himself and noticed his skin was pearlescent. He could see the grass through his boots, though the ground felt sturdy beneath him. He wondered if he landed on the wrong plane so that he could observe without being seen. That seemed like something a Val would have been able to do. In fact, it must have been how he'd watched the Agostonna's for years before he went to work for them as the weapons master.

Stuck in his musings and trying to force the memories to surface, Hunter almost missed Faria as she sprinted away from the Fae and back toward the mountains. He tried to solidify his molecules, tried to picture himself back on the right plane. With a slight vibration, the heat of the perpetual late spring melted into his skin and he knew he was back in the real world.

He followed Faria's signature and sieved his way to her. She was fast, faster than he'd remembered her being and it took him several attempts to get to her again.

"Where are you going, Princess?"

He expected snark, but what he received was her falling into his arms, tears pouring down her face. "Shh, love. Let's go back home."

TWENTY

ANDER

Jumping across the length of Anestra proved exhausting to Ander. The further the distance, the more energy was required. He'd been to Anestra plenty of times before, keeping himself hidden as he spied on whoever Darroc sent him after. He'd lived in the caves where Darroc kept his lair on the border of Wendorre for a time when he was younger, so he could easily visualize the edge of the Barren Plain where apparently the Great War took place a thousand years ago.

Now, however, Ander was on a ship with Endo, Nellie, Johanna, a few shifters, and several warlocks who all worked together to help the ship fly across the water. Well, Nellie didn't do much of anything other than shout out her idea of nautical terms that had no meaning and laugh to herself when everyone gave her exasperated looks. His *Drogosterra* flew overhead, and as he leaned against the railing of the ship watching the ocean as they sped through it, he would have given anything to be up there rather than stuck on a boat with everyone else.

"I'll let you take a ride," Nellie said, sidling up next to him. Freckles were sprinkled across her cheeks from the sun reflecting on the open water.

He raised his eyebrow at her.

"I mean, I'll let you ride me if you need the thrill."

"I don't think your queen would approve."

"I—wha—no," Nellie stuttered. "I only meant that you keep looking longingly up there, and I'm only down here so I could keep a closer eye on Suspect McGee, but I can take you up there if you need a break from this." She gestured her hands vaguely at the ship and sea.

He wondered how much he should open up to her, but he found whatever budding friendship they had to be easy. She had no expectations of him and looked at him like a person rather than Faria's son, or a Val prince, or Darroc's pet, or a murderer. Had anyone ever really seen him?

"I'm just tired," he settled on. The railing was slick with sea spray, and as Ander went to lean an elbow on it, he slipped, his torso suddenly leaning heavily over the water.

Nellie quickly grabbed his shirt and pulled him back, the momentary concern in her eyes melting into humor. "Saved your life." She grinned at him.

"Hardly. I wasn't in danger and I have excellent reflexes."

"Oh come on, you old grump. You owe me some feelings for that one." She turned to the open water and leaned against the railing, patiently giving him the time he needed to say more if he wanted to.

"I just don't feel like I belong here. Or anywhere, really. With Darroc at least I knew my place and purpose after a while. Here, I'm expected to help people who in my lifetime never helped me. They didn't even exist for me."

"I know what you mean, to an extent." Nellie cleared her throat and turned around, leaning her elbows against the railing with her legs crossed in front of her.

Ander wondered how she got to be comfortable in a body she wasn't allowed to live in for so long when he couldn't seem to manage to fit into a body he'd never had to hide.

"My mother moved us around so often, most of the time it was as if she was running from something. I didn't really have a home base or friends I could be with for longer than a few months at a time. Every year, though, we'd go back to New York to be with my mother's clan for a few weeks. I'd always received hateful looks and felt unwanted until Tommy. But even that was short-lived."

The waves thrashed against the side of the ship as they continued at a fast clip.

"You know what it's like to know your mother was murdered and then you get blamed for it just because you're different?" the anger in her voice told Ander she still had wounds that needed to heal.

Maybe he chose the right person to be vulnerable with, for once.

"And then to be banished from the only people I had left in the world in a way that basically equated to death?" Nellie continued, indignant, "It can mess with you, that feeling that you're not good enough to be with or belong anywhere."

Ander pulled out a chocolate bar he'd snagged earlier from Jane's house and split it with Nellie. "Cheers to that, friend. I know that feeling well."

Nellie squealed and tossed her half in her mouth. "You're all right, kid," she said, chocolate staining her teeth. She laughed and leaned over the railing, letting the wind whip through her curls.

Ander watched her, in awe that she felt so heavily about her past, yet found little joys in life. Their histories had a bit more in common than he realized, and if she could be happy and radiate the bright yellow aura of positivity, then perhaps he could try to look for the best in things, too.

"Whoa," Nellie said. "Iceberg! Dead ahead!" She winked at Ander. "Titanic reference."

"What is happening?" Johanna came over and asked. "These waters are tropical. There is no iceberg."

"I know, I just always wanted to shout it. Also, there's an island."

Ander glimpsed several pieces of land that started to come into view. They weren't anything special, though they weren't called the Bone Isles for nothing. Apparently, this was a frequent spot for shipwrecks to the point where people disappeared and were assumed dead. No bones were ever found, according to the stories.

"This doesn't look anything like the maps," Endo shouted over the wind. "There should be three or four, not—" He pointed to each as he counted. "Eight? There definitely shouldn't be eight of them." He took a step back from the ship railing. "If those rumors were true, then perhaps the one about the sea creatures was true as well. I'd keep from the edge if

I were you."

Ander wondered if he'd be able to sieve to the islands to look around, or at the very least maybe he would take Nellie up on the offer to hop on her back so he could get a better look. There was something odd about the air. It smelled the same, though the wind was hot instead of the cool breeze they'd become accustomed to. Now and then the scent of vanilla and cinnamon would pass by, which was also unusual for the middle of the ocean.

The waters were a beautiful teal blue and schools of rainbow-colored fish swam in between the bright pink and purple coral, the seagrass flowing gently in the current. Ander studied the ocean, mesmerized, as the fish seemed to almost glow. Without warning, the water flowed like inky coal, and a foul scent rose from the sea as if the fish were festering in the sun.

The ship slowed on Endo's command. "Something isn't right here," he said, almost to himself.

Ander resisted the urge to roll his eyes. A blind ant could see something was wrong.

Everyone waited with bated breath, unsure of what malicious act might befall them. Perhaps they would find out the reason why it was called the Bone Isles. Ander didn't feel confident enough in his fickle abilities to jump the crew somewhere safe in time.

Nellie seemed to have the same idea, as she readied her stance, prepared to shift at the first sign of attack. Ander felt the change in the water a second before something hard knocked against the ship, causing them to lose their footing.

It happened again twice more in quick succession. Ander's *Drogosterra* growled from in the air, and he felt a question cross his mind as if she was seeking permission to attack whatever creature lurked beneath the waters.

Ander pulled out one of the longer daggers he kept in a holster on his belt and removed his shirt, preparing to jump in the water before the others could be placed in danger. He felt certain he wouldn't die from whatever it was, not with his ability to recover from injury quickly, and he wasn't ready to have his *Drogosterra* locked in a fight with the unknown. He'd rather take the risk himself, and maybe in the process the others would start to trust him as well. It made him uncomfortable to realize how important that was to him.

"Whoa, whoa. Hang on there killer," Nellie said as she watched him jump onto the ship's railing. She grabbed his bicep, pulling him back to the safety of the deck. "Wow, how often do you work out? I mean—Faria would never forgive me if you were killed by some man-eating octopus or something. I volunteer as tribute—Hunger Games reference."

Before anyone could stop her, she took a running leap off the side of the ship. Nellie's special brand of shifter magic dotted the air with its peppery scent. Before she could fully transform into whatever sea creature she thought appropriate, a large, gray tentacle lashed out of the water and attached to her chest.

Nellie gave a blood-curdling scream.

"Nellie!" Marisa yelled, running toward the railing. She looked as if she, too, would leap after Nellie before Endo snatched her waist, willing her to stay on board.

Without thinking, Ander quickly jumped off the side of the ship. The freezing, stinking waters chilled him to his marrow. He grabbed Nellie, sheared off the tentacle, and quickly sieved from the water to the back of his *Drogosterra*, who had already dived toward them at Nellie's scream.

Ander, already exhausted from the earlier shifting through time, swayed where he sat upon the rough, scaly back of his dragon. He patted her neck in thanks then shifted his attention to a moaning Nellie. Ander carefully wrenched the tentacle free from her chest, sharp needles pulling at her skin as he removed it. The area was already bright red lending quickly to a bruising purple color. He leaned down and inhaled. The tang of poison filled his lungs.

"If you wanted in," Nellie said weakly through a moan. Her skin was already taking on a gray color. "All you had to do was ask. Consent … is … everything." Her eyes fluttered and she felt limp in his arms.

Ander, still unsure of how to properly communicate with his *Drogosterra*, shouted words in his mind, hoping she'd understand that he was going to take Nellie to healers he knew in another realm and for her to bring everyone else back to land in the meantime. He received the briefest hint of approval before he jumped realms with Nellie in his arms.

He wasn't sure why he decided to take Nellie straight to another realm rather than find his mother who might have been able to heal her just the same, but two particular guardians had stuck out in his mind and he needed them, immediately. He hoped their hatred for him didn't hold them back from giving his new friend proper care.

TWENTY ONE

NELLIE

There were two things Nellie noticed at once: First, she was lying in a bed, not hovering in mid-air with a tentacle sticking out of her like a barbeque skewer. The second, she realized she was back with the humans on Earth. Though her eyes were closed, her realm had one very distinct sound other realms didn't: Police sirens. *Okay, Earthbound again … How?*

Nellie could hear soft murmurings of people talking near her and attempted to stand up, or at least cover her naked breasts because Earthbound or not, she at least expected dinner before exposing herself to the room. The walls spun as she tried to sit up and the muted conversation faded in and out.

"Lucky she wasn't a siren …"

"It won't kill her but she'll feel like shite for a while …"

Ander's familiar baritone spoke, a comforting rumble of thunder in the confusion, "Let me scan her. I can make sure the toxin is gone."

"Absolutely not. If you think I'll let you touch another chosen one, you're out of your mind."

"She's right, Ander. One wrong move, one wrong thought, and it can harm her. She's too important to interfere with."

"Interfere?" his voice spiked in anger, which Nellie thought was completely justifiable. "I brought her to you for Fate's sake. If I didn't interfere, she could be dead or worse."

"He can touch me," Nellie said, or she thought she said it, but her tongue felt thick and her words came out funny. "I trust him." Nellie finally cracked her eyes open to see two people she'd never met before hovering over her while a soft glow left their hands as they scanned her body. "Everyone has cool scanning abilities and all I can do is—"

"Be anything you want to be, which is all anyone ever dreams of in life, isn't it?" Ander smiled gently at her. "I'm going to place my hand on your forehead and see if I can detect anything that shouldn't belong in there, okay?"

Nellie laid still, mostly paralyzed from the chest down with her girls flopping about for the world to see, but he politely looked into her eyes and had asked permission to touch her forehead. The bar was set so low these days, for human men at least. But she appreciated a male who didn't make things weird. Nellie nodded her head as best as she could and felt blankets slide up to her neck.

Ander bent down to her ear and whispered, "I've already seen it all anyway since you decided to get frisky with my dragon, in case you forgot."

Nellie knew he was attempting to distract her from both the weirdness of the situation and the fact that she'd nearly died or at least that was what she gathered. She appreciated the gesture. She slid her eyes over to see who the other voices belonged to, but could only see bright pink hair and nothing else.

Ander placed his hand along her forehead, the tips of his fingers just grazing her temple. What she would give for a massage right now. She always seemed to have inappropriate thoughts at the most inopportune times.

A slow trickle spread from where his hand touched her skin and spread down the length of her body like warm honey. Whatever he was doing, he could keep doing it. A girl could relax like this, especially after a near-death experience. She lazily watched his face, waiting for a sign of anything to give away what he saw inside her body, but he was as infuriatingly stoic as his father.

Finally, Ander sighed, and the warm feeling receded up her body toward his hand. He blew out a frustrated breath and shook his head. "If you had thought to turn into a siren …"

"I have no idea what they look like," Nellie said. "I haven't seen Marisa and her clan in the water, yet. Honestly, I was just going to turn into Nemo or something." She paused, waiting for a response. When she received none, said, "Disney reference."

Pink Hair snorted then mumbled to herself, "I just spent how many hours trying to save a chosen one and the genius wanted to turn into a fish. Against a weapon that was created and bred for the complete annihilation of the siren species."

"Oh, my gods." Realization struck Nellie. "Endo brought Marisa, just like he wanted to. He insisted she'd be able to see what was under the water and explore the islands for us. Is she okay? Do you think he knew? He totally knew, right? He had to have known."

"Actually, I have a theory," a girl's voice said from the corner of the room.

Nellie realized she was in a bedroom and that girl must have generously donated to her cause.

"I suspect that Darroc made a few deals with some dangerous people in other realms. Power in exchange for information or something like that. Just as he tried to make a deal with the clan leaders to fight for him when the time came."

"Sorry, who are you?" Nellie asked. She was happy her limbs were slowly starting to regain their feeling. She looked between the girl and the two healers of some sort, then up at Ander.

He exchanged a knowing smile with the girl and then glanced down at Nellie. "That's Jane. I tried to kill her with an arrow."

"These are my guides," Jane said. "I'm one of the chosen ones on earth to protect against the apocalypse. There's a bunch of us, but I'm the one from this sect. Nice to meet you."

Nellie stared at her. She was familiar and Nellie knew she'd seen her somewhere. Ander almost killed her with an arrow … "Oh!" she exclaimed. "I've seen you before. Moira showed me and Faria when you"— she turned her head to Ander—"shot a black arrow straight through her heart. You're Callie's cousin! From Florida!"

"I am!" Jane nodded. "And, yes, I haven't quite forgiven him, yet."

"The way you looked at me last night told me that I'm forgiven," Ander said, cocking a half smile at her.

"You wish, loverboy."

Nellie couldn't decide if she thought the exchange was cute or if she wanted to puke. Pink Hair looked the same.

"Enough of that," Pink Hair said. "If your theory is right, Jane, that means the veil between realms is either paper thin or completely gone in some areas. That means no protection, and whoever Darroc promised something to is going to come and collect."

"Actually, the veil has already come down. Earlier when I was flying as a *Drogosterra*, I went through several different realms, I'm sure of it, before I landed back in Anestra. It was just a pocket in the sky—first I was flying underwater, then through a crazy storm, etcetera. It went on for a few moments, but then returned to normal."

They all exchanged a look.

"It is finally coming to pass," the male healer said. "We all have our roles to play."

Nellie wanted to find out more but a wave of exhaustion hit her.

"You will still feel the effects of the toxin, chosen one," the pink-haired healer said. "It will rush through your body as we work to expel it from your bloodstream. Sleep now and we will take care of this."

Nellie didn't argue, nor did she want to, because it had in fact been a long while since she slept well, and falling into nothingness without a worry or memory of the trauma from the past few weeks sounded perfect to her.

"ARE YOU SURE YOU'RE FEELING OKAY? I felt awful leaving as I did," Ander was saying as Nellie started to come back to life.

Jane's guides were sprawled on the ground in a corner of the bedroom whispering among themselves. Ander and Jane leaned against her desk near the window. The late afternoon sun filtered through the blinds in the bedroom, creating orange bands of light and shadow across the walls.

"I'm fine, really," Jane replied. "From what I understand, I woke up just after you left. I felt more awful that you had to go without eating first. There's leftover pizza in the fridge if you want some."

"No, I appreciate it, but I would have suffered through a few bites last night. I never understood humans' obsession with pizza. The cheese is—"

"Epically delicious, you complete wackadoo," Nellie said, sitting up. "And I'm starving as fluff so if you feel like sharing your 'za, Jane, please, for the love of the goddess, bring me the whole box."

Jane laughed. "After what you've just been through, you can have whatever you want." She closed the bedroom door behind her, leaving Ander and Nellie alone.

"Hungry much?" Ander said.

"Are you freaking kidding me? With all the shifting and the nearly dying, I could literally eat you right now."

"Ah, bestiality and a cannibal. Nice."

"How are you?" Nellie asked, ignoring his attempt at jokes. "You shifted everyone, brought me to a different realm. When was the last time you had anything to eat? Or slept?"

Ander shrugged. "I don't know. Time is still messed up between realms ... a few days? Maybe?"

Nellie inspected him as much as she could in the lower lighting. He had dark circles under his eyes and his skin was sallow. Even the golden halos in his eyes were dim. "You look wrecked, my dude." She thought about it for a minute then said, "My prince? Can I call you my dude?"

Ander shook his head. "I'm no prince, and before you go in on me about it, let me remind you that you just said I look wrecked. I'm not really in the mood to talk about it, am I?"

"Okay, okay. You also seem a bit hangry ..."

"I've got pizza!" Jane said as she tossed open the bedroom door. She handed Nellie a heaping plate half filled with reheated slices, the other cold straight from the fridge. "Wasn't sure which type of person you were so thought I'd do both."

"I could honestly kiss you," Nellie said, her eyes filling with tears of happiness. She took a bite of each and chomped happily.

Ander looked on in disgust.

"And for you," Jane handed Ander a serving platter, "a deli sandwich, pickles, chips, fresh fruit, and cheese stick. It's what I pack for lunch at school and was the best I could do."

Ander looked down at his platter as if he wasn't sure what to do with it then back up at Jane. "Thank you," he said hesitantly before chucking a few grapes in his mouth.

"Don't tell me you don't like a classic American teenage lunch, either," Nellie said. "What *do* you like?"

"To be honest, I just like to be fed."

He probably didn't mean it to come out as heartbreaking as it did, but Nellie ached for him, anyway. She had no idea what horrors he faced with Darroc. Maybe he hadn't been fed at all.

Jane cleared her throat, ready to dispel the awkward silence as they chewed their food when the two guardians popped back into the room.

"Saved by the bell," Nellie said to herself. She flashed Ander a quick grin before stuffing her face again.

"How were they?" Jane, who knew what her guides had been up to, said. "Can they be healed? Will my blood do it?"

"Actually," Ander interrupted, "I think I can just replicate what Jane's cells did. I know I can do it."

"Even if you can," the male guide said. "My name is Santana, by the way," he said, turning to Nellie with a smile.

Whoa, did he just hear me wonder what his name is?

Santana winked at her then continued, "Even if you can, you can't go to each of the millions of humans and shifters on this planet to heal them. It's obvious, for one thing, and no one has that type of energy reserve."

Ander slammed his plate down on Jane's desk. "I have to do something! Please," the desperation in his voice lingered in the air, and as one, everyone turned to the healer with the bright pink hair.

"Lindy …" Santana said. "He has proven not to harm Jane, and now he saved another chosen one in Nellie. If he could somehow examine what needs to be done, we could ask Dr. Zhiv to take a look."

"Who's Dr. Zhiv?" Nellie asked with a mouth full of food. She needed to slow down in case Darroc decided to randomly show up. She laughed to herself picturing her vomiting all over his stupid face because she was too full when she shifted. Actually, she might be onto something. She took another bite.

"Dr. Zhiv is a trained vet, but we discovered he had a gift for healing. He could perform miracles—healing cancers that were impossible to treat, and his recovery rate for his surgery patients is nearly three times quicker than the average. We've asked him to help with what's going on."

"Getting an animal doctor to treat humans, nice."

"We must utilize whatever works, and he works." Lindy turned to Ander. "And there is one person you can see if you wish."

"Let's go," Nellie said, wiping the crumbs off her hands. "I just need to get dressed."

"Slow down there, eager one," Santana said. He placed a hand on Nellie's shoulder and she felt a rush of calm run through her. "You are still healing. There's no need to risk catching this disease, even if we might finally have a way of healing it."

Ander put his jacket back on and removed something from his pocket. He walked over, dangling her mother's locket in the air between them. "I kept this safe for you, but I thought you might want to hold onto it until I return."

Nellie smiled gratefully and fingered the locket, the warmth of his body heat still pressed into the gold. She had almost forgotten about it, again. She clasped it back around her neck. "Thank you. And hurry, would you? If I'm missing out on too much of the hot gos back home, I'll be pissed at you."

Ander chuckled and as one, they all popped out of existence.

Nellie drummed her fingers on the bedspread and glanced outside, the shadows thickening in the dusk. She wasn't sure how long she'd been in that bed, but she could at least stretch her legs for a little while.

She gingerly placed her feet on the floor, wiggling her toes and taking stock of the aches in her body. Her chest was still sore and she felt as though she'd been run over by a semi, but the food helped with her energy levels. She shuffled over to the window. Second floor, which meant a ton of stairs to climb down and then back up again before anyone noticed. A slight breeze trickled in through the open window, rushing across her face. The fresh scent of pine swayed her decision.

Though it felt like it took half a century to finally make it outside, Nellie immediately felt rejuvenated in the elements. The wintry air was crisp, but the promise of spring was in the fresh floral scent radiating from the surrounding woods. She was surprised at Earth being on the cusp of a new season when just a few days prior they were entering the winter. She wondered when time would balance between realms, or if it was always that way with the human realm. Perhaps that was part of the secret to living longer in Anestra. Time manifested differently so the body aged differently.

Nellie moved to the tree line, choosing a spot on a felled log to sit on. She absentmindedly toyed with her necklace, thinking about her time on Earth, both growing up and more recently, and realized she no longer felt as though she belonged there. Anestra was her home, Faria was her home. The sister she never had, the queen she was willing to die for.

Nellie closed her eyes, taking in the rustling of chipmunks on the dead leaves blanketing the forest floor, the birds singing a lullaby to each other, and the distant screeching of bats. Even the occasional siren as an emergency vehicle raced toward another tragedy. She would miss this place, the pizza, the bad Chinese takeout, and the way everyone in the city was both polite and rude at the same time. How does one say a final goodbye to an entire realm filled with so many people, cultures, religions, and species that she never planned on seeing again?

Her thumb snagged on the edge of her locket and Nellie sighed, removing it to take a closer look. Maybe she should bury the necklace as well since she wasn't able to choose a final resting place for her mother. She looked closer at the divot on the side, giving a slight pause when she realized that her locket opened. She pressed it firmly until she heard a small *click* and the locket swung open on silent hinges.

An old, stained piece of cloth was folded inside. Nellie carefully opened it, mindful to keep her touch delicate so as not to ruin whatever it was. On the cloth was some sort of writing in another language. Nellie had pored over enough documents with Faline to know that what she held was not of this realm and thought it curious that it was hiding in her mother's locket. Her mother had worn it no matter what for as long as she could remember. Nellie wondered if this was why they were always on the run, always moving from place to place. She barely ever finished the school year and it was impossible for her to make friends. Perhaps this was why.

Nellie carefully placed it back into the locket and slid it on her neck. She'd have to ask Faline if she knew what it was or do her own research when there was time to think about such things.

"What are you doing out here?" Ander's voice preceded his body as he appeared next to Nellie, his cheeks a bright pink. He seemed to be out of breath from some sort of exertion and the golden glow in his eyes was bright with excitement.

"Just saying goodbye to Earth. I don't think I'll make it back here again."

"Not even for the pizza?" Ander teased.

"Nah, I'd gone five years without it and I just ate enough to keep me satiated for another five. Besides, the food in Anestra is way better than anything they've got here." She stood and brushed the dirt off the back of her jeans. "What happened with the sick guy?"

"I was able to replicate what happened in Jane. Lindy is taking his blood to the vet now. I don't know what will happen from here, but she assured me this will change the tides and start to reverse the damage that was done." He smiled brightly.

Nellie's heart stuttered. She'd never seen him smile before, let alone be excited about anything. It brought out the male she imagined he would have been if he had grown up with them.

"I'm ready to go back. Have I gotten the all-clear?"

"Yes, but take it easy," Santana said, walking down the yard to join them. "You don't want to experience another shock of toxins, or much of anything for the next few days at least. Sleep as much as you can, and if the pain resurfaces or gets to be too much, tell Ander immediately and he'll let us know."

Nellie jumped into his arms, embracing the strange guide and his wonderful branch of magic that saved her life. "Thank you. I'll be sure to kick serious warlock butt in your honor."

Ander grabbed Nellie's hand, its heat radiating into hers as she took one final look at the first place she had ever called home.

TWENTY TWO

FARIA

My home is built on a lie.

Faria and Hunter landed in the middle of the sloping lawns of *Mentage*, surrounded by her people breaking their backs trying to gather enough food, tonics, armor, weapons, clothing, and protection all in the name of their land—in the Agostonna name—and not one of them understood what that meant. What her name meant—a descendent of the same goddess who forced the Fae to give up their lives, their power, so generations after could reap the benefit.

The cold wind whipping around them was a shock to her system as she took in a deep breath preparing to replace her mask of calm indifference, one her mother wore so often. Did her mother feel the same burden? Did she know the truth about the land she inherited?

Flocks of people swarmed them once they noticed the queen had returned. Shouts for her father, for Faline, and for the remaining Royal Guard were passed along as healers elbowed their way closer to check on them, older elves asked repeatedly if the Forsaken had returned, young kids jumping in excitement asking what they looked like, workers shoving plates of food in their faces.

It was nothing but chaos. Faria felt the pressure build in her chest as overwhelm threatened to consume her until—

Relax, Princess. A warm caress drifted down her spine as Hunter sent a comforting wave through the bond. *They have been waiting for their queen. You can do this.*

Faria gave a slight nod and squeezed Hunter's hand, readying herself to say something, anything to bring order amidst the madness, but a shrill whistle stopped her.

"Enough of this," King Dennison said as he made his way through the crowd. "Time is short. You all have jobs to do. As soon as there is an update, your queen will call for you. Until then, we prepare, we rest, we keep going. Without the havoc."

A few people looked humble and the children walked away, dejected.

"Wait," Faria said. The crowd paused, eager to hear from her. "Once I have shared what I learned with my father and the Royal Guard, I will help prepare tonics, meals, and sharpen weapons." She smiled warmly at them, keeping her tears at bay. They deserved so much better than her. "And I'll answer whatever questions the little ones have of my adventures." The children whooped in joy and everyone dispersed, much happier than moments before.

Faria would find time for them, she promised herself. They needed to know that she did care about them, that she was willing to sacrifice whatever it took to save them and preserve the land.

Fury over what the goddess had done spread through her at the reminder. "Father, we need to talk," Faria said, careful to keep her voice low. "We have a serious problem."

"We know about the mountains," Dennison replied. "Nellie could see them when she flew north."

"It's so much more than that. We should meet in the Council Room, immediately." Faria strode with purpose toward *Mentage*.

Hunter kept pace with her. Dennison tried to field away passersby who stopped to watch their queen.

Faria made an effort to nod her head to those who bowed to her. "Where is the Guard? They will want to know. And where is Nellie?"

"I ordered them off as soon as the two of you left. There is much land to keep tabs on, and they are the best ones to demand answers. I sent Ander off with Endo to explore Widow's Passageway and Nellie—"

"Is here!" Nellie's disembodied voice shouted in Faria's ear. She turned to the side and came face to face with her friend, who happened to be carried in the arms of … her son?

Hunter paused mid-step at the sight of them. "What is happening here?"

"Relax, daddio, there's nothing weird going on between me and your son."

"I was referring to the giant bruise on your chest," Hunter replied, "and the fact that you seem incapable of walking yourself."

Faria's eyes searched Nellie's body, quickly noticing what Hunter pointed out. Impulsively, she grabbed Nellie's arm and pushed her magic into her, trying to find the source of the problem.

"I'm fine," Nellie said. She nudged Ander with her free elbow. "Put me down, you oaf, so I can prove it to them." She walked a few feet with Faria still hanging onto her, but Nellie quickly lost her breath and swayed where she stood. Three sets of hands reached for her, Ander's being the first to steady her. "There no … need to fuss."

"I repeat," Hunter said, his anger mounting, "what is happening here?"

Ander wouldn't look directly at Hunter when he spoke, but rather to a spot slightly over his head, "She was attacked by … some sort of sea creature. I am still uncertain."

Faria narrowed her eyes at her son. She didn't know him well enough to know when he was lying, but he definitely knew more than he was letting on.

Ander continued, "Her body was flooded with toxins. I took her straight to two guides I know who have miraculously healed people. I thought they might know what to do."

"Why didn't you bring her to me?" Faria tried to keep the accusation and hurt from her voice. If anyone could heal someone dying, it would be her. That was proven with Moira just weeks ago.

You healed bleeding wounds, Princess. Hunter spoke logically through their bond. *The toxins in Nellie could have done insurmountable damage, especially from an unknown creature. We can't be sure it isn't driven by some sort of dark magic. We should be grateful he thought so quickly.*

Still, it upset her that she wasn't the first person her son thought of, but strangers. *And yet,* she thought, *I am a stranger to him, too.*

"Can we pick this up inside?" Nellie asked. "It's cold as fluff and I am dead tired. I need all the hot gos before I pass out."

"The gods have awoken."

The fire in the hearth crackled merrily while everyone gathered in the room collectively held their breath. Faline, bless her, seemed to be the only one who fully grasped what that meant. Her eyes were wide and she ran her hand over her perfectly coiffed hair as if patting down the tiny pieces would somehow change the news Faria brought to them.

"The Crystal of Light is gone," Faria continued, speaking clearly so each word penetrated through their disbelieving minds. "I presume Farrah took it back once she was awoken by her consort, Alexei."

"Question," Nellie chimed in. She sat at the table in the center of the room, her head resting gently in one hand as the other played with the locket around her neck. "How do you know, for certain, that her consort was the one who woke her up?"

"That's who it was," Ander whispered to himself, though somehow his voice still rumbled over the crackling flames.

"That's who who was?" Faria asked.

He looked up at her, his eyes blazing with sudden clarity. Faria was in awe every second she was in the same room as him, breathing the same air as him. To be with someone who was a part of her, the essence of her and Hunter's best selves, took her breath away.

"The guy in the volcano. The one who took the Flame from me."

The image of the male who had hovered over Ander as Faria entered the chamber flashed through her mind. Ander had been in a prone position and the male, dressed in black, had shimmered above him. He bowed at Faria then disappeared. She had been too concerned with Ander's well-being to give it a second thought. She scanned through the memory, trying to pin down the details of the male's face and compare it to the statue past the mountains but the details were too blurred.

"I can't remember," Faria said. "I was too focused on making sure you were okay and getting out of there."

"It was him, I'm sure of it."

"It does make sense," Hunter said, stepping next to Faria.

A buzz crackled from his skin. Soft tingles raced down her arms, numbing her fingers, and causing tiny sparks of flame to dance along her fingertips. She folded her hands in front of her to quell the embers of magic before anyone noticed. The look on Nellie's face let her know that she'd definitely noticed.

"If Farrah took back her Crystal then it makes sense that Alexei wanted his Flame," Hunter said. "He might have even needed it to wake her to begin with."

"Okay, so the gods have awoken," Dennison said, getting them back on track. "The question is, where are they? Why haven't they made themselves known? And we still have Darroc to worry about plus his beasts and whatever else he might have planned."

"There's some speculation that he made deals," Nellie said, rubbing her chest.

Concern flooded Faria and she made a mental note to keep a close eye on her friend for any other sign of weakness.

"Deals with other people or creatures in different realms," Nellie said, her voice growing tired, "and that now perhaps they're coming to collect."

"Who has this speculation?" Faline asked, her eyes filled with equal distress as Faria.

"A friend of mine who is a chosen one to protect Earth in the apocalypse," Ander said. "She and her guardians believe more surprises will be coming."

Hunter cleared his throat. "Actually, we might have an even bigger problem than that."

Faria took that as her cue to say the truth that cut her to the marrow: "The Fae are alive." She paused for effect and wasn't disappointed by the shocked silence pressing down on her. "There is some sort of ... magic— stronger than magic—that has frozen everyone in place."

"Everyone?" Faline asked. "What do you mean by everyone?"

Faria felt her throat start to close as the tears threatened to fall. "Elves. Val." She looked at Nellie's horrified expression. "Shifters." She cleared her throat before continuing. "There is a large group of Fae whose magic is pouring out of them and into the land. They have some sort of protection around them. I couldn't break it no matter what I tried. But they could hear me, I know they could. They were aware and they seemed to be in pain."

"What kind of sick fu ... uh ... freak would torture them like that?" Nellie asked.

"Farrah," Faria said. "She must have done it to ensure the land survived for her offspring."

"Offspring?" Wil asked.

He had been quiet until then, but Faria saw him exchange a look with his partner. Reed nodded his head, as if in answer to Wil's question. Both turned wide eyes to her.

"The Agostonna's are direct descendants of Farrah and Alexei."

"Do you mean to tell me that my best friend is part goddess?" Nellie asked, looking at Faria as if she had three heads. She turned slowly to Ander. "And that my friend's son, my prince, who has seen me in the nude, is part god?"

"Excuse me, what?" Faria demanded.

"Let's focus back on the issue at hand," Dennison said. "Sweetheart, it doesn't matter if you were descended from a goddess or a toad. We all came from somewhere and no one will treat you any differently, with the exception of being their queen. Right?" Dennison looked pointedly around the room and waited for the few mumbled yeses before continuing, "Great. Faline, what is this about the Fae? Do the Secret Keepers know?"

"Absolutely not, Dennison. You know I would have mentioned it when we needed them in the previous battle, let alone a thousand years ago. I certainly wouldn't have wasted my time trying to trace their whereabouts."

"So we know Darroc will return soon, possibly with friends from other realms. Farrah and Alexei are awake and have retaken their power. We can't know if they are friends or foes, so we will err with caution until or when they appear. We cannot do anything about the Fae until Darroc is taken care of. Unless there's anything else, we must focus on the elements we can control."

"There is one other thing," Hunter said. He turned to face the room, looking each person in the eyes before finally letting them fall on Faria again. "While past the mountains, Faria and I discovered recorded history of this land painted in Farrah's temple. The creation story, the evolution of Farrah and Alexei's love, and the conflicts that arose. One particular image depicted a group of what we believe to be warlocks banished for their repeated use of sacrificial blood magic."

"Warlocks? In the time of the gods?" Enis asked. "That seems off from our histories."

"There is much that is wrong," Faria said, bitterness coating her tongue as she spat the words. "Hurry and get on with it, Hunter. You know what still needs to be done."

Patience, Princess, the words whispered across her mind.

"These warlocks were heretics who believed themselves to be the rightful inheritors of Anestra because they were created here by the gods. They were furious at being denied their right because of a baby that was born, and from what I gather, they were a danger to the Agostonna line from the beginning."

"Wait …" Nellie said, her eyes unfocused as she processed what Hunter was saying.

Faria was at a loss on where he was going with this and once again urged him through the bond to spit it out.

"You're saying that these warlocks … Did they mentor Darroc or something?" Nellie asked, obviously quicker at understanding than Faria was.

"I have strong reason to believe they set Darroc on the path he is on, whether it was through directly teaching him darker magic or else setting the right things in his path, in an attempt to weaken the Agostonna's so they could eventually take over."

"That's quite the long game they're playing," Dennison said. "How do you know all this?"

"I started to put it together after reading the history written on Farrah's temple but it wasn't until I saw them again that it all clicked."

"Them? Again?" Faria asked. "Hunter, what are you saying?"

He faced her, reaching down to twine his fingers within hers. The heat of his palm soothed a part of her, but trepidation still took the lead.

"It's the Elders. The people who have locked away my memories, my abilities. The ones who tried to keep us apart, who threaten to unmake me if I disobey."

"For the love of Pete," Nellie said, interrupting Faria's rushing thoughts. She peered over at her friend and noticed her pale complexion, the sweat along her forehead. Nellie's lips were clenched and white as if in pain.

Ander casually grazed his fingers across her shoulder and almost immediately color returned to her face. *Interesting.*

Nellie gave him a grateful smile before continuing. "Are there any other revelations? Is anyone possessed by an alien? Any other animal or creature or god or crazed group of lunatics we need to worry about?"

Everyone looked surprised at her outburst.

Faria found it funny in an overwhelmingly unfunny way. She'd love to throw a full-blown tantrum then put herself to sleep the way Farrah did and she wasn't even officially queen of her own land yet.

"Look, I'm sorry," Nellie said, "but Hunter, my dude, why didn't you just destroy them all? I know you've got it in you."

"They claim they are the only ones who can unmake Darroc. But to do so, they need to first step on this land."

A chorus of "No" and "Absolutely not" rang throughout the Council Chamber.

Faria's head ached from the noise, from the heightened emotions, the lack of food, and not enough sleep. She rubbed her temples. "Enough," her voice rang with authority, though it was hardly raised above the din.

"Of course they will not be allowed on this land. I have a feeling that so much of the protection placed within the land was because of them. We must focus. If there is yet another group of people who are a danger to us, or more breaking through realms to help Darroc, then we must finish the ceremony so I can be accepted as rightful queen immediately."

Faria thought about all that still needed to be done. Preparing her people, securing the land, figuring out the warlocks' magic swirling through her veins, being accepted by the land, and preparing endless amounts of tonics and healing potions. Training that *Drogosterra* to fight and possibly even finding others to help. Freeing the Fae, saving those frozen on the other side of the mountain. She felt pieces of her crack under the pressure, the stress of which was nearly at the shattering point.

"We will do the ceremony tonight, when the moonflowers in the Spring Garden bloom," she said, quickly making a snap decision. "I must first visit with my people."

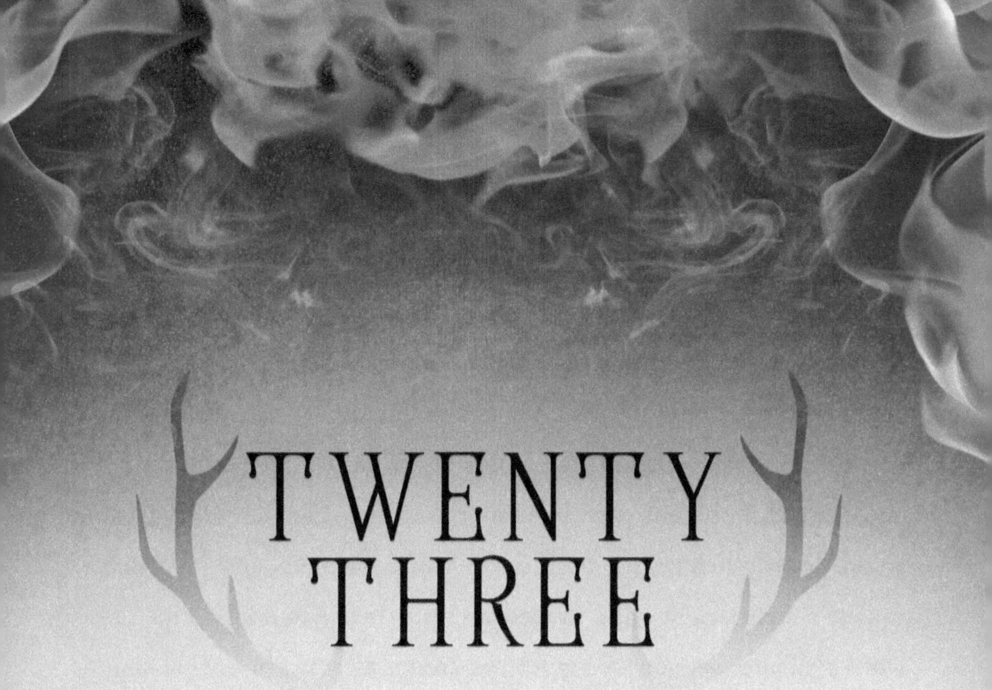

TWENTY THREE

FARIA

The Spring Garden at night was as close to a heavenly experience Faria ever thought she'd have the pleasure of experiencing. Night-blooming jasmine and moonflower gave a soft glow in the moonlight, guiding Faria past the jade fountain toward a trellis covered in deep violet roses lined with delicate black veins. She inhaled, allowing the fresh scents to calm her nerves as she focused on the moment rather than the inevitable hardships to come.

Faria had spent the afternoon walking among her people, visiting with the shapeshifters, tending to the sick, healing those who needed something more than the tonics they were given. She'd strolled through the empty streets of Athinia, missing the music playing through the taverns, the smell of fresh, sweet bread no longer lingering in the air.

Those she did pass were quiet, haunted, and scared.

She was young and had failed at so much in her short tenure as leader of their world, but she vowed to do right by them. Darroc had to be defeated. The Fae had to be liberated. The Elders had to be decimated. Perhaps with all the magic the Fates believed she should be blessed with could be put to better use after the impending battle was over.

Faria inhaled, allowing the aroma of the garden to ease her worries, and instead looked at each person around her. Her father and Faline stood directly before her, both dressed in dark pants and long-sleeved tunics, a lightweight cape draped around their shoulders. Her father wore a smaller version of his former crown as a symbol of passing on the reins. In his hands was the black satin pillow with the Val dagger gleaming in the moonlight. Faline held in her hands her mother's crown. Diamonds and rubies winked at her, as if mocking her for needing to take the responsibility she avoided accepting for years.

Footsteps brushed against the snow-laden ground outside of the Spring Garden, the light swishing noise muted against the murmurs of excitement. Part of the reason Faria wanted to see her people was to invite them to watch outside of the stone wall of the Spring Garden if they wanted to. She had balked at tradition for as long as she could remember, but seeing her people broken reminded her that they needed some sense of normalcy to unite them.

It was a good decision, Princess. Can you feel their energy?

Though it was dark out, Faria needed no extra light to see the elves, humans, warlocks, and shapeshifters crowding around the perimeter, each of them wearing smiles or hiding quiet laughter as they joked with their neighbors. She appreciated Hunter's reassurance, especially during a time when so many decisions she had yet to make were uncertain.

Faria caught Jamison's eye and he smiled at her. She was glad to see he was making a speedy recovery and was well enough to stand during the ceremony. Seeing the remnants of his injuries helped focus her. She needed to gain acceptance from the land so the shifters could be added to the Contract, and then she could worry about protecting the borders between realms from potential invaders.

Faria removed her boots then knelt on the stone pathway in front of her father, pressing her fingertips into the dirt on either side of her, and rested her forehead against the ground. She could sense a shift in the air, and a sudden stillness, as if the earth itself was aware the ceremony was upon them. Her nerves ratcheted as she thought of all the ways it could go wrong again, but she concentrated on the scent of the soil beneath her fingertips, the water from the freshly fallen snow, the pine and spice of the Forest of the Dawn, and a fresh burst of wildflowers on the wind. She was surrounded by everything she knew and loved, and despite the shocking truths she had discovered, it was still her home.

Please accept me, she begged the land, the Fates, the gods, whoever was listening. *Please accept me as the rightful ruler of this land so I can save the Fae and protect my people.*

The energy shifted as her father started the ritual, and whatever words he spoke activated the land.

If she concentrated, she could hear a low humming through the ground, as if the pebbles and dirt and insects and roots of life were all connected. A warm sensation rose from where her fingertips rested and into her body.

"Faria, repeat after me," Faline's voice took on an intonation of grave ceremonial importance, "I, Faria Alina Agostonna, swear that I will protect and serve the peoples of Anestra and all who inhabit here to the best of my abilities."

Faria's mouth was dry. She peeled her tongue away from the roof of her mouth to repeat the words back at Faline. Cold prickles of sweat started at her temples despite the magic in the humid air that helped the plants to survive.

"I swear that I am the true and rightful heir to the Agostonna throne, that the Fates have decreed my trials passed, and that through the blood of my ancestors, the land will know and recognize that I speak true."

Hunter raised the Val dagger from the satin pillow and murmured something in his language over it. The gold in his eyes illuminated and the crimson sheen of the dagger reflected off its glow.

Faria glanced at the others around her. Nellie nodded in encouragement while Ander stood at attention, his brows drawn over his eyes. Faline waited patiently for Faria to echo the words back so Hunter could complete the ritual.

Faria repeated the words, her voice strong with conviction, "... decreed my trials passed, and through the blood of my ancestors, the land will recognize that I speak true."

She thought of the Fates and the constant lingering threat they had posed to her over the course of the last year. Knowing now they were some part of the gods and goddesses' consciousness, that it was truly Their will that she was influenced by, Faria felt some sense of clarity and trepidation. Why hadn't they made an appearance yet? She *had* passed the tests, though she wouldn't be surprised if They came up with some last-minute caveat and were waiting right until this pivotal moment to pull the rug out from under her and prevent the ritual from finishing.

"Please," she whispered to the ground. "I pray to the goddesses, the Fates, and all my ancestors who come before me. I promise to take care of the land, to protect it to the best of my ability, to care for my people, to surrender my desires to help the land thrive. I know I am unworthy, but please accept me as the heir to the queendom to pick up where my mother left off to keep this land and these people safe within my care for the years to come."

The humming ceased and the onlookers murmured.

Maybe it was wrong for her to stray from what she was supposed to say, to say whatever it was she wanted to instead. *What does it matter, really?* she thought. *A little extra begging to the universe might help.*

A hint of amusement trickled down the bond and Faria looked up at a smirking Hunter *I wouldn't mind a bit of begging.*

Faria rolled her eyes and held out her hand, ready for him to slice her palm with the dagger he still held aloft. She knew he was trying to distract her so that her anxiety wouldn't run wild with thoughts she couldn't control.

When this is over, Princess, I'll show you what control really means.

When this is over, you're going to have to come up with a new name for me other than Princess.

Oh, I have several I'd love to—

"Ahem, Hunter," Faline said, interrupting their silent conversation.

"The dagger."

Hunter gave her a look that suggested the conversation wasn't over then cupped her hand, his heat burning through her. At his touch, the humming that had ceased began anew, birds in the distant forest came alive with chirps and songs Faria hoped were of celebration rather than of an omen. The night-blossoming flowers surrounding them multiplied and grew, and a faint purple light emanated from Faria and Hunter where he touched her.

"Here we go!" Nellie's voice barely penetrated through the cacophony of noise and sensation that overtook Faria. "Watch your parents, dude. This wild stuff has been happening since way before you were born."

"Hush," Faline chastised.

A breeze picked up between the two Val, further creating some sort of barrier between them and the rest of the world.

"Do it," Faria said, her heart racing as the anticipation built. "Let's hurry and make me a proper queen."

"As you wish, Princess." He bent over and sweetly kissed her forehead before slashing open her palm.

Deep crimson rose to the surface of her skin, and Faria quickly placed it down on the dirt path she kneeled upon. The cacophony of sound and vibration ceased until all was left silent as if the world's breath was stilted like sunlight through a canopy.

Tense moments unraveled like a spool of thread and though she didn't know how long it was supposed to take, Faria refused to acknowledge anyone around her, if only to not see the disappointment written on their faces. Worry suffused her but she had to believe. The sacrifices she had made for her people, to do the right thing, to please her mother, to prove she was fit to rule. She'd lost so much in just a few short weeks and had given most of what she could to the realm. And there was still more left to give, she knew. She had no choice but to make it work. To lead the armies, to somehow make it to Wendorre, despite there probably being a trap set up for her so the warlocks could thrive again, to hope they would follow her as a foreign queen they'd never met, to make sure they were taken care of just as much as her own people in Anestra.

And to make sure the shifters thrived, no matter where they ended up, to update the Contract and have them sign it, to make sure there was enough food, to make sure the people who fled from the threat of Darroc returned so they could resume their normal economic practices so they could all thrive.

All of that and more—convincing Ander to stay with her as an Anestrian, taming a *Drogosterra* or perhaps its entire Weyr, if it came to it. Dealing with the Elders and the gods. She would do it all, whether she was the queen or not. She would not abandon her people.

And then there was Hunter. The things she was willing to sacrifice for love, for a chance to be with him scared her. They might have been mated by circumstance, by the Fates, but this time she had to choose her people, wholly and without reservation. She knew Hunter would be there for her no matter what happened. She would try not to worry about the hurt in her heart, the depth of her despair she had felt for months agonizing over his absence and his presumed lack of care. She'd spent a long time lost in her grief that she loved someone incapable of loving her in return and she would not do the same to her people any longer.

She would bond with her land, with the earth she walks upon, with the air and ocean and salt of the dirt and magic in the stones and every ounce of what made Anestra a breathing, evolving entity. She'd have to trust that the rest would fall into place. She was tired of fighting the Fates, of trying to create her own destiny.

If they were meant to be together, if she was meant to be with anyone at all, she'd have to trust the Fates' design. They were cruel and heartless, but if all else failed, maybe Farrah and Alexei would look down on them with empathy and give their blessing. If they didn't turn into the type of gods that destroyed their creations.

Faria's blood continued to flow into the ground and she waited in the silence. She could no longer hear the rush of life through the dirt, could not feel the warmth of light that suffused through its minerals. She could no longer smell the essence anymore or sense the people standing around her. In fact, she was surrounded by a void so immense and unimaginable she couldn't tell if it was an image trapped in her mind or if she was swirling in the infinite space of Nothing.

Hunter? Faria's mind, her soul, reached for him but it was like he ceased to exist. Fear clawed its way into her marrow and panic welled within her.

A blast of heat rippled through her body followed by an icy chill that seeped through her pores and settled into the roots of her soul. She was on fire. Every ember of herself was set ablaze with cold flame and blazing fire. A song threatened to burst forth from her lungs if only she had the breath to sing it. An odd sort of chanting filled the dense space and Faria attempted to open her eyes but was blinded by the light emanating from … her. It poured out from her body until it was swallowed by the darkness beyond.

The indecipherable chanting increased and something unnatural caressed her skin. It was a kiss across her brow, a shadow of a hand on her shoulder, an embrace enveloping her body and she was overcome by an infinite amount of love and hope as it consumed her.

It was relentless; the chanting was too loud, the fire too bright, the pain too cold, and the different sensations battled with each other until finally a scream erupted from her and she shuddered as her body collapsed back onto the ground.

Faria's ragged breath burned her sides as she clutched the soil beneath her, her lungs seizing from within as she let the pain take over until every last agonizing stab of it filled the empty spaces inside. A rush of magic suffused through her skin, her blood, her very essence, splitting her apart until she rose in the sky and a violent light burst from her.

A rush of voices filled the space now teeming with life. Her magic, the entirety of it that had been an itch under her skin, locked in a chest deep within her was finally free. It was euphoric and she radiated with the glow of the goddesses, shimmered with the iridescent markings of the Val, blazed with the fire of the phoenix.

The magic settled back within her, satisfied that it had finally made its true appearance. Faria felt strange, her molecules buzzing with the new energy she had. Just as she regained her equilibrium, images flashed behind her eyes.

Her mother, warning her to stay away from the Gate of all Realms, Ander as a baby sleeping in her arms the only time she held him, Faline, fixing her hair before one of the many dinners she was forced to attend. Disembodied voices accompanied the memories, along with the desire to consume more of the time she had lost.

"*Well done,*" the words echoed in the endless chamber as The Fates surrounded her, Their hissing voices echoing her lost loved ones' sentiments. "*You passsssed, Queen Faria Agostonna. You, who are elf-born, Fae-blessed, Val-made, goddess reborn. You have earned the right to defend your realm from the true evil that lurksssss in the shadows. Use your powersss wisely.*"

The darkness started to fade and Faria, frantic for answers, shouted, "Wait! Why have the gods awoken? Where are they?"

The final word rang in Faria's ears as she became aware of her surroundings, the moonlight whispering against the stone and dirt beneath her feet: "*Everywhere.*"

TWENTY FOUR

NELLIE

Well, that's something you didn't see every day.

Faria's outstretched arms lowered back to her sides, the ghostly image of dark wings of fire receding with the action. As one, the warlocks who looked on fell to their knees, murmuring "My queen" endlessly. It was creepy as heck.

Nellie didn't fully understand their hive-mind actions but she suspected it had something to do with the fact that her best friend looked like a freaking phoenix. Endless questions rolled off her tongue, but they were stopped at the sudden sight of food being passed around and music starting up. She wasn't aware there would be a party after but things had been stressful and she was hungry, so a midnight celebration sounded fine to her.

"Faline," Nellie asked as they reached for a finger sandwich on a passing platter, "not that I'm complaining, but how do we know the land accepted her as queen? That whole levitation thing wouldn't have worked for Amira, right?"

"The land would have recognized her blood as an imposter and leeched all the powers from her until she was barely a husk of herself." Faline reached for a chocolate-covered strawberry and took a bite as if she didn't just say the land, what Nellie walked on and even spit on sometimes, had the ability to destroy someone so thoroughly, in the magical sense.

Nellie walked over to a recently erected drinks table and casually took a flute filled with elderberry wine and poured some onto the ground. "There you go," she whispered. "A nice treat for you."

"What are you doing?" Endo appeared from the darkness, clutching his own goblet and looking curiously at Nellie.

She hadn't seen him since Ander took her to Earth to be healed by Jane's guides, but he appeared to be unharmed. He wore dark pants and a shiny teal shirt that brought out the ocean in his eyes. His dark hair swept over one side of his forehead and his sun-kissed skin glowed even in the moonlight. He was handsome, and Nellie tried to feel anything of what she did before towards him, but it just wasn't there.

"I'm paying tribute to the land, lest she deem me unworthy," Nellie tried to joke with him, to be at ease so he wouldn't sense her thoroughly; she didn't wish to be in his presence. "When did you return?"

"Perhaps an hour after you and Ander disappeared. Riding in the claws of a *Drogosterra* is not for the faint of heart." He ran his hand through his hair, looking around her. "At least we discovered there is something dangerous in the waters. Now that we know, we can strategize better for the upcoming battles."

War strategy. That was what he wanted to speak about? "Did you know that something would have harmed Marisa? Is that why you brought her?"

"What?"

"That thing. I learned that if I were a siren, it would have killed me within moments of stinging me." As it was, Nellie still felt weak and a tremor of pain passed through her every so often. She knew her body was trying to rid itself of the toxins and if that was how she felt days after intensive medical healing, she couldn't imagine what that death would feel like to a siren.

"Nellie, come on." Endo stepped closer, reaching for her hand. "I was just being practical; I couldn't have known—"

Nellie jumped back from him before he could touch her. There was a moment of awkward silence between them then. "Endo, I don't feel that way toward you anymore. You must sense that from me, given it's one of your abilities to know the emotions of people."

"I know you are suspicious of me, but—"

"But nothing," Nellie interrupted him. She didn't want to have this conversation anymore. She admitted her feelings were gone and he acknowledged he knew and that was all that needed to be said. "We can be friends and work together, but that's all I can offer you. I've seen too much in the past few months and lost too many people to ignore the things that make me happy. Time is fleeting, you know?" Nellie could feel herself start to ramble but was saved by someone throwing an arm around her neck.

"There you are, Nellie! I believe you owe me a dance."

"Reed! I could kiss you," Nellie said as soon as they were out of Endo's earshot. "Like, just full-on tongue in mouth."

Reed chuckled. "I don't think Wil would appreciate you assaulting his partner."

"He can join! What do I care?"

"What am I joining in on?" Wil danced his way over, holding two glasses of wine, and handed one to Reed. String instruments played a lively song and dancers started flitting about to the beat.

"Nellie proposed a three-way," Reed said. "Wouldn't that be interesting?"

Wil choked on a sip of wine, splattering crimson on his tunic. "I'm … Yes. That would be interesting. Why is this being proposed?"

"Oh, your love here saved me from Endo. I didn't realize they were back. Where's Marisa? And the *Drogosterra*?"

"Marisa watched the ceremony from the back of the crowd with us," Reed said. "She wanted to skip the party so she could strategize with her clan how best to fight in the water. We're to bring them to one of the lakes to start practicing tomorrow."

Nellie was uneasy about that. If they got hurt or killed, she didn't know what she would do. They felt like hers to protect and sending them into that type of danger where she knows the outcome felt wrong. "Is there no other way?"

Reed shook his head. "They're confident, and it's their choice. As soon as the Contracts are signed with the shifters in the morning, they are free to do as they wish. Speaking of, Jamison and Tommy have been talking about what to do as well. They heard the rumors of shifters being stuck on the other side of the mountains. None of them has shifted since they've been here so they wanted to start practicing as well."

Tommy. Nellie almost forgot her former mate was here. She'd been so preoccupied with the revelations and not dying and of course needing to train the *Drogosterra.* It slipped her mind to make sure they were adjusting to the realm okay.

"I'll try to make time for that this week," Nellie promised. "I'll have to train the dragon, however that's meant to happen, but I'll be sure to work with the shifters, too. We all will need to learn the best way to fight with her."

"Ahh, yes. The *Drogosterra.* Ander sent her away to hunt in the north for a while," Wil paused to take a sip of wine. "I don't think she enjoys being around people, yet. When they returned yesterday she all but dropped them in the field before rushing away."

They watched the revelers in quiet contentment. It had been a while since Nellie had seen so many people relax and have fun, or just laugh. She wasn't sure what it was like in the weeks that she and Faria were on Earth, but in the debriefing they received, it seemed like a grim year for everyone. It was nice to watch children play tag in between the legs of their parents and Nellie saw more than one couple forget that almost everyone in attendance had excellent low-light vision.

It was only a fraction of what it used to be, but Nellie could feel the Anestrians start to heal from this one moment of joviality.

Nellie watched as Faria walked among her people, allowing the warlocks a bit of extra time to touch their foreheads or exchange words with them. It was strange to see her being worshipped in such a way, and a bit sad as well. They'd been deprived of a queen for so long, it seemed like they missed a mother's touch.

"Have the warlocks' powers returned?" Nellie wondered aloud. "They don't seem different."

Enis joined them, a plate of cheesecake in her hand. "It's as we suspected. Faria will have to go to Wendorre to restore the magic there."

"Is that honey cheesecake?" Nellie's mouth salivated at the thought. "As in, the honey cheesecake I've been frothing for since I returned here?"

"Yeah, there's special wine as well, fire whiskey, loads of things—"

"Cool, cool, but where did you get it from?"

Enis chuckled and pointed over her shoulder. "It's back there on one of the tables. It's going quickly so—"

"On it!" Nellie swerved in between running children, dancing couples, and a random juggler that popped out of nowhere and made it just in time for the last slice to be served. *Winner.*

Nellie was just about to dive in with a forkful when nearby exclamations of surprise stopped her. She looked up in time to see the blurred outline of someone pressing their way through the crowd, heading toward the Forest of the Dawn. The figure turned slightly and Nellie recognized the profile of Ander in the moonlight. She wondered if it was too much to be around everyone at once like this and wished she had a way to support him.

Making a snap decision, she turned to a passing server.

"Hey, do you happen to have a candle on you?"

TWENTY FIVE

ANDER

Several events surprised Ander after the ceremony.

First, there was the random midnight party. Platters of sandwiches and desserts made their rounds through the crowd and several tables filled with more late-night snacks and drinks were erected seemingly out of nowhere. Musicians with string instruments started playing songs and laughter filled the air.

That was of course, after the second event he didn't expect to happen, which was his mother turning into a phoenix, or some iteration of one.

She had been kneeling on a stone placed in the dirt pathway in the Spring Garden and appeared to be frozen. Her eyes were shut, though he could see them rapidly moving under her lids. Everyone around him held their breath, silent other than a random cry from a baby and its mother murmuring comfort.

Her head shot back and her eyes flew open, a golden fire blazing in them. She levitated a few inches off the ground, which was creepy as hell to see, and her arms stretched wide as the faint mirage of wings emanated from her. His mother's face was euphoric and the energy bursting forth through her was enough to make most fall to their knees.

The fervent whisperings and shouts of exaltations filled the night sky. Warlocks supplicated with their foreheads pressed to the ground and young children danced around parents whose faces displayed expressions of shock and hope. After the image of dark wings of fire dissipated, Faria had touched back down to the ground, the embers in her eyes faintly sparkling.

The celebration started shortly after which was when the third event he didn't expect to happen occurred.

Nellie held his hand.

He wasn't entirely sure how it happened, either. The music, the dancing, the magic crackling in the air, on top of his already heightened anxiety at the possibility of Darroc or the gods or anyone showing up again made his *malosin obsinae* agitated enough to rise to the surface of his skin. Ander sought a way out of the crowd, dodging between children and pushing others out of the way before he did something irreparable to them. His powers had been difficult to control for months the deeper into the Change he had been, and the development of the *malosin obsinae* and the flashes of rage that accompanied it had complicated his already emotional outbursts.

Ander breathed deeply, willing his body to calm itself. He could feel the distress of his *Drogosterra* through whatever bond it was they had now and her worry rippled across his mind. He tried to assure her he was okay. He had sent her off hunting after they briefly reunited earlier and he certainly didn't want her returning now thinking that he was in grave danger and accidentally harm someone.

He was close to the Forest of the Dawn, so close to hiding among the trees where he could take the time to regain control but he could feel it, the darkness taking shape, readying to shoot out of him.

Gentle fingers slid against his, cool against the heat suffusing him and the rage lowered to a dull simmer while a new feeling gave rise. He looked down at their hands, at her fingers intertwining his, her thumb rubbing soothing circles against his skin.

"Hey, *loverboy*," Nellie teased, referring back to what Jane called him. "Where are you off to in a hurry?" she kept her tone light.

He could feel concern emanating from her. She might not have been an elf or Fae, but he had the feeling Nellie could sense others' emotions. She certainly always knew when he needed someone. When he needed her.

"I, um," he stammered, uncertain how much to tell her. He was so open with her before, why was he having such difficulty in speaking to her now?

"It's the *malosin obsinae*, right?" Nellie asked him. "I could feel it rolling off of you during the ceremony and when you tried to disappear, I knew something was up. It's all the *people*, isn't it? I mean, I love a good party and all, but can we at least talk about your mother looking like a freaking dark phoenix? That was hot, am I right?"

"You're rambling," he said, but he appreciated that quality about her.

The more nonsense she spoke, the more he became caught up in her energy, mesmerized by the way her nose crinkled the more excited she got, the smile that seemed to come so easily when she didn't think about it. He had known her for just a short time, but it was these moments that he was growing to appreciate. Nellie was strange, but she comforted a piece of him that never quite knew how to relax.

Nellie bit her lip. "I know, I'm sorry. I ramble when I'm nervous. Or stressed. Or tired. Or hungry. Speaking of …" her voice trailed off and she lifted her other hand, a plate of dessert illuminated faintly in the moonlight. "Honey cheesecake! I cannot tell you how *long* I've been craving this."

"You found me so you could show me the cheesecake you're about to eat?"

"No, silly!" She released his hand. Ander felt suddenly empty.

Nellie pulled from her back pocket two forks and a candle. "Do you have fire magic? I didn't think this whole thing through, but I figured that since there was all this food and music and all that's missing is a balloon or two, and—"

"What are you going on about, Nellie?" Ander asked.

He was nervous about accidentally hurting her with his *malosin* but he extended his hand over the candle she placed in the cheesecake, calling a flame to his fingertip, and placed it against the wick. Once it ignited, Nellie took a step back and held the plate aloft between them.

"Happy belated birthday, Ander Agostonna!"

Ander looked down at the cheesecake and then up at her, confused at whatever this was that she was doing. He didn't recall when his birthday was since time passed differently between realms, and he certainly didn't expect his mother's friend to remember it either.

"Come on," Nellie said, her beaming smile losing a bit of its shine. "Make a wish!"

A wish. She wanted him to make a wish on the flame he just conjured. Ander never understood the human tradition of wishing for food. Things happened or they didn't. He'd been across enough realms to know the only way to get the world to react to you was for you to create action first.

"Okay, never mind. This was silly." Nellie made to blow the candle out, her shoulders drooping slightly.

The background revelry spurred him into action. It was a celebration, and though it wasn't his celebration, he appreciated the gesture.

"No, it's okay. I just never did this before." He gazed into her hazel eyes, noting the freckles that dusted her face. What was it about her that settled something in him? He blew out the flame and took the proffered fork.

"This is going to be the best thing you ever put in your mouth, I swear on the goddess. It's so creamy it'll just slide down your throat."

"Nellie," Faria's voice rang out, saving Ander from having to come up with a response. "Please tell me you aren't talking to my son about what I think you're talking about."

Ander smirked at her, wondering how she would respond.

"Depends," Nellie said, giving him the side eye. "What do you *think* we were talking about?"

Ander quickly stuffed a bite of cheesecake in his mouth to avoid having to take part in whatever conversation was to follow. *Damn*, he thought. *That does melt in your mouth.* The salty crust contrasted nicely with the sweetness of the cheesecake, and he took his time savoring every second of it.

Nellie gave him a look of satisfaction. "I know. So good, right?"

Ander soaked in her happiness at sharing something she loved with him and the wall he'd built inside to protect himself started to crumble. They stared at each other long enough for his mother to clear her throat.

"I don't know what's happening here, but I was hoping for a word, Ander."

"I will totally leave, okay? Ander, you hang on to that. Happy birthday." Nellie awkwardly shuffled backward.

He knew she'd lurk behind a tree or something to listen in. She seemed the type.

"Birthday?" Faria's eyebrows drew close as she stared at him in abject horror. "I haven't … Has it passed?"

"I don't know," Ander replied quickly. "I don't know what all this is but I guess it would be around now. The Change started a while ago, so I think in other realms I've been eighteen, maybe even nineteen."

"Nineteen." Faria nodded.

An awkward silence followed.

Nellie, who never actually left, said, "To be fair, Faria, I've been seventeen for like, five years. What is age, really but just a number." She glanced sidelong at Ander who quickly took another bite of cheesecake.

"I just … I didn't think …" Faria floundered before continuing, "Well, anyway, I just wanted to thank you, Ander. Thank you for staying, for helping, for your quick thinking in saving Nellie's life. Anything you still have yet to do. I recognize that you owe us nothing, and I just wanted you to know that though you technically hold the title of prince, I expect nothing from you until or if you're ever ready."

What should he say to that? Of course she shouldn't expect him to take up a title he never wanted. "Thank you," he settled on. "I appreciate the lack of pressure."

A breeze passed between the three of them, carrying the scent of caramel popcorn. Ander was at a loss as to how to make the moment less strange than what it was. Luckily, Nellie piped up, "Speaking of pressure, did you give Hunter the business?"

"The business?" Faria asked. "What do you mean by that?"

"What she means," Hunter said, approaching from the forest, "is if you told me off for whatever it is you've been upset about, even though I have proven my love and loyalty relentlessly."

"Well," Faria said, "I do believe I am still waiting for an apology for at least not properly communicating with me about pretty much ... anything."

"That's right, daddio," Nellie interrupted. "No communication, that's the problem these days, wouldn't you say so, Ander?"

Ander tried to keep up with the conversation but an incessant buzzing sounded in his ear that thankfully distracted him from the conversation. He wanted nothing to do with getting into his parents' communication issues, of that he was certain.

The simmering rage he felt dimmed as a sharp pain started in his abdomen and slowly spread outward. He wondered briefly if there was something wrong with the cheesecake when a steady pulse radiated from his chest. Ander clutched his heart though he knew there was nothing wrong with it. It was something much worse.

"What is it?" Nellie asked, placing her hand on his shoulder.

Ander dropped to his knees and immediately the faint glow of his mother's healing paired with the green of his father's hovered inches above him. It wouldn't work because what he felt was not something that could be healed. Another lance of heat tore through him and his head pulsed with warning.

"I can't get to him," Faria said, her voice frantic. "I don't know what's wrong."

"It's not you," Nellie said. She looked into Ander's eyes.

A double vision of beauty swam before him.

"Is it him, Ander?" Nellie asked.

Ander panted, trying to keep his breathing and fear under control. He couldn't show up in front of Darroc in a state of panic. The calmer he was, the better. "It's him," Ander said. "He's calling me."

He disappeared.

PART IV

TWENTY SIX

FARIA

There are different types of aches when it comes to being a mother. The ache of having to leave them before they're ready, their haunting cries filling the mother with guilt as she tries to walk away. The ache of them leaving before the mother is ready, their eager faces alight with the possibilities of a future filled with freedom. And then there is that unique pain that Faria had hoped to never feel again; the ache of watching her child leave, knowing he didn't want to go.

Faria had the honor of motherhood ripped from her. Any love that could have been bestowed, any dreams she could have nurtured, disintegrated like motes of dust the moment Darroc had stolen him as a newborn. She'd had to come to terms with learning that he lived an entire lifetime without her, that she missed all of Ander's firsts, his cuddles, and the joy of watching his personality take shape. She'd missed out on the opportunity of loving him properly.

It was one thing to watch him leave of his own accord, such as when he left quickly following the bonding to his *Drogosterra*. She would never stop someone from leaving who didn't want to be around her or her land. But to see the fear in Ander's eyes as he'd said that Darroc was summoning him and being unable to stop him, *again*, from suffering at the hands of her former husband, was enough to make her snap.

Faria fell to the ground on all fours, the cold seeping through the thin material of her pants. Jagged stones stung her palms, their sharp edges like hornets breaking the barrier of her skin. She breathed deeply, swallowing down the impulse to shoot flame or ice at anyone who came too near. Ander was *just there* and despite the power of the warlocks, the phoenix, the elves, and the Fae running through her system, she still could not protect her son. The only thing left that she could do as a mother was taken by Darroc again.

Her fingertips grew hot and the earth beneath her hands scorched the ground. Faria knew that she had the capability of rendering anyone she wanted to dust, but she had to remain clear-headed and lead not with emotion, but logic, something that wasn't her strong suit. She swallowed the ache of knowing she couldn't help Ander in that moment, because if Darroc was strong enough to summon him, that meant he'd be on his way soon. She had to be the matriarch now and protect her people.

The presence of more bodies approaching pressed upon Faria, and she straightened, coming to her knees before anyone else could see her on the ground. She had to remain a symbol of strength as the moment they waited for was upon them. Three of the Royal Guard, Johanna in the forefront and Wil and Enis in the back, headed toward Faria, but her blessed mate intercepted and immediately told them what happened. She took advantage of the moment to gather herself.

Faria knew she should have a plan, but for all the magic she possessed, not one ounce of it could help her strategize a winning battle. She left that to Hunter, who once commanded the Val army, and knew her father, who led the Anestrian army, would take over the logistics. Instead, she stepped away from the group, willing the flames dancing upon her fingertips to recede.

"Hey," Nellie presented the plate of half-eaten cheesecake. "This seems ridiculous now."

"Did I really miss his birthday?" Faria asked. Would there ever be one moment where she didn't fail at motherhood?

"Don't beat yourself up for it. We've all missed out on so much. Plus, even with more Val in existence, time hasn't stabilized yet as it should have, and even if or when it does, that doesn't mean it will all run concurrently. Even he doesn't know exactly how old he is. We will likely miss out on many more events if we travel to other realms."

A breeze shifted through the trees, the leaves whispering secrets indecipherable even to the keenest elven ears. "We have to get him back," she said, determination steeling her voice. Faria paced in a circle, her boots melting a path on the frosty grass as she contemplated the best course of action.

She looked from Nellie to Hunter, still conversing with members of her guard, and shook her head. They weren't prepared. There was still training with the *Drogosterra* and the shifters and the Contract and—

Don't worry, Princess, Hunter's voice traveled across her mind. He crossed his arms while he and Johanna went back and forth on how the front lines should be set up. *It will all be figured out. First, the Contract to prevent anyone from turning on the shifters, and vice versa. Then training until the moment arrives. We have prepared in all other ways.* He nodded at something Johanna mentioned then gave Faria the side eye and winked.

He was right; there was no point in worrying about what had not come to pass yet.

"Nellie," Faria turned back to her friend who was surprisingly stoic, considering what had happened. She was used to her frantic energy, not the veil of doom Nellie now wore. "I heard Enis give orders to Wil to report back to my father. It will soon be chaos here." She stopped, considering if it was worth it to ask Nellie this favor or not. If she succeeded, it could change the tide of the battle if it should come to that. "I want you to go to the royal library. Search the archives there. See if there is anything about the last war, the Elders, anything that might help us win this. The Spell of Unmaking, even. It's a long shot but I don't want to say we didn't try."

"You know I'm all for it, but we have … hours, maybe? That won't be nearly long enough." Nellie rubbed her eyes. "Okay. Okay. The Nellinator is on it."

Nellie seemed more tired than usual, her pep not quite hitting where it usually did. Faria knew she had been through so much in the past few weeks, but her sass and humor had never wavered. Now, however, it was obvious the last events had taken their toll. Nellie's pale complexion was covered with beads of sweat breaking.

"Hey, wait," Faria said, placing her hand on Nellie's forearm before she turned to go.

Immediately a blue glow emanated from where their skin touched.

Faria sent a rush of healing power through her friend, trying to find the source of what caused her malady. "Are you all right?"

"Sure," Nellie said, the color slowly regaining in her cheeks. "Thanks for the boost. I'll be fine." She started to walk away but turned around, a fierce look of determination in her eyes. "We will get him back, Fifi. He can't take him from us again."

NELLIE

Goddess above, I feel like shiitake.

Nellie stood in front of an ornate fireplace in the royal library, willing the crackling flames to heat her icy skin, but short of falling directly into the fire, she felt she couldn't get close enough. That freakshow that stung her did more damage than Nellie had expected, and though both Lindy and Santana told her she needed to relax and heal, Nellie didn't think it would be quite as bad as it was. She was grateful that Ander had noticed and gave her immunity boosts when she was too weak and too stubborn to ask.

But now he had been summoned to Darroc's side, a harsh reminder that while the frivolity they had experienced during the celebration was necessary, it was also short-lived; a reality they were forced to endure until

Darroc, the gods, the Elders, and any other potential threat was taken care of.

Shivering, Nellie turned away from the crackling fire and observed the spread of tomes, manuscripts, pieces of parchment, and illustrations laid before her on one of many tables in the royal library. She was surrounded by scores of bookcases filled with leather-bound books and huge pieces of framed artwork ranging from family portraits to elaborate landscapes of what she assumed was Anestra she had never seen before. Candelabras were affixed to the stone walls while thick patterned rugs covered the floor. Fires were lit in each of the hearths situated every few feet along the walls. The scent of dust and ink competed with the spiced bark from the burning logs. Shadows grew and contracted in flickering relief.

Nellie had spent the better part of an hour acquainting herself with the layout once she got over the shock of how vast the royal library was. Nellie didn't know how Faria expected her to find "whatever" they needed to help, both because of the expansiveness of the room and also because nothing appeared to be in any apparent order.

The lack of labels slowed Nellie down, but she found some order within the chaos when she happened upon an elaborate floor-to-ceiling bookcase filled with nothing but the most shocking and spiciest romance novels Nellie had ever come across. Titles such as *When the Wyvern Calls* and *Taming the Beast* were tame compared to *Two Fae, One*—

"Amira, you dirty dog," Nellie whispered to herself. She loved that her former queen, and from the looks of it, many others, were into so many … expressive forms of coupling.

She'd lost more time than she'd cared to admit blushing her way through one too many deliciously inappropriate scenes. Once she remembered her task, however, Nellie started pulling the titles she could understand that seemed as if they had anything to do with Anestra's history, the Agostonna family line, and most importantly, the Great War from a thousand years ago. If Darroc was the same driving force behind the war back then as he'd claimed, then Nellie was sure she would find evidence of the Elders or their influence somewhere within those pages.

But it was dull work and her bones felt brittle with the chill that refused to leave her. The moment Ander had left, Nellie felt imbalanced, like something crucial was missing, like whatever it was that regulated her freaking body temperature.

A distant clock chimed the hour: 3 AM. Nellie had maybe another hour of extensive research to do until she could catch an hour or two of sleep before training Ander's *Drogosterra*. Sighing, she unraveled the nearest scroll and continued to work.

"Do you think all that drool will smudge the ink on thousands year old parchment?"

"The oils from our skin ruin the ink so you can be sure that puddle has destroyed whatever was there."

"Should we wake her?"

"Nah, give her a few moments to realize there's a stack of pancakes and another slice of honey cheesecake in front of her."

Nellie's eyes flew open and she peeled her cheek away from the parchment she had pored over a short while ago. "You could wake the mangled corpse of an elephant with how loudly you're whispering." She cringed internally at the mess she made of the document, hoping no one cared to know what food was given to the armies during the Great War.

Nellie eyed Wil and Faline standing in front of her, both wincing at the state of the parchment. The dark circles under their eyes let her know that no sleep was had between them.

"What are you two doing in here, anyway? Oh my gosh, am I late?" Nellie stood, feeling the weight of a blanket slide from her shoulders. She glanced at it, wondering if she unconsciously searched for warmth in her sleep.

"I came to help you a few hours ago," Faline said, resting a hand on her arm.

A wave of calm washed over Nellie and she smiled gratefully up at her adoptive mother.

"Did you find out anything useful?"

"Short of discovering that Amira was into some kinky things, no. Nothing."

"I thought as much." Faline sighed and gathered up the tomes and manuscripts. "I wasn't able to find much either, except a passage from a journal belonging to a young warlock who resided at *Mentage* during the Great War. All they said was the warlock prince had changed himself so much through endless blood sacrifice and experimentation both on himself and others, that he was not a warlock at all anymore. That much we suspected. They went on to say the Spell of Unmaking was the only way to destroy him, which I believe confirms what the Elders told Hunter."

Nellie rubbed her temples. The little sleep and a lot of celebration the night before was doing a number on her. How much wine did she drink? She felt worse than the first time she and her former mate Tommy got drunk at a clan gathering when they were sixteen. The only real recollection she had from that night was how acquainted she was with the bushes.

"That warlock didn't happen to have the Spell of Unmaking in their journal, did they?"

"No, but it has been told many times that only Darroc knows it. Although, we now know the Elders do as well. Hunter informed us last night that he had first-hand experience at being unmade by their hands."

Nellie couldn't fathom the amount of pain and leftover trauma he must have suffered at the hands of the Elders. It blew her mind that he still felt like he needed to listen to whatever they said. They bound his powers and kept him from his mate. As far as she knew, his memories were still locked. And then those freaks had the audacity to ask to return to this land? Nellie didn't know much, but it seemed as though one too many blood sacrifices made them certifiably insane.

"Are you all right, Nells?" Wil asked as he returned from shelving a stack of books goddess knew where in the chaos she had made. "You're pale and sticky looking."

"Is that how you won Reed's heart? By telling him how sticky he looked?" She didn't doubt he was wrong. Nellie tried ignoring her racing heartbeat and the increasing strength of the dizzy spells that wracked her, but she knew something like that wouldn't get past elven senses.

"Maybe you should skip the training," Faline started. "It's not even necessary—"

"No," Nellie forced out.

The other two looked at her in surprise, no doubt taken aback by her outburst.

She was a jokester, someone people didn't often take seriously, but she didn't need to be coddled. She would get better eventually. "We can't put it off. We have no idea when Darroc is coming, and I at least have to make sure the young dragon can listen to directions. I'm heading there now."

"Did you want to tell Faria about the journal?" Faline asked, holding it out to Nellie. "At least give her an update and maybe she can give you a little boost."

Nellie grabbed the journal from Faline and scanned the section that still lay open. The only known written copy is in his Book of Undead. She wondered how the heck a random warlock would know that, but then was reminded of last year when Hunter had a mind to search Darroc's caves for that spell book. He knew that was where it could be found. There must have been some legitimacy to the warlock's claim.

"Got it. I'm outtie."

It wasn't until she left that Nellie realized she hadn't touched the cheesecake.

"Goddess above, you look awful."

Faria immediately placed her hands against Nellie's skin, the heat of her magic finally allowing a bit of the cold to ebb away. Nellie sighed in relief as she felt a burst of energy return. Moments before, she had handed Faria the journal, who skimmed the words and nodded her head silently. Undoubtedly, she had told Hunter what was found through their mind magic. Nellie wished she'd had that with Ander. Not in a mating way, of course. That would be weird. Just in a normal, we're-friends-and-I-want-to-make-sure-you're-okay way. Obviously.

"I feel like monkey butt, I can't get this chill to leave my bones, and I'm exhausted, but I need to train the little welp. Where is that dragon?"

"Hunter said she's been unsettled since Ander left. He has a suspicion that she could feel whatever it is Ander is going through." Faria rubbed her chest as if it ached.

Nellie watched her friend close her eyes and bite her lip in worry.

"The *innulum* is telling me he's okay, though the connection is distant. I don't think he's still in this realm, or if he is, he's being blocked somehow. I think he might be caged."

White, hot, protective fury blasted through Nellie at the thought. Knowing the trauma Ander had suffered at Darroc's hands, and then picturing him caged, nearly sent her in a spiral of hate. Instead, she nodded at Faria and allowed the rippling change to rumble through her as she shed her human skin for *Drogosterra* scales.

Nellie rose into the mid-morning sky and allowed her inner eyelid to slide down, protecting her vision from the elements. The icy wind pelted her wings but she felt warmer in her body. She allowed the fire in her belly to heat her through then veered north, where she suspected Ander's *Drogosterra* was waiting.

Tiny specks moved along the land below her as Nellie glanced every now and then at the Anestrians preparing for whatever battle may come their way. It was hard to predict what Darroc might have in store for them. More of his creatures, certainly, but perhaps more unholy magic that they couldn't anticipate. The Elders were something to worry about, as well. Hunter seemed confident that they couldn't re-enter the country without Faria's permission, but Nellie doubted it.

They were playing the long game and had been for centuries, which meant they had eons to prepare contingency plans for every scenario they could think of.

Nellie rumbled low in her chest, allowing the fire in her belly to expand and fill the empty spaces within. It helped to have a built-in furnace but she couldn't stay a *Drogosterra* forever. She yawned, allowing herself a small roar and tiny sparks to flicker from her snout.

Where are you going? The thought trickled over Nellie.

She swooped around, looking for her dragon friend. She saw nothing but thick gray clouds above and an endless sea of golden forest below. The *Drogosterra* continued, *You fly so slowly when there is danger. Do you know how to battle?*

Where are you hiding? Nellie stopped gliding and hovered mid-air, trying to listen for any sounds of wings flapping or breathing. She could hardly hear past the wind rushing through the clouds and even that sounded muffled. *I'm not in the mood for games, kid. And what do you know about battles, anyway?*

We were created for such things, remember? Your kind has little memories but ours are long. I heard one of your leaders tell you to train me but there is no need. I was bred for battle. It is perhaps I who should train you. I cannot have you in the way or harmed because you do not know what to do.

There *would* be more sense in her learning from the beast created to fight and protect, rather than her training it. Who was she, but a creature that imitates others? And Faline did try to tell her it wasn't necessary. Nellie didn't care in that moment. The less she had to think, the better. The muffling in her ears progressed into a dull buzzing sound and her head started to pound. Multi-colored spots danced in front of her eyes.

The dragons soared together in silence for a time, and Nellie's head grew heavier with each moment that passed. Her wings faltered and she had to consciously remind herself to keep flapping them. The icy wind raged on, forcing Nellie to swerve between the currents. After a time, she lost track of where they were. North, wasn't it? She looked around for a landmark: a mountain range, a lake, the forest, perhaps, but the day grew darker and her vision swam. She wondered what Ander was forced to endure in that moment.

Can you feel him? Ander?

Only from a far distance. My Val is very cold and very … annoyed. But I think he is well. I shall contain my anger until the one who keeps him is near. And then I will roast him.

Good … good. Gods, she was so tired. How much longer did they have to fly? Nellie couldn't tell how far the Forest was beneath them but she was sure it wouldn't hurt too badly if she crash-landed. *How adept are you at catching things?*

What should I catch, friend?

Me.

Nellie passed out.

TWENTY EIGHT

ANDER

He put me in a godsdammed cage.

Ander sat chained to a stone wall in a cave he had to assume was in a mountain on some freak of a realm he'd never been to. The darkness was thick and unforgiving, even his advanced lowlight vision couldn't decipher his surroundings, outside of impenetrable bars of pure ice. Whatever Darroc had encased him in was drenched in the bitter stench of dark magic. The wrongness in the air nearly suffocated him.

Judging from when waves of hunger struck him, Ander gathered it had been about three days since Darroc left him in that cage. Though he was confident Darroc had not attacked Anestra, Ander grew more concerned the longer he was trapped.

It was terrifying being in Darroc's presence again. He'd shown no sign of the torture he had endured at Moira's hands, but the flames from the sconces had danced across his ripped robe and his pale skin, highlighting the crazed look in his eyes. Deranged. Before Darroc had been cold and calculating, patient. He used to keep his rage to a low simmer. Being with Darroc was like being in a room full of venomous snakes the moment before they decided to attack.

After being summoned, Darroc had immediately thrown Ander into the prison he was in. Spittle flew from his mouth as he demanded explanations for what happened to the Eternal Flame. Instead of waiting for a response, Darroc had magically ripped the answer from his mind. Ander had felt a chilling burn shred through his thoughts, his memories, bringing him back to the day he tried to take the Flame for Darroc.

"Who is he?" Darroc had whispered in Ander's ear as he smoothed one thin finger down Ander's cheek. "The one with the golden eyes. He is not Val."

Ander had tried to keep quiet, tried to think of anything but what the answer was but to no avail.

Darroc had let out a wheezing laugh, his stale breath brushing against Ander's skin. "A god come back to life? Well, he is no match for me."

Darroc pulled out his Book of Undead, slashed his arm open, and allowed the thick, gelatinous sludge to leak from his veins. It hit the ground with a hiss, then Darroc had recited the words from the open spell book and crimson runes glowed near his feet.

"You will stay here until I see fit. And if you are somehow able to break that chain, these runes have more purpose than just caging you in or shielding you from other magic users. Cross these and they will strip the very life force from you." A high-pitched giggle had escaped his mouth, echoing around the chamber.

Ander had searched his face for any trace of the saner male he once knew but there was no recognition.

Darroc's eye twitched. He rested his face against the ice bar of Ander's prison and sighed with relief. "It's so refreshing, isn't it? This ice. It's so hot, so hot, so hot, all the time burning, but for this. You should thank me for bringing you here." He giggled again then left Ander with nothing more than a crust of bread.

As soon as Darroc had disappeared, the cave Ander was plunged into total darkness. Now his food was gone, he was freezing, and more than anything, he was pissed. He was the son of a Val prince and Queen of Everything. Two of the most powerful beings in Anestra. Did that count for nothing?

Ander didn't even know how to seek the help he needed. The place in his mind where his *Drogosterra* resided felt like the ghost of what used to be there. He could faintly tell she was alive, but outside of that, there was nothing. The *innulum* was the same. The carved feeling in his chest reminded him that something was missing and it was more than a minor annoyance. He rubbed the area to soothe the ache.

His attempts to draw fire to his frozen fingertips proved fruitless since he could not reach the well of magic within him. His strength did nothing against the steel clasped against his wrist, which he assumed was what prevented him from using magic, and he was unable to sift through time. He shivered uncontrollably, his teeth clacking, body convulsing with the cold. The pitch of night surrounding him did nothing to ease the chill or anger rising within him. He refused to piss in the dark as he had been doing for days. He was done being tethered to a deranged animal like Darroc.

Darroc was completely off his rocker. There was no way he had enough sense left in him to keep anything useful out of Ander's way. His ego wouldn't allow him to do such a thing. If Ander was able to break the chain then maybe he could finally access a piece of his magic and at least get out of his prison cell. Then surely he would find something, a spell book, perhaps that he could attempt to use.

Sitting with his back against the iced stone wall, Ander breathed deeply and allowed his senses to fully open. Darroc didn't think ahead when he left Ander plunged in darkness as it only strengthened his advanced hearing. He allowed the silence to wash over him, patiently waiting for the moment it shifted.

He had no real sense of time in his dungeon, but Ander guessed a few hours had passed when he heard it: A slight whooshing sound to his right. His heart beat faster, hoping he was right, that he heard wind whispering through an overlooked opening, that Darroc was as careless as he had hoped.

What did that mean for him, though? Even if there was a fractured opening, it didn't change that he was still chained to the wall, behind bars that appeared impenetrable, and surrounded by weird runes that would strip him of his magic.

Ander slammed his head against the wall in frustration and tried to focus on the ghost of connection he had back home.

Home.

Was that what he considered Anestra now? His home? He hadn't known one growing up. He'd always been with Darroc, but they'd jumped realms for years. He'd stayed in Wendorre for a time, in the labyrinth of rocky shoreline that Darroc had secretly claimed as his lair, but Ander had been confined to one area. He'd snuck out to explore a few times when he was a kid, and a few more when he started to realize what abilities he had, but even then it never felt like home.

The Anestrians hadn't been welcoming to him, though he understood why. For most of them, he'd been with the enemy for over eighteen years. They probably suspected him of being just as evil, or Darroc's spy at the very least. But there was something about being in a place where magic was heavy in the air, where both beauty and flaws thrived, where people felt hope. Maybe that was what he was after. A flicker of hope after a lifetime of darkness.

Before he'd hardly had enough time to contemplate it, but being alone for three days allowed him ample time to consider that it felt nice being near his mother and knowing there was someone else like him—his father, though they hadn't spent much time together. He still didn't get why his *Drogosterra* chose him, but he understood the bond was sacred and was grateful to have something feared and revered on his side. Why hadn't he named her yet? Rhayna. That was what he would call her.

And then there was Nellie.

She was odd but had been there for him, a silent beam of support as he struggled in their realm. She was funny and loyal and said whatever came to her mind. She was a beacon of light, and he found himself gravitating toward her as if she lit his path home. His mother was lucky to have someone like Nellie in her life. He'd only known her for a short while, but he knew she … That she …

Ander shook violently, coming out of his reverie. His numb limbs bore down on him and the frozen air started to heat. How long had he been out of it? He hadn't remembered falling asleep. But he was so comfortable, the first time he'd been able to relax in days, so it wouldn't hurt to … close …

She is dying.

He no longer felt hunger, he realized with relief. Or thirst. Just tired, so … tired. The nightmares wouldn't plague him, at least. The exhaustion was too much for …

She will not last the night, Princeling.

Who won't last the night? Ander didn't know. There was no one in his life. Just him, the darkness pressing on him …

Ander Agostonna, son of Queen Faria Agostonna and her consort the Val Prince Hunter d'Valero, Protector and Heir to Anestra and its surrounding territories, future king to all that is yet to come, you must save her.

Why were there so many titles attached to his name? What was in a name anyway? Shakespeare, he remembered, asked that question. He'd once had lots of time to read human literature growing up. He'd like a book now, actually. After he woke from his nap …

Fight it, Princeling! the words rang through his head, the voice echoing where knowledge and memories used to reside.

Princeling? Was he a prince?

Open your eyes.

The command pressed through him and he felt his heavy lids start to rise. A bright azure flame swam in his double vision, shocking to his senses after days of being a blind man. His eyes stung, but he was unable to give in to the urge to close them.

Golden orbs appeared in a haze above the flame.

This is going to hurt, Princeling. But then that abomination will have no control over you anymore. Breathe deeply, my child.

"What?" Ander croaked, his voice thick with disuse for so long. "What will hurt?"

The collar of his shirt ripped down to his chest and before he could protest, searing, white-hot pain burned through his flesh, his blood. His essence was on fire as he watched a tiny drop of flame melt into his exposed skin. Ander screamed, his voice breaking as his body convulsed. It was too much, worse than anything he had endured with Darroc, worse than what he imagined being unmade would feel like.

He couldn't tell how long the torture went on. Hours of sheer agony must have passed. He must have been on the cusp of dying for no one could endure for as long as he had. Ander's vision flickered and a face that looked so much like his, like his father's, but with eyes of liquid gold, appeared before him. The god who took the Flame from his grasp in the fire realm. Alexei, Farrah's consort.

"I know you," Ander whispered.

You are not dying, Princeling, but she is. The Flame integrated within you and broke the bonds with the abomination. With it, you now have the power to save her.

Ander's hands gripped the dirt floor on either side of him and tried to use them as leverage to stand up, shaking with the effort. He tipped over, his arm bending awkwardly beneath him. He was too slow to regain the feeling in his limbs to make much progress.

"Who is dying?" A shot of dread tore through him and he swallowed down the panic burning his throat. "Not my mother?"

No, child. Can you not feel her?

Ander was starting to get pissed off at the god floating before him as if they had all the time in the world to chat away. He felt his *malosin* build beneath his skin.

Wait.

He felt his malosin.

He hadn't been able to do that since he'd arrived. If he could feel it, then surely—

A pulse of distress rippled through him as he felt Rhayna for the first time in days. She seemed frantic but very much alive.

Alexei said his mother was fine. Who else …?

Time is short, Princeling. The bonds that tie you here are no longer. Save her. She has the key to the their demise.

"Why me? Why have you come to me instead of saving her?"

You were both dying. No one would have found you in time. Now both of you can be saved before he destroys everything.

"Why can't you just destroy him? You're a god, are you not?"

Even gods have limitations. Our energy is needed elsewhere.

"Will you not help us, then? You're leaving us on our own?"

Not helping? I just gave you a piece of my power. Do not think that is nothing.

A retort pressed against the tip of his tongue before the god spoke to him again, giving him a warning this time.

Ander, what is given can be taken away. Do not forget that.

Alexei disappeared, leaving Ander in a shroud of darkness again, but it didn't matter. He could feel the realms as he had before. Stronger, even. He flipped through them in his mind like pages in a book until he came across the one he needed. He turned inward for a moment to locate his *Drogosterra* then closed his eyes and flashed out of his forsaken prison, hoping he wasn't too late.

TWENTY NINE

FARIA

"Again."

Hunter walked through the rows of archers in training, correcting the form of the shifters who'd never held a bow before. Faria stood in the stands of the arena, frustrated at not helping them herself.

You can't do it all, Princess.

Faria internally rolled her eyes and swallowed the impulse to remind Hunter she was the most powerful being in existence at the moment. With the exception of the gods, but she didn't want to give voice to that thought. It wasn't comforting to know the extent of power that ran through her veins, though it was a relief to anticipate releasing much of it into Wendorre once she stepped foot on their land.

I helped train them on Earth, remember? I have a rapport with them. Nellie, more so. Do you think she's doing well with the Drogosterra?

To be honest, the Drogosterra won't be much of an issue. They're bred for battle. It was more for optics, to ease the people's worries that she would go rogue on them.

Annoyance flittered through her. *Why waste anyone's time on optics?*

They needed every hand they could get and sending Nellie off on training for appearance's sake was an extreme misuse of time. Had she known, she wouldn't have allowed it, especially not with Nellie as weak as she still was.

Faria had given her a healing boost and felt a bit depleted after. It took much more energy than she had expected. They needed to figure out more information on the creature that poisoned Nellie. She hated to think of the potential carnage it would cause to others who weren't as powerful.

To answer your question, putting our people's minds at ease will reassure them we care for their safety and well-being. And they'll be more focused on fighting their opponent rather than looking for fire to rain from the sky.

Faria looked at the group of Anestrians sweating under the mid-morning sun. They had been training for hours, long before dawn. Those who weren't actively training rotated shifts between the kitchens and the healer's tents, or went off on supply runs. Small groups had broken away to prepare for the journey to Carenek Peaks, Mercy Bay, and along the border of Wendorre. Her father sent word to the Dwarves who live under Carenek Peaks, but the response wasn't promising, and they no longer could hold out hope for the Fae to come to their aid now that their fate was known.

"Hey." Marisa climbed the stairs to where Faria stood and awkwardly curtseyed. "Umm ... your majesty."

It looked strange to see that gesture from someone in jeans, but Faria liked the style and made a mental note to add a pair or two to her wardrobe.

"Stop that," Faria said, pulling her friend closer to her. She lowered her voice, "What are you doing?"

"Showing you respect," Marisa replied. "As everyone should now, regardless of friendship status. And it's good for the optics."

Faria pursed her lips and analyzed Marisa's appearance further. Her dark brown hair was disheveled, her tan skin paler than it had been on Earth. Faria lightly touched Marisa's shoulder, the faint blue glow from her fingers looking for an illness to explain the change in coloring.

"I'm fine, Faria. I just need to get back in the water. We all do."

Shortly after Ander disappeared, Faria had visited each of the shifters to go over the Contract and have them sign it. It felt archaic, a strange tradition given what they learned about those who performed too much blood magic, but none of the shifters complained. They had sliced their fingers and pressed their blood to the parchment. Once it made contact, Faria felt a piece of her magic change. It was hard to describe, but a shift in energy that allowed her to feel the life force of the shifters. The most important aspect of the Contract was that once it was signed, no one could intentionally harm another without physically harming themselves. It was an excellent way to ensure safety but it also ensured conflict regulation, which was why it was imperative for the shifters to sign immediately. If there were any altercations due to prejudices, they could at least be assured that neither the shifters nor the Anestrians would be harmed.

A thick, down jacket hugged Marisa's body and a canvas bag sat at her feet. Faria looked again at those in training and noticed none of the shifters belonged to Marisa's clan. "Are you leaving already?"

"We are all ready to go, with your permission. It has been far too long since we've been in the ocean and we'll have a lot of training of our own to catch up on."

"Do you want me to send Nellie to you when she returns? Perhaps she can train with you and help—"

"Not to interrupt, but that girl needs to be in the air as a *Drogosterra*, as far from the water as possible."

"You know that creature can kill sirens," Faria said. She was concerned for her new friend and didn't want any more harm to come to the shifters. They had been through so much already, and with the rest of the war still to come, she didn't want to risk unnecessary loss.

"All the more reason for us to train as soon as possible. We have a few tricks up our sleeves." Marisa gave her a small smile. "I wanted to ask you a favor actually."

Faria swallowed a sigh. "Queen for half a day and already being asked favors?" She gave a small smile. "What can't wait until after?"

She wants you to come with us on the journey to save travel time and help me conserve energy.

Faria shifted her eyes to Hunter, his back facing her as he prepared for a new training rotation. *Is it really Marisa who wants this favor, or you?*

You have to learn how to sieve through space and this is the perfect opportunity to learn.

He wasn't wrong. There hadn't been time with everything that had happened in the past few hours. She still felt the magic from the acceptance ceremony the previous night settling into her. *Show me.*

Amusement trickled through their bond. *Does this mean you forgive me?*

It means show me, Prince. And I still haven't received an apology.

"Hello, Faria?" A hand waved in front of Faria's vision. "Did you hear anything I said?"

She focused her attention back on the shifter. "I'm sorry, Marisa, I've been so distracted. What was the favor?"

"I was hoping you'd come with us to Mercy Bay." Marisa tucked her dark hair behind her ear, hesitating. Faria had never seen her confidence shaken like that.

"The people at *Mentage* might be accepting of us now, and I know we just signed the Contract, but I think it would be helpful if you made an appearance, showed your support to have us there."

Faria was dumbfounded. She stared open-mouthed at her friend until she realized people were probably watching her and promptly closed it.

She knew, of course, that she was now the ruler of *all* of Anestra, but her mind had been so preoccupied with the people at *Mentage* and in Athinia that she never thought about those protecting the port city, or any of her borders. What type of information were they getting? Did they know the land accepted Faria and now she was technically their queen?

Did they need more weapons or armor? She knew nothing—

Calm yourself, Princess. Your father and I have everything sorted. We stationed well-trained soldiers all along the border, and the people in every city, village, and in between are up to date on the major events. We've had systems set in place for a long time.

Faria closed her eyes and breathed deeply, letting the scent of baking bread from the kitchens and the distant tweeting of birds in the Forest of the Dawn soothe her. The sun's rays washed her in their warmth. "Yes," she responded, "I think that's wise. I will go."

THIRTY

HUNTER

"Again."

"We've been at this for nearly an hour already," Faria complained. "It's wasting time. You should just start bringing them to Mercy Bay."

Hunter and Faria stood on the field at *Mentage* next to the training arena. Dozens of Anestrians milled about, either working on their training or else blatantly watching. The shifters waited on the side, a few packed belongings waiting by their feet. The sunlight grew shorter as Hunter tried to teach Faria how to access the Val's unique sieving power.

"They need their queen and you need to master your abilities. It wouldn't be advisable to have me transport you when you should have the same power. People might question your ability."

"They can question all they want," Faria replied, blowing a stray hair away from her face. "At least we would be there."

Hunter had a feeling the watchful eyes of Faria's people were making her somewhat nervous. He loved Faria, but she needed to learn how to block out the excess noise. At the moment, that meant everyone staring her down. It didn't matter if they watched the most powerful ruler they'd ever had flounder at her failed attempts at sieving. She had nearly limitless power and it would benefit them from seeing her start from the bottom and master it.

"You can do this, Faria. Close your eyes, find the place inside that is home to Val magic. Once you access it, you'll be able to do what you wish on a whim."

Faria closed her eyes.

Hunter watched her face relax into a blank slate. The worry lines around her mouth eased and as she exhaled, her shoulders relaxed from against her ears. Footsteps sidled up next to him, and Hunter turned to find Dennison. He wore thick leather armor and had a sword holstered to his hip. A bow was attached to a back quiver of arrows next to him. His eyebrows were drawn in a tight frown.

"What's wrong?" Hunter murmured. He carefully raised a wall in his mind to try to keep Faria from listening to his thoughts.

Dennison looked like he had bad news to share and he didn't want to alarm Faria or distract her with something that could be out of her control.

"We just had a report come in from one of our sentries in the northern outpost of the Forest," Dennison murmured. "Said he saw two

Drogosterra flying toward the sea."

"All right, so Nellie is doing what was asked of her. What's wrong?"

"He said one of them hovered in the air for a long while, unmoving, and then its wings collapsed and it fell from the sky."

Hunter's heart quickened. They couldn't lose anyone, least of all their most powerful shapeshifter or a *Drogosterra* that could change the tide of the battle to come. "Was it an attack?"

"He doesn't believe so. The larger *Drogosterra* swooped down to try to catch the smaller one. Said he'd never seen anything move so quickly, she was practically a blur in the sunlight. But then there was a thunderous sound, like a clap of thunder." Dennison paused, as if hesitant to speak the next words aloud. "They both disappeared."

"What do you mean, disappeared? Did they crash into the Forest?"

"No. He ran toward where they should have landed but there's no trace of them."

Hunter ran a hand through his hair, pulling slightly at the roots. There was more than one problem to worry about. Nellie had been sick, Hunter knew, and still, they asked her to train the *Drogosterra* for show, of all things. Hunter was angry at himself for not paying closer attention to the signs of illness, taking it more seriously. He thought the boost Faria had given her would have been enough.

But then to have them both disappear …

Faria and Hunter were already missing their son, and now their best friend was gone as well. The list of enemies who could have caused their disappearance was endless. The gods? The Elders? Did Darroc somehow figure out how to tap into the bond Ander had with his *Drogosterra*? It was impossible to know.

"What needs to be done?"

Dennison shook his head. "Someone needs to stay at *Mentage*. You and Faria leaving is risky enough, and I will not leave these people here without proper guidance. Besides, I'm the commander of the army and I need to remain where the army is. Endo is already on his way to the border of Wendorre, and Enis went to Mercy Bay ahead of you all. I'll send Faline and Wil, but no one else."

"We need to keep this quiet until we know what is happening." Hunter thought about it. While he knew Marisa and her clan needed to get to the ocean, he didn't feel right about all the detours. "Maybe I should stay and investigate—"

"Investigate what, *mate?*" Faria appeared between him and her father, a smug look on her face quickly replaced with suspicion. "Why are you two whispering over here? What happened?"

"What has happened, my darling," Dennison said, wrapping his arms around her, "is that you learned how to sieve over short distances." He kissed her rosy cheek and she smiled up at him.

Gods, she is so beautiful when she smiles, Hunter thought. He cleared his throat. "Do you think you can do it over long distances now?"

"I could probably sieve to the moon if I wanted to." Her arrogance was back in full force now that she'd mastered that skill.

He liked knowing that pieces of her personality were still the same despite the trauma she had endured.

"But yes, I think I can. Is it the same when traveling with someone?" Faria asked.

They gave a parting wave to the former king and walked to the waiting shifters, their anticipatory energy pulsating in the air. It was hard not to get wrapped up in their excitement. Even Faria seemed flush with it.

"It is the same, but more energy will be required to make up for the force of the energy displacement. Try with one person first."

Faria raised her eyebrow and grabbed onto Marisa and a younger girl, both with heavy bags in tow. "Race you there."

He was glad she felt playful, but Hunter had the weight of the world's problems caving in on him. He had to stay focused and find Nellie as soon as possible.

Still, he could play along. "You five,"—he pointed at the closest shifters to him and gave them a cunning smile—"let's show her how it's done."

Mercy Bay was Anestra's second largest city besides Athinia, though they couldn't have been more different. Athinia was a place for education and the arts. Entire blocks were carved out specifically for painters, musicians, jewelers, and the like. The largest library on this side of Carenek Peaks had hundreds of books devoted to the study of alchemy, sociology, architecture, medicine, and more. Restaurants from every culture imaginable filled the air with sweet and savory scents that enticed even the most stoic of people for a cheeky treat. Gardens and places of worship were sprinkled throughout the city, and any specialty shop imaginable had storefronts, ready to greet the public.

Mercy Bay was nothing of the sort. It was known as a city for workers, rather than the city for dreamers like Athinia. Situated directly on the Sea of Aurelia, the coastal city was damp with sea mist, and despite there being many restaurants to choose from, none could produce a scent that overtook the seaweed and brine that permeated the town. Trading ships were docked along the bay, mostly empty as the seamen made their way to the ample taverns, inns, and adult establishments to take care of their hunger and other needs.

Most of the city's shops were specialized for seafaring, such as nautical instruments, rigging, and various preserved foods. A large, octagonal building was located centrally in the city and acted as a community center of sorts. The Trading Council discussed trade policy there, weekly markets were held there, and jewels and other fine treasures were often sold or auctioned in that building.

Everyone lived and worked together, and those who didn't have money used the barter system, the same as in Athinia and throughout the rest of Anestra. It was always busy, no matter the time of day, but that particular day held more excitement with the threat of battle looming over them.

Hunter appeared next to Faria, giving her a smug smile at having sieved five others along with him, but she paid him no attention as her eyes were focused toward the ocean. He followed her gaze, wondering what caused the shocked look on her face when he saw rows of warlocks, elves, and humans on their knees in reverence to her. The warm sea breeze drifted through his hair, bringing with it the scent of brine.

"How long did it take them to notice you were standing here?"

Faria looked at the scores of Anestrians before her. Dozens more became aware of her presence and fell to their knees in the sand or grassy embankments. She lifted a brow at him. "Considering I landed right in the middle of some sort of mass pilgrimage, one second, maybe? Where did all these people come from?"

Hunter turned in a circle, taking in the overflowing cobblestone streets, the crowded docks, and people hanging out of the windows of the inns and adult establishments. No one had seen Faria in well over a year, even longer than that, and now their elusive queen was right in front of them. "They're here for you, Princess. Your father put out a call to arms. This looks to be anyone able to fight who didn't come before."

Why should they come for me? Faria's voice whispered through his mind. Her need for private conversation let him know her confidence from moments before had been shaken. *They don't even know me, not really.*

You are the queen, Faria. You hold immense power. It ripples off you in silent waves. Many of these people did not come before because they were scared and you were gone. Now you're here, unannounced, as they prepare for battle. It helps them to have proof of your power.

I should say something to them, she said. *What should I say?*

"Queen Faria." Enis ran up the grassy embankment, the sun glinting off her metal armor as she quickly bowed in front of both Faria and Hunter. "Thank the goddess you're here. There's something wrong with—"

"The water," Marisa and Faria said in unison.

As one, they stared off into the distance.

Marisa's breathing quickened. "There is something happening to the water."

"Yes, that," Enis agreed. "The fish have been gone for days, and—"

"No," Marisa breathed. She started vibrating, her body buzzing with some power of the shifters Hunter didn't understand. Marisa, transfixed, stepped toward the sea. It caused a ripple effect in the shifters next to him, and soon they all followed suit.

Faria's hand snatched onto Marisa's arm. "What is happening?"

Marisa pulled out of her grasp, and, glassy-eyed, resumed her walk. "Something comes. It is calling us. I don't think we can stop it."

"Try harder," Hunter forced the words from his mouth as he, too, tried to keep the shifters from leaving. A few Anestrians closest to them slowly rose to their feet, exchanging an uneasy look between each other. "You don't know what's out there," Hunter said.

"That's what I've been trying to tell you," Enis said, grabbing hold of the youngest shifter. The girl turned and bared razor-sharp teeth at Enis. "What the f—look, something has been happening to the water. It's more than the fish being gone. We have reason to believe there is a thinning of the veil between realms occurring right in the ocean. It's like what has happened near Widow's Passageway. Islands appearing out of nowhere, the bright colors of dulled—ouch!"

The girl nipped at Enis' fingers, blood shedding. Instantly, the young shifter fell to the ground, shrieking and grabbing her head as if it were splitting open. Tears leaked from her eyes as she begged, "Please make it stop, make it stop."

Murmurs rustled through the crowd as they watched the shifter writhe in pain. Faria knelt next to the girl and sent a comforting energy through her. "It will stop as soon as you no longer wish ill intent on another. This is what happens when you break the rules of the Contract. No one is allowed to purposely harm another, little one."

"I didn't, it wasn't, I'm sorry, Faria, I'm sorry. Please make it stop."

"It wasn't entirely her fault," Marisa said, her attention divided between her clanmate and the ocean. "There is a compulsion." A shudder ripped through her body. She gripped Hunter's shoulder, her nails sharpening to points and digging into his skin.

"A compulsion to protect or to do something stupid like walk directly into a trap?" Hunter asked. He controlled his breathing, trying not to let this unknown threat shake his composure.

Soft whimpers escaped the young shifter beside Faria as her pain subsided. Faria got back on her feet then stilled, her head cocked to the side as if hearing something no one else could. Hunter scanned the area, his senses hyper-aware as he tried to pick up on what worried her.

What is it? he whispered in her mind, unwilling to alarm those closest to them. *I can't sense anything.*

Faria's eyes shifted back and forth, seeing something that wasn't there. *Earthquake. Wave. Portal. Gods. Earthquake. Wave. Portal. Gods. Earthquake—*

Hunter shook his head, unable to make sense of her ramblings. He thought she was having a vision and tried to see the images her mind was interpreting, but he could grasp nothing but blurring images and a sense of foreboding. Faria gasped and shot toward the water, her body all but disappearing with her speed. Seconds later, rumbles reverberated from deep within the earth, sending a rippling effect through the ocean and onto the shoreline.

A few elves closest to the water shouted the alarm and lined up in a row next to Faria, who stood at the water's edge with her arms raised to her sides. Hunter still didn't know what she was prepared to do, but he understood well enough what the first two parts of her vision had been.

Earthquake. Wave.

The earthquake just happened and now …

"Get the children to safety," Hunter barked, immediately taking action. He didn't know how long they had. Seconds, perhaps, to do as many preventative measures as possible. Dark clouds rolled in from the horizon, lightning flashing in the menacing sky. "Shield your homes, the businesses. Now!"

Warlocks and elves scrambled to do his bidding, falling over each other while trying to help those who didn't have the proper magical ability to do it themselves.

What do you need, Princess? Tell me how to help.

A tinge of annoyance trickled its way down the bond. Her thoughts were still scattered and she no doubt classified him as a distraction. Faria turned her face to the sky as the first few droplets fell from the rapidly approaching storm.

Waves crashed angrily along the shore and the rock cliff face outlining Mercy Bay. Salt and mist sprayed and rain pelted down against the ships docked at the port as they swayed listlessly to the side. The shifters broke free of Hunter and Enis' grip and followed Marisa into the quickly receding shoreline.

"No!" Faria shouted over the noise of the storm. "Do not enter those waters!"

Thunder crashed overhead followed by an unnatural silence.

Hunter searched the skies and along the horizon for whatever was to come. Was it the Elders? They had a flare for dramatics. Or was it something more? Farrah and Alexei, come to ruin their creations? Or worse. Whatever portal Enis referred to that Faria saw in her vision. He knew of many realms, but none were accessed through an underwater portal. The Gate of all Realms was the only way to access them unless one was a Val with the power to sieve through realms.

It's coming, Hunter. It's going to destroy this city and then the creatures will come. I've seen it all.

We won't let it happen, Princess. He knew there was nothing they could do, though. Their power would be completely decimated from trying to hold that amount of pressure at bay. For all the magic they had, they still were not gods.

I'm going to try something. Trust me.

Do not give too much of yourself, Faria. We do not know what this is and you will be needed elsewhere. I will—

I will save my people, Hunter.

Faria glanced over her shoulder, searching until her eyes landed on him. Waves of love crashed through the bond, more than she had revealed in over a year. It was the first time he grasped the power of her feelings for him. He was overcome, wondering how a person could love another with so much intensity, but then he realized she mirrored what he felt for her as well.

Years of denying and tempering feelings rushed through him and he sent it right back to her. Everything neither of them had been willing to say was understood in that moment. He poured his forgiveness to her and she took it, giving back to him endless acceptance of who he was and what they could be in the future.

The hard edge to her gaze softened and then she turned back to the ocean, to the ever shrinking shoreline, to the powerful force of nature that was moments away from shattering them all, and she let her power loose.

THIRTY ONE

NELLIE

oly heck on wheels, I'm dead.

Nellie tried to stretch but found herself with little feeling from the neck down, striking a sense of deja vu from a few days ago. She refused to open her eyes to look upon whatever horrors had befallen her and instead tried to make sense of where she was. Judging by the soft padding beneath her and the bright sunlight threatening to pierce her closed eyelids, she'd guess she was still outside. The scent of wildflowers and sea mist surrounded her and a soft *whump* of hot air covered her naked body every few moments. Apart from what she knew to be the sound of the *Drogosterra* shifting her body weight on the grass, everything else was eerily silent.

Nellie mentally took stock of her injuries as much as she could without the ability to move outside of breathing. Her head felt as though it'd been run over by a semi, her throat grated like sandpaper when she tried to swallow, and she had the extreme urge to brush her teeth. She couldn't tell if anything was broken. Dizzy spells wracked her, and she realized that even if she had the ability to move, she was likely too weak to do so.

A stray thought filled her with dread. Had she caught the virus plaguing the shifters on Earth? Were these her last moments, frozen in time, in whatever realm they were in?

Speaking of last moments, Nellie remembered flying with the *Drogosterra*, of her telling Nellie that there was no need for training because *Drogosterra* were created for battle and protection, and then Ander's sweet dragon diving to save Nellie as she passed out.

But, even if the *Drogosterra* was able to catch her, that didn't explain where they were or how they got there. Nellie had been on a full death dive toward the Forest of the Dawn, but she knew with absolute certainty that was not where she lay.

A shadow passed over her face, easing the aching brightness enough so she was encouraged to slowly peel her eyes open.

"What the fuck!" Nellie exclaimed, shock rippling through her at the sea of jade surrounding a halo of sun staring down at her. "Ander?"

"I didn't realize you knew that word," he replied, a tight smile straining his face. "I thought you were more on the prudish side."

"Was it all the times you saw me naked or my offer to let you ride me that gave off that impression?"

"It was this crimson blushing your cheeks while talking about it."

"Ha. I am not blushing," Nellie stammered. "And for the love of the goddess, can you please explain to me why in all heck I am in the buff, again, and how you are here?"

"What I'd like to know is why you're naked with Rhayna again. This is a strange habit of yours and I don't kink shame, but I don't think I can allow it to go on much further."

Ander's head dipped out of her line of sight, but she felt feather-light touches against her bare midriff followed by a warm caress trickling just underneath her skin. She was faint with relief over seeing him alive. If they were alive. Wait, was she dead and he was her afterlife because … she could do worse. No complaints from her.

"Hey, loverboy, not that I'm not thrilled to see you, and I'm glad you finally gave your dragon a name, but how did you get here? And where is here, exactly?"

"We're still in Anestra, on the other side of Carenek Peaks. How I got here is a long and complicated story. How we got to this particular location, was thanks to a god, and to answer your previous question, I had to strip your clothes off to properly heal you."

He came back to her line of vision, his forehead creased with worry lines. Nellie thought it odd someone his age would have them, but after all he'd been through … "Ander, what happened to you? Where's Darroc?"

He ran his hand through his hair and for the first time, Nellie noticed sweat beading along his temples. He wasn't wearing his signature leather jacket from what she could see, and if the dark circles under his eyes were any indication, he hadn't slept for days.

"Let's talk about me after. The state you're in is … concerning. I'm releasing some of the magic I used to numb you. I need to see what your pain level is at."

"Since when did you become a wonder doctor?" Nellie asked through gritted teeth as the pain she thought was tolerable amped up. "Gods it feels like acid is running through me. What the fu—fudge is happening?"

"How long have you had these black ribbons flowing from the source of the attack?"

Black ribbons? She could barely remember her own name at the moment, and he wanted her to remember if she noticed skin discoloration? She was a shapeshifter. Her skin always changed. "Uh, listen, Ander, I'm sure you've been through a lot, but you know what I am, right? That, uh … It's sort of my job to—"

"Hey, smartass, look at your chest. How long has it been like this? Days?"

Nellie whimpered in pain as she leaned forward enough to look down and audibly gasped. The wound on her chest looked almost like a three-pronged plug that had been impressed on her chest bone. Tiny pinpricks where the razor-sharp teeth of the creature's tentacle had attached were a deep crimson, and extending from them was exactly what he had said; dozens of thin black trails spread out toward her shoulders and down her stomach. She tried to sit up to see more but screamed in agony at the attempt. It felt if she had no skin, as if every nerve were exposed to the elements.

"Shit," Ander said. He started pacing in a circle, his hands clasped on the back of his neck. "How the fuck did he give me the power with no explanation on how to access or use it."

She wanted to ask who "he" was but was distracted as Rhayna shifted to the side, revealing a giant unmoving waterfall. Nellie carefully lifted herself on one elbow, sucking in air at the stabs of pain with the movement, to get a better look. Looming over them to her right was a sheer rock cliff that extended at least a hundred feet into the sky, if she had to guess, and continued down beyond what she could see. To her left was a wide field of wildflowers with rolling hills in the distance, and above her was a brilliant blue sky.

Nellie looked back at the waterfall. The unmoving water wasn't quite frozen. There was no sheen to it the way it would be if it were made of ice, but why else would it pause in its movement? The water should have been thunderous as it crashed against whatever pool of water was below them. Unease gripped her.

"Are you sure we're still in Anestra," Nellie whispered, suddenly afraid to use her normal tone, "because this is freaky."

"Yeah, if you think that's weird, wait until you see what's past those hills."

Nellie didn't want to know what other sick surprise was lurking on that side of Carenek Peaks. Perspiration licked at her the more she thought about it. "Ander, um, I think we should go."

"Hey, are you okay? Your heart is racing." Ander hovered his hands over her chest. "These black veins are starting to pulsate."

"Why am I still naked?" Nellie asked breathlessly. She tried to suck down as much air as she could before she suffocated. Night fell before her eyes, and she thought she heard a strange howling in the distance. "What's that noise?"

"Nellie." Ander slapped her cheek a few times. "Nellie, open your eyes! There is no noise besides us talking and breathing. We are the only ones awake."

"Awake?" Nellie slurred. "It's dark now and I'm still … It's cold."

A wet snout pushed against her body, the touch causing spasms of pain to ripple through her. Nellie opened her eyes and bright sunlight filled her vision again. She tried to turn her head to the side, but the movement was slower than her brain wanted her to go. Rhayna huffed warm breath over her. A drop of saliva splashed down her arm.

Ander muttered to himself, "Why would he give me … as if I should just know." He ran his hands through his hair, pulling at the ends in frustration. "He said I needed to save you. He rescued me, told me to save you, and now we're here and I can't fucking save you."

"Language, loverboy," Nellie whispered. "I'm a strong independent woman. I don't need saving. I need … clothes." Yes. That was what she needed, of all the things she could have wished for in that moment. But she didn't see the purpose in keeping her exposed, unless … "Unless you love looking at me, in which case, ask for my permission, you dirty dog."

"Nellie. You. Are. Dying. You're naked so I could follow the source of the black veins, and now I must use them as a gauge for whether what I'm doing is working or not. We've been here for hours and—"

Ander's voice dimmed as the howling Nellie thought she heard became louder, echoing in the haunting stillness. Her eyes shot open, but the emptiness pressed further in on her. She remembered that chilling sound and a trickle of fear spread through her.

"I think … perhaps … Darroc—" She couldn't finish her sentence.

The thought of Darroc or any of his creatures arriving in Anestra now, when she was unable to see or shift and according to Ander, was dying, was more than terrifying. Nellie reached around her, feeling for something solid to grab to help pull herself up, but she could barely tell if she was lifting her arms.

"Nellie, stop flopping around for a minute, I need to try something," Ander's voice was clear next to her ear and she could smell the perspiration coming off of him. "I'm going to numb you again so you hopefully won't feel much."

"But ... Darroc ..."

"He. Isn't. Here," Ander said, his voice straining with the effort of whatever he was doing to her. "I would know."

"Stop," Nellie said weakly. "Ander, I think ... I think it's too late for me." She knew death was hovering above her, waiting for the perfect moment to be let in. She didn't have the strength to fight it, and if Darroc was on his way, Ander needed to conserve whatever energy he had left after being imprisoned for however long it was, rather than wasting it on her.

"No," Ander forced out the word, letting the stubbornness he undoubtedly got from his parents shine through. "I have the ability. He said it. I felt it and can feel it still, burning within me. I know I can ... I can save you."

What words did she have to express her final thoughts? There weren't any that would encompass the entirety of what she felt, for him, for Faria, for Anestra—the people and land that saved her when she thought she was left for dead. Whether the Fates orchestrated her arrival to that realm or if it was sheer luck that the Gate of All Realms dumped her on

Anestra's doorstep that day, she didn't know, but Nellie was grateful for the people she met, the experiences she had, and the life she lived. She wasn't ready to call it quits—her body was doing that for her—but she could enter the Beyond knowing she tried to live her best life.

"No offense, loverboy, but you said you've been at it for hours. And I can't—" Nellie stumbled over her words as another wave of pain racked through her. "I can't have you put all your energy into me when Darroc—"

"Dammit, Nellie!" Ander yelled.

Beside Nellie, Rhayna huffed an irritated breath, or at least Nellie imagined she was irritated. Female solidarity and all.

"I already told you, I'd know if he were here," Ander said.

"I can hear his creatures," she whispered, tired of conversation. "If you were saved, wouldn't he know where you were?" Nellie's breathing became labored and her thoughts slowed to a trickle. "I need my necklace. I don't want to leave without my mother's necklace."

"You're wearing it, Nells." Ander brushed the hair back from her forehead, the touch little more than feathers drifting along her skin. "Don't you dare give up now. We need you." There was a slight pause as Ander pressed his cheek against hers, his voice a low growl in her ear, "I need you."

Nellie tried to quip something clever back to him, but she couldn't bring herself to speak anymore. Or think. Or breathe, even. *It's nice to be needed*, she thought. Even nicer was not having to do anything anymore.

A low lamenting growl brought her back from the brink of nothingness as a wet snout shuffled across her face. She couldn't think why Rhayna was so sad. She wondered if something happened to—

"No!"

An impact across her chest sent reverberations through her body and she had a silly thought of the audacity Ander had to not let her die in peace.

"I have the power of the gods inside me. I'm not letting you do this."

A muffled crackle sounded in Nellie's ears. A spark of warmth entered her fingertips, trailing up her arm and toward her chest. The stabbing pain she felt minutes ago receded into a dull throb. Dark shadows displayed across her eyes. It was the first time she could see since losing her vision, though it had still barely returned. A bright light flared in her short range of sight. A rush of power swam through her.

"It's working," Ander said. He pressed his hands along her exposed chest.

She longed to make an inappropriate comment, but she was more excited that she could *feel* his hands against her chest.

"The lines are fading. Nellie, I think I'm doing it."

"Great," Nellie whispered. "Really didn't want to die naked in this creeptastic place." She swallowed thickly, her throat feeling like she ingested cat litter. "You wouldn't happen to have water on you, would you?"

Nellie slowly turned her head toward Ander and blinked against the growing brightness of her vision. Thank the goddess she was starting to see again, and what a sight to open up to. Ander's profile was little more than a silhouette against the muted sky but the golden halos in his eyes blazed with a flickering flame.

"Little busy here," Ander panted. Sweat dripped down his temples and as her vision cleared, she noticed how pale and sickly he looked. "I think I've almost got it."

Nellie's leg twitched in response and she noticed her body bathed in heat that had been absent previously. She felt warmer than she had in days. "Maybe you should slow down, loverboy," she said, concern growing for him the longer she stared at him. "You look like how I feel."

"That's a strange way to thank the person saving your life."

Nellie attempted to sit up for the first time since regaining consciousness on that side of the Carenek peaks, gingerly raising her head while Rhayna assisted with the tip of her wing to Nellie's shoulders. She leaned back, using it as a brace, and waited for a wave of dizziness to pass.

Ander's hands hovered over her chest, a fiery glow reflecting against her skin. He pressed against her, and she felt flames lick her wound, cauterizing it closed. At once, the dark veins running through her disappeared.

With a gasp, Ander collapsed to the ground next to her, breathing heavily with the force of the exertion the healing required.

"Are you all right?" Nellie asked. "Because you can't heal me just to die. Pretty sure that's against the rules somewhere."

A chuckle escaped him, then another, until Ander was overcome with uncontrollable laughter. His eyes still glowed, but the fire in his hands had faded. Despite that, a light seemed to shine through him and the more he displayed his unguarded joy, the more beautiful he became.

As much as she wanted to bask in that rare show of happiness, Nellie was tired, weak, thirsty, and still more exposed than she wanted to be. "All right ... first, toss me my shirt. I refuse to allow you the honor of looking at all this hotness right now. Second, what's so funny?"

Ander passed Nellie her shirt and shook his head, staring earnestly into her eyes. "I don't know how I did it but gods, it was incredible. The rush of power, the joy I felt as it yielded to what I wanted."

"Okay, you're starting to sound like a villain mastermind in the making. Let's go back to more sane territory and tell me from the beginning what happened."

Ander sat up and faced her, a hint of a smile remaining on his lips. "I was trapped for days. Darroc, who is a complete psychopath by the way, left me in the dark, magically chained to a wall in a cage of thick ice and no way out. All of my abilities were shut and I was dying of hypothermia. And then he came."

Nellie was horrified by what he'd experienced in just a short time, but she leaned forward, riveted by his story. "Who came?"

"Alexei."

"Pardon me? Farrah's concubine, the creator of all of this." Nellie gestured wildly. Rhayna readjusted to keep her from tipping over. "He appeared to you? What happened?"

"He told me you were dying and he sent me to save you. He freed me, Nellie, from Darroc. His compulsion, the blood connection we had, the magic keeping me locked away in that hellscape of a realm. He gave me a piece of the Eternal Flame—and gods the pain! But he said it was the only way to save you and then he sieved me from my cell and grabbed you two out of thin air and plopped us here before disappearing again."

"He gave you the Flame? So that's why you kept going on about having the power of the gods."

"It's just a small piece of it, but yeah. And he was right about me saving you, although we would have saved hours if he'd taken the time to tell me how."

"If he could do all that—give you a piece of his power, snatch us out of the air, save both of us from dying—why hasn't he gotten rid of Darroc or the Elders?"

"He said this was his version of helping and their energy has been focused elsewhere."

Nellie considered that alarming thought. If there was something more vicious that required their attention than eliminating Darroc or the Elders, could they stand a chance against what was to come? She shivered, not from the shadow of death, but the fear of the unknown. Nellie looked around at the unsettling stillness of their surroundings. It could have been beautiful and probably was once, but this place felt like a tomb despite evidence of fervent life beneath the immobility.

"We should get out of here. I feel like I've been licking sand for the past hour. I need fresh, not frozen water. And we should probably check in with everyone. I really thought I heard Darroc's creatures." Nellie gripped her necklace, a comfort to her as she shook off the ghost of the reaper. "I have a bad feeling—wait."

Ander stood and with an assist from Rhayna then helped Nellie to her feet as well. "Are you sure you're okay to go? You can ride Rhayna and I won't even make a joke about it."

"No," Nellie faced Ander, her mouth dropping in horror. "You said you're free of him. The blood bond is broken."

"Yeah ... so?"

"So there's no way to tell …"

Rhayna's sudden growl finished her thought as an apparition appeared next to them.

Darroc's cruel voice sliced through the silence, "Well, isn't this interesting."

THIRTY TWO

FARIA

Muffled shouting. Rain pelted her face, soaking her clothes and seeping into her skin. Ships creaked through gusts of wind. Despite all that, an eerie silence descended as the shoreline rapidly receded.

The destruction she saw in her vision was unlike anything Faria had ever witnessed before. She wasn't under the false impression that she alone could stop the devastation heading their way. Nothing but the gods themselves could control an ocean. But if she could at least hold it at bay long enough to give the others a chance of surviving, then she would do whatever it took.

She had the ability to control multiple elements. She now had the knowledge that a little blood magic could strengthen one's powers. It was all the encouragement she needed.

Faria let go of the chains she kept locked on the source of her magic and finally let the full strength of it loose.

The sudden onslaught of unbidden power brought a rush of euphoria, and even with her feet sinking in the muddy sand, hail pelting her face and the terror of not knowing who was powerful enough to cause such a catastrophic event was nothing compared to how good it felt to have the full strength of her magic running through her veins. Faria squinted through the downpour and watched with stunned horror as a mountain of water rippled and grew until nothing but a black fortress pressed steadily toward the shoreline. Her power gushed from her in a bright violet light, meeting their impending doom with an electric crackle that echoed like a lashing whip.

"Line up!" Faria screamed over the crashing thunder. Lightning flashed and for a moment she thought she saw shadows of movement in the wave, but the light faded too quickly. "Those with elemental magic. Steady the rain! Calm the winds!"

Watching her power clash and travel down the tidal wave gave her a heady feeling. It was one thing to feel the strength of her magic but another to watch it in action. Still, even the momentary pause it gave the water wasn't enough to save her people. She needed more, something stronger.

Faria thought of ways she could combine her power with those of the other elves on the frontline with her but immediately rescinded that idea. She didn't want to be like the gods, forcing the Fae to leech their power into the land to sustain the magic.

The only person she was willing to sacrifice was herself, but Faria had the sense to recognize it wasn't the time for that. She still needed to release the warlocks' magic in Wendorre and save the Fae, and she refused to allow whatever this was to defeat her before all her people were safe and free from this terror.

Faria's breathing was strained and beads of sweat mingled with the rain pelting her forehead. The longer she blasted her magic, the more her energy depleted.

Alarmed shouts reached her and though she didn't want to break her concentration, Faria needed to make sure there was no other immediate danger to focus her attention on.

A band of warlocks encircled the sirens, trying however they could to prevent them from entering the water. Faria focused her attention on Marisa, who was writhing on the ground. As clan leader, she should have been able to hold the others at bay, but the more Faria watched, the more she realized her friend was in trouble.

Marisa whipped her head to the side, making eye contact with Faria. She gasped as she watched in horror as Marisa's body flashed between human and what Faria had to assume was her siren form. Claws and razor-sharp teeth sprouted and receded, glistening pearlescent scales erupted on her skin before disappearing. Most shocking was Marisa's dark hair and eyes transitioning to hot pink, a horrifying contrast to their current darkness.

Faria spared another glance over her shoulder searching for Hunter. Once she saw he was sufficiently distracted, she turned to the elf next to her. She quickly took in his features and demeanor to determine if he was willing to do what was asked of him. His golden hair was dappled with white, letting her know he was at least a few centuries old. Though he was tall and broad-shouldered, exhaustion was evident in the stoop of his shoulders and the way his arms shook from his usage of power.

"Excuse me," Faria yelled over the storm. "What's your name, sir?"

"Gordon, your highness," he shouted back.

"Gordon, I need you to do me a favor, immediately."

Gordon dropped his arms to his side, heaving a bit as he did so. Rubbing the water from his eyes, he said, "Anything, my queen. What is it?"

Faria licked her lips. She could taste the salt of the ocean and an undercurrent of fire. She hesitated slightly, worried others would overhear. "Do you see that dagger next to my hip? The one with the black hilt?"

Gordon looked at the dagger, then back into her eyes. "Yes, what of it?"

She swallowed, both nervous about her request and with the increased desire to quench her thirst. Her magic was dehydrating her. "Remove it and slice my palm open."

"Your highness?" he questioned, looking at her uncertainly, then shifted his gaze off into the distance. "Are you sure?"

"I said immediately, Gordon." She searched for Hunter, who suddenly stiffened and glanced over his shoulder. *Goddess above*, she needed Gordon to hurry before Hunter realized what she wanted. "Now. Please."

Gordon grabbed the dagger from her holster. After a moment of contemplation, he moved quicker than she would have expected and slashed open Faria's palm. Her magic faltered, the violet light that was once poured from her now staggered against the tidal wave.

Faria felt Hunter slam against her mind, trying to stop her or speak reason with her before she slid her palm to the ground, but he was too late. She knelt on one knee, held one hand in front of her, and slammed the other against the muddy sand, allowing her essence to pour into the earth. Her energy, waning only moments ago, resurged throughout her body.

At once, the world froze. The wind stopped shouting and the rain held in place, translucent droplets hovering in midair. Horrifying deja vu of the other side of Carenek Peaks flashed through her mind, and for a moment regret beat at her chest. She was using blood magic, she knew, and though it wasn't her first time, she was now doing it with full access to her power. What if she did as the gods did and surrendered everyone to a frozen prison without their consent?

"What the absolute *fuck* did you do, Princess?" Hunter appeared next to her, holding two children in his arms.

"Get them away from here," Faria gasped, barely sparing him a glance. The last thing she needed was to have her anger mixed with the blood magic. Who knew what catastrophe would result from that? "It's too dangerous!"

"Yes. It is too dangerous," he said through clenched teeth. "Do you even know the repercussions if your blood mingles with that dark magic?"

A memory from a lifetime ago resurfaced from when she tried to figure out where the wasting spell on her land had come from. Then, she could tell the dark magic was reading her own, though she stopped it before it could get a firm grip on her.

Hunter was right; she had no idea what would result from her mixing her blood with this land.

"Look at Marisa, Hunter. She's practically feral." Faria released the walls in her mind, just enough to speak to Hunter without feeling his simmering rage. *We have absolutely no idea what will happen to them if they enter those waters. Something is calling to them. Focus on what's most important.*

What's most important, Hunter said, his voice a bomb moments from detonating, *is that the queen of this land and the most powerful being outside of the gods just released her magic into waters infested with dark magic. The irresponsibility—*

Faria slammed the walls back in place, effectively shutting Hunter's chastising out, and allowing her magic to carry on the currents until she reached the point where it clashed against the wave. She closed her eyes, curiously feeling for the source of dark magic. She felt an answering interest and cautiously pulled back, just enough to get her bearings.

Confusion filled her as she tentatively reached out again, feeling for Darroc's energy. It normally felt akin to brimstone and fetid sewage with a mask of something sickeningly cloying. This, however, was alluring, seductive. It was power with ripples of menace, though it didn't feel like dark magic. It simply … was.

She pulled back, reorienting herself back in her body, refocusing on her surroundings. Her magic was still flowing from her, only this time she let it simmer in the currents and willed them to neutralize the water. The eerie silence continued as she poured everything she was into that single task, but still, the wave did not budge. There was a pause and Faria felt like whoever's power she was trying to combat was waiting to see what she could do. Whatever it was found her amusing.

Fuck this.

Fury rose in Faria as she thought of the demented being who found amusement in the devastation of her country. Amusement over killing thousands, including innocent children. Amusement over her pouring every ounce of her essence just to keep this piece of her country alive. Faria's *malosin obsinae* rose to the surface, spurred by the flame of fury burning through her. She felt it press against the boundaries of her skin as if it were looking to be free of its physical cage and Faria welcomed it, allowing the darkness to spread throughout her body and beyond. The light of her magic changed from bright violet to a deep crimson as the shadows from within mixed with her power.

And then she felt it—a taunting.

Feelings that were not her own rippled through the currents in the ocean, seeping into her magic, drawing into her being. It was laughing at her. Faria's own emotions were starting to spring out of control and she watched electricity crackle between her fingertips, then shoot up to the sky followed by a crash of thunder.

This time, she created the storm. This time, she manifested the gusts of wind shooting toward her unnamed enemy. This time, she controlled where the rain slaughtered the ground.

Faria watched as the sparks between her fingers shifted to black flame then heard the shouts of surprise as she rose in the air, aided by her dark phoenix wings. And from them burst forth more of that crimson light, illuminating the waters in a bloody shadow, halting the progression of the wave, forcing it to turn back to calm waters once again. Faria knew she'd won—not when cheers erupted, not when the compulsion on Marisa's clan ceased, but when that forsaken laughter turned to surprise and disappeared altogether.

It was then Faria recognized how spent she was, how much energy had been used, and when the phoenix wings her *malosin obsinae* formed finally drifted back into her body, Faria crumpled to the ground.

Elf and warlock alike rushed to her side, but none were quicker than Hunter, who pressed his hand against the back of her neck and ran a healing wave through her. Though her breathing was still ragged, she no longer saw spots before her eyes and Faria watched as the cut on her hand stitched together as if it was never there to begin with. Knowing she was healed, at least physically, Faria met Hunter's eyes and gave a slight nod.

They just witnessed a miracle fit for the gods, Princess. It's okay to show them weakness along with your strength.

It isn't that, Faria responded. She had an uneasy feeling. The seas were calm, the storms had cleared, yet there was something off. It felt like whoever or whatever it was *let* her control the tidal wave. She was a player in their game, not the victor. *These celebrations make me uneasy. Something still isn't right.*

She thought back to the vision that flashed just before the wave came. Earthquake. Wave. Then there was—

A shocking column blue beamed up from the center of the ocean straight into the sky and extended off to the horizon. As the flashing light receded, an otherworldly image appeared in the sky of an underwater fortress illuminated by sporadic eerie green light. It wasn't that the image of an underwater scene was written in the sky that was frightening, but that it was clear a portal to another realm had opened and they had seemingly no way to close it. Screams of terror resounded in the night.

On instinct, Faria sieved to Marisa and tried to grab the closest siren to her to get them out of whatever harm was on the way. As she reached for her, a chilling note rang out by a single voice. It was soon joined by another until an ethereal chiming echoed along the seafront. Faria turned in a circle searching for where the voices came from, but nothing seemed out of place. Scores of Anestrians lined the beach and beyond the city's cobblestone streets. Buildings glimmered with the sheen of protection and warlocks stood guard next to them, seemingly ready to use what little magic they had to reinforce the shields' weaknesses.

Archers were scattered on the docks, bows at the ready. Wind whipped through flags on ships, the breeze carrying with it the same scent as the magic she felt. It was musky, seductive, addicting.

Hunter appeared next to her, his nostrils flared. "I just warned your father that Mercy Bay is under attack and to prepare for a battle at *Mentage*, just in case. What is that smell?"

"I don't know … Marisa, *no!*"

The siren had reached forward and was mere inches from touching the water when the force of Faria's command resulted in her using the Voice—an ability to inspire compulsion. The recipient had no choice but to listen to what was commanded of them, yet when Faria expected Marisa to comply, there was little more than slight hesitation before she shifted into a beautifully scaled creature and slid into the water. The rest of her clan followed suit, despite Faria's attempt at Voicing them as well.

"What's wrong, Hunter? Why isn't it working?"

"It's that singing. Where is coming from?" His eyes glowed with golden light.

Faria watched as his canines sharpened into points like that of the Fae. His features grew starker and his *malosin* spread out from him, causing those nearby to cower in fear.

He continued, his voice taking on a guttural tone, "They must be stopped."

"What's happening to you?"

Just moments ago, Faria thought she had everything under control, if only for a second. She'd saved the city, she protected her people. Now the sirens were outside of her reach and she had no way to get to them. A portal to another realm was open for the gods knew what creatures to fall through. And that incessant music, the seductive scent, overpowered the rest of her rational thought.

"I was made to protect you," Hunter said. "This is what I must become."

"Look!" someone shouted. "What is that?"

"It's a monster!" another called out.

Faria sighed in exasperation before facing the ocean again. She was exhausted, thirsty, and drenched from the storm, and she knew her magic was down to the dregs after what she had just done. Still, she had to deal with the choice she made and had to confront whatever was to come with a steady hand.

Darkness had descended and storm clouds lingered, blocking any light the moon could have provided, meaning only the sinister glow from the other realm provided any clarity into what might be lurking within the depths. Faria had to wait only a minute before she saw what brought fear into her people's voices.

Appearing from the water was the most frighteningly beautiful face Faria had ever seen. Dark hair, glowing cerulean eyes, delicate cheekbones. Its body soon appeared, and though it was shaped as an Anestrian would be, she knew it was not of her realm. It smiled at her, revealing a mouth full of razor-like teeth. From behind its arms snapped two long tentacles which it aimed at her. Faster than light, Hunter swiped the blade of his sword through the tentacles before they could implant themselves on her. Unholy screeching filled with pain and rage echoed in the night, and as the creature shrieked, Faria noticed at least a dozen more appearing from beneath the surface of the water.

She looked down at the tentacle twitching in the sand and noticed the sharp prongs on the underside of them. It was shaped in the same pattern as Nellie's wound.

"They are what attacked Nellie that day. The creatures that nearly killed her." Faria started to shake with heart-stopping terror. "Those guides that tried to heal her. They said—"

"It was lucky she wasn't a siren or else she'd be dead," Hunter finished for her.

"Oh, gods." Faria tried to step toward the ocean to meet the creatures head-on, despite having no idea what they were capable of besides spreading the poison within their sharpened prongs.

A hand on her shoulder stopped her.

"The sirens must fend for themselves, Faria. Until we can control the threat of the hundreds here."

"Sacrifice the few for the many?" The thought made her sick.

"You know it's what we must do," he said. "Besides …" He removed one of his Val daggers dripped in *Drogosterra* blood to reinforce the strength of the blade and whipped it at one of the creatures nearing the shoreline. He hit his mark straight through the creature's left eye. It staggered but kept walking.

A volley of arrows soon followed.

Hunter looked at her, a feral gleam in his eyes. "The war has begun."

THIRTY THREE

ANDER

How could he have been so stupid?

The moment Ander was free, everything had been a whirlwind of pain, stress, and grief. He'd just gone through immense torture at Alexei's hands having the Flame placed within him, then was transported without a moment of reprieve to the other side of Carenek Peaks and dropped in front of a field of immobilized Fae. He had scrambled away from them, but before he could shake off the horror and dread, he'd heard Rhayna's lament and found her and Nellie just behind a hill in a field of perpetual sunlight. The scene felt wrong, to have golden beams shine upon a body that was gray and nearly lifeless.

Ander hadn't had time to think beyond trying whatever he could to access the power of the Flame and save Nellie as Alexei said he'd be able to do.

Not once did he think about what being broken from Darroc's blood bond truly meant. Even though Ander was no longer forced to do Darroc's bidding, that also meant he had no idea where Darroc was at any given time or all the ways Darroc could spy on him.

And now, with Darroc's apparition in front of him, he realized his greatest mistake. He thought he'd be free of Darroc, but this was the evil warlock who raised him, who tortured and murdered innocent souls of every species to create the perfect monster, who transformed himself into something other. To think that Darroc wouldn't have a way to find him, or at the very least, spy on him, was incredibly short-sighted.

Ander whipped around to the sound of Darroc's voice, stepping in front of Nellie to protect her from both the apparition and the very real creature growling in front of them. "How did you find me?"

Darroc's image was that of his disguise as the Prince of Wendorre. His face was young and deeply tanned with sharp features and bright purple eyes. He was dressed in a simple tunic and leggings and even appeared to be wearing boots. He shimmered in the ghostly way of apparitions being there in conscious thought but not physically, but Ander didn't miss the crazed look in his eyes.

"The better question, son, is how did you break free? And *when* did you receive the Eternal Flame?"

The creature standing next to Darroc bared its teeth, its mouth frothing against its muzzle. Rhayna growled behind him in warning, but it only seemed to excite the beast further. Ander took in its matted fur, the lopsided way it held its body. He noticed a gash on its side, deep enough for it to have been a killing wound, with the area around it festered and black. This creature shouldn't have been alive, and yet it was animated in front of them.

Nellie had caught on to a similar thought. "Hey," she said, "shouldn't that thing be dead?"

"Ah," Darroc's voice said, his gaze zeroing in on Nellie.

Ander stiffened and moved again so she was out of sight. Rhayna took her wing and used it as a shield to further block Nellie from Darroc's view.

Nellie's muffled "Hey" was eclipsed by Darroc's next words: "You know I spent months wondering why your scent was so familiar though I'd never seen you before. But then I heard you speak and—" Darroc cut off, laughing menacingly. "I knew immediately where you came from. She was clever to hide you from me."

Ander's panic rose and his need to protect Nellie was at the forefront. She'd already known Darroc had murdered her mother, but Ander had been certain that Darroc never knew Nellie's origins. If he put two and two together …

"I know what you did to her, you sick freak," Nellie's voice was strong behind the barrier of Rhayna's wing.

"Tsk, tsk. That's no way to speak to your … creator," the declaration rang in the still air.

Ander had known Darroc created all shapeshifters. He had abandoned what he thought were failed creations on Earth and eventually, they evolved into the clans Nellie grew up with. He wasn't sure how much Nellie knew of her history, but Darroc loved to hear himself talk so he was undoubtedly ready to reveal his plan. Ander couldn't help but feel this was just a distraction for something more. He looked at their surroundings but nothing shifted, and there were no other sounds besides the deranged psychopath in front of him and the creature growling beside him.

"I know you created the shapeshifters," Nellie said. "You want me to call you daddy or something?"

"That's not my thing," Darroc replied, a crazed smile on his face. "And that's not what I meant. I gave Maggie the same spell I put on Faria when I'd thought she had become impregnated with my child. But then she somehow escaped the cell I kept her in and was able to evade me. For sixteen years I searched for her and my child, yet when I caught up to her, she revealed that she terminated the pregnancy and then I tore her heart out." Darroc cackled.

"You sick motherf—"

"What do you want, Darroc?" Ander cut in. The last thing he wanted was for Nellie to fall into revenge mode when they still weren't sure what they were up against. "Why aren't you physically here?"

Darroc gave a long-suffering sigh. "I expected more from this conversation. Oh, well."

The creature paced around them and Ander felt Rhayna focus on it so Ander wouldn't have to.

"If I were really there, I'd never have learned that you hold a piece of the Flame, now. Excellent information to have. The second reason," Darroc paused a moment as if listening to something on his end. "Ah, yes. Does the name Faline mean something to anyone?"

Nellie's cursing ceased and thunder rumbled from deep inside Rhayna. Bile rose in Ander's throat. He willed Darroc not to say the next words that threatened to leave his mouth.

"Or how about … What was it again?" Suddenly Darroc's apparition disappeared and was replaced with the image of a mangled body, shreds of flesh hanging off a skeleton of meat and gristle. Darroc's disembodied voice continued, "Do you recognize this one? Hm? I'm just so bad with names … Let's ask Faline, shall we?"

"You sick bastard," Nellie whispered. Rhayna lowered her wing, allowing Nellie to move forward.

Ander grabbed her arm, twisting her to face him. "Don't look at this, Nellie."

Nellie's eyes were wide and unfocused, her freckles stark against her bloodless face. Ander glanced over her shoulder as the image panned over to the body of a slight female, her normally pinned hair hanging loosely and matted with blood. Her eyes were gouged and her fingers bleeding from where her nails were ripped out. Ander's vision swam. It wasn't anything he hadn't seen before, or done on behalf of Darroc in the past, but this was her. Faline.

"Nellie," Faline's agonized voice scratched in the shocked silence, "don't look, child."

Nellie's breathing turned to quick panting and Ander watched as her eyes took on a crazed look, her skin pale as the blood drained from her face.

"Ander," Nellie's voice was filled with tortured pain, "please."

He didn't know what she was asking for. Please don't let her turn around? Please let her see to believe it was real? "Nellie, I'm sorry."

"This is quite boring," Darroc cut in. "It's too late for your darling adoptive mother, just as it was too late for … Ah, yes. Wil, was it?"

Silent sobs racked through Nellie's body.

"What are you doing, Darroc?" Ander said. "What is the point of this?"

"I'm having fun," the words were said succinctly and dripped with evil. "This was to bide my time. But … time's up."

Faline, on some intuition of knowing what that meant, said, "Nellie, I love—"

A strangled cry followed by the sound of flesh tearing through bone. Nellie gasped, releasing a wailing moan of grief and fury as she collapsed to the ground at Ander's feet.

Ander watched as Darroc took a bite from Faline's still-beating heart, muscle and sinew ripping with the action. He chewed and released a sound of ecstasy then said, "I wouldn't delay if I were you. *Mentage* is calling."

The apparition disappeared. At once, Rhayna let out a burst of fire and brunt the remaining creature to ash before running her snout along Nellie's back in a comforting gesture.

Nellie lay in fetal position on the grass, the sun beaming on her prone body. She was in shock, Ander knew. He felt something similar, along with rage, desperation, hopelessness. He barely knew these people, but they were his mother's friends and family. They were people of her land—their land. And while he didn't know if he wanted to stay and live as a prince, he did know he failed them, somehow.

"Nellie." Ander gently lifted her into his arms and held her close. "I don't know what to do here. We need to check on *Mentage* but I don't want to rush you. I'm also not willing to leave the Fae unprotected."

"The Fae?" Nellie asked weakly, staring at him with dead eyes. "You mean the immobile ones Faria was talking about? They're near here?"

"Just over that hill," Ander said, gesturing with his head. "And I don't know how long Darroc spied on us or what he saw. But we need to figure out our next step, and fast."

Rhayna let out a sudden growl at the tree line in the distance. Ander placed Nellie on the ground and watched an influx of emotions pass over her. Grief, fury, then a calm acceptance. She shifted without hesitation to a wolf and sniffed at the air, her hackles raised. Ander knew she would grieve later when there wasn't another threat to worry about. Nellie sniffed the air again and sat on her haunches. Curious, Ander scented the air as well and zeroed in on any unwelcome movement in the immobile land.

Nellie shifted back to her human form whispered, "I think it's people. I smell dirt and sweat but no hint of magic. Could it be humans?"

Ander shook his head and headed in their direction. Now that he understood how to use the flame, he was careful not to wish any ill thoughts toward a potential ally. He stepped through fields of wildflowers, casually pushing insects suspended in the air out of his way and stopped just short of the pathway leading back to the peaks.

Ander's *malosin* simmered beneath his skin and he felt his body try to change into more of a predator out of a need to protect. He was able to hold it at bay long enough to say, "Show yourself before my dragon turns you to ash."

With silent footsteps, a group clad in shining armor walked out of the forest, axes and bows resting by their sides. The tallest one in the lead stopped short, giving Ander a surprised look of recognition then proceeded to get down on a knee in what appeared to be fealty. Ander cautiously approached with Nellie a few steps behind.

"My prince," said the stranger in a deep, guttural voice. "It is an honor to meet you."

"Who are you?" Ander cocked his head. "Why do you think I'm your prince?"

The stranger stood, though the others behind him remained on their knees. Though he was tall, he still only came to Ander's chest. A thick beard covered his lightly wrinkled face, and his bright eyes twinkled the longer he examined Ander.

Finally, the stranger said, "Forgive me, you are just the spitting image of your father. Hunter and I have known each other for a great long time. There's no mistaking it."

It was unusual for anyone to speak to him about his father in a kind way. Up until recently, the only 'father' he knew was Darroc. And to have someone accept him so wholly as a prince, despite him being away or committing the crimes he had made him feel like maybe he could belong.

He shifted uncomfortably. "What is your name?"

"Ah, right. Sorry. My name is Thuuk, leader of the Dwarven clan under the mountain. Or we used to be under the mountain until that happened." He cocked his head vaguely in the direction behind him to indicate the split peaks. "Since our city has been cleaved by what Dennison informed us was the Goddess, we decided it was finally time to join you."

"That's right," Nellie said, her voice dripping with distaste. "Didn't you say several times that it wasn't your problem, that you didn't want any harm to come to your people, that you empathize but too bad for us?"

Thuuk had the sense to look embarrassed. "Yes, that's true. The last time we fought in a battle was during the Great War a thousand years ago, but we cannot stay away any longer. We received urgent news from Dennison just a few hours ago."

Ander crossed his arms in an attempt to keep his *malosin* under control. His emotions were running high as it were, and he didn't want to lash out at them for being the bearer of what was certain to be bad news. "What is it?"

"First, Faline and Wil are missing—"

"Dead," Nellie's sharp voice cut him off. "They are both dead at Darroc's hands."

Thuuk hung his head and the others behind him stood up, murmuring their shock. "How do you know?"

"We had a run-in with him," Ander said, keeping it short. "What is the second thing?"

"Mercy Bay is under attack by an unknown source. Faria has lost control over the sirens and she has already used most of her magic reserves."

"What?" Nellie gasped, horrified. "How is that possible?"

"Hunter popped back to *Mentage* to give Dennison a quick update. We don't have any more information than that."

"We have to go," Nellie said frantically. "We need to find the sirens, help Faria, she can't do this on her own."

"There's one more thing," Thuuk said. "The messenger said just as he was leaving *Mentage* to deliver Dennison's plea for help, he heard ungodly creatures and screams coming from the Forest of the Dawn. He believes *Mentage* is under attack, as well."

"Shit," Ander said, folding his hands behind his head.

He started pacing, running through the different scenarios. If Darroc overthrew *Mentage* he would have claim over the throne, especially since he and Faria never officially terminated their marriage. But both his parents were in Mercy Bay, and it sounded like there was little hope on that front. He couldn't be in two places at once.

"Okay," he said, settling his eyes on Nellie. "We have to secure *Mentage*. If Darroc takes it, it's game over."

"Absolutely not," Nellie said through clenched teeth. "*Mentage* is a glorified house. I am not letting my friends, or anyone else, die because of a *house*. We go to Mercy Bay."

Ander didn't want to separate from Nellie. Though he was fairly certain he healed her of the illness that was killing her, she'd just been dealt with two heavy losses, and he wanted to keep an eye on her. Still, he didn't see how it was possible when both *Mentage* and Mercy Bay needed them.

"All right," Ander said, finally making up his mind. "I'll go to *Mentage* while you go to Mercy Bay."

"Of course, I will," Nellie said. Her body started to shimmer as she prepared to shift. "Don't worry about me, loverboy." Then she turned into a *Drogosterra* and shot into the sky.

Rhayna beat her wings, preparing to leave as well.

"Where are you going?" Ander asked. He didn't think she'd want to leave him as well, but he knew better than to try and stop any female in his life from doing what they wanted to do.

She sent a feeling of comfort to him and then took off into the sky after Nellie.

Ander tried not to worry about why she would leave when they needed her most, but she was bred for battle, after all, and if they were splitting up, then perhaps she needed to go somewhere to prepare.

He turned his attention back to Thuuk. "Have you explored this entire area?"

Thuuk nodded. "We know what lies here."

"Then you understand that I don't feel comfortable leaving them unprotected, especially now that Darroc has found a way to infiltrate the country once again."

Thuuk turned toward his clanmates and sized them up. "Who volunteers to guard the Fae?"

At least three dozen dwarves pounded their axes against their chest plate.

Thuuk shook his head. "Loyal to a fault. We can spare a group of ten. Decide amongst yourselves who will remain here." Thuuk sidled up next to Ander. "Glad it's not me that has to stay here. This whole place feels like a grave, doesn't it? It's too horrifying to be this beautiful. Didn't think this was how it would be."

Ander didn't know how to make small talk with strangers, so he made a noncommittal noise and once the dwarves said their goodbyes to their clanmates, he said to Thuuk, "I don't mean to be presumptuous, but we can't waste any more time. I'll take you guys in groups of eight. Any more than that and I risk losing too much energy."

"Of course, Prince Ander."

Swallowing down the fear of what was to come, Ander waited for the first eight dwarves to hold on to whatever part of him they could reach, and he left for *Mentage*.

THIRTY FOUR

ANDER

Mentage was a bloodbath.

Chaos rang as rabid monsters swarmed out of the Forest of the Dawn, meeting their demise with *Drogosterra* blood-soaked weapons—the only way to kill the creatures. From the sky swooped giant hawks, snatching people from the ground, or gouging them with their talons. Shifters teamed up with elves to fight the creatures while the warlocks used what magic they could as protection. Screams rang in the night—screams of dying, screams of terror, screams for help. The ground was littered with bodies and gristle and the distinct tang of death hung heavy in the air.

The first time Ander showed up with the dwarves, he landed in the thick of battle, though his companions didn't seem to mind. The second their boots squished on the guts of their enemies, they joined in the fight and seemed exhilarated to do so. Ander had spared a moment to locate Dennison but couldn't distinguish one elf from the other amid the never-ending stream of monsters pouring from the forest.

Exhaustion ripped through Ander after retrieving the dwarven clan. It took him a total of six times laden with stout beings covered in heavy armor and weapons, and though he'd sieved greater distances, he had never done it so many times in succession before with that many people. It was disorienting to go from the chaos of battle where the sound of death was deafening to a beautiful sun-washed field of silence, so when Ander returned for the final time, he'd barely swerved in time before a mangled muzzle latched onto his throat.

"Watch it!" someone yelled as they skidded past him and collided with a creature that was half bear half human.

Gods what was he doing standing in the middle of the field? He hadn't eaten in at least three days, possibly more, then spent most of his energy healing Nellie and transporting the dwarves. He had no weapons, no armor, and barely any magic left. If Darroc showed up next to him at that moment, Ander would barely be able to swat him away, let alone do anything to cause damage.

Gruff hands grabbed the back of his shirt and yanked Ander away from a swooping, rabid eagle. He looked over his shoulder at his savior and made eye contact with his grandfather. Dennison kept a firm grip on him and led him off the field, ducking and swerving out of the way of more creatures, swinging axes, or those wrestling the beasts to the ground. The tang of blood and sweat turned his stomach and recalled the horror of what happened to Faline and Wil.

Dennison didn't let him go until they were back near the Spring Garden where the scent of jasmine and honey tried to mask the devastation a few fields away from it. Three large tents had been erected near there, and he allowed himself to be led into the first. As soon as he walked in, all sounds of battle had ceased and his ears rang with deafening silence.

The tent was divided into different sections. One area had a washing station set up with a few tonics and a healer standing at the ready. Another area had a few tables and chairs, and yet another had pillows and rugs to sit on. Ander assumed this tent was meant for people with minor injuries with hearts of stone, crumbling under the weight of war. He was surprised to be the only person in there.

Dennison led him over to the healer, who bowed her head at both of them.

"My lord," the healer said quietly. "My prince. How can I serve you?"

That was yet another person who called him a prince in the past hour. He grew up with nothing; how could they expect him to adapt to this lifestyle simply because of who his parents were?

"Ander needs a healing elixir and then we both need a private moment if you don't mind."

The healer rummaged through bottles filled with brightly colored liquid and pulled out a small golden vial. "Take the whole thing, please, Prince Ander. It will help you for the next twelve hours, at least."

Ander eyed it suspiciously then unstoppered it. It smelled like syrup, but he knew better than to trust anything that had the appearance of being safe. "What exactly is it?"

"It will heal most minor injuries," the healer explained. "If you are hungry, it will satiate you and if you are tired it will give you a short energy burst. The more powerful your magic is, the more it will help you."

Ander didn't know if he could trust these people, but he doubted Dennison would have led him somewhere to take him out of the game so easily. And he was starting to sway on the spot. If Dennison didn't have a firm hold on his shoulder, he would have crumpled where he stood. He took the elixir and downed it in one gulp.

The effects were immediate. A rush of healing energy spread through his blood, and he could feel each part of minor damage within his body heal. The ache of exhaustion disappeared and he no longer felt hunger or thirst. His magic stirred within him where moments ago it was lifeless. It didn't heal every part of him; he was still furious, confused, and scared. The images of Faline and Wil mingled with every terrible thing Ander had been forced to endure, but at least he knew he could help fight.

"Thank you," he said, handing the empty vial to the healer. "What is your name?"

"Jerome, Prince Ander," the healer replied. He bowed his head and made to depart to give Ander and Dennison privacy.

Ander reached a hand out to stop him. Even though he had no intention of ruling the queendom in the future, he still didn't want people to dislike or fear him. "Jerome, thank you for this. But please, call me Ander. I'm just Ander."

A small smile appeared on Jerome's lips, revealing a dimple on his cheek. "Your mother insisted on the same, and now look at her. I'll be right outside if you need me."

Once they were alone, Dennison turned to Ander and enveloped him in a bone-crushing hug. Surprise flickered through Ander. He'd never been the type to allow touch. No one had ever wanted to touch him anyway, but as Dennison embraced him, Ander could feel the relief and love pouring from him. He awkwardly patted Dennison's back, unsure of how to handle so much emotion.

"What happened to you?" Dennison asked. "How did you escape?"

"Is this the best time to discuss this?" Ander might have had a healing burst, but he certainly hadn't forgotten the entire battle happening right outside the tent's walls. "We should get back into the creatures."

"We rotate our fighters. Some come to this tent for quick healing and solitude, but you'll find most are in the other two to eat or seek more serious medical intervention. I was part of the rotation out and soon I'll check on the injured and help the kitchen with food if they have need of me."

It was such a foreign concept to Ander to be part of a community that was so organized, yet did everything they could to help each other. He was used to survival of the fittest, to staying out of Darroc's way, kill or be killed. Here, though, it was the complete opposite.

"We aren't whole if all of us aren't whole, Ander," Dennison said, reading the confusion on his face. He led him over to the tables and poured them each a cup of water.

Ander drained his, then Dennison poured him another, leaving the pitcher on the table between them.

They sat in silence for a moment, before Dennison said, "Can you tell me what has transpired?"

Ander shifted in his seat and kept his eyes on his cup, shifting it between his hands if only for something to do. "Darroc used the blood bond to force me to him. I ended up in another realm, in a mountain made of ice. He had me chained to the wall, which drained me of my magic, and runes on the floor that would unmake me if I were to find some way to escape. And then he left me there for three days until I was rescued."

Dennison kept his face carefully blank. He was a strategist and ruler, and Ander had no doubt that he was trying to find some sense of weakness in his enemy. "Who rescued you?"

"Alexei, Farrah's consort." Ander expected a flash of surprise or other emotion from Dennison, but after receiving none, he continued, "I was dying of hypothermia, unable to use my magic, and had no way to escape. Alexei appeared to me and told me I had to keep fighting because I was the only one who could save her."

"Faria?" Dennison demanded.

Ander shook his head. "Nellie. The illness from the creature in the sea was killing her, and I was the one who could heal her. Alexei forced a piece of the Eternal Flame inside of me which burned the blood bond with Darroc and allowed me full access to my magic again, and then some. He flashed me out of the prison and I ended back here."

Dennison stared off to the side, contemplating. "We received a report from the north. A *Drogosterra* was falling to the ground, while the other dived in what appeared to be an attempt to catch it. Then they both disappeared out of thin air. I'm assuming that was Alexei's work, as well?"

"I landed on the other side of Carenek Peaks, directly in front of the Fae. It was exactly as my mother reported. Their magic is draining into the ground, but they are immobilized. I believe they are also fully conscious as well."

"One problem at a time. Then what happened?"

"I heard Rhayna, so I followed the sound of her cries and found Nellie in her human form on the ground. I immediately got to work trying to heal her, but she seemed to be getting worse. Alexei never told me how to access the piece of Flame within me and no matter what I did, Nellie was closer to death with every minute that passed. It took hours, but I was finally able to heal her."

"Thank the goddess for that," Dennison said.

It was the first time Ander had seen or heard any emotion from him since his embrace, and it was telling how much Nellie meant to the former king.

"Why isn't she with you?"

Ander stood up abruptly and started pacing in small circles, working himself up to sharing the part he'd been dreading. "Okay," he said, sitting back down across from Dennison. The space felt too small, suddenly, and Ander was finding it difficult to breathe. He took another sip of water. "Darroc's apparition appeared then. I'd forgotten that without the blood bond, I would no longer be able to sense when he was around. It had been like that for years; I just didn't think—"

"Spit it out, Ander." Dennison crossed his arms and leaned back in his chair. "I am a patient man, but there are still things both you and I must do this evening."

"You have to understand, he's crazy now. Whatever Moira did to him … he's not sane. Before he was cruel and calculating. Now he's nothing short of deranged. And the things he will do … has done." Ander took a steady breath. "He spoke about himself for a while and revealed some things about Nellie's mother. And then he … *dammit.*" Ander slammed his fist on the table, the glasses jumping from the impact. "Darroc tortured and murdered Wil and Faline. He showed us their bodies. Then he mentioned that we might be needed at *Mentage* before he disappeared. Just as we were leaving for here, Thuuk and his clan found us and relayed the message about Mercy Bay. Nellie went there to be with Faria and I brought the dwarves here."

Dennison stared blankly at him for a moment, letting the words process. "You're sure that Fal—Faline," his voice cracked, "and Wil have gone into the Beyond?"

"Yes. I'm sorry."

Dennison stood from the table and approached Ander, grabbing hold of his arm, and pulling him to his feet. His grandfather embraced him again, only this time it was out of comfort rather than desperation.

"It is I who am sorry," Dennison said. "You shouldn't have had to see them like that. You shouldn't have had to endure what you have at his hands. I'm so sorry, Ander."

Before Ander could properly react, Dennison let him go and said, "You may remain here and help where you can, if you wish, but then I need you to go to Mercy Bay."

"But Darroc—"

"He won't come here," Dennison said. "This is a distraction, as you said. He wanted to split you and Nellie up and he succeeded. I fear for my daughter. I cannot leave our people here and I must defend *Mentage*. Without it, we are nothing. Without Faria, we are nothing. And, despite your hesitation, without you, we are nothing."

"But—"

"We have more than enough Val weapons to destroy these creatures. We have enough healing elixirs to help our people. You delivered us the dwarves, who are excellent fighters. We are better prepared this time. Something terrible is happening at Mercy Bay, Ander. There is a reason why Darroc didn't want you there. Please, protect my daughter."

Ander placed his hand on Dennison's shoulder, nodded once, then left.

THIRTY FIVE

NELLIE

Her heartbeat to one word only. *De—stroy. De—stroy. De—stroy.*

Every tragic thing that had happened to her went back to Darroc. She had no lasting relationships when she was younger because they were constantly on the run, which she now knows was because of Darroc. He murdered her mother. She was banished from her clan—the leader of which worked alongside Darroc—and faced a fear worse than death when she was forced through the Gate of All Realms. Her being forced away from her mate, away from what she thought was her only chance at having a lasting connection, was because of him. Her existence—because of him.

And now his reign of terror was a cycle on repeat.

Her adoptive mother, the sole person in all the realms who knew what she was, took her in without fear. Faline raised her and taught her the ways of the realm and how Anestra functioned. Faline made sure Nellie knew how to protect herself by encouraging her to take part in archery and defense lessons. Faline encouraged her friendship with Faria, allowed her to get into mischief, comforted her through the pains of pretending to be someone and something she wasn't.

Nellie flew quickly through the currents in the air, letting her fury and grief spur her on. She allowed her thoughts to stray to darker places, giving her imagination free reign over the revenge she would exact on Darroc. Burning him to ash would be too quick and painless a death. Once she figured out how to immobilize him, she would do every single thing he did to Wil and Faline, but slower. With intention.

A strong upwind draft brought with it the briny scent of the sea and Nellie could make out tiny pinpricks of light increase in frequency the closer she approached. A sick sense of glee with a dash of anticipation built with every mile she passed.

Somewhere deep inside, Nellie knew this wasn't her. She didn't do revenge, she wasn't a torturer. Faline wouldn't want this for her. But Nellie was entering her villain era and she was tired of being the funny, happy, positive person people expected her to be. She was tired of suppressing her feelings, of making sure everyone else was okay first.

This time, she would do what was best for her.

Colorful flashes of light in the distance caught Nellie's attention, and she slowed and descended underneath a layer of storm clouds until she hovered close enough to make out what they were, but far enough away to remain hidden. Magic users.

She swooped down allowing the fire in her belly to build as she readied her attack. She drew up short, her eyes finally giving detail to what caused pain-filled screams to fill the night. Dozens of the most beautiful creatures she'd ever seen were interspersed between city streets, the docks, and the shoreline. They all looked similar with dark hair and angular features, and if it wasn't for the ... *What the fluff, are those tentacles?* Nellie would have been sure they were some type of elf or Fae. She watched for a moment as one of the creatures sprang a tentacle on the closest person, latching itself to their chest, just like what happened to her.

Holy crow, they were the same creatures from Widow's Passageway. Baring her teeth in a snarl, Nellie allowed the fire to shoot from her chest as she dove toward the creature, careful with her aim. At once an unholy screeching came from the monster as it caught flame and ran for the sea. To Nellie's satisfaction, it shriveled in the sand before it could touch the water.

More shouts of alarm mingled with cries of surprise as Nellie found a spot large enough for her to land. It was easy to tell who the enemies were, as it seemed most magic users were aiming for the sea creatures. *Okay, so all I have to do is burn them each to a crisp, and then Darroc will be pissed enough to show up. Easy.*

Just as she locked onto her next victim, a voice yelled her name: "Nellie, wait!"

Hunter ran up to her and placed a hand against her scales. She felt his attempt at healing her, but she was no longer sick. The only thing she needed was a nice dose of the blood of her enemies.

"Change back, please. We need to talk."

Nellie growled but quickly switched to her human form. She glanced down, grateful her clothes were still intact. Small miracles. "What is it, Hunter? Did you see what I just did to that one? Let me kill them all and we can call it a day."

"For every one you kill, three more walk out of the ocean. We can't put the sirens in any more danger."

Nellie noticed the strain on each of the magic users' faces. They weren't trying to kill the creatures; they were holding them at bay. That had to mean ... "Marisa? The others?"

"We haven't had eyes on them for nearly an hour. These creatures have taken our entire focus. That, and whoever is behind this attack."

"You mean Darroc?"

"No." Faria appeared next to them. "I don't recognize this energy, but it isn't Darroc's. What are you doing here? Where's the *Drogosterra?*"

"I don't know," Nellie said, distracted. If Darroc wasn't behind the creatures, who would it be? The Elders? That didn't make sense. "After I left Ander—"

"He's back?" Faria grabbed Nellie's shoulders. "I haven't paid attention to the *innulum.* He's ... yes. He's near, thank the goddess. Is he harmed?"

"Maybe just mentally like the rest of us," Nellie replied. Faria and Hunter exchanged a glance then looked at her. "Don't talk about me in your heads, it's rude."

"What happened, Nells?" Hunter said. "I sent word to Dennison that we were under attack, but all was well on his end. And now that Ander has returned, what's wrong?"

Nellie took a deep breath and counted to ten before responding.

Faria was her queen and Hunter her consort or whatever, and she was required to deliver information clearly and succinctly, regardless of how much she'd rather scream at the two of them to let her flay the tentacles off the sea creatures.

"Faria," Nellie said, putting her patient mask in place. She grabbed her friend's hand. "I was seconds away from dying then Ander showed up and healed me. It's a wild story but I'll let him tell it when he's ready. Faline is ..." A sob tore through her but she took a deep breath and continued in a robotic tone, "Darroc tortured and murdered both Wil and Faline. He alluded to *Mentage* being under attack, so after Thuuk and his clan found us, Ander and I agreed to split up. He brought the dwarves to *Mentage* and I am here. I don't know where Rhayna is, but I assume she went with Ander.

"Now I am filled with rage, hate, and bloodlust. I humbly ask you, my queen, to allow me to kill these fuckers so we can be done with them once and for all."

To her credit, Faria looked only slightly less than shell-shocked at the news of Faline and Wil's death, but she watched her queen straighten her back and turn to face the water once again. "There will be time to grieve, but now is not it, Nellie. We need clear heads and pure hearts. There is something controlling these creatures, but you've seen Darroc's handiwork. He doesn't have this capability."

"These creatures kill sirens, Faria. Let me shift into something that will allow me to see and fight underwater. They need me."

"Every person here needs you, Nellie. Marisa and the others were under an extreme compulsion that I was unable to break. They are either fighting or they are lost. I know that sounds cruel," Faria said, continuing before Nellie could interrupt her, "But please. I just used every ounce of magic within me to hold that ocean at bay, and whoever was behind it taunted me. The only reason we aren't dead is because it allowed us to live."

Nellie looked around at the scores of Anestrians fighting. Most of them were everyday citizens, sailors, or shopkeepers. Tavern owners or farmers. They weren't all scholars, or fighters, even though every citizen was trained as much as they wanted. They just lived a life of peace and enjoyed Anestra's prosperity. And yet they were gathered, fighting, and dying for Faria, for their country.

Gods she just wanted to murder things, but Faria was right. "What do you want me to do?"

"Isn't this cute?" a cruel voice cut in. "How easily you comply for her, yet you're like a feral kitty when it comes to me."

Well, there goes my pure heart. "It's about time you showed up," Nellie said, creeped out by Darroc's disembodied voice. "Where are you hiding this time?"

"Right in front of you."

Hunter and Faria stood at once in front of Nellie as if they wanted to protect her. She shook her head and pushed her way between them. Rain started to fall, making it even harder to see in the darkness. They stood upon a grassy hill right before it sloped down to the sandy shore. To their right was the city and in front of that were the docks and cliff face.

Nellie scanned through the elves, humans, and warlocks fighting the creatures or else working to protect the city and help each other to safety, but there was no sign of Darroc. She'd just realized the three of them were isolated from everyone else at the moment and how stupid that was.

Hunter whispered something under his breath and Nellie felt something like a warm blanket encircle her.

"Clever Val." Darroc appeared a few feet before them, not bothering to mask his appearance this time.

His face was long and thin, the bones jutting out at odd angles. His red eyes glittered with malice and as he smiled, his thin lips revealed a set of razor-sharp teeth. *What was with every villain having sharp teeth?* He wore robes that clung to his thin frame in the rain and pulled back his hood to reveal patches of white hair against a severely scarred scalp.

"My protection spell is stronger than yours, so I'd suggest not trying to fling any fireballs at me this time. I'm … less forgiving of flame, these days." Darroc gave a high-pitched laugh and continued, "Do you like those creatures? Beautiful, aren't they? I'll admit I had some help with that one."

"What's the matter, Darroc?" Faria asked. "You're really that angry that the warlocks' magic doesn't work for you? Do you think killing your people is a way to gain their loyalty?"

Darroc looked down at the frenzy and chuckled to himself. "What's that expression the humans like to say? Something about a pot and kettle? You'd know all about sacrificing the few to save the many, wouldn't you?"

Hunter called a fireball, bouncing it in the air above his hand. Darroc bared his teeth at him then giggled again. Nellie recalled Ander describing him as deranged, which was spot on.

"Our son helped me with them. It's true. When he was younger, I brought him to another place ruled by different gods than here. I'd met one of them centuries ago in my quest to make the perfect warlock. Anyway, we struck a deal. I help him destroy his brother's playthings, and then he will come to my aid when I call." He gestured to the creatures before them and the ocean beyond. "As you can see, he delivered. My creation kills sirens, and now he has come to my aid as well. He did fail at drowning you all, which is unfortunate, but you will perish in the end, anyway."

"I've had enough of this," Nellie said. She was bored, tired, and wanted to end him if only so he'd stop talking. "No one cares. Let's move on to the part where we kick your butt."

"You won't succeed," he said, rolling his sleeves up. Darroc snapped his fingers and waited a moment. "But by all means, try."

A howl erupted in the night and from the field and city streets beside them, Darroc's monsters appeared.

The fighting began.

THIRTY SIX

HUNTER

If there was one thing they could be grateful for, it was that Darroc was shockingly predictable.

Though he didn't expect Darroc to turn up at Mercy Bay, or for there to be a battle at Mercy Bay at all, he knew they'd have his creatures to contend with. Hunter was grateful he had the foresight to forge as many weapons in *Drogosterra* blood as possible and distribute them throughout the country. Nearly every person down there, male, female, and child, had at least a dagger or more, so he knew they were well prepared for those monsters.

What they didn't anticipate, however, were the tidal wave, nature of the sea creatures, or the general inability to kill anything without consequences. They probably could have dealt with just the rabid monsters or just the sea creatures, but both would put them at a serious disadvantage.

Nellie shifted into a *Drogosterra* and immediately a monster charged at her. She dipped and flew upwards, opening her jaws to tear rabid flesh from bone. Another swooped down from the sky and Nellie twisted, clamping on its belly. Guts poured from the air in a morbid pirouette.

Go fight with our people, Princess. I'll take care of Darroc. Faria made no move to get out of harm's way. *Go!* he snarled at her and she visibly flinched. *You will not do any other idiotic thing like fighting a warlock without magic. Take your anger out elsewhere.*

"I'm stuck," she said through clenched teeth. Her body jerked as she tried to move her feet. "I can't go anywhere."

"Ahh, yes," Darroc said, circling them. "You can thank me for that as well. I think you'll find that neither of you will be sieving anytime soon."

Hunter narrowed his eyes and tried to sieve as well, finding he couldn't do it. "How can you do that? Only the Elders have that ability."

"The Elders ... yes. Banished for too much sacrifice, blood magic, and ill intentions, but they were warlocks, were they not? If they figured it out, what makes you think I wouldn't have, especially when I had a Val at my disposal to experiment on."

Hunter's *malosin obsinae* erupted from him unchecked and daggers of darkness shot straight at Darroc. Without waiting to see how he would parry the attack, Hunter pelted Darroc with fireballs straight to his chest. Darroc simply laughed as everything Hunter threw at him dissipated inches before reaching him.

The stormy night was accentuated by occasional bursts of fire from

Nellie mixed with the snarling of rabid creatures and the sacrificial song of death.

We need the Spell of Unmaking, Hunter. Nothing will touch him.

Well, we don't exactly have a spare copy, do we, Princess?

Frustration and anger spurred him on, throwing everything he had at Darroc. Faria removed her daggers and flung each one at him, the only thing she could do without the freedom of movement. Even with her innate ability to always hit her mark, none penetrated Darroc's defenses.

"What's it like, *Queen* Faria, to have the power of every magical species the gods created, and you still can't defeat me?" His mirth died down and with it came a sense of foreboding Hunter couldn't shake. "Let's play a game, shall we?" Darroc snapped his fingers again and three sea monsters emerged from beyond the hillside with their tentacles wrapped tightly around Endo, Enis, and a child from the city.

Hunter stiffened. Poisoned prongs were held just above each their hearts. Endo had tears streaming down his face. He was a traitor in Darroc's eyes, and Hunter and Endo both knew there would be no escape for him, regardless of the game. Enis stood with her back straight, chin up, ever the soldier she was. The child, to her credit, simply looked around. Panic set in.

"Choose."

Faria was a storm within skin, her energy crackling as the space between them became suffocating. "You're sick."

"This one," Darroc said, grasping Endo's shoulders, "this one is a traitor two times over. It would be a favor to us both to be rid of him." He walked to Enis and caressed her hair. "This one is feisty. She'd be most satisfying to play with." He stopped next to the young girl and bent over so he was at eye level with her then slowly ran his finger down her cheek. "But this one ... I do have a soft spot for children."

Bile rose in Hunter's throat at the thought of Darroc near another child. He tried to think fast, to figure out in what way they could access their powers or do anything to prevent this twisted idea of a game.

Nellie let out a ferocious roar and dove toward them, letting out a stream of fire directly at Darroc, but even that missed. She swung back around, thrashing her tail to the side aiming her poisonous spikes at his back, but it veered right and almost pegged Enis instead.

Lightning struck the ground, too intentional to have been nature's calling. Hunter whipped his head to Faria whose teeth were bared, sweat dripping down her face. Her *malosin* hovered outside of her body and Hunter felt a rising call in his own.

"I'm going to destroy you," she said, straining with the effort of trying to use magic that wouldn't respond.

Another bolt of lightning struck; this time close enough to them that Darroc's robes were singed with the electric heat. The momentary victory was cut short when Darroc plunged his hand straight through Endo's heart.

Endo's eyes widened in surprise before he crumpled to the ground. Memories flooded with bittersweet remorse. They trained together, got drinks together, and shared the occasional male or female if the mood suited. Despite what had transpired between them, Hunter considered Endo one of his closest friends and he knew in time they would have gotten back to where they were before the warlock rebellion started.

He also knew, from the moment Darroc brought him out, that Endo wasn't going to survive that night. Faria shook beside him, her *malosin* pulsating with the rage she barely kept contained.

Darroc licked the blood from his fingers. "Hm, mediocre flavor from a mediocre warlock. Disappointing." He dropped Endo's heart with a squelch against the grass then moved down the line. "Who's next?"

"Don't touch them," Faria said through gritted teeth. "What is the point of all this?"

Darroc paused as if considering his response, then let out a booming laugh. "The point? Now everyone can see that I am more powerful than you, even with all the magic possible for you to possess. I still immobilized you and your little prince with a single thought. Look at how my beasts massacre your people. I did this, and you are still incapable of stopping me."

Without warning, he turned and snapped Enis' neck. The crack echoed in the shocked silence, broken only by Faria's gasping breaths.

Nellie let out a lamenting wail then tried once again in vain to set Darroc on fire with a heated blast. She landed forcefully, rocks and dirt spraying over them. Deep crimson glowed from behind menacing teeth as she prepared another stream of fire but was stopped by a command from behind them.

"Nellie, don't." Hunter whipped around to find Ander approaching them from beyond the hill. Fear sent icy shards of trepidation straight to Hunter's heart. Relief that his son was safe diminished the closer he stepped toward Darroc's maniacal tantrum.

Nellie growled low in warning, but she paused in her advance.

Ander walked up to Faria and stood next to her, his arms crossed as he stared daggers at Darroc. He appeared unscathed, if not exhausted. They all were.

"What are you doing here?" Faria asked. "*Mentage?* My father?"

"All is well," Ander replied, his voice low. "They are under attack but it's being handled."

"Ahh, our son has decided to show up," Darroc said, his look of amusement settling into something colder. Hunter's *malosin* thrashed against the confines of his skin as the need to protect Ander defied any other instinct he had. "You are actually quite adept at killing for fun. Would you like the honors of this last one?" Darroc ran his finger down the child's cheek. "Just for fun?"

Nellie snapped her jaws in Darroc's direction. Darroc stepped on Enis' lifeless body before stopping in front of the child. Screams of the dying down in the bay and city streets mingled with the snarls of Darroc's creatures in the air, while the sea monsters silently thrust their prongs into unsuspecting victims' faces.

We need the Elders. Faria's grief washed over him. *Look at the bay. Our people are dying, their magic depleting. We can't do anything to touch him. He's going to keep killing everyone I care about until there's nothing left.*

Despite her logic, Hunter knew the Elders and knew they'd somehow be worse than Darroc. If Farrah and her sisters banished them centuries or millennia ago, the danger far exceeded anything Hunter or Faria was aware of.

There has to be another way. We can't risk our people.

Who will be left after tonight? I will not stand around and do nothing when I have a solution.

Then Faria, with some innate understanding that Hunter couldn't quite grasp, sliced her palm open once again and placed it to the ground. "I will allow the Elders to enter these lands to perform the Spell of Unmaking."

As one the world around them quieted. Dying screams simmered to whispers, rabid growling was little more than a grumble. Nellie's screeching roar was cut short. Waves crashing against the break wall told secrets to the stone.

Hooded figures appeared around Faria, Ander, Hunter, and Darroc, their faces shrouded in darkness. Nellie was forced behind them, an invisible barrier erected between them. The tension was thick as Darroc looked between the twelve Elders, shock registering on his face. As one, they started chanting, their voices rising and falling like the tide in a murky sea. Trepidation gripped Hunter as he remembered being on the receiving end of their wrath.

The splintering crack of broken bone could barely be heard above the ear-piercing shriek that tore from Darroc's throat. Flesh ripped; tendons snapped. The chanting grew as if frenzied by the pain of their sacrifice.

Faria watched with rapt attention, her *malosin* vibrating with excitement. This time, Hunter didn't feel his own respond in kind. Something wasn't right. He scanned the bloody beach and field beyond, watched as his comrades fought and died, as the sea creatures flung their prongs into the Anestrians' chests.

As each shred of Darroc's being was ripped from his body, his creatures slowed and started to fall, allowing the Anestrians enough time to stab them with their Val weapons. Though nothing happened to the sea creatures, Faria's people seemed to be filled with a second wind, allowing their magic to bolster once more as hope came back to them. Despite that, apprehension still filled Hunter.

Ander sidled closer to him, murmuring low so the Elders couldn't hear. "Something's off … I can't access my powers."

Hunter stared into eyes that were the exact mirror of his own, right down to the tiny blue freckle at the edge of the golden halo. The mark of Val royalty. He hadn't seen it in another in nearly a millennia. He swallowed hard. "Your mother and I could access only a shadow of our powers since Darroc arrived."

Ander slashed his head to the side. "It isn't that. I have a piece of the Flame inside me. It burned through the area of dark magic Darroc put in place. It's only now that these … beings are here." He gestured to the group of males, their chanting still rising and falling with the power of the spell. "Are you sure they're all here? Someone has a hold over me, an awareness I've never felt before in all my time with Darroc, across any realm."

Hunter scanned his son's face, trying to make sense of what he was saying. If he had a piece of the Flame, then he had been in the presence of Alexei, meaning he would have known if it was a god that controlled his powers. And it wouldn't make sense for Alexei to give him his Flame, then render it useless when it mattered. Hunter couldn't begin to fathom deplorable beings Darroc and Ander had dealt with over the years, but given Darroc's surprise at the Elders' arrival, he couldn't have come across them before, which meant …

Hunter whipped his head back to the Elders. Darroc was barely a husk of himself, nothing but skin and shrinking bones that would soon pop out of existence. But Hunter didn't care at that moment, too busy counting the cowled figures surrounding him. *One two … six … eight … ten … eleven.* Eleven. Where was the last?

Hunter searched the field around them, the bay below them. Then he noticed something odd. All the shifters were in their human form, and none of the magic users appeared able to use their abilities. They all looked at each other in confusion. Even the sea monsters had given a slight pause as if they didn't expect the onslaught of power to halt. Nellie slammed to the ground with a dull thud, her jaw dropping in shock.

It wasn't just Ander that couldn't access his magic. It was everywhere.

A lone figure shifted from the shadows, lowering his hood as he approached Faria. His gait was slightly wobbled as if he were unbalanced, but Hunter could never mistake the voice that preceded his face.

"Well, now that's taken care of, we have much to discuss."

THIRTY SEVEN

FARIA

"Queen Faria, so good of you to invite us back to our rightful land."

"Who in the gods' name are you?" Faria asked, her arms poised as if ready to strike. Magic burned through her, and though her *malosin obsinae* shrouded her, the other magic she possessed did little more than simmer.

"That's an odd way to thank your savior," the male replied. His gravelly voice was charred paper turned to ash by overuse. "You're welcome, by the way."

"Jacobi," Hunter said.

Faria spared a quick look at Hunter, her heart giving an odd flip to see him standing shoulder-to-shoulder with their son. Gods, they looked so much alike. Ander's features were slightly more angular, and he had Faria's lips, but the hair, skin tone, the eyes were all Hunter. Their stature was the same as well as they both stared venom at the one Hunter called Jacobi.

"What have you done?"

"What have *I* done?" Jacobi barked out a rough laugh, then rubbed his chest as if the action pained him. "My son, the male I guided through the past thousand years, who kept you as safe from harm as I felt was necessary, who attempted murder on all of us"—he gestured to the hooded figures behind him—"wants to know what *I* have done."

"You're the one who locked Hunter's powers." Faria seethed. "You're the reason I believed him dead."

"Yes, yes, all for worthy cause, is it not? Look at how it all played out. You two are together again, no harm, no foul."

"No harm?" Faria asked through gritted teeth. "No harm? I would have destroyed the realms if it meant he would come back to me."

"Hmm ... yes. But those annoying Fates deemed it necessary for you to have a child, and something more to live for, did they not? It has all worked out so beautifully."

"Thinking Hunter abandoned me after I was forced into a bonding ceremony is 'working out?' Seeing him lay on the ground, dead and burnt straight to the bone is 'working out?' Having my son stolen and raised by a serial killer is 'working out?' Knowing he lived an *entire life* without the love and guidance of his parents is 'working out?'"

"You are quite emotional, Queen Faria," Jacobi said, a cruel smile twisting on his lips. "The Fates had always looked out for you, did They not? They brought this one"—he tossed a hand in Nellie's direction—"to you years ago. If They had not, would you have been able to navigate the human realm to locate your son? The Fates don't deal in smiles and rainbows. They deal in necessary actions for the greater good. Be grateful! I know I am. You needed to think yourself entirely alone and incapable, that there was no way for you to defeat Darroc, otherwise, you never would have needed our help and we would not be back on our rightful land."

"Are you saying there was no need to summon you?" Ander said, attempting to step in front of Faria but finding himself rooted in place. "That my mother could have defeated him?"

"Yes." Jacobi let the weight of that single word hang in the air between them. "Now that that's in the clear, Queen Faria, I believe you have something that is ours."

He glided toward her, the cloak he wore swishing lightly against the ground. Faria's mind raced the knowledge of her powers, which was limited, trying to figure out how she could have defeated Darroc. He locked down everyone's magic. She was still firmly rooted to the spot, unable to fight or defend herself if her life depended on it. Judging by the look in Jacobi's eyes, it depended on it.

What do I do, Hunter? We have no magic against him. Faria's heart rate increased and she wiped her sweaty palms against the sides of her pants, wishing there was some way to release the pent-up fear and anxiety of the past few months. *What can be done?*

He wants your power. He thinks they are the rightful heirs to the land. I don't know how to stop him.

Faria scoffed. *Yeah, well he can get in line. The land has already accepted me. What can he possibly do about that?*

"Well," Jacobi cut into their silent conversation, his face inches from Faria's.

She leaned back, eager to get as far away as possible while frozen in place.

"I could always bleed you out. That would be the ultimate blood sacrifice, would it not?" He inhaled as if smelling a sweet bouquet of wildflowers. "With every drop the earth greedily accepts, your magic would trickle to me."

"You dare threaten my mate," Hunter growled.

Faria looked at him, a mixture of fear and thrill running through her. Hunter's *malosin* rose like a beast behind him, his eyes shining gold fire. Next to Faria, Ander cracked his neck and turned, a pair of flames peering down at her. *What is that?*

"Ander," Nellie said, unable to stand from her prone position on the ground. "Can you use the Flame?"

He gave a guttural response, "Trying to come out."

Beyond them, screams of terror mounted as the sea monsters renewed their attack. Anestrians were unable to use their magic to hold them at bay or create protective shields. Shifters could no longer fight in their animal form. They were all stuck as humans, and they would eventually all die as them as well.

The Elders moved as one and positioned themselves along the cliff face overlooking the bay. New chanting started, though it sounded different than with the Spell of Unmaking. The remaining sea creature holding the young child and its companions hissed at the Elders, thick rivulets of black veins undulating under their skin.

"You know our histories, don't you, Hunter? We are demigods, born from the creation of Alexei and his brothers. This is our land, and seeing as Queen Faria has no heir." Jacobi eyed Ander and waited a breath as if expecting him to interject. "When she is gone, the power will revert to us, where it should have been given in the first place."

Hunter's beast of a *malosin* reached over his body in an attempt to attack Jacobi, but it was held back by the same resistant force. Faria tried to drown out the noise so she could reach inside of herself, to find whatever it was that Jacobi said would work, but she couldn't ignore the pleas for help. The clashing of swords. The shrieks of terror abruptly cut off by each final death blow. She had made a horrific mistake in calling the Elders there.

Desperation clung to her like a second skin. It wasn't due to the threat of death; she would die a hundred times if she knew her people would be safe. It was because of the deep-seated need to protect them. Gods, if only she could release the ferocity of what boiled inside her.

Jacobi pulled a thin blade from his sleeve, slender enough to slip between ribs, sharp enough that she wouldn't feel a thing. Ander and Hunter both let out feral snarls and even Nellie attempted to stop Jacobi's advance from where she lay. He kicked her in the jaw and continued as if it were of little consequence. She yelped and fell silent.

Ander went berserk, flames dancing on his hands. It was more magic than any of them had been able to use. Thunder crashed as another storm approached, winds picking up velocity. Faria's hair swirled around her and

Hunter's *malosin* shadow beast prepared another attack. The sea creatures crawled toward the cliff edge, hissing at the Elders along the way.

A calm settled over Faria despite the chaos of the storm, the thrashing of Darroc's monsters dying a slow death, and the screams of her people as the sea creatures plunged their prongs into them. The world around her moved as if in slow motion. She reached up and caressed Ander's cheek. He calmed under her touch.

"I love you," she whispered.

The only time she'd ever said those words to him. His eyes widened.

"Don't you dare," Hunter said, frantic. "Whatever you're thinking, Princess, don't do it."

She poured all the love she could muster through their bond and allowed it to rush through them. She swallowed his fear and let that fuel her, too.

And when the world resumed its normal speed, she was unsurprised when Jacobi whipped his wrist and slashed her throat.

Faria let out a slight gasp. She was wrong. The pain burned more than she thought it would. Her vision swam before her as her hands reflexively clutched at her throat, warm crimson flowing over them. Hunter roared, the pain echoing down to her soul. He would heal, she knew. He'd forgive her one day.

She sank to her knees and prayed to the goddess as her essence poured into the land, prayed to the entire universe that she finally did something right, then allowed the blessed darkness to consume her.

THIRTY EIGHT

NELLIE

An agonizing scream woke her.

A torrent of pain spread through her jaw to the back of her skull. Nellie still lay on the ground which was rapidly turning to mud under the relentless downpour. She opened her eyes, shielding them against the rain, her eyes blinded by flashes of lightning and bright green light.

Nellie looked down at herself, relieved that she at least wasn't naked that time before her eyes locked on Ander. He kneeled on the ground next to Faria, one hand on her neck and healing light radiating from him. "Come on, mom. Don't do this, not now."

"What?" Nellie gasped, sitting up. *Wait.* She could sit up. She crawled through the mud and something else, something darker staining her skin.

Was that ... blood?

She let out an anguished moan as the crimson liquid poured from Faria's neck and soaked into the ground. Bile ran up Nellie's throat and she heaved at Faria's feet, unwilling to accept what was clear before her. Hunter was on his knees, fists pounding the ground in rage as his scream threatened to split the world in two.

"A simple blade, Hunter. That was all it took to slay the Queen of Everything." Jacobi laughed, the other Elders joining in.

It didn't make sense. Faria was trained better than anyone, except perhaps Dennison and Hunter. There was no way she'd allow her throat to be slashed, that she would end her life so simply without knowing her people and family were safe.

Nellie shook her head, disbelieving, but Faria's lifeless body was starting to cool, her tan complexion pale and waxy. Her eyes were still wide open, and a small smile played on her lips.

Hunter rose and circled Jacobi and tossed his soaking hair out of his eyes. Deep golden light poured from them, casting eerie shadows against Jacobi's haggard face. Nellie looked back at Ander, still muttering, "Come on!" to himself as he tried to heal his mother.

"Ander," Nellie said, placing a hand on his forearm.

He shook her off and renewed his effort.

"Please, she's gone. We'll need your power elsewhere."

"Why would he give me the Flame if I can't save anyone with it?"

"You saved me," Nellie said. She stood up and held her hand out to him. "Jacobi and his freaks from hell need to be decimated. Will you help me do it?"

Ander heaved under the effort of using so much magic at once. He looked at Nellie and saw twin flames of murderous intent blazing in his own eyes. The Val were seriously scary when they were in kill mode. She wanted the power housed in that body to inflict major damage to the Elders.

He grasped her hand and then raised his palm toward the group of Elders closest to them, releasing a stream of fire. The rain hissed as it made contact and steam rose, but the flames didn't falter. Two Elders were set ablaze, but they doused themselves moments later. Meanwhile, Hunter it seemed anguish unlocked Hunter's power. He threw giant bolts of electricity at Jacobi, each one just missing him by a hair's breadth. Nellie felt her power stir inside her, but she was still unable to shapeshift into another creature.

Nellie looked beyond the Elders to the bay. Sea creatures still grasped people with their tentacles, tossing them high in the air before releasing them. Warlocks and elves were blocked from their magic and had little to no defense against the sea creatures. Luckily, Darroc's monsters seemed to have lost their fervor. Thank the goddess for small miracles.

Given that she wasn't a magic user herself, Nellie wasn't sure where she'd be most useful. There was a loud snap and Hunter gave a pained shout. His arm hung from his elbow at an odd angle. Ander threw a fireball at Jacobi, it was easily deflected. The other Elders kept their low chanting.

Nellie glanced down at Faria's body and—

Where was her body? She was there—throat slashed, eyes open, but now there was nothing but a pile of ash. Did Ander misdirect his flames?

How had she missed it? Neither of the Val seemed to notice as they were both locked in a magical war with Jacobi.

Wind howled as Nellie trudged her way through squelching mud to where Faria once was. The area around the pile of ashes was eerily calm. The wind didn't seem to affect it, nor were they soaked with the incessant rain. The ground was no longer thick with Faria's blood, as if the most tragic loss to affect the land hadn't just occurred.

A sound trilled from the distance. Nellie barely registered it, except it was so different from the thrashing of boats along the dock, waves smashing against the cliff wall, or cacophony of the dying. It was musical and haunting, creating a song both mesmerizing and chilling.

The Elders looked between each other, their chanting stilting as they registered more voices than theirs. Nellie rose to her feet and looked out along the bay. She shielded her eyes against the rain and focused on the portal in the distance. A flash of lightning illuminated the space enough for Nellie to see several figures pop their heads out of the water.

The music grew louder, competing with an agitated hissing noise coming from beach. Sea monsters fell to the ground, thrashing in pain. More lightning flashed and Nellie watched as the figures from the ocean drew closer to the shoreline. There were at least a dozen, possibly more. She found herself inching closer to the edge, desperate to know more about them. Their voices filled a void that festered within Nellie, replacing it with something euphoric and if she could get just a little closer then—

"Nellie, for the gods' sake," Ander grabbed her around the waist just as she dived off the cliff. Her reverie broke just in time to see she wasn't the only one affected. One Elder had toppled over the edge, splashing in the water and appeared to be torn apart by sharks or something worse. "What are you doing?"

"What the hell was that?" she asked, her heart racing. Of all the cool ways she'd envisioned her life ending, sharks were not on the list.

"Sirens."

"Oh, my gods. Marisa?" Nellie searched the waters, trying in vain to find her friend.

Ander tightened his grip on her. "Nellie, focus. I'm sure she's fine. We need to take advantage of the distraction while we can."

Nellie still leaned toward the ocean, despite the vise Ander kept her in. The call of the Siren was powerful, but he was right. She had needed ... something. Why had she come over? She gasped, realizing. "The song."

"Yes, I know," he shouted over the chaos. "I've been around them before, or their earlier kin. I know the damage they can do."

"No, oh gods, no, not that," Nellie wiggled, trying to get out of Ander's arms. "Put me down, you oaf. It's the song. *The song.*"

"What? I don't know—"

"The phoenix song," one of the Elders said. He panted on the ground at their feet as he also tried not to swan dive into the water. "These sirens, they are different. They aren't hurt by that which was created to destroy them. And this song, only they can—"

"That's it!" Nellie exclaimed. "Moira said if we needed her, we simply needed to sing the song. I thought she just died one too many times and was a bit confused."

"Moira is gone, Nellie. Darroc destroyed her. They can't be singing for her."

The clouds swiftly departed, revealing beautiful swirling cosmos above. The phoenix song reached its peak and the winds, the screams of the dying ceased. The earth cupped its ear, curiously waiting for—

"My *innulum*," Ander whispered, rubbing his chest. "I can feel it. *Her.*"

A motion behind Ander caught her attention. He whipped his head around, dropping Nellie in the process. The siren's voices cut off as they dipped back below the water.

A sudden blast of obsidian fire blocked Jacobi's next attack on Hunter, causing both males to stagger backward. Brilliant, sparkling ebony and gold feathers glittered as the dark phoenix blazed in her glory. She hovered before Hunter, her wings spread wide, and focused her fiery gaze on the Elder. Jacobi's eyes widened briefly before he cracked his neck and renewed his efforts of destruction, only this time against the phoenix.

The other Elders paused their spell casting, thrown by the appearance of a mythical creature. Without their spell, Nellie regained the ability to shift into her *Drogosterra* form, allowing her to see clearly in the night. She soared toward the cosmos, marveling at the swirling hues of violet and cerulean among a sea of stars before turning her attention back to the battle.

From this view, Nellie watched fire burst from the dark phoenix's spread wings, burning each attack Jacobi threw at Hunter and Ander. Nellie waited for the phoenix to rain ebony fire on the Elders, but she seemed more focused on taking the brunt Jacobi's magical attacks.

Exhaustion was evident in the Anestrians on the bay. Despite the monsters having lost their mojo once Darroc ceased to exist, they still managed to inflict damage on the elves, humans, and warlocks who fought endlessly against them.

Nellie had just prepared to dive down to help free a child from the clutches of a rabid wolf when suddenly the Elders resumed their chanting. Nellie was forced back into her human body once again. She free-fell with a scream, the ground quickly rising to meet her when Hunter whipped out a protective shield, causing her to bounce off the ground. Her teeth clacked and she bit her tongue, but was otherwise unscathed. And pissed the hell off.

She threw a grateful smile Hunter's way, but he turned back to the fight. Standing shoulder to shoulder, Hunter and Ander's *malosin* combined to form a cage for Jacobi. Once immobilized, they took turns tossing electrical bolts and spheres of fire at him. Nellie crossed her arm with a huff. What would it take to kill him?

He was the mastermind behind Darroc, planning the long game for well over a thousand years just for the opportunity to step back on this land. Nellie knew it would take more than a few balls of fire to destroy him. Maybe if the other Elders were gone?

If only Faline was there, maybe she would ... but it didn't matter. Rage and anguish filled Nellie again as she remembered all the loss they'd experienced that day. Faline and Wil, Enis and Endo. She might not have felt the same way about him as before, but he didn't deserve an ending like that. Like her mother had.

Nellie gripped her mother's locket, the keepsake holding so much more meaning for her now that she knew the whole truth. She was Darroc's offspring, and her mother died protecting her until the very end.

True family was created from love, not biology. It didn't matter if she was Darroc's offspring. Her mother and Faline were her real parents. Faria was her sister. Nellie felt like the luckiest woman in all the realms to have known a family as unique and loving as hers.

She sighed, refocusing on what she could do in the present to help those of her family who remained. The Elders had to be taken down. Magical attacks didn't seem to work on them, and she couldn't assume she'd make it close enough to cause them physical harm if she even could. There wasn't much she could do while in her human body, but as long as the Elders did their spell casting, no one outside of Hunter and Ander was able to use any type of magic.

As Nellie moved her hand away from her necklace, her nail got caught on the clasp, opening the heart pendant on a silent hinge. A tiny piece of paper fluttered to the ground. Nellie had forgotten all about it; it felt like lifetimes ago that she was on Earth recovering from the sea monster attack. She unfolded the paper, remembering that it was in a completely different language.

She never knew why her mother insisted on wearing that locket everywhere, or why she held onto something that wasn't from the human realm. But not even Nellie had known it existed and if her mother was willing to die without—

No freaking way.

Nellie searched the cosmos, wondering if the Fates were playing a long game of their own because she couldn't possibly possess even an inkling of luck to have what she thought she did in her hands. Fantastical galaxies stared back at her, in wondrous swirls of greens and purples, endless stars, ringed planets rotating lazily in their orbits. It was beautiful, but far less impressive than what her mother had done for her. For all of them.

For sixteen years, her mother had been on the run. And if Darroc had held her prisoner long enough to experiment on her, that means she must have been in his secret lair. And the one thing everyone kept discussing was if it would be worth it to search his lair for …

"The Spell of Unmaking," an unfamiliar voice whispered in her ear.

Nellie slowly turned, her hand gripping the tiny paper, worried the stranger was going to tear it away from her. Her fear melted away when she gazed upon the most beautiful woman Nellie had ever seen.

She was tall, much taller than anyone Nellie had ever interacted with before, with bright white hair pulled back in a tight bun on her head. A gold headpiece glinted off her dark skin and was dressed for battle in a tight one-piece suit with various pockets for weapons. Her high cheekbones and elongated ears seemed almost inappropriately elegant paired with bright violet eyes. She looked like life and death. The energy radiating off her brought Nellie to her knees and she bowed her head in a show of reverence.

A slender hand reached out and cupped Nellie's chin, raising her head to look straight into the eyes of the goddess Farrah. Warmth and peace unlike any Nellie had ever known filled her as she slowly rose to her feet.

"Am I dead, for real this time?" Nellie whispered, unwilling to break whatever hallucination she was having at the moment. Perhaps Ander hadn't healed her and this was a byproduct of the remaining poison in her veins.

"No, child. You are still conscious in this dimension, in this realm, in your same life."

"Ah ... okay. Interesting way to phrase that. I mean, what are you doing here? I mean, are you finally gonna help? I mean, not *finally*, you know, I would never question a goddess or the creator or you know, you, but I mean, you're here now so, you are, right?" Nellie really needed to learn when to shut up, but unfortunately, the creator didn't see fit to give her that impulse so was it really her fault?

"Yes, I brought help." Farrah stepped aside just as a portal opened behind her and a team of *Drogosterra* flew into the sky.

Nellie counted twenty, maybe more. They wasted no time snatching Darroc's monsters and clawing their way through their enemies, though Nellie noticed none of them spat fire on anyone. Nellie searched for Rhayna, whooping as she spotted the dragon tearing a rabid bear in two with her teeth. A rider sat upon her back, an equal look of glee on his face.

"Alexei," Farrah said, answering her unspoken question. "He has missed them and couldn't resist."

Nellie nodded as if it were completely normal to see a god riding a dragon and turned back to Farrah, waiting for some sort of instruction.

"Your Val king and prince can perform that spell together. The Elders should not be part of this life any longer." Her lips curled up in a snarl, revealing sharp canines.

"Okay ... Not that I'm complaining, but can't you just zap them, or something?"

Violet eyes turned to obsidian then back again as Farrah's facial features smoothed out into something less menacing. "Much energy has been spent across the realms, trying to separate and seal off different worlds my sisters and I had created before irreparable damage could be done. That abomination you call Darroc had been very busy over the last thousand years."

"Right ... okay." Nellie desperately wanted to know more, but she would have been pushing her luck if she kept questioning the will of a goddess. She couldn't believe she was standing in the presence of the freaking *creator* of this realm, and Faria's ancestor. "Um, one last question."

"No. There isn't time. I must save your queen before she is too far gone." Farrah stepped around Nellie and walked straight to the dark phoenix who hovered between Hunter and Jacobi.

"Well, Farrah, you finally decided to make an appearance. Seems a bit late. I've already killed your heir."

Farrah, classy goddess that she was, ignored Jacobi and whispered something in Hunter's ear. He looked back at Nellie, then grabbed Ander and jogged over to her, both out of breath. Their *malosin obsinaes* radiated immensely dominating energy.

"Um, okay, boys, mind reeling it back in. Kinda hard to breathe, here," Nellie said as her throat started to constrict. They complied, but barely. "I've got The Spell of Unmaking, so you know, you're welcome."

"Nellie, I could kiss you," Hunter said as he grabbed the paper from her and scanned the words written on the page.

"Hey, that's my line," Emmie replied. "Will it work on Jacobi?"

"Let's see," Hunter said.

Hunter quickly went over pronunciation with Ander, having him repeat the words back carefully. If there was one thing Nellie knew about spells, it was that saying the wrong word inevitably led to a different result. After Hunter felt satisfied, he and Ander stood behind the protection of the dark phoenix and started their chanting.

Immediately, the Elders choked on their words as if they were snatched from their throats. Fillets of skin sizzled, exposing rotted flesh. Ander and Hunter increased their chanting. Blood oozed from collapsed eye sockets, streaming down their sunken cheeks. Convulsing in paid, the Elders dropped to their knees, screaming as bones cracked, muscle tore, viscera blanketed the ground until they were reduced to nothing but ash. That, too, disintegrated until they faded from existence.

The effect was immediate, allowing the shifters to change back into their animal forms and finish off what the *Drogosterra* hadn't gotten to yet. Nellie felt her power stir within her, but she held off on shifting until she knew where she would be most useful.

Despite the spell wreaking absolute havoc on the Elders, Jacobi was the only one unaffected, curled within the shadowy cage the Val trapped him in.

Farrah stood next to the dark phoenix, her violet power pouring into the creature. Now that the chaos was slowly starting to switch over to their control, Nellie realized that the dark phoenix hadn't moved since she arrived. Her wings were stretched out in the same position, and she even hovered in the same way. The brilliant black and gold flames never dimmed, but she didn't seem able to do anything else, either.

Nellie watched intently as Farrah's power mingled with the phoenix fire and seeped into the creature. She knew that this was Faria, but she couldn't fathom her queen turning into something that was beyond logical existence. They had seen hints of a phoenix within her, of course, after Moira gave her the warlocks' power, and the ghostly image of wings had appeared when the land accepted her. Never did Nellie think that Moira would have given her this blessing, or curse, especially without any direction on how to control it.

Because that's what Nellie now recognized this as. Faria had lost control of her power and was trapped inside that body unable to do anything. Nellie should have known that her best friend would have done something entirely reckless to save their people. There was no way Faria was certain she'd even change into a phoenix. The risk on their people, on herself.

There had to be a way for her to come back from this.

The agonized screams of the Elders as their bodies were flayed in front of them dimmed as they each slowly disintegrated into nothing. As one, Hunter and Ander collapsed to the ground. Nellie ran over to them. "What is it? What do you need?"

"Water," Ander said. "Food," Hunter said. "Our energy is completely spent."

"Completely?" That worried Nellie. Jacobi was still survived it didn't look like Farrah was making much headway with Faria. "Farrah said Faria is stuck in that body because she has lost control of her power. We can't have everyone out of commission when Jacobi is still alive."

A *Drogosterra* landed beside them, kicking flecks of mud on their faces.

"Rhayna," Ander said, extending a handout. She nuzzled his palm as someone hopped off her back. "And *you*. You could have told me how to access the Flame, you know. Nellie almost died!"

Alexei cocked a half smile, surprisingly similar to the one Hunter gave to Faria when he wants to annoy her. "But she didn't."

He winked at Nellie as he walked by her and stopped next to Farrah. They looked at each other with concern. Alarm bells went off for Nellie. Farrah shook her head slightly then Alexei nodded and walked up to Jacobi.

"Alexei, my creator," Jacobi said, bowing his head slightly. "Have you finally come to reward me for all I have done in your name?"

"You are nothing but a flea, perched on a grain of sand, in the middle of the desert. There is no reward for you. You do not get to enter into the Beyond. Your soul will not find peace. And I will not spend any more time on you."

Alexei raised his hand in the air and made a fist. Within moments, Jacobi shrunk and with a squelching *pop*, ceased to exist.

"Are you freaking *kidding* me," Nellie burst out. She stomped over to Alexei in outrage. "All you had to do was make a fist? We went through all of this for ... That?"

Alexei cocked his head and examined her like a predator learning his prey. She swallowed and remembered that it was a god she spoke to and slowly backed away. "I mean, we owe you our lives. Thank you."

"Do you think we can be available at your beck and call, little one? We had to correct damage across twenty-one realms. Twenty-one. We had to completely destroy eight of those. There were portals that had to close before realms crashed into each other. There were other gods to contend with, more abominations to exterminate."

"Yes, absolutely, you're right." Nellie nodded earnestly. "I can see now that all of those things were done to protect this realm."

"You are not our only creations, nor our only failures," Farrah said, her voice tight with strain. Hunter stood next to Faria's dark fire and reached out to stroke her flames as if to soothe her.

"I can't reach her," he said. "I can feel her torment and confusion, but I can't enter her mind. How can this be? What can we do?"

"It was too much power too soon," Farrah said. "Trying to disentangle it is like trying to undo knots from spiderwebs. They all cling to each other, unwilling to let go. If she were stronger, she would be able to hold the barriers between powers. She cannot handle the weight of all this magic.

"The Fates deemed her worthy," Hunter said through clenched teeth.

"We are the Fates," Farrah and Alexei responded in unison. "We are the land. We made her heir." Their voices rang as if there were a dozen of them rather than two. The hair on the back of Nellie's neck stood on end. "But we are not infallible. We misjudged."

"No," Ander said, stepping next to Nellie. She gently leaned against his side to comfort him. "You have to help her. She can't remain like … this."

Farrah's hands dropped to her sides. "If I strip her of her magic, she will cease to exist."

"What about you?" Ander turned to Alexei. "She's the queen! You need her to rule. There has to be something."

"Princeling, Farrah is the creator. I am the destroyer. I cannot help her more than what Farrah has already done."

"Faria, you hear that?" Nellie shouted up at her best friend. "They're saying you're not strong enough. As if, right? So, can you prove them wrong? Please?"

"I doubt she can hear you," Farrah said. "She isn't human in there, or elf, or Fae, or even Val. She is something else entirely."

"No." Hunter's *malosin* poured from him and reached through her flames, embracing her fiery body with its dark spirit. Shadows surrounded her as more of his essence anchored her, calling her back to him.

"Your energy would be better spent by serving your people. I can feel the land past the mountains stirring." Farrah closed her eyes as if listening. "They will need guidance."

"What about the Fae?" Nellie asked.

"They shall remain that way evermore." Farrah's voice rang with finality.

Ander stepped closer to Farrah with disbelief on his face. "They're conscious! They can see, hear, and feel. You want to keep them trapped in that type of pain?"

"They made the sacrifice for their land. Without them, Anestra would not look like this."

Nellie looked around at the gore and guts soaking the sand, the broken windows and torn roofs of the shops in town, and the bodies that littered the ground. "No offense, but it's not looking too hot as it is."

"My mother will do something about this. If I know anything about her, it's that she will not let them live this way."

"Princeling," Alexei said gently, "your mother is gone. And we must go as well. There is still much damage to undo."

"Wait, you're leaving?" Nellie asked. "She's the queen! Your heir! Your daughter's daughter's daughter times like ... a lot! You're going to leave her like this?"

"I don't think so." Ander's *malosin* grew outside of his body as well, his eyes shining with the Flame as his joined his father's. He embraced his mother in the only way he ever could, the sight bringing tears to Nellie's eyes. She stepped up and reached her hand out to the flames and was surprised that they didn't burn her. She inched closer, allowing herself to be enveloped by obsidian fire, and wrapped her arms around the corporeal shadows of the Vals' *malosin*.

Please come back to us, please. Nellie wished with every fiber of her being that Faria could somehow hear their thoughts or at least feel how much they loved and needed her.

Magic came in all forms. It didn't have to be party tricks or powers with the ability to kill. It could be something as simple as love, as simple as needing and wanting another person to reciprocate that feeling. The simplest magic was what came naturally. Maybe they didn't always get along and they fought often, but their connection to each other was their anchor, their lifeline.

Farrah couldn't untangle the web of powers that melded together inside Faria, but if they could somehow bring her back to herself, Nellie knew that Faria would be able to do it.

"Come on, Mom," Ander whispered. "Come back, please."

Nellie watched through wavering flames as Alexei and Farrah held hands and disappeared. *Wow, they weren't kidding about leaving.*

"Let me in, Princess," Hunter said. "Come back to us."

The minutes ticked by and Nellie knew in the back of her mind that Alexei and Farrah were right. They were needed elsewhere and if Faria were stuck in her present state, maybe it would be more logical to come back to her after they dealt with the Anestrians coming back to consciousness on the other side of Caranek Peaks. Nellie also really needed to check on her shifters make sure Marisa and her sirens were safe.

A slight movement startled Nellie from her anxious thoughts. Obsidian flames flickered and slowly receded into the body of the phoenix. Nellie wondered how awkward it would be when the three of them were standing here holding onto a bird, but a moment later, black and gold feathers shed and the phoenix's wings slowly revealed shoulders, an arm, fingers. Long, wavy hair grew down its back and legs planted firmly to the ground. Faria was whole again.

"So quick to forget about me Nells?" Faria asked, her voice scratchy as if she'd been screaming for hours. "Rude."

"Holy shit, Faria!" Nellie exclaimed. She clung to her best friend, her sister, and tears poured down her face. "Oh, my gods, they were just useless, weren't they? Wait, I shouldn't say their names. What if they're still listening?"

"Did you just curse?" Faria asked. "Have you changed that much without me?"

"You should hear other words she knows," Ander said, winking at Nellie. "I was just as surprised as you."

Faria clung onto Ander's neck squeezing hard enough that Ander coughed with the pressure. She stepped back, her eyes shining with unshed tears. "You brought me back," she whispered. "You all brought me back."

"If you ever pull a stunt like that again," Hunter said, pulling Faria into his arms. "I'm going to give you a proper punishment."

"Promise?" Faria asked.

Nellie hooted while Ander made a sound of disgust and the four of them laughed for a moment. Faria quickly sobered up and looked around them. "The *Drogosterra* have returned? Does that mean there are more Val?"

Hunter nodded. "Before she left, Farrah said she could feel them stirring on the other side of the mountains. The land is finally waking up."

"And the Fae?"

"She said Anestra wouldn't be the same without them and refused to free them. Although if you ask me, I think we're in need of a bit of an upgrade." Nellie gestured to the bay below them. "And I'd bet a million bucks *Mentage* is looking just as rough."

Faria sighed. "There's so much to be done." She paused and considered the ocean. "Did she mention anything about what caused that tidal wave or the creatures from the sea?"

"Those creatures are from another realm," Ander said. He rubbed the back of his neck and shifted uncomfortably. "They belong to the Lord of Storms and Seas. He hired Darroc a long time ago to help him and ... well, that meant I helped him, too."

Faria looked first at Hunter, then at Ander, a horrified expression on her face. "I'm sorry," Ander said quickly. "I know it was wrong, there was nothing I could do. I tried to do the right thing, still. There was a woman trapped there and I freed her and—"

"Oh, no Ander," Hunter said, placing a hand on his shoulder. He looked into his son's eyes before embracing him tightly. "It is us who are so sorry for not being there for you."

"Oh ... it's ... you know."

Nellie watched the three of them, her heart aching. There was so much trauma to heal, so much damage to undo.

Faria wiped the tears from her face and took a steadying breath. "Right. We'll have plenty of time to speak about these things. If you want to, when you're ready," she added quickly.

"What do we do now?" Nellie asked. "Is the threat truly gone?"

"Yes, I believe so." Faria turned to face the bay and watched her people start pyres to burn the bodies of the creatures that littered the ground. "Now, clean up. We rest. We give thanks for what we have." Faria grasped Nellie's hand and looked at her boys. "And we start anew."

EPILOGUE

Wendorre was a wasteland.

Faria walked along the western coast, which she was told was once lush with marsh and meadowlands. Now, little more than dirt and sand crunched under her feet. Heat radiated in waves from the ground as the relentless sun roasted them.

Faria waited two days to go to Wendorre. She desperately needed to sleep and eat, then helped clean up the streets of Mercy Bay. Her people kept trying to supply her with fresh food, offers for her to spend the night in their home, but she gently declined. The magic coursing through her was too much and she could admit that Farrah was right. She didn't have the proper control over it, and she didn't want to harm anyone.

Now she walked the barren landscape that she supposed was hers, though she knew nothing about it. She still needed to create a council to take care of the day-to-day things, make sure everyone was fed and had proper shelter, care for the sick, provide educational and militaristic support. One thing at a time, though.

Reed walked by her side as a protector, though Faria invited him along to help distract him. His grief over losing his mate was palpable, and nothing but time and focus on other tasks would help him, at least in the moment. "How will you know where the right spot is?"

"I think it's just intuition. My fingertips are vibrating in anticipation. I think the magic knows it's home."

Faria wrapped her arm through Reed's, subtly sending a comforting wave of magic through him. Silent tears fell down his face, but he smiled down at her anyway. He patted her hand and sighed deeply. After a few more moments, Faria stopped.

"This is the spot."

She bent down and pulled a tiny dagger from her boot. She no longer had any desire to mess with blood magic, but knew this was the best way to draw the essence out. She closed her eyes and concentrated on the power of the warlocks that resided inside her. Once she had a lock on it, she sliced her palm and pressed it against the ground.

Faria kept her eyes closed and envisioned a verdant land filled with flowers and wildlife, rivers and lakes. She pictured abundant farmlands, a healthy people. The land drew the magic from her and with each moment that passed, Faria felt a bit lighter and more free.

"Whoa," Reed breathed from beside her. "Look at that."

Faria opened her eyes and smiled at what the magic had already created. She stood upon lush grass and bore witness to the ground sprouting wildflowers before her. In the distance, a dried riverbed flushed with water and she could hear the currents bubbling happily over the bedrock. She turned in a circle and welcomed the breeze that brought with it the fresh scent of land after a rainstorm.

She heard shouts and exclamations and waited as a group of people climbed over the hill and noticed her for the first time. She smiled warmly at their shocked expressions and internally groaned when they dropped to their knees. She'd get used to the reverence, one day, though she hoped she never would. She was still just Faria, despite the many titles she now held.

Faria signaled to the group of warlocks that came with her and Reed.

Tears streamed down their faces and their eyes were alight with sheer joy. "My queen," they said in unison as they, too, dropped to their knees.

"Please, stay with our people. Help them readjust and let them know I will return soon."

"Yes, of course."

"You really will return, right?" a shy voice asked.

Faria looked down at the young warlock. He was short with a boyish face that reminded her so much of Endo when he was younger. "Yes, you needn't fear. The magic has returned to the land now, and so long as I am your queen, that is where it shall remain." She took a step back from them and grabbed Reed's wrist. "Ready?"

Reed gave a short nod then she sieved the two of them to the other side of Carenek Peaks. "Don't you think you should have stayed, and I don't know, given them a speech or something?"

"Anestra is broken, Reed. And there is only one of me. The warlocks will regain the full height of their powers soon, and with their land prosperous once again, they will be busy getting used to their new way of life. Which means I have at least a day or two to sort out this mess."

They followed a curve in the river bend and halted in front of an assembly of beings crowding around Hunter.

Shortly after the Elders were unmade, Hunter was crippled with all the memories they had kept locked away from him. It took a while for him to sort through them and for the pain to dull into a manageable ache. Faria felt the residual effect through the bond, though he had tried to keep it from her. It was horrific, both to realize how much the Elders had kept from him, but also the mental and physical pain that would take a long time to manage.

Once Hunter realized that not all his people perished in the Great War as he believed for the past thousand years, he immediately went to them. He learned the Fates had transported those who survived there, and then they, too, were taken by Farrah's magic that froze the other beings.

Hunter had learned that they lost no time while frozen on the other side. They were alive but didn't age, and to them, it was as if they woke up from a long sleep. It was still disorienting, however, to appear in a new place and not be in the thick of battle and on the verge of sacrificing themselves as they believed.

Faria walked up to Hunter and grasped his hand. Immediately the frenzy quieted as they took in Faria's features and felt the power radiating from her. She took a breath to steady her nerves and tried not to dwell on how awkward she felt speaking to the legendary Val, who up until recently, thought was just an Anestrian myth.

"Hi, I'm Faria Agostonna."

Silence followed her declaration.

She continued, feeling the absurd need to clarify, "Queen of Anestra."

"You look so much like Queen Athinia," a Val standing off to the side said. "The same bone structure, same eyes. Even your stance. That's incredible."

"Queen Athinia was my great, great, great, great grandmother. I think. I have to admit I didn't pay much attention to my history, but I will work to rectify that shortly. I want to welcome you to the land ... or rather, back to the land? This is an unprecedented time for all who have lived within the past few centuries and there is much we are all adjusting to.

"With that being said, I want to assure you that Hunter and I will care for you in whatever ways you need. We want you to feel comfortable and safe."

"We are made to defend you, Queen Faria. The only thing we wish is to be given the proper resources to train so we can protect you."

She smiled gently at them. She'd forgotten for a moment that they were a war people, and while they desperately needed to replenish their army, she also hoped that they would find another purpose while they lived there.

"You are welcome to move closer to *Mentage* and use the training facility there, or we can build a new one for you here. There's plenty of space. Also ... " Faria looked to the sky and watched as a group of *Drogosterra* flew toward them. "I believe we found some old friends of yours."

Shouts and cries of exaltation rang out as they spotted the *Drogosterra*. Faria noticed a few of them had markings on their palm similar to Ander and wondered if any of the *Drogosterra* Farrah brought over belonged to one of them.

I'll work with them on the location and Drogosterra, Princess. I'm their king and commander, so they'll fall back on whatever I say,

This should be a collective vote, Hunter. Let them have a say.

Hunter squeezed her hand and called their attention again. Faria quietly slipped away as he slipped into commander mode and motioned for Reed to follow her along the path toward a small village situated near the river.

They came upon Nellie who stood on a giant boulder, speaking to a large group of shifters. "And then, they sent me through the Gate of All Realms! Can you believe it? As if I'd kill my own mother." Her arms were spread wide as she dramatically told her story. The shifters listened with rapt attention.

"So anyways, let's thank the Fates I ended up here and … oh, hey Faria."

As one, the shifters stood and crowded around Faria. They reached their hands out and pet or sniffed in Faria's direction and some even bared their necks at her. Hunter tried explaining that these shifters were much more in tune with their animal counterparts and often lived as some version of their two halves. Faria saw evidence of that when an older female with the body of a human with a long tiger tail approached her and purred deeply.

She felt Hunter's amusement trickle down their bond and Faria couldn't help but laugh as well. She wasn't used to that sort of attention, but she didn't want to make them feel like their culture was strange or didn't belong. "Hello, everyone. I'm Queen Faria ..."

She gave a similar speech as she did to the Val, adding that everyone would have to sign the Contract as soon as she was able to sort it out. They were just happy to be free to roam and live as they once did and happily agreed to it.

"I'll come back very soon, I promise," Faria said, excusing herself.

She walked up the path through a village and to a distant field beyond where Ander waited for her in front of the Fae. He hadn't agreed to live or accept his title as Prince of Anestra, or a Val prince, or anything really, but he was very involved in the rebuilding of Anestra. Faria didn't care what he chose as long as he wanted to be part of their lives and was immensely grateful he was there for what she was about to do.

She knelt on the ground in front of the nearest Fae and let the grief and anguish she felt from the past few days wash over her. She couldn't believe she lived her entire life not knowing or caring what happened on the other side of Carenek Peaks. She grieved for the entire lifetime they lost, for the people who sacrificed themselves for her.

Faria placed her forehead against the ground and breathed in. The magic of the Fae smelled like what she associated Anestra with. Ocean and vanilla, with a hint of cinnamon spice. It sickened her to know that the scent that brought her such comfort came at the expense of scores of Fae losing their lives in perpetuity.

Now it was her time to sacrifice.

"I release the magic bestowed upon me as the Chosen One, the magic the gods deemed me worthy of having. I give this back to the land so that I may free the Fae from their contractual bond to live out the rest of their days free from having to give any more than they are willing." She pressed her palms firmly into the earth and inhaled deeply. "Please accept my offering." As she released her breath, she blasted every ounce of magic she could safely give into the land.

Though Faria had briefly lost control when she was a dark phoenix, she never wanted it to happen again. No one needed that much power. Even after giving back the warlocks what belonged to their land, she still felt heavy with her own magic. She was queen of Wendorre, queen of the Val, and queen of Anestra, but she could rule as effectively with the abilities suitable to her race. All the extra she gave back and prayed it would be enough to release the Fae.

Time trickled on and Faria felt Ander kneel next to her then place his hand on her back. He sent a gentle healing wave through her, replenishing her exhaustion and hunger until she felt she could go as long as necessary. Her well of magic was depleting, and just as she hoped she wouldn't have to sacrifice every drop of it, she felt the ground shift.

As one, the Fae gave a collective sigh. They moved as though walking through water, trudging their way toward Faria. She knew they'd have to get their stability back after centuries of disuse, so she stood and waited patiently for them to get to her.

The one in front of her reached his hand out to her face in slow motion as if he were moving through syrup rather than the warm summer air and wiped a tear from her cheek. "Thank you," he whispered before breaking out in tears of his own. "Thank you, my queen."

Faria sat with them for hours and sent Ander for food, water, and healing potions. When they were ready, she explained what happened over the past few years and why she released them. She gave them the choice of living among them or by themselves the way the dwarves do. She admitted she didn't know much about their culture, and she didn't want to force anyone into something they didn't want to do.

Ultimately, they decided to stay in the forest on that side of the mountain, secluding themselves until they felt ready. The haunted look in their eyes let Faria know that it would be a long time, if at all, that they would be healed enough to join them. She made a mental note to never ask them for favors and only accept volunteer offers if they decided to approach her. As far as she was concerned, any duty or obligation they had to her and the land was fulfilled.

It wasn't until after midnight that Faria and Ander sieved back to *Mentage*. They were both emotionally and physically drained. They walked through the Spring Garden and Faria let the comfort of the scents wash over her.

They stopped at the jade fountain in the middle of the garden with the statue of the eagle, lion, stag, and phoenix. Faria sat on the edge and patted the space beside her. Ander complied, keeping a bit of space between them. Faria felt a twinge of sadness at that, but as with all wounds, they would take time to heal.

Ander cleared his throat. "Thank you for giving me your rooms to use while I'm here. I don't know how long I'll stay, but I appreciate it."

"You will always have a place here, Ander, whether you wish to accept the mantel as future ruler of Anestra or not. I'm happy you're here."

"What happens now?"

Faria shook her head. There was too much that needed to get done, still. "The clean-up effort, the Contract, making sure the shifters from Earth have found where they'd like to live. Repair and rebuild Mercy Bay, bring life back to Athinia. Eventually, I'll want some people on the other side of Caranek Peaks to learn the magic they used on that side. We're behind now from where they were a millennia ago."

That wasn't even the half of it, but he understood. "The memorial, too, right? For the fallen?"

Faria's throat constricted at the thought of all they lost. "Yes, we will form a section of the Forest of the Dawn specifically for the memorial. I'm thinking a large marble slab with the names of the fallen, and statues, perhaps." She wanted one of Queen Amira, at least, and was strongly considering others. "What will you do?"

Ander shook his head. "I'm not sure. I think I'd like to stay here for a while until I figure it out. If that's okay," he added quickly.

Faria's heart swelled with the love she kept repressed from the moment her son went missing and allowed the relief to wash over her as her cold heart started beating again.

She looked at her son and drank in his features that were so much like his father's, but hers as well. She recognized herself in him and felt the joy of watching a piece of her heart breathing outside of her chest. "I love you so much, Ander."

He stared at her and slowly placed his hand on top of his. "I love you too, mom."

There was a rustling in the bushes ahead of them and a single eye peered through. Faria smiled. "I see you, Nellie."

"I wasn't spying, I swear," Nellie said, climbing over the hedge. "I … lost something."

"You mean your mind?" Hunter appeared next to her, putting an arm around her shoulders. "We've been aware of that one for a while."

Faria leaned her head on Ander's shoulder and watched the night flowers bloom around them. She didn't know what tomorrow would bring, but she had her health, her people, and more than anything, she had her son and all the sacrifices made over the past few months were worth every second to have him by her side.

Finally, Faria found her place in the world, and with her family by her side, she knew she could conquer whatever came next for Anestra.

THE END

ACKNOWLEDGEMENTS

I almost didn't finish this trilogy. I thought I was done with writing and spent quite a bit of time trying to figure out how to bow out gracefully, or at least quietly.

That, obviously, didn't happen, despite the universe's best attempts at it, and I can attribute that to a few select people who remained a beacon of light in the darkness.

To JP McDonald – my critique partner, my sounding board, my rock, my anchor, my everything I've needed. I would have given up every day, every hour, if you weren't a constant pain in my behind. You kept me rooted in reality, constantly gave me perspective, reminded me of my goals. Every time I was adrift at sea, you found me. Thank you for sacrificing your time to read through the horrible slog of a first draft and providing insight where I couldn't be bothered. This book wouldn't have seen the light of day without your endless guidance, no matter how often I forced it upon you.

To Kiraka Davis – what have I done to earn your friendship? There is no way that I can reciprocate the level of love and care you give to our friendship, from your weekly check ins, to hyping up anything I plan to do, no matter how small. Your insight into the development of this book was invaluable and I am so grateful to have your presence in my life.

To Julia Scott – what an absolute godsend you've been this year. Thank you for bearing with me, for taking on projects last minute, for doing everything possible to help me reach my deadlines, for absolutely killing it at what you do. Without a doubt, I would have no reason to publish if the universe didn't guide me to you.

To so many in the bookstagram and writing community who have been a constant support as I slowly lost my sanity this year: Jessika, Lilian, Greg, Zaid, Bex, Ethan, Sam, and so many others. I don't know where my writing journey will go from here, but I'm so grateful for the constant check-ins, the distractions, the support, and all of the love.

ABOUT THE AUTHOR

EMMIE HAMILTON is a writer, mother, and amateur candle maker. Her favorite pastime is creating worlds others wish they were born into. She received her MFA in Creative Writing from Southern New Hampshire University and has been previously published by Pure Slush Press and various non-fiction outlets. Chosen to Fall is her debut novel.

You can connect with her on Instagram @authoremmiehamilton or visit her website www.emmiehamilton.com for the latest publication information.